I0818212

The New Jerusalem

The New Jerusalem

Third Book of Cup of Christ and the Forgotten Disciple Mystery-Thriller Trilogy

JACK HOLT

The New Jerusalem

This is a work of fiction. Apart from the historical figures, any resemblance between fictional characters created by the author and actual persons, living or dead, is purely coincidental. Any theological views or philosophies are the opinions of the characters and not necessarily those of the author. Any factual errors are the responsibility of the author.

Holt Publishing ™

For information, questions, or comments, contact
jackmholt.com
jackmholt21@gmail.com

ISBN: 978-1-7355283-6-6 (hardcover)
ISBN: 978-1-7355283-7-3 (paperback)
ISBN: 978-1-7355283-8-0 (e-book)

Cover and interior design
Deborah Perdue, Illumination Graphics

Other Books by Jack Holt

The Cup of Christ Mystery/Thriller Series
The Cup of Christ and the Forgotten Disciple
The Tree of Life
The New Jerusalem

Introduction

The high history of lé *Sangraal* has never been told by any mortal man since Saint Joseph de Arimathea wrote these sacred words about our Lord and Savior. However, I declare to all men and women who wish to own this book, if God allows me to live in good health, it is certainly my intention to bring His story together.

If God blesses my holy quest, these parchments will be found.

—Lord Robert de Borron
Anno Domini 1190

The High History
of *lé Sangraal* and the Forgotten Disciple
is Dedicated to My Patron and
Brother-in-Law
Comte Gautiér de Montbéliard

—Lord Robert de Borron

Dedication

To my loving wife, Carol, who had patience for the last twelve years listening to me speak about my book. Also to my late mother, Charlotte, who gave me the interest to write, and my late dad, Jack, who had a great thirst for history.

Acknowledgments

I would like to acknowledge author Stephen Lawhead, for inspiring me to write my first book in The Cup of Christ trilogy. His tireless research in Celtic lore and the legends of King Arthur motivated me to create my own ideas.

Dan Brown, author of *The Da Vinci Code*, provided the inspiration for me to use symbols, codes, and arcane terminology.

I am grateful for Joanna Penn whose success as an independent author contributed to me taking the same route.

Thank you to my indefatigable graphic designer, Deborah Perdue, and her assistant Tara Thelen from Illumination Graphics, who used their artistic abilities to capture my book's vision. My sincerest gratitude to Reverend C. Allen Colwell for his counsel. Glastonbury Abbey Trustee and archeologist Dr. Roberta Gilchrist for her scholarly input on the Glastonbury Abbey structures and grounds.

I offer my humble thanks to my great taskmaster, Pam Johnson of Pam the Editor. Without her helpful advice and developmental editing, I would not have accomplished this writing journey. Also to my copyeditor Joni Wilson who kept me in the proper boundaries of literary grammar. Last but not least Gaye Mack, my spiritual guide for ideas from Glastonbury Abbey.

My printing company, IngramSpark, offered great advice about getting my book published for all those who love historical fiction and mystery thrillers.

Jack Holt

The New Jerusalem

"I saw a new heaven and a new earth. The first heaven and the first earth had disappeared, and so had the sea. Then I saw a New Jerusalem, the holy city, coming down from God in heaven. It was like a bride dressed in her wedding gown and ready to meet her husband."

—Saint John the Writer
Anno Domini 96

Anno Domini 37

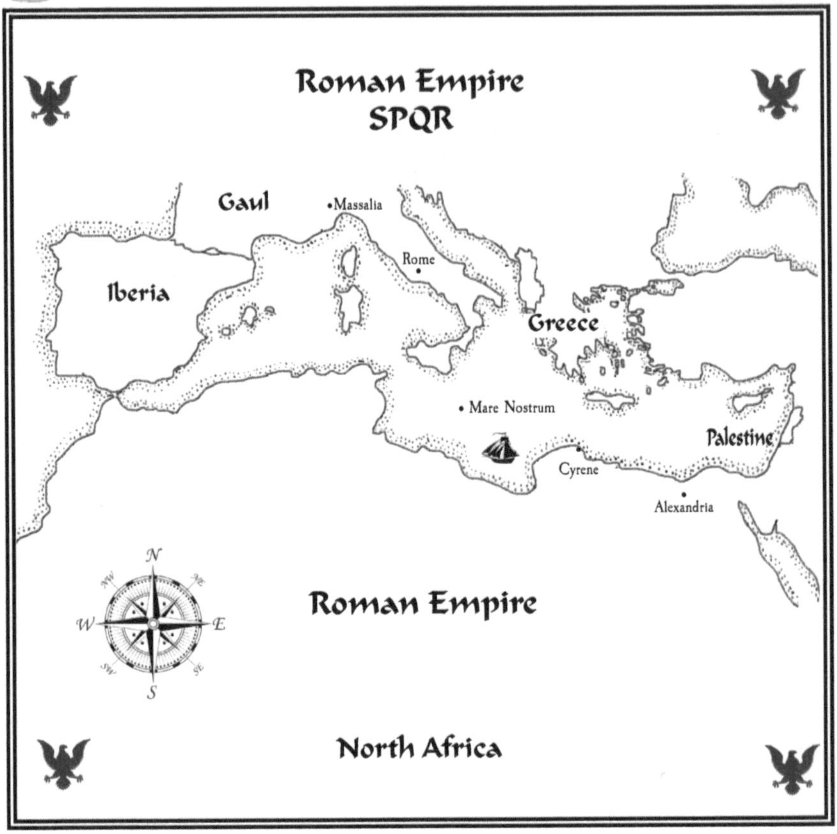

Roman Empire
SPQR

Gaul
Massalia
Rome
Iberia
Greece
Mare Nostrum
Palestine
Cyrene
Alexandria

N
NW
NE
W
E
SW
SE
S

Roman Empire

North Africa

Anno Domini 1190-1191

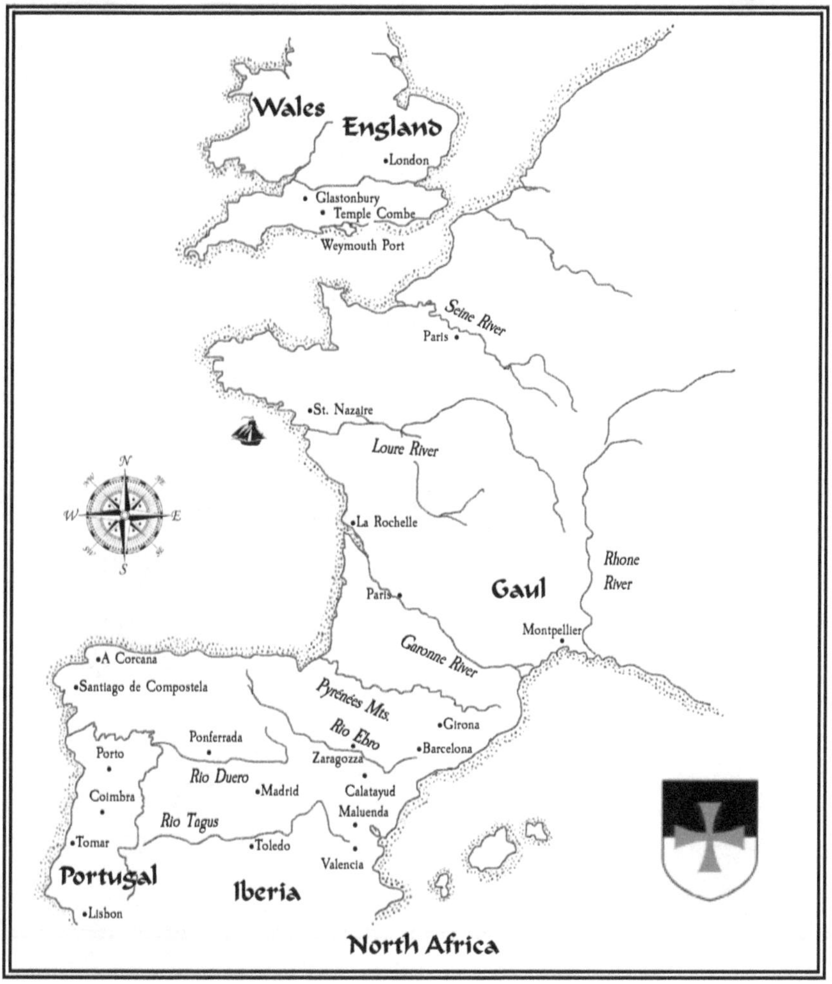

Wales
England
•London
• Glastonbury
• Temple Combe
Weymouth Port
Seine River
Paris •
•St. Nazaire
Loure River
N
W
E
S
•La Rochelle
Rhone
River
Paris•
Gaul
Montpellier
Garonne River
•A Corcana
•Santiago de Compostela
Pyrénées Mts.
Rio Ebro
•Girona
Ponferrada
•Barcelona
Porto
Zaragozza
Rio Duero
•Madrid
Calatayud
Coimbra
Maluenda
Rio Tagus
•Tomar
•Toledo
Valencia
Portugal
Iberia
•Lisbon
North Africa

† Anno Domini 37 †

Anno Domini 1191

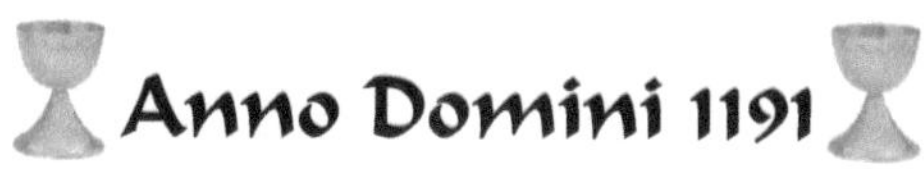

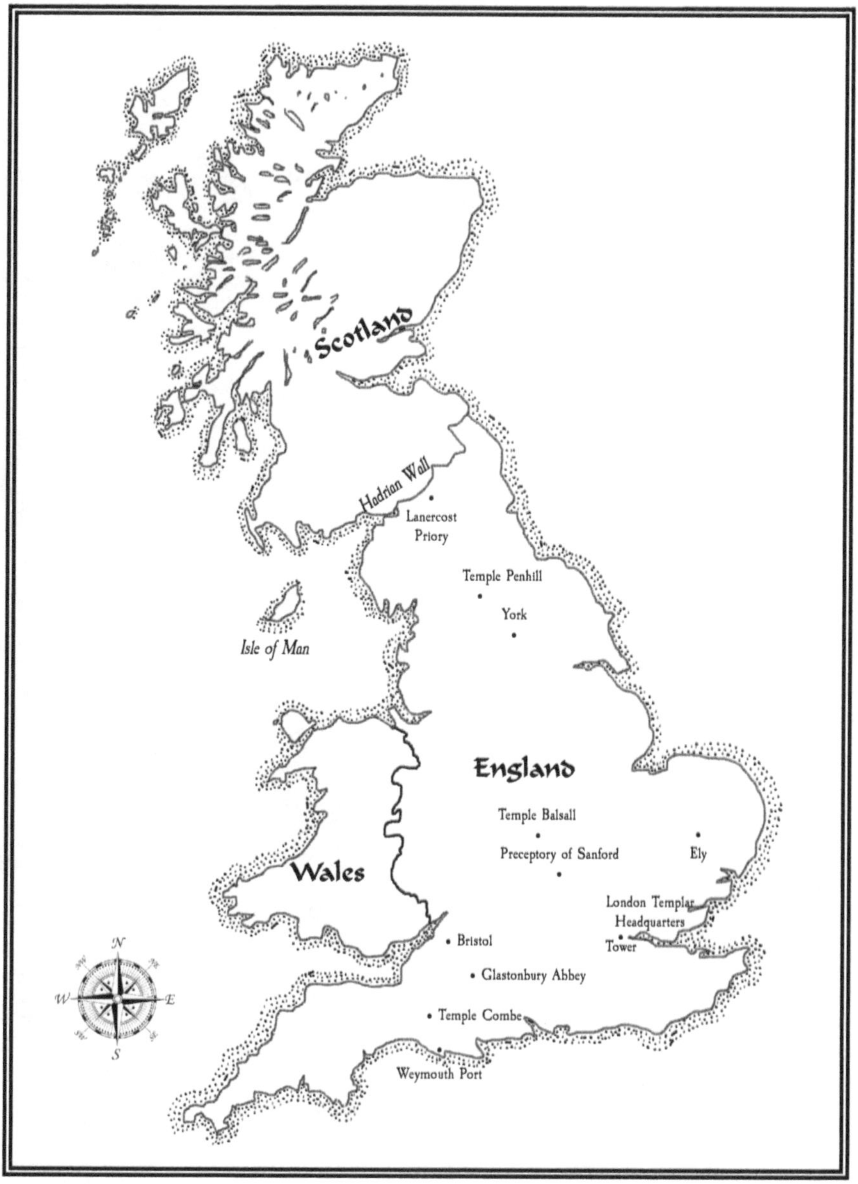
Scotland
Hadrian Wall
Lanercost Priory
Temple Penhill
York
Isle of Man
England
Temple Balsall
Preceptory of Sanford
Ely
Wales
London Templar Headquarters
Tower
Bristol
Glastonbury Abbey
Temple Combe
Weymouth Port
N
S
E
W

The Principal Characters of the City of Jerusalem and Palestine *Anno Domini* 37

Alein Yosephe—son to Yoseph of Arimathea, partner in his father's business

Barabbas—the murderer set free by Jewish Sanhedrin, instead of Jesus the Christ, released by Pontius Pilate

Clotho—Greek woman, early follower of Yoseph of Arimathea, living in Palestine with new baby and wife to Georgeus

Eli of *Yerushalayim* (Jerusalem)—camel and cloth merchant; with two sons, Eliyah and Isaiah

Eliyah—son of Eli, the camel and cloth merchant

Enoch—infant son of Hebron and Enygeus; also name of Old Testament prophet who walked with God and didn't die

Enygeus—sister to Yoseph of Arimathea, wife to Hebron

Georgeus—Greek husband to Clotho, early follower of Yoseph of Arimathea, living in Palestine with new baby named after Yoseph of Arimathea

Hebron—brother-in-law to Yoseph of Arimathea, overseer to Yoseph's merchant business, husband to Enygeus

Herod Antipas—tetrarch of Galilee-Perea; one of the sons of Herod the Great

Herodias—wife of Herod Antipas and the woman who had John the Baptizer beheaded

Herod Antipas—tetrarch of Galilee-Perea; one of the sons of Herod the Great

Isaiah—Eli's son

King Arviragus—ruler of the Celtic Silures

Lazarus (Eleazar)—resurrected from the dead by Yeshua ben Yoseph (Jesus the Christ), brother to Miriam and Martha, later follower of Yoseph of Arimathea

Miriam of Magdala—landowner, mystic, student of Rabbi Yeshua ben Yoseph, a new friend to Yoseph of Arimathea

Miriam of Nazareth—niece to Yoseph of Arimathea, mother to Rabbi Yeshua ben Yoseph, widow to the late mason and carpenter Yoseph of Nazareth

Nicodemus—member of the Jewish Sanhedrin ruling council, scholar, lawyer, old friend of Yoseph of Arimathea

Philip—one of the twelve disciples chosen by Rabbi Yeshua ben Yoseph; also good friend to Yoseph of Arimathea

Pontius Pilate—Roman procurator of Yehudah (Judea)

Rabbi Yeshua ben Yoseph—itinerate preacher, mystic, biblical scholar, son of Miriam of Nazareth, rumored to be the foretold *Maishiach* (Messiah)

Shimon bar Yona—also known as Cephas (the Rock) or Peter; brother to Andrew, fishing merchant

Shimon the Zealot—half-brother of Rabbi Yeshua ben Yoseph and apostle; also later follower of Yoseph of Arimathea

Thomas Didymus—apostle of Rabbi Yeshua ben Yoseph; also a later member who joined Yoseph of Arimathea

Yohanan bar Zebedee, the Writer—disciple of Rabbi Yeshua ben Yoseph, biographer, a close friend to Rabbi Yeshua

Yohanan Marcus—writer, student of Rabbi Yeshua, his two-story home used for the Seder (Passover meal)

Yohanan the Baptizer—cousin to Rabbi Yeshua ben Yoseph. He foretold Rabbi Yeshua as the Messiah, and he would baptize his disciples with the Holy Spirit. Yohanan was possibly Essene trained. He had a son named Zechariah and, after Yohanan's beheading, his son was raised by Yoseph of Arimathea's family.

Yosa—daughter to Yoseph of Arimathea

Yoseph ben Caiaphas—high priest of the Jews; head of the Sanhedrin

Yoseph of Arimathea—richest merchant in the Mediterranean region, member of the Jewish Sanhedrin ruling council, uncle to Miriam of Nazareth, great uncle to Yeshua ben Yoseph of Nazareth

Zechariah—orphan son of Yohanan the Baptizer, toddler second cousin to Rabbi Yeshua ben Yoseph

The Principal Characters of Frankish Gaul and the Levant *Anno Domini* 1190

Baroness Marie de Borron—wife of Lord Robert de Borron; mother to Robert's sons, Brian and Henri; sister to *Comte* Gautiér de Montbéliard

Cardinal Folquet de Marseille—archbishop of Toulouse, former troubadour, head of the Roman curia

***Chevalier* Marcel de Tournay**—seneschal to Cardinal Folquet, archbishop of Toulouse

Commander Armound de Polignac—Templar leader at the commandery of Carcassonne, old friend of Grand Master Gilbért de Érail

***Comte* Gautiér de Montbéliard**—former Crusader, writing benefactor to Lord Robert de Borron, brother-in-law to Robert de Borron

Grand Master Gilbért de Érail—Iberian grand master of the Poor-Soldiers of Christ (Knights Templar)

Hughes de Montbard—Templar squire, great-nephew to Saint Bernard de Clairvaux, under the command of Grand Master Gilbért de Érail

Muhammad Nur Adin—former emir from the Levant, constable of the Templar horses in Gaul, scout.

Richard I, *le Coeur de Lion*—king of England; duke of Normandy, Aquitaine, and Gascony; lord of Cyprus; *comte* of Poitiers, Anjou, Maine, and Nantes; overlord of Brittany; reign 1189–1199

Robert de Borron—lord of *Château* Borron, poet, writer, troubadour, swordsman, from Northern Burgundy

Robert de Sablé—grand master of the Templar's entire order, reign 1190–1193

Saladin (Salāh ad-Din Yūsuf ibn Ayyūb)—Muslim Kurdish Suni sultan of Egypt, Syria, and part of Palestine; led a great army against Christian crusaders; reign 1174–1193

Sergeant Guy de Béziers—Templar scout, former seaman, under the command of Grand Master Gilbért de Érail

Sergeant Jacque de Hoult—Templar scout, under the command of Grand Master Gilbért de Érail

✠

The Principal Characters of Iberia (Spain) *Anno Domini* 1190

Admiral Hidalgo de Fernando—admiral of the Templar fleet and uncle to Commander Juan Felipe

Alfonso II (the Chaste)—king of Aragón; conde de Barcelona, Catalonia, Provence, Cerdanya, Y Roussillon; husband to Queen Sacha; brother-in-law to Princess Helena

Alfonso VII—king of Castile (Toledo); late brother of Princess Helena

Alfonso VIII—king of Castile (Toledo); nephew of Princess Helena

Averroes (Ibn Rushd)—polymath, philosopher, Islamic scholar, jurist, grand *mufti* of Córdoba

Chamberlain Rodrigo—chamberlain to King Alfonso II and Princess Helena's bastard half-brother

Commander Juan Felipe—commander of the castle fortress at Ponferrada and nephew to the admiral of the Templar fleet

Deborah—Jewish lover of Gilbért de Érail; mother of Jeremiah Santiago de Compostela

Esperanza—lady-in-waiting to Princess Helena of Aragón

***Frère* Carlos**—armarius, scribe, cantor of priory and castle of Calatayud

***Frère* Chaplain Jeremiah Santiago de Compostela**—Templar chaplain, scholar, son to Grand Master Gilbért de Érail

Gerard de Ridefort—infamous tenth grand master of the entire Templar order (1184–1189) who lost the battle of the Horns of Hattin in Levant

Helena—princess de Aragón; *marquésa* de Barcelona, Castile, y Provence; widow of the martyred principe Pedro, late brother to King Alfonso II of Aragón

Joanna—twin sister of Deborah (deceased) and aunt to Chaplain Jeremiah de Santiago and sister-in-law to Grand Master Gilbért de Érail

Marshal Poncho Díaz de Vivar—Templar ancestor of El Cid and carried El Cid's sword, Tizona

Miguel—*hermano*, *Frère abbé*, *abad*, abbot of San Pedro el Viejo in Huesca, Iberia; traveling companion of Lord Robert de Borron

Noir Ombre—War dog trained by Muhammad and Lord Robert de Borron

Pedro Bernardo Ramón—principe de Aragón; Marqués de Barcelona, Provence; martyr of the Battle of the Horns of Hattin in the Levant; late brother to King Alfonso II (The Chaste); late husband to Princess Helena

Prior Etienne—manager, wine merchant, sommelier of Princess Helena's vineyards

Sancha—reina de Aragón; Condesa de Barcelona, Catalonia, Provence, Cerdanya, y Roussillon; also spouse and queen of King Alfonso II (The Chaste)

Suleiman—one of the assassins of the *Hashishiyya*

Yitzhak, Isaac the Blind (Rabbi Yitzhak Saggi Nehor)—his name means much light, he is a seer, Jewish mystical leader, philosopher, and teacher of the Kabbalah

The Principal Characters of England
Anno Domini 1190-1191

Abbot Henri de Sully—abbot and overseer of Glastonbury *Abbaye*, 1189–1193

Cernunnos—Merlin, Hern, and the Green Man; a supernatural being with powers of shapeshifting, a seer, and the ability of immortality

***Frère* Ambrosius**—armarius, scribe, cantor at Glastonbury *Abbaye*

***Frère* Cedric**—brother (blood) to Sergeant Jacque de Hoult, an accountant, residing at the London Temple

Grand Master Guillaume de Newham—leader of the London Temple with jurisdiction over England

Guillaume de Longchamp—bishop of Ely, lord chancellor, chief justiciar of England, legate to Rome

Guillaume le Maréchal, earl of Pembroke—good friend of Grand Master Gilbért de Érail and King Richard the Lionheart's marshal and fixer

Preceptor Roger de Shelborne—commander of the Templecombe preceptory and friend of Grand Master Gilbért de Érail

Saint Dunstan—most venerated saint of England from the 10th through 11th centuries, abbot of Glastonbury Abbey, artist, silversmith, and archbishop of Canterbury

The Principal Characters of Britannia, Gaul, and the Mediterranean Sea *Anno Domini* 37-43

Adair—Celtic Druid priest in diaspora from Britannia and friend of Yoseph of Arimathea

Alein Yosephe—son to Yoseph of Arimathea, no longer a partner in his father's worthless business

Ammon—Jewish name means "hidden one" and is the evil Barabbas

Azazel—Jewish demonic name means "hot desolate place"

Barabbas—the murderer set free by Jewish Sanhedrin, instead of Jesus the Christ, released by Pontius Pilate

Bedwyr—Celtic clan chief for the Glass Isle or Avalon

Beli—Arch Celtic Druid; name means "shining one" and grandson to Adair

Clotho—Greek woman, early follower of Yoseph of Arimathea, living in Palestine with new baby and wife to Georgeus, traveled with Yoseph to Gaul

Eli of *Yerushalayim* (Jerusalem)—camel and cloth merchant; with two sons, Eliyah and Isaiah

Eliyah—son of Eli, the camel and cloth merchant

Enid—Druid priestess and great granddaughter of Adair

Enoch—infant son of Hebron and Enygeus; also name of Old Testament prophet who walked with God and didn't die

Enygeus—sister to Yoseph of Arimathea, husband to Hebron

Finn—Arch Druid of southern Britannia and old friend of Yesha ben Yoseph and Saint Yoseph of Arimathea

Georgeus—Greek husband to Clotho, earlier follower of Yoseph of Arimathea and traveled with him to Gaul, has a baby named after Yoseph of Arimathea

Hebron—brother-in-law to Yoseph of Arimathea and husband to Enygeus; now a teacher

Hiram of Yoffa—captain of the ship *King Solomon*, son of the widow Tabitha (aka Dorcus)

Isaiah—Eli's son

King Arviragus—ruler of the Celtic Silures

Lazarus (Eleazar)—resurrected from the dead by Yeshua ben Yoseph (Jesus the Christ), brother to Miriam and Martha, later follower of Yoseph of Arimathea and bishop of Marseilles, Gaul

Marcella—related to the late Queen Cleopatra and handmaid to Martha

Martial—friend of Lazarus, follower of Saint Joseph of Arimathea, shipwrecked sailor

Maximus—friend of Lazarus, follower of Saint Joseph of Arimathea, shipwrecked sailor

Miriam Cleopas—one of the Mirams at the crucifixion and later preached in Gaul; also, one of the *les Maries de le mare*

Miriam of Magdala—former landowner, mystic, student of Rabbi Yeshua ben Yoseph, an old friend to Yoseph of Arimathea, preached and taught many years in a cave near Baume, Gaul, as an anchorite teacher; also, one of the *les Maries de le mare*

Miriam Salome—possible sister to Yeshua ben Yoseph (the Christ), was at the tomb, traveled to Gaul where she drifted ashore with the two other Miriams (*les Maries de le mare*)

Nathan—good friend of Yoseph of Arimathea and Lazarus, follows Yoseph to the Glass Isle

Nicodemus—expelled member of the Jewish Sanhedrin ruling council; now a rabbi, apostle, and old friend of Yoseph of Arimathea

Philip—first apostle of Gaul and good friend to Yoseph of Arimathea

Philo—mystic, theologian, philosopher, Jewish leader in Alexandria, teacher of the Kabbalah, good friend of Yoseph of Arimathea

Sarah—from the ancient land of Abyssinia and the line of queen of Sheba, handmaid to Martha and Miriam of Magdala in Gaul

Saturninus—teacher and preached Christianity in Toulouse, Gaul

Shimon of Cyrene—friend of Yoseph of Arimathea and Nicodemus; carried the cross for Jesus the Christ

Sidonius—aka Restitutus, the man born blind and preached in the upper Rhône Valley, Gaul

Tabitha, also known as Dorcas—clothing maker and widowed mother of Captain Hiram

Thomas Didymus—apostle of Rabbi Yeshua ben Yoseph; also a later member who joined Yoseph of Arimathea and left for India and became an apostle

Trophimus—bishop of Arles, Gaul; commissioned by Saint Philip of Gaul

Yohanan the Baptizer—cousin to Rabbi Yeshua ben Yoseph. He foretold Rabbi Yeshua as the Messiah, and he would baptize his disciples with the Holy Spirit. Yohanan was possibly Essene trained. He had a son named Zechariah and, after Yohanan's beheading, his son was raised by Yoseph of Arimathea's family.

Yohanan Marcus—writer, student of Rabbi Yeshua, his two-story home used for the Seder (Passover meal), later becomes a pupil of Philo of Alexandria

Yosa—daughter to Yoseph of Arimathea

Yoseph ben Caiaphas—former high priest of the Jews; past head of the Sanhedrin

Yoseph of Arimathea—richest merchant in the Mediterranean region, member of the Jewish Sanhedrin ruling council, uncle to Miriam of Nazareth, great uncle to Yeshua ben Yoseph of Nazareth; now a Christian teacher (rabbi), apostle, penniless

Yudas Iscariot—treasurer, disciple for Rabbi Yeshua ben Yoseph, rumored to be a member of the Sicarii (daggermen), a group who assassinates Roman officials, later died by suicide

Zechariah—orphan son of Yohanan the Baptizer

PART ONE

Death Lingers

CHAPTER I

Kingdom of Aragón

Winter

Anno Domini 1190

I placed my steaming clay bowl of *café* on a protruding stone block, while sitting down, and focused my eyes on Suleiman's departure. He disappeared from my sight down the steep hilltop as fast as a male hare chasing a female in springtime. Quickly, I dashed to the portcullis just as it was lowered, thwarting my attempt from further pursuit. A sudden cold wind heightened my thinking as I observed him abandon his cart, and then gallop his horse down the treacherous fortress path. He wore the same distinctive clothing that I now remembered from both Vézelay and Huesca.

I grabbed my bowl of brew, gulped it down, and raced off in search of Grand Master Gilbért to tell him whom I just observed. I noticed *Abad* Miguel coming my way.

"*Pax vobiscum*, Lord Robert," he stated. "Are you upset about something?"

"*Oui*, and I urgently need to see Grand Master Gilbért. Have you seen him this morning?" I hoped he would say *oui*.

"*Si*, he is at the training grounds practicing with his big Damascus sword. Just follow the metallic sound of striking swords, you will find him there."

"*Merci* for the information." I nodded to him and ran toward the *clanking* sound of swords. On the far side of the large keep was a fenced practice area, which to my surprise held both Gilbért and Chaplain Jeremiah. Each man wore full chain mail that covered a bulky aketon coat while fighting each other as if it were a matter of life or death. Chaplain Jeremiah was quick as a cat as he sidestepped his *père's* thrust, yet Grand Master Gilbért instinctively backstepped his thrust as the blade tip found empty air. A steaming exhale of breath came from each man in the cold December morning. Each had beads of sweat dripping from the tips of their noses. Their focus was on the fighting arena, and they didn't see me approach until I started waving my hands back and forth. Grand Master Gilbért glanced in my direction but didn't stop his slashing movements. His *fils* continued fighting, not noticing my signal as he struck his *père* across his shoulder with the flat blade of his sword.

"*Halte*," shouted Grand Master Gilbért, as he dropped his sword on the frosty ground. "What's wrong? You appear distressed, Lord Robert, and you have black circles under your eyes." He wiped his face with a cloth a young squire just handed him.

"*Oui*, you are correct on both counts, but it's not the lack of sleep that concerns me. We need to speak in private as soon as possible."

"*Abbé* Jeremiah, please take my sword," he said, "then meet us in the parlor right before Terce." He reached down, grasped his sword, and threw it toward his *fils*, who caught it with the quickness of an eagle.

"What's troubling you, *mon ami*?" Gilbért asked, as we moved toward a stone alcove.

"I think the *qahwa* Moor vendor has been following us since we left Huesca. Possibly even before I met you," I added.

"What makes you think that?" Grand Master Gilbért inquired.

"Do you remember me describing the strangely dressed Moor

I glimpsed one night back at Huesca?"

"*Oui.*"

"Remember, Commander Sancho gave him a sack of coins there at the old mosque; while hidden I observed his strange clothing. I viewed the same, red-colored boots and red sash covered today by a brown tunic and black mantle. He was the same height and weight as the man at Huesca. However, what caught my observation was his diminutive size. Back in the woods at Vézelay, one of the three men who murdered your sergeant fits his small height. I never ascertained their faces, and the vendor had a black cloth around his head, which only exposed his eyes."

"Are you positive it's the same man?" asked Gilbért as he rubbed his beard.

"Absolutely, I recognized his voice from Huesca, and he became suspicious when I stared at his attire. After I paid him, he mounted his horse, left the fortress, and seemed to vanish from the rocky hilltop. This showed me at once he was an excellent equestrian just like the ones at Vézelay. Is this one of de Tournay's scouts who is trailing us?"

Grand Master Gilbért gazed down at his boots in deep thought.

"*Non, mon ami*, this smells of the cardinal. Your description of his clothes and riding abilities sounds familiar to me, but I don't think he is entirely a scout. Did he have a *jambiya*-style dagger similar to Muhammad's?"

"*Oui*," I quickly answered, "but the handle was plainer."

"We must speak to *Abbé* Jeremiah about his attire. He'll give us his scholarly opinion on this man's clothes. Follow me to the parlor and we can further discuss this new incident."

Hurriedly, we both bound up the tower steps and reached the parlor room breathless. Grand Master Gilbért entered first and sat next to the fireplace.

"Was the *qahwa bon*?" he asked as I sat down in front of him.

"*Oui*, it was excellent. The drink is amazing, the cloudiness of my still sleepy mind vanished. What do the Christians of Iberia call the drink?"

"They call it *café* and others say *coffeé*," he replied with a slight smile. "Do you think this Moor is trying to poison me and my men?"

It was an unexpected question I hadn't anticipated, which sent fear through my body. "I think he is shadowing us to see if we will find the next *Sangraal* parchments. He or whoever is aiding him needs me alive and won't kill me or the rest of us until our quest is completed. Though I fear the cardinal may kill others who aren't essential to our trip to Toledo."

"Your good reasoning makes sense and I agree with you, but we must be aware of the cardinal's ruthless ever-changing tactics."

"What kind of ruthless tactics is the cardinal using now?" came *Abbé* Jeremiah's question as he entered the room.

"*Baron* Robert and I were discussing a strangely dressed Moor posing as a *qahwa* vendor who is spying on us. What do you know about the local dress, customs, and daggers of the Moors?"

"I know some of their clothing styles and weapons. Please explain more, Lord Robert."

I repeated the description to Chaplain Jeremiah, not leaving out the slightest detail. He sat at the end of the table with his hands clasped under his chin, listening to every word, mirroring his *père's* contemplating mannerisms.

"I'll leave for the scriptorium and discuss this with my armarius, Carlos. He may have some answers or books that could help us."

He sprung up from his seat, quickly rounded the table, and exited the parlor.

"I know my chaplain will find an answer. He hasn't failed me yet." We then both moved closer to the roaring fire.

It was just a short period of time before he returned holding a dust-covered book and placed it on the table. Meticulously, he unstrapped the small leather belts holding the book's contents together and slowly opened it.

"Where did this book originate?" I asked, curiosity pulling on my mind.

"Carlos told me it came from a great Muslim library at Cordoba. It says here on the first page, *Ahl al-bayt* or the People of the House authored this book. It's referring to the great prophet Muhammad's bloodline. It states on the second page that this book helps those who seek the *haqiqa* or inner truth."

"What specific members is it referring to?" I asked.

"The Prophet Muhammad had a daughter by the name of Fatima, and she later married Muhammad's cousin, Ali. Thus, Muhammad's bloodline continued through this marriage. Ali became the first Imam of the Muslim faith. The Shiite sect of Islam started with Ali and his wife, Fatima. The scholars have told us that before Muhammad died, he passed on secret knowledge to Ali. The Saracens call this secret knowledge *nass.*

"What does the word Imam mean?"

"It means 'supreme guide or leader of the Muslim faith that originated with *Allah's* authority.' The Shia Imams are said to interpret the hidden meanings of the *Qur'an*, which is called *bāṭin.*"

Abbé Jeremiah paused for a moment, turned one of the red and green-colored designed Moorish pages, and perused it, before speaking.

"What I am seeking is a section of epistles called the *Rasā'il Ikhwān aṣ-Ṣafā'*. It's a collection of fifty-two epistles divided into four parts that discusses all the known sciences, including astronomy, geometry, and music. In addition, there are treatises on philosophy, religion, the cosmos, and eschatology. Ah! Here it is. I will read this opening line for you, Lord Robert. 'He who knows himself best knows his creator best.' It's at the heading of an epistle, which speaks of the Brethren of Purity. It further states this group has learned the way to enlightenment. The goal of the student is to purify his soul and achieve salvation, which he accomplishes by studying a combination of Greek philosophy, Christian ethics, Sufi mysticism, which is another sect of Islam, and Muslim law. The book tells of nine degrees of wisdom administered by *daìs.* The *daìs* are the direct representatives of the Imam."

"What does all this esoteric information have to do with the Moor who has been tracking me and my companions?"

"Lord Robert, let me continue. We may understand what motivates him and how many more are like him. Please bear with me."

I nodded my agreement and Chaplain Jeremiah continued.

"The word *daìs* means 'summoners.' They summon their pupils to teach them the nine secret degrees."

Suddenly, he stopped speaking with his eyes widening.

"How can this be?" he asked while turning several pages forward. "The pages explaining the nine degrees are expunged, they aren't here. Please forgive my lapse, however, there's an *ulama* or Muslim scholar in Toledo who knows about the nine degrees. We will speak to him when we arrive there."

His momentary pause to gather his thoughts gave me a brief opportunity to ask about an update on the *Sangraal* parchments. "Chaplain Jeremiah, when you were in the scriptorium, did you ask *Frère* Carlos how the book was progressing?" I prayed to myself its completion might be earlier than we thought.

"He said he's ahead of schedule and you'll have the bound parchments tomorrow."

"I am sorry to interrupt you . . . you were saying something about a scholar you know in Toledo who could tell us more about the Brethren of Purity." I hoped the scholarly *abbé* wasn't offended at my numerous interruptions.

"*Si,* there are two scholars there who could be of service to our quest. One is a *Judio,* and the other is a Moor I just mentioned. The *Judio's* name is Isaac the Blind or Rabbi Yitzhak Saggi Nehor, which means of much light. The Muslim's name is Averroes or Ibn Rushd. After we return the *Marquésa* Helena to Zaragozza, we'll plan our trip in more detail. In the meantime, I will contact *Hermano* Enriqué at our commandery at San Servando. Chaplain Enriqué knows both men and we can use the *castillo's* good library.

"Where is Muhammad Nur Adin?" I asked, wondering why he wasn't here to help us.

"Before we came here, I sent him a note to track the *qahwa* vendor you saw. I hope he'll have some useful information. He should be back by Vespers, and we can defer any discussion until he returns. Let's proceed to the *chapelle;* we have already missed Terce and now it's time for Nones."

Quickly, we adjourned and proceeded to the *chapelle* with my mind still trying to comprehend all the information from the dusty old tome. The Brethren of Purity was the name Commander Armound de Polignac mentioned at Carcassonne to beware of. So far, I had concluded the Brethren of Purity was a violent and secret organization, yet I feared to hear more.

Ringing bells suddenly distracted my thoughts as they announced the daily office of Nones. Helena jumped up from a kneeling bench in the *chapelle* and her dark brown eyes met mine as she hurried out a side door while holding her chaplet beads.

After the service, I returned to my cell and found a note on my writing table. Upon examining it, the folded paper had a red wax seal embedded with the royal crest of Aragón. Quickly, I broke it, and my nose caught the fragrant rose-vanilla scent of Helena. My fingers carefully unfolded the note, and I began to read its contents. She requested my presence in her room as soon as I returned from Nones. Hurriedly, I washed my face, then combed my hair, after which I put on a clean Templar surcoat, and exited my quarters. I bound up the spiral stairway with my rapid heartbeat anticipating our meeting. What new illuminations would she reveal today to surprise me? My hand forcefully pounded on the door and then I announced my name.

"Roberto, please come in," came her silky sounding voice. Upon entering, I observed she was by herself.

"Where is Esperanza?" I inquired, surprised to see her alone.

"Lord Robert, at least you could say hello and give me a proper greeting," she said in a mild rebuke. "My subjects are better mannered than you."

"I am sorry, Helena, for my poor manners. I wasn't expecting you to be alone. Again, please forgive me for my thoughtlessness."

"You're forgiven," she said with a sly smile. "Just for your information, Esperanza is mending some of my riding dresses; otherwise, she would have been here. Now sit down and tell me about the mysterious parchments you're having *Frère* Carlos make into a book."

I was surprised. How did she know this? Had he disclosed to her our secret?

"You can remove that silly surprise expression on your face," she stated, this time with a crooked smile. "You should know me by now to realize I have many sources who will divulge information to me, and *non*, *Frère* Carlos didn't betray your secrecy."

"I must admit, Helena, you have better information than the evil cardinal." I shook my head in disbelief.

"As I mentioned earlier, the royal family members of the *Royaume* de Aragón's survival depends on punctual accurate information about our enemies as well as our financial interests. It's a live chess game we can't lose. Now tell me more about this holy book."

I was in a dilemma; how much should I divulge? Yet, I had sworn to secrecy not to speak of the book or its contents. Did she know everything or was she bluffing to gain further information?

"For expediency's sake, do you have any idea what the book contains?" I asked.

"*Non*, only it's a copy of something written by a man at the time of our Lord and Savior, Jesus the Christ," she answered, while crossing herself.

"*Oui*, that's true, but what do you know about the saint, Joseph de Arimathea?"

She thought a moment then replied.

"He was the man who dressed our Lord in a burial shroud after taking Him off the cross. In addition, he placed Jesus in his own sepulcher, from which our Lord resurrected himself from His human death."

"*Oui*, you are correct again, Helena, but there's more to this man's life than in the twelve verses of the four Gospels of Saint Jerome's translated Bible."

Her eyes widened. "I think you have found something about Saint Joseph de Arimathea that nobody else knows." She gave a sly grin.

"You're right, but I can't say anymore. I've been sworn to secrecy and my mortal soul may be at stake if I reveal any further information."

I hoped my statement would deter her demanding curiosity.

"What did he say in his parchments, Robert?" Once again, she didn't give up but pressed on for more answers. Her weak smile now turned into a frown of frustration.

"One last piece of information; there may be additional parchments written by Joseph de Arimathea. However, let's discuss your vineyards that you want to show me." I hoped to change the subject and stave off any more questions. Helena had a way of making me say things I knew I would later regret.

"One final thought, Robert. It's apparent Cardinal Folquet won't stop until you and Grand Master Gilbért lead him to the additional parchments, if they still exist. What is written on these parchments, and the importance of its worth, the cardinal must greatly value in pursuing you here and losing his numerous *chevaliers*. His evil and greedy heart is his fuel to follow you to the ends of the earth. Beware, Robert, he is a godless man and a cardinal in title only.

"So, you want to know more about my vineyards, *oui*?" Helena suddenly changed our topic of conversation. "I have many large oaken casks at *Château* Maluenda holding my *vino*. There are fifty workers tending the fields and fermenting the grapes, which the *moines* at the nearby priory supervise. The *moines'* expertise and assistance have made the vineyards quite profitable for everybody in *Roi* Alfonso's *royaume*.

"Now, I have a question for you, Robert. When will *Frère* Carlos have your codex completed?" She still was not giving up.

"Soon," I replied.

"I need to depart in several days," she stated. "Both the prior and I are to meet and plan for a large shipment of *vino* sailing to England. It's urgent the shipment arrives . . . before our Christ's Mass."

"*Frère* Carlos will have the tome completed tomorrow and we could leave any time after the holy book is returned to me."

She gave a quiet sigh of relief.

"My *château* is a retreat away from the obfuscation of court life and at Maluenda I feel like a normal woman. Overseeing my vineyard is always a good excuse to flee from the burdensome responsibility of royal duties."

"Tell me, Robert, how did you meet your *épouse*? Was it an arranged marriage?"

"*Non*, it was the *comte* who introduced us, while I was entertaining at his court. Her graceful young countenance and lovely shape captured my eyes and heart. It wasn't because she was a *mademoiselle* of high degree, but her kind demeanor. She didn't dominate our conversation yet wasn't shy. Marie had the patience to examine with care and comment with pertinent thoughts. She would speak her mind, just like her *frère,* in a convincing fashion, which wasn't emotional in nature. It's quite uncannily similar to you, for I feel you and I have known each other far longer than a week."

"You're too kind to a lonely woman," she replied, reaching for my hands, and grasping them in a tight warm grip. Both our eyes met, and we each smiled, while Helena still maintained her grip. It felt good to have a woman touch me once more, yet I could see in her eyes the sadness of losing a soul mate. I concluded we both longed for something we couldn't have, just as she released her hands from mine.

"Robert, I have enjoyed speaking to you this afternoon; let's meet here tomorrow. I suspect we'll be departing the day after tomorrow for my *château*. For now, *au revoir,* Roberto," she said, translating my name into her native language.

We both rose for me to leave. Her closeness filled my nose with her wafting vanilla-rose scent, which permeated the entire room. Her full breasts brushed up against my surcoat with each step she made toward her door. Quickly, we reached her room door, she turned to face me with our eyes staring at each other. There was a moment of hesitation before she released my arm. After the *clanking* of the released lock, she turned once again toward me, gave me a kiss on my cheek, and then retreated into her room. My giddiness overcame me, and my heart raced with excitement as I started back to my room. Was our loneliness capturing us in its snare? Yet, I knew her beauty and our common interests were propelling me closer to her too, yet still reflecting on the faces of Marie and my two *fils*.

CHAPTER II

After opening the door of my cell, an unexpected familiar voice startled me. "Did you enjoy your meeting with the *marquésa*?" asked the surreptitious Grand Master Gilbért.

"*Oui,* but how did you know?" I was a little surprised to see him in my room.

"These ancient Moorish walls speak to my fellow *frères.* Nothing is hidden in our holy domain. Don't worry, Lord Robert, I am not spying on you. Daily, I receive many different items of information. Some of it's worthless to me, yet I must be diligent when there's a traitor in our midst. The only caveat I might add to this conversation is don't divulge any *Sangraal* information to *Marquésa* Helena. If you remember, *mon ami*, I didn't want *Abbé* Jean Saint Gauden to know about our quest, for fear the cardinal's men would torture him. The *marquésa* is a powerful woman, both in rank and determination, yet the less she knows, the fewer people we'll have to protect."

"Is it true after tomorrow we are departing for Helena's vineyards?"

"*Oui,* I just received word from Muhammad, and he said he lost the trail of the *qahwa* vendor."

I couldn't believe the great Saracen prince and scout couldn't track down any mortal man, which left me feeling troubled.

"Muhammad said he was *taqiyya,*" Grand Master Gilbért stated.

"What does *taqiyya* mean?" I asked, fearing I didn't want to know the definition.

"It means one who is concealing himself from what he purports to be. He's a 'shapeshifter' and can disguise himself as anything or anybody."

This left me quite puzzled and didn't make any sense. "You are confusing me, please explain further."

"The vendor was a spy, but not just an ordinary spy, for he was sent here to kill or capture one of us at the proper time."

"Whom was he sent to kill?"

"It could be any of us. If I knew more about who sent him, we could be better prepared to defend ourselves and who they are targeting." Grand Master Gilbért's pinched face stare unsettled me.

"Why not the obvious answer? The cardinal sent him."

"I don't believe the cardinal sent him, for this man was trained and schooled in the Levant, however, I have been wrong before." Our warrior-*moine* leader then pulled on his bushy beard.

To my chagrin, our list of enemies seemed to grow larger by the day, leaving me with more doubts about completing our quest.

The next day Helena and her lady-in-waiting, Esperanza, met me in the parlor. They entered the room a short time after the divine office of Nones.

"*Bonjour*, Lord Robert. Did you sleep well last night?" Helena smiled while glancing at Esperanza.

"*Oui*, better than the previous night, although my cell was quite cold. Not like the warm *crackling* fire we have here before us. I see that it snowed last night. Will this make our journey to your *château* difficult?"

"*Non*, there's a level road and most of it travels along the banks of the Rio Jiloca to my *château*. It's one day's journey from Catalunya and I would dress for the colder weather. The winds off the rio are quite strong, making our ride uncomfortable, yet we should reach Maluenda before nightfall. Grand Master Gilbért told me we would have extra Templar *chevaliers* escorting us to my *château.* He didn't say why we need this additional escort. Do you know why?" She gave me a coy smile, leaving me with the impression that she was testing my response.

"*Oui*, he knows that the cardinal may lay another trap for us before we reach Maluenda." I knew my lie wouldn't deceive Helena too long, for her sources of information were superb. I believed her spies were better than Grand Master Gilbért's informers. Yet, I couldn't confirm either, leaving me with a conundrum. Should I confide in her what Grand Master Gilbért told me about the *qahwa* vendor? Her safety greatly concerned me, especially after I felt responsible for several deaths.

I gave in. "He thinks the *qahwa* vendor is a spy and called him a *taqiyya* or 'shapeshifter.' Yesterday he visited us here at the fortress and a short time later he left when I recognized him from Huesca. He was sent here to kill or capture one of us, for what reasons I can't say. It could be for the *Sangraal* parchments, to stop or slow our quest, or hold you, Helena, for ransom. I just don't know, but Grand Master Gilbért thinks it isn't one of the cardinal's killers." I wondered if my mouth had said too much.

"You have a spy in your midst, Roberto," Helena said, "and it's one of the grand master's men, yet I don't know which one."

"Your sources couldn't specify?" I asked, not surprised she knew.

"*Non*, however, have you seen any suspicious behavior by any of his men? What about his Saracen scout? He's from the Levant and would seem connected to this *taqiyya.* In addition, he is gone for long lengths of time."

"What you say is true, but I still can't believe any of my companions would betray us. There aren't any braver or more trustworthy men anywhere than Grand Master Gilbért's men. Each would die protecting one another and a good example of this was Squire Hughes. He threw his body in front of a crossbow quarrel protecting one of his fellow *frères* and died. I still curse Marcel de Tournay each day for the young, martyred squire's death. As for Muhammad's loyalty, Grand Master Gilbért risked his life to rescue him from certain death. He is indebted forever to the grand master for protecting him from harm's way."

"*Mon ami*, please be careful, I fear for your life even more, since you are a family man and have two handsome *fils*. Your quest is quite important, but don't leave an *épouse* and two children without a *père*." Helena reached and grasped my hands and then kissed them.

A small tear of sadness rolled down her cheek as we both sat down then staring into each other's eyes. Only silence prevailed, with each of us searching for answers. However, I knew some of our questions about each other were similar but different. Our eyes didn't want to depart, but Esperanza's quiet cough broke our intense gaze. We turned our faces away, while still holding our warm hands together and glanced at Esperanza.

"Your *Altesse*, please forgive me for interrupting, however, we must prepare for our journey tomorrow. It's time we leave, Lord Robert, and I wish we could speak longer, but my *altesse* and I have many details to complete before we depart tomorrow. It's my duty to see the servants are ready upon our arrival at Maluenda. Perhaps after we arrive at my *altesse's château*, we can converse some more." Esperanza smiled.

I hated to release my grasp from Helena's soft hands, yet reluctantly I stood to escort both women to the *Marquésa* Helena's room. Helena tightly grabbed my left arm, while Esperanza did the same to my right arm. All three of us strolled toward her room down the dim-lit stone corridor. Upon reaching their door, both women turned to face me, smiled, and slowly released their tight grips from my arms. Helena unlocked the door and both women disappeared behind it, with Helena's rose-vanilla fragrance still lingering in the hallway. I didn't want to leave but toyed with knocking on the door to see if Helena would speak to me after the office of Compline. Yet, once again in my mind's eye I saw Marie's face and I had to meet *Frère* Carlos in the scriptorium at that time. Deciding not to knock, I left for my room to update my journal, after which I rested some before Compline and meeting the dwarfish *moine*.

Compline was over quicker than I anticipated, letting me reach the scriptorium before the final rays of sunlight. There I met *Frère* Carlos, who was sitting at his slanted desktop, yet it was too dark to copy any parchments. Instead, he was grinding with a mortar and pestle some reddish-orange concoction on a small flat table. On one side of the flat table were penknives, pumice stones, awls, and a reading frame. I didn't see any finished book lying on his slanted desktop and now feared he hadn't finished the *Sangraal* book.

"*Bonjour, Frère* Carlos," I said with a lump forming in my throat. "What is this reddish-orange liquid you're producing?"

"*Bueno tardes* to you, *Señor* Roberto," he replied.

"It's crushed ladybugs, red ants, and a little olive oil. This makes excellent ink for our red-colored illuminations. All our writing inks and illumination colors come from the surrounding countryside. One of our *frères'* full-time duties is to seek out a goodly supply of plants and insects to use here in the scriptorium. However, you didn't come here to hear me lecture about our ink-making process. You want to see the completed tome of the *Sangraal, oui*?"

"*Si,* oh, I mean *oui,*" not realizing the learned *moine* spoke my native language. His philological skills, both ancient and modern, let him shift from one foreign language to another, without any difficulty.

"*Señor* Roberto, please follow me down this corridor and I will lead you to my fellow *frères*, who have completed binding the *Sangraal* codex. One of my companions is the finest tanner in Iberia and used the best calfskin leather to bind the holy parchments."

We moved a short distance and approached a window facing an open cell, or as the holy scribes called it, a *carrell.*

"This *moine* sitting here is *Frère* Seamus. He is from Hibernia and our expert illuminator. The other *moine* standing next to him is *Frère* Enriqué. As I mentioned earlier, he is a foremost tanner."

"Lord Robert, you have a great precious God-given gift," the redheaded Hibernian stated. "Divine intervention has entered your body to remember so much detail. In addition, the speed you can write and the ancient words you can translate onto parchment."

"*Si*, it's a miracle, for you have surpassed *Santo* Jerome in speed when he translated our *Santo* Bible into Latin," *Frère* Enriqué commented, his dark eyes widening with wonder.

"*Bonjour* and *merci beaucoup*, holy *frères*," I replied. "However, my divine gift is solely for understanding the will of our Lord, Jesus the Christ, and His disciple, Saint Joseph de Arimathea." There was a slight pause in my conversation, allowing ourselves to make the sign of the cross, to honor our Savior and His servant.

"It's both odd and a blessing I can translate the many ancient words Saint Joseph has written, but no other languages, other than my native tongue and the Latin language. Even the Latin language has changed somewhat in the last twelve hundred years." I strained my neck looking for the revised tome. "Enough discussion, *mes amis*. Where is the *Sangraal* book?" I inquired, my body trembling with anticipation.

Frère Carlos ambled over to a small wooden cupboard, stopped, reached into his surcoat pocket, and pulled out a ring of keys. He partially stooped over, unlocked a set of doors, after which he reached in, and with much circumspection grabbed a dark cloth sack. Slowly, and with reverence, he turned to place the sack on a table nearest me. My entire body ached to see what the cloth sack's contents would reveal while praying for the small *moine* to move faster. Each of his footsteps seemed mired in deep mud and each of his knees seemed frozen. I drew nearer the table just as he placed the sack on the wooden tabletop. Slowly, he reached into the cloth bag and withdrew its contents.

"Behold the words of God, *Señor* Roberto!" *Frère* Carlos exclaimed for all to hear.

"*Mère de Dieu*!" I too shouted. Then came my deep gasp of amazement, as all three *moines* crossed themselves once again. The holy codex's shiny brown binding was exquisite in the last fading rays of sunlight. Instantly a sense of relief and happiness overtook my entire being, prompting me at once to say a prayer of thanksgiving.

"*Señor* Roberto, our Excellency Grand Master Gilbért described to us how the old *Sangraal* book appeared before it was stolen from us. However, I am sorry we couldn't replace the precious jewels embedded in the old book's covers by our Cistercian *frères*, but I know you will like each page's illuminations," *Frère*

Carlos said with a toothy smile of accomplishment. I embraced each one of the hardworking artisan *moines* and told them God had guided their hands and my companions wouldn't forget their holy work. After much praise to my fellow scribes, the book beckoned me to peruse its cover and contents.

"Let me hold the book and see the many illuminated pages." I lowered myself to a bench alongside the table. Carefully, my fingertips felt an embossing in the smooth calfskin leather covering. To my surprise, it was the same symbol as the one found in the cave at San Juan de la Peña. My fingers counted the five fish designs, along with the five petals of the cinquefoil flower and the five-pointed star. Slowly, I turned the many bound parchment pages, wondering how I had completed such a momentous task. My eyes sharply focused on the Celtic-designed illuminations bordering each page of Saint Joseph's original words that I had copied. Their twisting ornate animals, people, and plant characters seemed to glow and move before my sight. There were orange-colored fish endlessly intertwined with one another. On numerous pages, the corners had blue-colored triquetrous highlighting each new page number, followed with a bronze-colored designed chalice decorating the tops of the first paragraph of all beginning chapters. All the cups generated yellow rays of light from their interiors, and at the end of each chapter a green-leafed tree, with knotted tree roots inextricably interwoven with an identical tree turned upside down below it. All my senses embraced the smell of the new leather, the sounds from the *crinkling* parchment pages, the touch of the embossing, the multitude of the colors, and even the taste of the leather after closing the holy book when I kissed it.

"Bless you, *frères*, for I know God and His Holy Spirit were in your hearts, hands, and sight this past week."

"*Señor* Roberto, we are like you, humble servants of God and His Son," *Frère* Carlos said, bowing his head and crossing himself. "Please accept the *santo* book." Carlos gestured with his small hands. "May God protect you on your quest, my *amigo*."

Slowly and with reverence, he handed me the heavy *Sangraal* codex, pausing momentarily before placing it into my arms. "Let me show you out of our scriptorium, it becomes quite dark in here after sunset. You may become confused, so follow me."

I said my good-byes to the other two *moines*, embraced them, and then turned to follow *Frère* Carlos out of the scriptorium. Once we reached the entrance, he paused and spoke.

"*Pax vobiscum, mon ami,* I know I won't see you again, but God has told me you will find what you seek." We embraced one last time.

He closed the large arched door and at once I strolled back to my room. The new leather smell of the codex exhilarated my nose upon approaching my room; knowing quite well I wouldn't let it out of my sight. I failed to continue to the holy office of Vespers, but stayed in my cell until after Compline, studying the magnificent artwork designs on every page. I knew the *moines* who bound this holy book couldn't read the ancient words of less than twelve hundred years ago, yet their hearts told them the purpose of the holy words.

CHAPTER III

My eyes blinked for sleep and the last candle in the cell sputtered its oncoming demise, letting me know it was time to retire. As my head caressed the straw-filled pillow, thoughts of tomorrow's visit at *Château* Maluenda and Helena's vineyard momentarily prevented me from falling to sleep, yet the anticipation didn't last before I fell fast asleep.

I awoke the next morning before dawn, anxious to leave on our visit. Reaching for the foot of my bed, the touch of my fingertips rubbed over the *Sangraal* bookbinding, letting me know it was still there. Cautiously, I packed the holy book into a waterproof cow's gut pouch and placed it into one of my saddlebags. Then, I changed into warmer clothes, which were fur-lined boots and gloves. After I finished dressing, I grabbed my saddlebags, approached my small wooden door, and quickly left the cell.

I met Grand Master Gilbért, Sergeants de Hoult and de Béziers in the bailey grounds next to the main keep. Small misty clouds of breath came from their mouths as each spoke something. Muhammad was absent as usual while scouting ahead for any ambushes. *Abbé* Jeremiah and *Abad* Miguel trotted up next to me on their horses holding the reins to mine.

"*Seigneur* Robert, I seized the liberty to have your horse saddled so we can start right away," *Abbé* Jeremiah said, handing me the reins to my horse.

"*Merci,* chaplain, for obtaining my horse. It appears we'll have cold weather today."

"*Si*, the dark clouds behind us are heavy with snow." He was gazing toward the jagged light of the morning dawn. "Grand Master Gilbért is in the armory and will arrive soon.

A thunderous *clopping* noise drew my attention, which forced me to turn around in the saddle. Racing up behind us, on horseback were Grand Master Gilbêrt with ten Templar *chevaliers* and ten Templar sergeants all holding lances and crossbows. The sudden show of force gave me an immediate sense of protective confidence, yet did our warrior-*moine* leader know something I didn't know?

"Where is *Marquésa* Helena?" I inquired of Grand Master Gilbért.

"Your *Altesse* is waiting for the rest of her courtiers. As you well know, women of high degree expend time on being presentable," he said with a bearded grin.

Just as the bells for Prime rang, there came the *rumbling* sound of wagon wheels from the stables accompanied by *whinnying* noises from the horses. First came the royal carriage with six palace *chevaliers*. Three rode in front, followed by three behind the carriage. Suddenly, the window curtains parted and there appeared Esperanza waving to obtain my attention. I waved back while searching to see if Helena was in the carriage. A second, yet smaller carriage appeared and fell in behind the palace *chevaliers*. This carriage already had its curtain pulled back, exposing the interior of the cabin. All I could see were lesser ladies-in-waiting and their *amants,* yet once again, no Helena.

"Lord Robert, are you searching for *Marquésa* Helen?" Gilbért asked, while rubbing his beard with nervous frustration.

"*Oui*," I answered, suddenly hearing a single galloping horse approaching from behind. A snorting Andalusian steed pulled up beside me revealing Helena as its rider.

"*Bonjour* and *bon matin, Seigneur* Robert," she said, her voice full of anticipation. "Are you ready to proceed to my *château*?"

"*Oui,* and I hope you slept well last night."

"Quite well, *merci beaucoup*, for I fell asleep knowing all my tasks were completed for today's visit. Sleep came fast and deep and now I am exhilarated by our ride. After you escorted Esperanza and me to my room, I sent a note by messenger instructing my staff to ready themselves upon our arrival today."

Then she spurred her horse's flanks. The big white animal raised himself on his hind legs and then raced forward for all to follow her lead. Helena's regal presence on horseback was impressive, yet more spectacular was her horse-handling abilities. She had complete control of the swift Andalusian as we galloped through the portcullis, passed the barbican, and made our way onto the steep narrow road. Once on level roads, the morning sunlight darted in and out of the dark clouds, letting on lighter occasions to see what she was wearing. Her head, shoulders, and part of her arms displayed a red-hooded brown fur-trimmed cape, which had a gold serpentine clasp holding it together at her neck. Under her cape was a thick ink-blue colored long sleeve brocade dress. For warmth, her hands displayed brown calfskin gloves, with matching colored leather boots. Inside her hood, she wore a white veiled wimple and kerchief circling her face. The top portion of her forehead bore a gold filigree-designed jewel-encrusted circlet, letting everyone know she was a royal member of the *Royaume* de Aragón.

Suddenly, she turned her horse facing toward the palace *chevaliers*, her oncoming courtiers, our warrior-*moines*, and shouted something in her native tongue. Instantly, one of the palace *chevaliers* galloped forward holding the royal flag of Aragón, with its large designed quartered shield bearing a red cross-topped oak-leafed tree in one quarter on a gold background. The second quarter, adjacent to the first, bore a silver fitchée cross in its quarter on an azure background. Directly below the first quarter, the third had a red Saint George cross that had four royal Moorish heads evenly spaced in the quarter. The fourth and final quarter had four red stripes on a gold background. The same royal crest that first greeted me at the Aljafería Palace. The huge multicolored *flapping* flag was an impressive sight blowing in the strong early December wind.

"Lord Robert, I hope you find my *château* comfortable, even though the food is sparse," she said with a grin, after falling back to join me. "Holy Advent has restricted our eating choices and supply, however, my beloved head cook will surprise us with some permissible selections. We can rely on some excellent aged *vin* from my vineyard, along with superb living accommodations, which after staying in *moine* cells, my *château* will seem like paradise. In addition, your quarters are quite tranquil and conducive to writing, if so moved. Your room has two large hearths, four windows giving you plenty of daylight, numerous large tables, several chairs, wool-made Moorish rugs, a quite ornate canopied bed, and the use of my main hall when you desire."

"*Merci beaucoup,* Helena, for thinking about my holy work and creature comforts," I replied, now feeling quite obligated to give her something in return. "Will your head cook have a supply of *qahwa* or *café*?" I was thinking about my capacity for alertness to update my journal.

"*Oui*, he has a sufficient supply of beans to roast for our entire entourage and even have some leftover."

Without warning, Sergeant de Hoult shouted to Grand Master Gilbért. "Your Excellency, search to the left of the horizon! I see a lone rider racing toward us!"

Grand Master Gilbért reached for his spyglass from his saddlebag. Quickly, he raised the tubular instrument to his eye, peered through the strange device, paused, and then announced it was Muhammad. "It appears he has urgent information, for his horse is quite lathered with sweat." He abruptly put the spyglass back into his saddlebag.

"Sergeant de Béziers, have the *roi's chevaliers* prepare for battle. I will inform our *chevaliers*." He spurred his horse to seek out the rest of his warrior-*moines*. Just within an eye's blink, my ear caught the metallic sound of swords withdrawing from their scabbards, with my fighting reflexes doing the same. Out of the corner of one of my eyes, my vision caught the Templar *chevaliers* bearing horizontal lances and quickly moving to protect our flanks. Half the warrior-*moines* followed Sergeant de Hoult to the front of our column; the other half quickly followed Sergeant de Béziers and galloped to our rear, while the palace *chevaliers* encircled the *marquésa.*

"Your *Altesse,* may I have your permission to command your *chevalier*?" Grand Master Gilbért urgently asked of Helena.

"*Oui*, you may," she quickly replied.

He turned his horse, spurred its flanks, and rode toward the leader of the royal *chevaliers.* He shouted something to him, the leader acknowledged Grand Master Gilbért, then shouted to his men. Instantly, they backed up their horses closer to Helena and closed ranks, forming a tight thorny circle around their *marquésa.*

Once again, Grand Master Gilbért spurred his horse and raced out to meet Muhammad, while the Templar marshal assumed temporary command of the Templar and royal *chevaliers.* After a short time, both men returned up a rocky side trail with their horses' nostrils flared from exhaustion.

"Lord Robert, some twelve unknown riders are following us!" Grand Master Gilbért announced for all to hear. "In addition, there are similar numbers hiding in a deep ravine ahead. It's quite important we stay close to the riverbank and not break ranks if attacked. I want all of you to follow my orders without hesitation!"

"Grand Master Gilbért!" Helena exclaimed. "Find me a sword promptly so I can protect my courtiers and fear not, I can use a sword with the best of the royal *chevaliers.* My late *mari* taught me how to defend myself."

Helena's demand amazed me, not because she was a *princesse* of Aragón, but the similarities between her and *mon épouse.* It was uncanny that I had trained *mon* Marie too, to fight and defend herself with a sword. Both women had the brazen fortitude to kill a man to protect themselves.

"Your *Altesse,* I can't allow you to have a sword," Grand Master Gilbért sternly stated. "I know how excellent your swordsmanship is, yet you and Lord Robert de Borron are too valuable to risk capture. My men won't allow this to happen, and your *chevaliers* will agree with me." Immediately, there was a resounding "*sí*!" from the voices of the men guarding the *marquésa*. Helena shook her head in disgust and then lunged for the nearest sword rider in a vain attempt to grab his weapon. Once she failed, she retreated farther into the thorny circle of lancers.

With caution, we slowly moved forward on the trail for another league, all the while shadowed by the unknown horsemen following us along a distant ridgeline. They neither wore discernible tunics nor carried a recognizable banner. The surrounding terrain became steeper as we progressed closer to Helena's *château*; finally seeing the mystery horsemen disappear. Was this a good sign or a deception?

Château Maluenda was perched on the top of a high plateau hill next to a valley that Grand Master Gilbért called El Ebro. At the base of the *château* was a small village with roofs of rust-colored clay tiles.

"Stay alert, Lord Robert and Your *Altesse*!" shouted Grand Master Gilbért. "If anything is to happen, it's now. They don't have enough men to attack the *château*, yet I fear for the villagers. Spur your horses and follow my lead!" He motioned with his left arm for us to race up the *château* road. The entire entrance road erupted with what sounded like rolling thunder, as thirty *chevaliers*, sergeants, and two royal coaches sped onto the narrow drawbridge. Luckily, we had dodged any ambush as our entourage quickly approached the square-shaped towers. Helena screamed for her gate sergeants to raise the portcullis, which happened instantly, just as the royal *chevaliers* galloped up to the raised barrier. Quickly, she yelled orders to her men, who were hiding behind the merlons, to arm their crossbows to fight. Suddenly, ten men appeared holding armed crossbows in front of each crenel. Her horse reared on his hind legs, sensing a forthcoming battle, and then galloped into the bailey area of the *château*. The *rumbling* sounds of her courtier's wagons followed her as they bounced over the timbered bridge. Grand Master Gilbért, his marshal, and I were the last to cross the drawbridge, just as Helena ordered her guards, who were stationed above the murder hole, to hastily raise it with the *clanking* iron chain.

Château Maluenda sat on a steep plateau, with two sides of it impossible to scale, letting me see a great distance above the roof-topped houses. Grand Master Gilbért and I jumped off our horses. Quickly, I searched around the bailey area for the steps to the *château* front embrasures; I spied them, and then darted toward the steps. Once we reached the embrasure landing, the entire valley floor was visible overlooking Helena's large fiefdom.

"Lord Robert, observe below that last hill into the village," Grand Master Gilbért said, pointing with his chain main-covered gauntlet. "There are the unknown followers who were tracking us." He reached for his spyglass from his opened saddlebag. To me, the image appeared like a small black snake slithering toward us ready to strike.

"*Oui*, they're the cardinal's men," came his quick terse comment. "I have an idea what they'll do next." He handed me the tubular glass-topped instrument. "Observe, you can just see the bottom arm of the cross of Toulouse on their saddle blankets."

Carefully, I rested the spyglass on the embrasure ledge and focused on its length. He was right; the round, yellow-colored knobs of the cross were slightly visible. "You said you knew what they were about to do next. What did you mean?" I watched their horses race closer to the village.

"They'll capture the village people and hold them hostage and kill them if their demands aren't met. *Mon ami*, we both know what those demands will be. I must alert my men and the *marquésa's chevaliers* to stop these evildoers. Lord Robert, hurry and tell her *altesse* to have her men lower the drawbridge, for her village is under attack. In addition, alert the royal *chevaliers* to attack the cardinal's men before they enter the village. We need to snuff those *bâtards* out instantly before they capture the villagers."

As I hurried down the stone steps to the bailey, Helena had already anticipated my message. She yelled directly to the sergeant of the guard, who immediately had his men release the *clattering* chain of the drawbridge. Slowly, the wooden bridge lowered with pawing horses behind it ready to race across. Yet, to my surprise, a lone guard on the highest tower raised a large red flag and vigorously waved it in the direction of a lone tower amidst the village houses. Out of the top of the square-shaped village tower, came a man replying with the same-sized waving red flag, which was followed by the ringing of bells. Right away, the villagers came out of their houses and scurried toward the lone square tower. Rapidly, a door at the bottom of the tower opened, which let the village people enter.

"So, this is their means of escape from the murderous bands of marauders and now the cardinal's men," I stated to Grand Master Gilbért. "It's quite a clever means of escape. I assume once the entire village is inside, they will withdraw the ladders keeping anybody from capturing them."

"*Oui,* that's correct, Lord Robert," came the reply not from the Templar grand master, but from *Marquésa* Helena. To my surprise, she had rushed to the battlement to oversee the threat to her subjects. Quickly, we rushed down the stone steps along with the grand master's marshal. There they were waiting for us, at the bottom of the steps, with saddled horses. With a single leap I mounted my horse, and then heard Grand Master Gilbért shout, "Lord Robert, you must stay here!" But I didn't want to hear him. Instantly, he shouted to his men, "Kill all the cardinal's men, and don't seize any prisoners!" Then came the thunderous pounding of our horse's hooves racing across the wooden bridge.

In unison, we cried out the names of Saint Michael and Saint George and shouted Psalm 115. It was a glorious sight as we rode down the steep trail from the *château*. Out in front of the charge was Grand Master Gilbért, followed by the Templar *chevaliers* with their gleaming pointed lances. Closely surrounding the grand master was his marshal with a tight knot of warrior-*moines* carrying their black and white flag called the *beauséant*. The Templar lancers struck the cardinal's men with a sudden grinding *clank*, which caused many of them to retreat. The remaining cardinal's men drew their swords only to meet the royal *chevaliers* who hacked them to death. The Templar lancers galloped after the remaining cardinal's men and knocked them off their horses and then speared them. However, to my chagrin, the cardinal's seneschal, Marcel de Tournay, had hidden another estimated sixty *chevaliers* behind a flanking ridge, which now thundered toward us with raised swords. I had hidden in the last group of Templar *chevaliers*, and now realized that was a mistake.

"We are outflanked!" I yelled above the din of battle.

CHAPTER IV

Grand Master Gilbért glanced in my direction but didn't seem concerned with me being there as he rounded up prisoners. Was this his normal battle reaction, which I had seen before, or something else? To my left side and in the direct sunlight, shadowy figures appeared on the opposite ridge. Was this more of the cardinal's men surrounding us? I prayed not, as a lump formed in my throat. Quickly, I raised my hand to block the sun to see how many we faced. To my horror, some of the men carried crossbows, while others had longbows. They marched out forming two horizontal ranks, longbowmen in back and crossbowmen in front. Then to my relief Grand Master Gilbért ordered them to shoot, realizing they were Templar bowmen. De Tournay's *chevaliers* suddenly reined in their horses and turned with wide-eyed expressions of horror, but it was too late. Loud *hissing* sounds erupted after the bowmen released their arrows, which covered the sky with their dark needle-shaped shafts. Then came a simultaneous thud sound, followed by shrieks from both the riders and their horses. Only a diminutive group of *chevaliers* survived the airborne stingers; the rest fell to the ground like human and horse pincushions. It was over, we had defeated the cardinal's men, with no loss of life. The enormous blood spilt metallic odor wafted across the battlefield. De Tournay and his marshal turned with a few guards and slowly slithered behind the ridge, like the cowardly snake he was.

"Lord Robert," Grand Master Gilbért said with a pinched crimson face. "You defied my wishes and came out here to fight. Leave now, I don't have enough men to protect you if de Tournay comes back with more *chevaliers*."

With great frustration, I spurred my horse and galloped toward *Château* Maluenda, only stopping to order the sergeant of the guard to lower the drawbridge. After entering, Helena met me and ordered one of her squires to help me dismount.

"What do you think of my protection plan, Robert, for the villagers?" she asked as we climbed up the steps to the embrasures. Casually, she reached for my drawn hand and tightly grasped my palm. My body still clenched with anger at Grand Master Gilbért's rebuke.

"I think it's a *bon* plan and I wondered what purpose your lone tower held when we first arrived."

I didn't pull my hand away from her comforting warm grip yet succumbed to her gentle fingertips touching mine. Her intoxicating rose-vanilla perfume locked my hand to hers, preventing me from releasing my grip. Once reaching the first merlon, she turned toward me, and her bluish-gray eyes held me in her trance.

"Robert, I can see in your face and manners, you're a true Poor-Soldier of Christ, even though you are married. God's will supersedes our free will and His love for us is beyond all human love. You see yourself as a seeker of truth, yet God has made you into His sword to cut away evil and ignorance too."

Helena was right and how intuitive were her instincts. She seemed to read my mind and knew my heart as my hands grabbed her waist, pulled her body toward me as I breathed in her pleasant smell, and then embraced her. It was a dangerous emotional move on my part, but for the moment my guilt didn't exist. We held each other tight until we heard footsteps coming toward us on the wooden steps. Hastily, she released her hands from my back and spoke.

"Grand Master Gilbért is a wise man for not pursuing de Tournay," she stated while glancing away from my gaze. "He is a cautious man and always thinks of his men's safety, not unlike the fool Grand Master Gerard de Ridefort, who was responsible for my *mari's* death at Hattin. One day soon, he will oversee the entire order of the Poor-Soldiers of Christ and leave us to return to Jerusalem. What will the *Royaume* de Aragón do without his counsel and bravery? I fear for our safety, Lord Robert." A tear of sadness rolled down her cheek.

"I am quite positive he will visit your *royaume* when necessary," I replied, reassuring her of Grand Master Gilbért's long attachment to Iberia.

"I heard my name mentioned," came a voice behind the steps. Grand Master Gilbért nodded to Helena. "Your *Altesse,* we captured several of de Tournay's men. What do you want to do with them?" Grand Master Gilbért asked. "I hope you're quite pleased with our results."

"*Très bien, mon* Grand Master, but don't kill them. Quickly secure the scum to the *oubliette*. Maybe we can later obtain some information. Right now, I am too angry to interrogate them."

Immediately, he shouted to several of his sergeants Helena's wishes, which caused the handtied prisoners to butt heads with their captors. However, it was a futile attempt to escape from their donjon fate, which brought racing royal *chevaliers*, who threw several of the prisoners to the ground and kicked them. Helena shouted at her guard to stop and ordered them to hobble the prisoners' legs.

"Lord Robert and Grand Master Gilbért, please follow me to your quarters," she said in a terse manner, still seething with anger. Helena didn't say another word as we left the battlement and advanced down the stone steps to the bailey area. There we met her chambermaid and Esperanza followed by *Abbé* Jeremiah and Muhammad.

"What are you planning on doing with your prisoners?" Grand Master Gilbért asked.

"We will discuss this after supper tonight. Until then, you must make yourselves presentable for court. Please follow me down the end of this corridor to your rooms." She held a flickering lantern in her hand. Her chambermaid assisted by pointing to each door where we would stay.

"Grand Master Gilbért, there's a *chapelle* in the keep for your order to perform their divine offices. After Vespers, we will meet in my great hall for supper, yet for now, refresh yourselves and if you need anything to make your stay here comfortable, just ask for my chambermaid."

Quickly, she turned to leave, followed by Esperanza. My eyes stared at her shapely hip movements as she marched down the narrow hallway, causing my heartbeat to race and my manhood to increase. Her well-proportioned physical features, combined with her high intelligence and assertiveness made my face hot with racing blood. The vulnerability of her loneliness, or maybe mine too, left me in a dangerous predicament. I feared I could no longer control my lust for Helena and knew each additional day we were together something might happen. I didn't like my position and silently prayed to stay loyal to my *épouse*. Avoiding her was impossible, for now, she was an integral part of our quest. Helena had resources at her disposal we didn't have in seeking out the possible whereabouts of the next set of *Sangraal* parchments. The city of Toledo was likely where they were hidden.

"Lord Robert, are you hearing what I just said?" Grand Master Gilbért asked while flashing a scowl on his face.

"*Non*, I apologize for my inattentiveness. My mind was distracted. What did you say?"

"*Oui*, I can see you were distracted by the *marquésa*." He grinned, which simultaneously turned into a frown. "I want us to stay here for just a few days. The weather will worsen soon and will make traveling difficult. In addition, *Marquésa* Helena doesn't know how ruthless the cardinal's men can be. Let's move outside to the bailey area and discuss this matter away from traitorous ears."

Instead of returning to our rooms, we both traveled back down the spiral stone steps, then exited into the cold cloudy afternoon air. With long steps, I quickly followed the grand master of Iberia across the open bailey area until we came to some partially hidden steps.

"Follow me up these steps to this less noticeable battlement," he said, as he quickly darted up the wooden steps, and then reached the crenels without taking a breath. His indefatigable stamina never ceased to amaze me.

The allure was devoid of royal guards, leaving us quite alone, with the howling wind our only other companion. We hunkered behind a large merlon, with both of us casting our gaze out over the red clay-tiled rooftops of the village below. The battlement curtain wall fell straight down ending itself on a sheer cliff face, which the rocky escarpment descended some distance to the village floor. This explained why the wall had no guards. Only pigeons or hawks could assault this battlement.

"Lord Robert, back at Zaragozza we discussed the possibility of a spy or spies among our fellow *Sangraal* comrades. We were to devise a plan to reveal the traitor or traitors, yet I didn't feel the palace was the safest place. The *roi's* fortress has too many secret passages for somebody to hear a trap we might conceive."

"Do you have any suspicions in who this could be?" I asked, reluctant to hear his answer.

"*Non*, that's what troubles me. My men have fought with me for numerous years and not once disobeyed me. Their honor and courage are beyond reproach, and I never questioned their loyalty. Muhammad is the oldest companion of our small group of fighters, and I saved his life many years ago. We're both aware of the traitor Ramáirez Sancho back at the Huesca commandery, which I had arrested and thrown into prison. What I plan to do is give out a fake order each day to one of our companions, using both you and me as bait. Each of us will accompany this person on an assignment concerning the *Sangraal* parchments. The bogus information should be just enough pertinent knowledge so the cardinal's men will act on it. This will include the *marquésa* in our web of suspicion."

"Why her?" I quickly retorted. "She can't be in league with the cardinal; her spies constantly give her information on the cardinal's machinations. Besides, the cardinal doesn't want just me and the *Sangraal* parchments, but also *Roi* Alfonso's *Royaume* de Aragón."

"That's the point, *mon ami*. Some of her spies work for the cardinal and she doesn't know it, but I do. However, I don't know their names. Spying is a complex profession, though dangerous, yet quite financially lucrative. We need to sift out all the brigands, spies, and traitors, which will help her too and the *roi*. Lord Robert, will you aid me with these baited traps?"

"*Oui*, but this isn't a job I seek pleasure in, yet it would be easier if it was an unknown man or men of the cardinal's *chevaliers*."

"I agree, but don't forget we have a higher purpose here in helping our Lord and Savior," Grand Master Gilbért chided my quickly forgotten memory.

We continued standing behind the merlon, still cold and hearing the howling wind, while we tried to converse on our trap. We agreed I would accompany Chaplain Jeremiah back to *Château* Calatayud to retrieve some valuable information on the next *Sangraal* parchment location.

"Muhammad will accompany both of you, but I'll only tell him I left a map there for him to retrieve. In addition, he will think both of you are with him to obtain the *marquésa's* forgotten luggage."

"However, won't that sound unusual?" I asked, thinking it didn't make any sense. "A Saracen prince, a *seigneur* from Burgundy, and a Templar chaplain to retrieve a royal portmanteau would appear and sound incredulous."

"*Non*, not if the portmanteau contains crown jewels!" The grand master exclaimed with a wrinkled grin on his scarred face.

"When do you want Chaplain Jeremiah and me to leave?"

"Tomorrow at first light and also I will inform Muhammad later tonight about leaving. When you return tomorrow night we'll know if he is a spy or not. Now let's return to our rooms, wash, rest, and prepare for *Marquésa* Helena's supper banquet."

I unlocked the door to my room, still thinking of what we had spawned to test Muhammad's loyalty. It left me with a feeling of deceit and unease, knowing I would have to face him tomorrow.

Gazing around my room, it was quite pleasing as I observed a roaring fire emanating from a large stone fireplace. Directly across from the fireplace I spied a large wooden four-poster bed. There in one of the corners of the large room stood an ornately carved wooden commode. The widest stone wall in the room had a long buffet with a silver decanter of *vin* placed on it along with two silver chalices. At the far end of the buffet was an ewer of water, a washing bowl, and two towels, which I used promptly to wash my face, then combed my hair, and finally brushed the dirt off my tunic with the remaining towel. After completing my ablutions, the thick feather bed drew me toward it, which enticed me to rest from the numerous days of hard riding. For a while, I lay across the soft bed contemplating what we had experienced in the last six or seven days. My thoughts prompted me to drift in and out of sleep as I reflected on *mon épouse* and two *fils,* and suddenly a loud knock echoed in my room.

"*Seigneur* Robert, you are requested by the *marquésa* to appear at her *altesse's* supper," announced a deep unknown male voice from behind my door. "It will commence at sundown; don't be late." Quickly, I jumped up from my bed, checked my mantel and tunic for cleanliness, and then proceeded to my door. Immediately, I stopped myself, thinking to hide our *Sangraal* book and my personal journal. Slowly, my eyes surveyed the room for a suitable hiding place; stopping to gaze upon the featherbed ticking. I drew my dagger, moved toward my bed, and cut out a large hole on the underside of the mattress. After completing this task, I carefully hid my saddlebags deep inside the mattress by covering them with the thick feathery down. Afterward, I carefully straightened the bed comforter and once again proceeded to leave. After locking the door behind me, I pushed on it to see if the lock worked, and then headed down the dark stone corridor.

Upon reaching the steps, I met Helena's chamberlain. He wore the same royal crest on his tabard, which the rest of *Roi* Alfonso's guards and household members displayed. The man stood the height of a giant standing bear, with no visible neck and a huge head that sat on his broad shoulders the width of a doorway. His large size prevented him from leading me alongside him down the narrow spiral stairway, yet he directed me where to proceed upon reaching the bottom of the stone steps.

"*Señor* Roberto, please turn left, it will lead you into the great banquet hall where you will be announced," he said with his deep bellowing voice echoing throughout the tower.

When it came time for my entrance, the chamberlain raised his long-jeweled staff and pounded it on a large square-shaped block of wood and shouted out my name to the already seated courtiers. *Marquésa* Helena sat elevated in a pointed back oak wooden throne. Slowly, she nodded her approval as I seated myself at the end of a long trestle-shaped table. Directly across from me sat Grand Master Gilbért and next to him sat Muhammad dressed in the finest green, black, and white silks, which were quite befitting for his princely status. On each side of them were seated *Abbé* Jeremiah and *Abad* Miguel. At the end of the table, and closest to me was another large, pointed back throne chair, which was vacant revealing its carved escutcheon design of the *Royaume* de Aragón. Each arm of the throne ended with the carved face of a turbaned Moorish head. Slowly, Helena rose from her throne, with the assistant of her ladies-in-waiting and headed directly toward the smaller throne chair. To my seated right, the empty chairs quickly filled with the numerous ladies-in-waiting, assisted by young squires. Esperanza sat down next to me on my right, while Helena remained standing, waiting for me to seat her, so I thought. Yet, everybody at the table immediately rose to their feet and bowed their heads, while several trumpets blared out announcing the beginning of the banquet.

"*Abbé* Jeremiah, would you say the blessing over our food, and *Abad* Miguel, would you say the benediction after the meal?"

Helena asked of both holy men.

"*Oui*, Your *Altesse,*" both men said together.

After the blessing, she extended both her arms and then motioned downward, letting us know when to sit.

"Lord Robert de Borron, I see you're refreshed after spending some time in your room. How do you and Grand Master de Érail like your accommodations?" she asked, motioning for her gigantic chamberlain.

"*Très bien*," we simultaneously replied.

"My room is quite peaceful and spacious, which will make it conducive to writing and updating my journal," I continued in praising our accommodations.

"All of you will enjoy our banquet, for my cook has done an excellent job in preparing it for tonight's occasion." Helena's chamberlain bent down to hear her orders. He, in turn, clapped his hands and an army of servants rushed out into the great hall carrying silver trays of steaming baked bread and silver bowls of various fruit. Quickly following them scurried another large contingent of serving maids bearing silver flagons of *vin*. Carefully, the young women poured the garnet-red liquid into a large silver chalice and placed it right next to our place setting. Just as I sipped my first taste of *vin*, the music started, catching my ear with a slow familiar rhythmic sound. However, I couldn't remember the name of the musical piece, yet the melodic quality of the dour sound kept asking me to name it.

As I glanced toward *Abbé* Jeremiah, his pleasant grin and hand motions as he spoke were identical to his *père's* voice and gestures. I wondered if others recognized the same similarities.

"Lord Robert," came Helena's voice, dislodging me from my gaze. "You seemed preoccupied with some inner thought. Is my banquet boring you?"

"*Non*, Your *Altesse*, quite the contrary. I am astonished by your excellent *vin*. It's the best I have tasted on my journey, and I must confess the bouquet and smoothness is far superior to our *vin* in Burgundy. It's obvious why *Roi* Richard *le Coeur de Lion* desires this excellent *vin* for his *royaume*."

My stomach growled with hunger as I broke off a large section of the hot yeasty smelling bread and started chewing its soft warm texture. To my surprise, after swallowing several pieces of the crusty bread, my tongue tasted the bread's unexpected filling.

"Was the bread baked with cheese?" I asked with my mouth watering for more.

"*Oui*," replied Helena. "It's goat's cheese and some of the other loaves have cow's cheese. My cook and I thought this would be appropriate for the Advent season supper. The *vin* and fruit taste well with the different cheeses and bread. In addition, I included the orange-colored succulent fruit you desired so well at the royal palace."

In front of us was a large silver bowl mounded high with the ball-shaped fruit, emanating its sweet perfume smell. My wine cup never emptied, and the orange fruit bowl always stayed full. Our conversations among us grew louder and merrier with each refilled cup of *vin* and the music seemed to disappear from my ears. My heart and eyes pulled closer to Helena's every word. Her striking appearance was more alluring than when I first met her at *Roi* Alfonso's court. An ink-blue veil framed her hair and face, with a wimple and kerchief of a contrasting gold color. Holding it all in place was a blue velvet roll intertwined with gold threads on her head. She had me bewitched, for my eyes never left hers and my heart raced trying to burst forth from my chest. Slowly, she bent across the table and her sweet wine breath whispered into my ear.

"Robert, it's quite important I speak to you after the banquet ends. My chamberlain will call on you at your quarters and escort you to my room. There I will tell you more details."

I wondered what she was about to say. Fearing it was unwelcome news, yet praying it was good news. I could see Grand Master Gilbért reflected the same furrowed brow of concern I felt on my face.

The evening banquet continued for a short while longer until the entire court had satiated their appetites. *Abad* Miguel, who on the word of Helena's chamberlain, rose to say the benediction. After completing his blessing of the court, her chamberlain escorted Helena out of the banquet hall first, followed by her courtiers.

As I ambled back toward my room, Grand Master Gilbért stopped me.

"*Mon ami*, what did the *marquésa* whisper into your ear?"

"Little, only that her . . . chamberlain would arrive . . . later tonight and escort me to her royal chambers. She said she had something of utmost importance to tell me. That's all I know at this point. I am hoping it's good . . . news instead of bad."

"Please keep me informed and beware of her guile, Lord Robert, if it concerns Cardinal Folquet or lé *Sangraal* parchments. Wake me early before you depart for *Château* Calatayud if she reveals anything of importance. I am returning to my room, for now, sleep is beckoning me to embrace it," he said with narrow glazy eyes. "*Bonsoir, mon ami*, I will see you early tomorrow before first light," he stated with a weak grin upon his face as he unlocked the door.

CHAPTER V

The *marquésa* was right about the potency of her *vin,* for I missed the keyhole to my room several times before unlocking it. Then staggered across my room to reach my bed, it appeared to move farther away upon approaching the feather mattress. Slowly, I lowered myself upon the large bed, fearing not to damage the hidden *Sangraal* book.

I don't remember falling asleep, but my ears aroused me with a loud pounding knock on my door, followed by a booming voice.

"*Seigneur* Robert de Borron," came the chamberlain's sonorous voice. "You are requested to accompany me to her *altesse's* royal chambers. Please open now, she has urgent information for you!"

Quickly, I jumped from my bed, and then reached for a brush, to brush my hair, after which I straightened my surplice, and headed for the door. Upon unlocking it, Helena's chamberlain covered the entire entrance to my door, while staring straight into my eyes. With one of his hands the size of a ham, he pointed down the corridor where we were to go. He stood at least two heads taller than I did, which with each of his massive strides quickly passed me as he led me down the tower steps, only stopping at an entrance to another corridor, which was narrower than the one leading to my room. At the end of the hallway was a solitary large wooden door with the crest of the *Royaume* de Aragón painted on it. The chamberlain slowed his stride, ambled toward the door, paused, then raised his enormous fist, and lightly knocked on the door.

"Your Alteza Helena, *Señor Baron* Roberto is here," he announced in a surprisingly quiet voice.

There was a moment of silence, followed by the *rustling* sound of a dress and light footsteps.

"Please enter, Lord Robert," came her muffled voice.

The royal chamber door opened with Helena's silk cloth-covered arm motioning me into her room. Her chambers were the size of three of the guest rooms, with a noticeable size stone-carved fireplace emitting a *crackling* fire. Once she closed the door and locked it behind me, the heated room caused my face to flush. On each side of the fireplace, supporting the long stone mantel, were two stone-carved statues of life-sized *chevaliers*. Directly opposite the fireplace, stood an intricately carved wooden bed supporting a full-length canopy above it. The bed's size could sleep at least four people in comfort.

"Roberto, please come and sit with me on my daybed," came her soft-sounding voice. "I have two cups of *vin* prepared for our conversation. Please sit here." She pointed with one of her sparkling gem-encrusted fingers. Her loose chestnut-colored hair cascaded over her bare shoulder, exposing its wavy thickness. The wimple she had worn earlier wasn't there, which now revealed her long graceful neck.

"I am glad you came after my long and stomach-filled banquet, for I am about to show you a mysterious drawing. It could be of some importance to your quest or maybe not. It has been an enigma to me for numerous years; please pardon me while I fetch it from my trunk."

She handed me a filled cup of *vin,* then she briskly walked across the long room to a large leather-covered truck. Quickly, she reached for a large key from her dress sleeve, bent down, and slowly unlocked it. She raised the lid, stood up for a moment to survey the trunk's contents, bent down again, and retrieved a rolled parchment.

"My late *mari,* Pedro Bernardo, bless his martyred soul," she stated, which prompted us to cross ourselves, "received this parchment from an old *mère supérieure* at a convent near the *monastère* at San Juan de la Peña. Once, many years ago, he spoke of this peculiar drawing, saying the nuns gave him one to hide. Pedro said a rustic-dressed hermit gave it to them from the Pyrénées Mountains. The old *mère supérieure* brought it to my *mari* when the hermit never came back to retrieve it. She thought maybe he could tell her the meaning of the arcane symbols."

Carefully, with her long fingers, she placed the unrolled parchment on a long trestle table placed in the center of her chambers. "Roberto, what do you think these symbols mean?" Helena stared at the parchment.

Quickly, I bent over the table to observe the contents but staggered backward with disbelief. Could my eyes be deceiving me? The parchment had the same drawn designed symbol, which *Abad* Miguel had shown me at Huesca. The seal design was identical, with the exception of seven additional stars clustered together below the roundel. The seven stars were similar in shape to the larger center star, still shaped like a pentagram star, but smaller in size. The drawing even had five fish designs at each juncture of the cinquefoil petals. Concentrating further, I now counted a total of eight stars and five fish, which were both of Saint Joseph's sacred numbers given to him by our Lord and Savior, Jesus the Christ. My hands began to tremble with excitement and right away Helena placed another full cup of *vin* on the table.

"It appears my parchment drawing has had a great influence on you," she stated with a slight grin around her rosy-colored lips.

"*Oui*, see here, all the stars are five-pointed and totaling eight. The fish are identical-shaped and total five. Both these numbers are clues given only to Saint Joseph de Arimathea and not to any other disciples. This includes even the great Saint Peter. However, Mary Magdaleine knew of them first and she helped him interpret their meanings. Don't you see, these numbers are telling both Saint Joseph and me about his future ministry, which may be written down on the next set of parchments?!" I exclaimed, not thinking Helena understood me.

"Is this something you learned from Saint Joseph's Gospel?" she inquired, moving closer to the parchment and me.

"*Oui*, both the numbers five and eight, our Lord, Jesus the Christ, gave in secret to Saint Joseph to ponder their true meanings. It's another clue in helping us search for the location of the next *Sangraal* parchments."

I had said more than I should have to Helena while fearing I couldn't trust her. In addition, even if she were innocent of any nefarious actions, what knowledge she already knew might jeopardize her life. It left me with a dangerous predicament, which I didn't want to shoulder. I knew I shouldn't say anymore.

"I must show your drawing to *Abbé* Jeremiah and *Abad* Miguel the first thing tomorrow morning. Did your late *mari* receive any more information from the nunnery before he put on the cross?" I asked, hoping she would have additional information.

"The sole thing he told me, right before he left for the Levant, was it had something to do with the history of Toledo and was a holy symbol. *Mère supérieure* may have given him that information when she handed it over to him for protection. Roberto, that's all I know."

"Could we contact the old *mère supérieure* for more information?"

"*Non*, she is now deceased and my *mari* said she never showed the drawing to any of her *soeurs,* fearing she would upset the bishop."

She smiled at me. "I am so happy you're pleased with my drawing. It thrills my heart to see you quite passionate about your quest and too many years have gone by since I shared something with another man." Helena reached for my left hand. Slowly, she grasped my fingers holding one corner of the drawing and then gave me a kiss on the side of my cheek.

"Roberto, since you've arrived, my spirits have been lifted each day in anticipation of seeing you," she said as tears welled in her eyes. Her rose-vanilla scented cologne made me swoon as both her arms encircled my chest and back. Helena's firm breasts were now tight against my lower chest and her warm body felt good rubbing against me. Immediately, my manhood rose toward her, pressing ever closer against my surcoat and her gown. However, my unholy lust came to a quick end by a loud knock on Helena's chamber door.

"Your Alteza, is there anything else you might need before I retire?" asked the booming voice of her chamberlain.

"*Ninguno,* Rodrigo, we still have plenty of *vino* and fruit. You may retire and *buenas noches*," she replied.

Rodrigo's heavy *thumping* footsteps echoed down the hall before going silent.

His interruption had pulled me away from my passionate temptation, keeping me from regretting any future actions. I knew Marie and my children were concerned about me and de Tournay could put them under his sword at any time. I had to stay focused on the drawing and our future quest to Toledo. Right away, we broke our embrace, and I continued studying the parchment symbol. Helena, with a demure move, reached for the silver decanter, refilled my cup, and then hers, followed by a long period of silence between her sips before she spoke once more.

"Roberto, I failed to mention another drawing, which *mère supérieure* gave my *mari.* All my *bon vin* has clouded my memory and it didn't seem important, for it's almost identical to the one in front of us. Let me retrieve it, it's in the same trunk and near the top. Quickly, she unlocked the leather trunk, grabbed the parchment, and hurriedly returned to the table. After carefully unrolling the yellowed parchment, she pointed toward two angels.

"The sole differences are these two angels," she said, while I helped her hold the four corners.

Once more, she had surprised me with her intuitiveness to help put together and explain the cryptic clues put before us.

"These are the same two chiseled angels holding the wheel in the archivolt at San Pedro el Viejo!" I exclaimed with excitement. "This drawing confirms we are on the right path for the next set of *Sangraal* parchments. Helena, see here," I said with my pointed finger trembling. "The five-pointed stars and the two angels are meant for us to search the heavens to guide our way. This is where our future clues may come from and lead us to our destination."

"Roberto, what do you think is the significance of one large star and seven smaller ones around it?"

"The stars I can't entirely say, but the angels I believe are Saint Gabriel and Saint Michael or possibly one of them is Saint Uriel, so I have been told. The five fish and five petals of cinquefoil represent the five wounds of our Savior. The number five has endless meanings, both pagan and Christian, yet the center has me vexed, along with the seven separate stars." I said no more.

"Could the larger star in the center represent the Bethlehem star that guided the magi to baby Jesus? It appears this same star is guiding you to the next set of *Sangraal* parchments you seek."

"Bless you, Helena, you're right!" I exclaimed. My excitement, along with the additional cups of *vin* caused me to embrace her slim waist. However, my long embrace was for appreciation, yet my body and mind thought otherwise. Her soft loose hair brushed against my face as we finally broke our embrace. Once again, I gazed upon the new drawing, hoping to keep my attention on the two angels. "This makes sense, the drawings are guiding us to the words of our Christ and Savior."

"Maybe *Frère* Carlos has a book in his scriptorium that could give meaning to the smaller shaped stars," she suggested touching the smaller stars with her long narrow fingers.

"*Oui*, that's another excellent idea, which I will mention to Grand Master Gilbért at dawn, for Muhammad, Chaplain Jeremiah, and I are planning on returning there tomorrow. We have a military matter that must be dealt with, and we can accomplish two duties at one time."

"But . . . what about our tour of my vineyards and *vino* presses, Roberto?" Helena implored. "This was one of the purposes we came here to my *château*," she said with a flushed face.

"We can still ride together and tour your vineyards after I return, which will be before sundown," I stated, hoping to calm her disappointment.

"*Bon*, I'll wait for you and have my horse ready when you return."

"Let me refill your cup, so I can toast you for your perceptive ideas you have given me." I reached for the decanter of *vin* with my arm brushing against her shoulder. I poured the garnet-colored liquid into her empty cup.

"Let's move to the settee where we can relax better." She grabbed my hand. "Roberto, I fear I am becoming drowsy, yet I want to hear more about the women of Northern Burgundy. Please sit here and tell me about their desires and fears, especially their desires in their men."

I didn't know where to start or what to say, but her drowsy-filled eyes beckoned me to reply. "The women prefer their men to be chivalrous, to protect their families and homes, and to support and defend their local parish churches."

"That's too general," she stated. "What are their womanly fears and dislikes of their men? What do they expect of their lovers and *maris* in romance?"

She left me in an awkward position, but I knew I had to satisfy her curiosity.

"To know a woman of Northern Burgundy is to know you."

"But I am a *princesa*, not all your Burgundy women are *princesas*, *non*?" she asked.

"True, but that's not what I meant," I replied. "They're proud of the large families they bear, a *mari* who's able to feed them, and a man with a tender touch. Women are no different in their pride, joys, and fears regardless of their social status. We desire the same things and to serve Christ."

We then crossed ourselves. Afterward, Helena's face drew up with disappointment and tears started rolling down each of her cheeks.

"I so miss not having children, Roberto. You're a blessed man in so many ways." Her voice cracked with sadness.

Slowly, she tilted her head on my shoulder and started sobbing with her wet tears. I didn't know what to say, instead, I held her tighter, and we both fell asleep.

We were awakened by a pounding knock on the chamber door,

which caused my instincts to reach for my sword, yet my hand was around Helena's waist. The royal *vin* had done its work.

"Your Alteza," bellowed the chamberlain in a resonant voice. "Grand Master Gilbért is searching for *Señor Baron* Roberto. He's wanted immediately!"

Helena bolted straight up from her slumber. With her eyes focused on the door, she replied in a clear anxious voice.

"He'll be there right away." She then jumped up from the settee, straightened her hair and dress, as she strolled toward the door. Quickly, she unlocked the door, then opened it. Rodrigo filled the entrance.

"*Señor* Roberto, you're to follow me back to your room. Grand Master Gilbért is waiting for you. Please come now." I felt some guilt for sleeping in Helena's chambers, but hurried to Gilbért's demands.

"Roberto, don't forget the scrolls, for you're to show them to Grand Master Gilbért," Helena said, while quickly handing them to me.

I said *au revoir* to Helena, promising to see her in the afternoon. Both Rodrigo and I hurried back to my room, whereupon reaching it, Rodrigo stood in front of the door and spoke. "Is there anything else you need of me?"

"*Non*," I replied. He said *adios* and left.

CHAPTER VI

Right away, I opened the door and viewed Grand Master Gilbért pacing back and forth in front of my fireplace.

"Where have you been?" he truculently asked. "Muhammad and Jeremiah are ready to depart and you're not even wearing your chain mail!"

I had anticipated his anger with me, and thought he was right. I knew the scroll drawings would placate his displeasure.

"Study these drawings while I change clothes," I said, carefully handing him both scrolls. I started putting on my chain mail, yet out of the corner of my eye, I observed his red-faced anger change abruptly to an openmouthed facial expression of wonder.

"Where did you acquire these drawings?" he uttered, with a loud voice of disbelief.

"Both drawings were given to me by *Marquésa* Helena tonight. They belonged to her late *mari*, *Don* Pedro Bernardo."

"Did she say where he obtained them?"

"*Oui*, the same abbey the other drawings came from, San Juan de la Peña. However, these drawings include a group of stars, which total eight and each bear five points. The numbers five and eight are the holy numbers that our Lord, Jesus the Christ, whispered to Saint Joseph, and he wrote of these numbers in his book. The two angels, framing the center star, are directing us to the next set of *Sangraal* parchments. We need to consult with *Abbé* Jeremiah and *Abad* Miguel right away."

"*Oui*, it's quite fortunate and timely you are traveling together today. I feel we'll solve several unanswered questions after you return from *Château* Calatayud, Lord Robert. Now you must leave, and I have spoken to Muhammad about your assignment. Have a safe journey and always search the horizon, *mon ami*. Oh, by the way, *Abad* Miguel wants to travel with you. I don't have any objection and he desires to speak to *Frère* Carlos about copying a manuscript. *Au revoir*, Lord Robert. I will pray for your safe return."

With much haste, I grabbed the scrolls, strapped on my sword, and dashed out of my room. As I rushed down the stone corridor, Helena's door slightly opened, and I saw her eyes follow me as I passed toward the spiral stone staircase. The late December sunrise hadn't cracked the horizon as I met three dark-mounted riders in the bailey area.

"We were worried about you, Lord Robert de Borron," came the familiar voice of Chaplain Jeremiah as he spurred his horse to leave. Right away, I leaped on my saddle and then stuffed the scrolls in my saddlebags, after which I grabbed my reins, and spurred my horse to leave. Our thundering horses' hooves split the early morning still air as we crossed the drawbridge and the last noise I heard came from the *clanking* chain of the portcullis.

In front of us, as usual, was Muhammad lighting the way with a pitch torch. The persistent moist stream from our breaths indicated the weather was colder. My eyes flashed back and forth looking for any ambushes. The sky was void of any clouds. After half a league of travel the sun rose above the distant hills, causing Muhammad to extinguish his torch. Each of our horses galloped along at a leisurely pace, snorting long streams of moisture from their nostrils as the day grew gradually warmer. The four of us said little, other than me mentioning the new scrolls and the symbols they contained. This elicited a curious discussion between the two holy men and what conjecture the clues meant. Both were quite anxious to reach our destination, so they might examine them at the scriptorium.

"Lord Robert, are they similar in design to the drawing we viewed at Huesca?" Chaplain Jeremiah asked.

"*Oui* and *non*," I replied leaving the chaplain with his tilted head waiting for more information. "I'll explain in more detail my hypothesis when we reach *Château* Calatayud."

We continued along the riverbank trail until I estimated we were about a quarter of a league from the Templar fortress. On top of a distant hill appeared what seemed like various sizes of white candles fixed motionless on the promontory of the hill.

"Riders coming!" Muhammad shouted to my surprise in my native tongue. "*Chevaliers* on that promontory," he continued, after putting the spyglass back into his saddlebag. Now I could see the white-colored candles starting to move at a rapid pace. Quickly, Muhammad drew his long scimitar, spurred his horse to meet them, and repeatedly shouted his battle cry, "*Allahu Akbar*!" We followed his lead and galloped behind him, yet his swift horse disappeared over the next ridge. Then to my dismay, he appeared once more but heading in our direction. This didn't bode well, however, I never knew him to run from a fight, no matter the number of men he faced.

"*Mujahidin, Mujahidin*!" Muhammad hollered, as his horse raced toward us. Quickly, he pulled in his reins, as his snorting horse pranced around me.

"Does anybody know what he is saying?" I asked of my holy companion as my consternation grew larger.

"He said they are the holy warriors of God approaching," Chaplain Jeremiah said. "Rest easy, Lord Robert, they're fellow Templar *chevaliers* patrolling this district and nothing more."

Their thundering hooves quickly approached, and Chaplain Jeremiah rode out a short distance to greet them. Upon seeing him, they reined in their horses and trotted over to greet him. At first, they bowed their heads in respect, after which they gazed toward *Abad* Miguel and again bowed their heads. We followed the *chevaliers* uphill with a steady gallop until we reached the square-shaped barbicans of *Château* Calatayud. There we met the leader of the patrol; it was Poncho Díaz de Vivar, marshal to Commander Joffre. Then, numerous squires rushed out to help us dismount from our horses.

"Lord Robert and *Abad* Miguel, please follow me to the scriptorium right away. I am afraid my curious anticipation has overwhelmed me," the young chaplain said, taking long strides across the bailey yard like his *père.* All four of us quickly followed and saw a spiral stair step entrance. We bound up the narrow steps, after which we stopped at the entrance to the scriptorium hallway. Halfway there, *Frère* Carlos met us with a large smile, which seemed larger than the rest of his small frame.

"What a surprise to see you, pilgrims, back so soon. You caught me just as I was leaving for the dorter to retrieve some special writing pens, but that can wait. Now tell me, what has brought you back so soon?" *Frère* Carlos said as he searched our eyes for an answer.

"We have received some new drawings to show you and hope you can explain their meaning," I stated, staring at Chaplain Jeremiah's anxious face.

"Well, take them to my writing desk, it's the last window on the right," he said, pointing with one of his pudgy ink-stained fingers. Right away, we moved toward his desk, where I spied several scrolls scattered underneath and many worn-out ink-stained quills scattered on top of a nearby table.

"Just push those dull nib quills to one side of the table," he said as I handed him both scrolls. Watchful, he unrolled the brittle parchments and his large brown eyes moved back and forth, momentarily focusing on the symbol designs with the scrutiny of a scholar.

"You have come across some quite unusual symbols. It appears of ancient origin, though one parchment appears slightly newer than the other. This one with the seven smaller stars, they were added later. It appears both Iberian Christian and Outremer in design style. The seven small five-pointed stars represent some ancient Greek or Persian symbols. My observation tells me it's a star cluster in a constellation and the larger eighth star represents the leader or primary star. The five circling fish are early Christian symbols, which all of you well know. The two angels and the five-petaled flower have me perplexed, yet it's easy to say the angels are Gabriel and Michael, but I don't believe so. What do you think, *Abad* Miguel and *Abbé* Jeremiah?"

Abad Miguel answered first. "I too agree with what you are saying, yet I believe one of the angels is the Archangel Uriel and the other is the Archangel Gabriel. Our mystery angels aren't protecting the wheel but trying to convey another clue to the whereabouts of the second set of *Sangraal* parchments."

"I concur with your conjecture, *Abad* Miguel," Chaplain Jeremiah stated. "And furthermore, in my university studies, *Santo* Gabriel is often called the 'cupbearer' of good tidings, along with his role as God's ubiquitous messenger. The old Persian magi had a comparable being in the zodiac constellation called Aquarius or water bearer. In addition, the Greek deity, Hermes, was Zeus's messenger."

"Lord Roberto, what do you say about this drawing?" *Frère* Carlos asked me next.

"They were recently given to me by *Marquésa* Helena, who inherited them from her late husband, *Principe* Pedro Bernardo. He received them several years before he died at the battle of Hattin. A now-deceased abbess at San Juan de la Peña gave them to him and she said she received the parchment drawings from an unknown hermit who lived in a cave in the Pyrénées Mountains."

"Lord Robert, I am afraid this information doesn't help me, though the drawing at Huesca and those at San Juan de la Peña both came from the same region of the Pyrénées Mountains. However, I have some splendid tomes on angels; I'll leave now and retrieve them." The small *frère* jumped up from his seat, and then ran to a dark corner of the library. He was gone but a brief time when he returned holding two large dust-covered books. Each he laid carefully on the long table next to the parchment drawings. His small fingers searched the brittle pages until he came to one section of the large book and stopped.

"Right here it shows similarly drawn angels holding a spoked wheel. It says one of the angels is Saint Gabriel, the messenger for God. The other angel is holding a scroll in one hand and holy fire is emanating out of his palm on the other hand. This is a separate drawing of the two angels holding the spoked wheel. It says he is the angel Saint Uriel, and his name means 'fire of God.' Saint Uriel is identical to the one holding the wheel but without the scroll and fire. See!" *Frère* Carlos pointed it out. "Here's the symbol for Gabriel's name, [illegible]. His seal means the 'water of life' or 'cupbearer.' His constellation sign is Aquarius, the water bearer from the ancient Persian magi. Uriel's seal or symbol is down at the bottom of this page. See it right there AŽŽ א ו ר א ל Ω ✠."

We stretched our necks over Carlos's right shoulder as he drew his ink-stained stubby fingers to it. Both symbols were seals I didn't recognize, yet my holy powers of translation didn't reveal anything.

"What about Archangel Uriel's constellation sign?" I excitedly inquired, as I searched for it on the old, yellow-stained page. With circumspection, Carlos slowly turned the page over and there on the next page was a drawing of a woman holding a set of chained scales.

"See, it says right here, the woman is the constellation Libra. She symbolizes a mediator like *Rey* Solomon from the Old Testament. In addition, there's a reference to the prophet and seventh patriarch from Adam, Enoch. God favored Enoch and the knowledge and wisdom from the Book of Enoch the Archangel Uriel gave him. The Book of Genesis says Enoch didn't die, but God lifted him up to heaven and there he traveled with God. This is after he taught our ancestors to read, write, and especially the principles of mathematics. His knowledge of the heavens and stars are far past our understanding. The apocrypha text says he wrote a total of 366 books on the future of mankind. His books predicted the coming of our Lord and Savior long before the later-day prophets of the Old Testament. In addition, he knew about the Second Coming of the Christ, just like the Bible says in the Book of Revelation, which Saint Gabriel announces by blowing his trumpet."

"*Frère* Carlos, what do you think all these drawings, symbols, and information have to do with finding the next set of *Sangraal* parchments?" I asked, noticing Muhammad carefully studying the pages. To my surprise, he answered first to my question.

"Chosen one, these beings also spoke to our Prophet Muhammad, may peace and blessings be upon Him. The Angel Jibril taught Him the holy words from *Allah*. The Holy *Qur'an* tells us such. In addition, there's a *surah* or chapter that mentions Enoch or, as the People of the House call him, Idris. He was a man of great truth and an old prophet to our faith; may peace and blessings be upon him."

His depth of knowledge never ceased to amaze me, and his articulation was superb in my native language. I longed to know more about this Saracen prince and his mysterious past.

"I am just a faithful scribe for God, and not a great theologian or philosopher, yet we *hermanos* are guardians of ancient books and their secrets," *Frère* Carlos stated, not answering my original question. Instead, he glanced toward *Abbé* Jeremiah for agreement.

"*Si*, I agree with *Hermano* Carlos and his responsibilities, however these signs, seals, and symbols are speaking to us of their higher indications. Each clue is building on the next, which is leading us to Toledo. Once there, all the bricks will come together, revealing the house where the next *Sangraal* parchments lay hidden. *Abad* Miguel, what can you add to our conjecture?"

"I believe we are missing one thing, which Muhammad just said. The chosen one among us, who is Lord Robert de Borron. We are here only to assist him, but he's the chosen person who will see the higher purpose of our quest. God has touched him with the Holy Spirit and only he will see God's higher meaning and purpose."

"Do you mean seeing into the future or something in the past?" I asked, quite baffled with what *Abad* Miguel had just said.

"Perhaps both, yet I am not certain, my *amigo*. It's your destiny and only you can seek it to its conclusion."

To my surprise, came a combined resounding reply of "*sí*" from my cohorts after *Abad* Miguel gave his wise counsel. "*Hermano* Carlos, could I have one of your scribes copy the pages of this book, before we leave?"

"*Sí*, *Señor* Roberto. When are you leaving?"

"Right after we retrieve a trunk that *Marquésa* Helena left in your guest room. Can you direct us back to the room and unlock the door?"

"*Sí*, I remember now, she indeed left her personal leather chest there. Let me give this book to one of my fellow *hermanos* to copy." Quickly, with his one arm, he motioned for one of his scribes to come forward. Hurriedly, a *frère* came forward and *Frère* Carlos spoke to him about what he needed. Afterward, he pulled out a large ring of keys from his robe and the dwarf armarius said to follow him.

Helena's former guest room wasn't far from the scriptorium, and we quickly arrived at the wooden entrance door. The small *moine* selected a large iron key from his ring of keys and placed it into the keyhole. Quickly, he turned the lock and then opened the door. To my surprise, there was an actual, brown-colored large leather chest with the royal escutcheon of the *Royaume* de Aragón. Apparently Helena indeed forgot about it. I glanced at Chaplain Jeremiah and noticed a slight smile on his face, which told me he outsmarted his *père's* ruse. Could he be the cardinal's spy? My entire body shuttered with apprehension, and I told myself this couldn't be possible.

CHAPTER VII

"Lord Robert, your face is pale as if someone frightened you. Are you feeling all right?" the young chaplain asked, while he and Muhammad lifted the chest to their shoulders and exited the door. *Abad* Miguel and I followed, as *Frère* Carlos followed me and then locked the door. I proceeded back to the scriptorium to retrieve the copies of the book drawings with their numerous odd symbols.

Chaplain Jeremiah said, "Lord Robert, meet us in the stables and prepare to depart. One of the squires will saddle your horse and we will leave now."

Both *Frère* Carlos and I arrived back at the scriptorium entrance just as his scribe completed my copies. The *moine* carefully perused both copies, thanked his fellow *hermano*, and placed the copies into a small stiff leather tube, which he then sealed with its leather cap. He handed me the leather cylinder.

"*Señor* Roberto, I hope we have helped you in some way on your *santo* quest. Chaplain Jeremiah said you wouldn't return this way on your return trip to Zaragozza but would travel a shorter route. Therefore, I will leave you with a quote by a fellow *hermano* like me, who lived in the sixth century after our Lord's birth. His name was Cassiodorus, who was a scribe like me, he said, 'Every work of the Lord written by a scribe is a wound inflicted upon Satan, for by reading the divine scriptures he wholesomely instructs his own mind. By copying the precepts of our Lord and Savior, he spreads them far and wide over the face of the earth.'

"You are a holy scribe, my *amigo* and don't lose sight of your precious gift. *Vaya con Dios* and *adios, Señor* Roberto, maybe we will meet again if God wills it." *Frère* Carlos reached out his hand to grab one of mind. However, I embraced him instead and gave him my farewell.

"*Muchas gracias,* my *amigo,* and *vaya con Dios* to you," I said, still embracing the small man.

Chaplain Jeremiah and my fellow cohorts were waiting for me as I approached the stables. They had already loaded the trunk onto a two-wheeled cart attached to a lone burro. Quickly, I mounted my horse, spurred him, and with my cohorts trotted across the drawbridge to start our cautious descent to the open road. My companions said nothing as we headed back toward *Château* Maluenda. We were just a third of a league from the *château.* Finally, the village outskirts appeared, where a feeling of relief came over me. After a short time, we entered the bailey grounds and Grand Master Gilbért met us.

"Lord Robert, did you experience any problems?" he asked as I dismounted my horse. "Please, accompany me around the bailey before you leave with *Marquésa* Helena. I am anxious to hear your report and what the new scroll drawings revealed."

"It appears Muhammad or *Marquésa* Helena isn't one of the traitors and I assume you never suspected *Abad* Miguel or Chaplain Jeremiah," I whispered.

"*Non*, I suspected everybody, but you. My ruse tells me my suspicions are now down to one possible traitor out of two men. It's either Sergeant Jacque de Hoult or Sergeant Guy de Béziers. This disheartened me to come to this realization, yet our lives and spiritual welfare are at risk. My traps will continue, *mon ami*, even if you aren't aware, but trust me. Lord Robert, you have an engagement with the *marquésa* and must leave while there's remaining daylight. I don't like this visitation to Helena's vineyards. De Tournay could capture you anywhere among the grapevines. Use your time wisely;

tomorrow morning we leave for Zaragozza. It will be a shorter route back and only I know the way, so have your belongings ready to leave. After you return tonight, we will speak about the scrolls and their symbols' meanings. For now, enjoy your sightseeing with *Marquésa* Helena. *Au revoir, mon ami;* see you tonight."

Quickly, our military leader left to help unload Helena's crown jewels, leaving me pondering which of the two sergeants were guilty of treason.

"Roberto," came Helena's voice taking me from my rumination. "Are you ready to leave? Please hurry, we have little daylight left."

"*Oui,*" I replied, feeling quite tired from riding since early in the morning. A smile came over my face, thinking that here I was remounting my horse for an insistent proud *princesse*.

"I have my *caballeros*, along with Grand Master Gilbért's *chevaliers* and sergeants to accompany us at a distance. Do you think this is sufficient for our late afternoon ride?"

"*Oui,*" I acknowledged, at the same time raising my body and stretching my neck to see if Sergeants Jacque and Guy were among the escort. To my chagrin, there they were behind the Templar *chevaliers.*

"In addition, I have you as my protector and champion, *oui*?"

"*Oui*, you're right and I know you're prepared to defend yourself without my assistance."

She again rode a large, white-colored Andalusian horse, which pawed the ground with one of its front hooves. His metallic bit made a *clacking* sound against his teeth, signaling to his rider he was ready to leave. Helena wore a red velvet riding dress with a silver-linked chain around her waist. On her left hip was a slender-shaped dagger enclosed in an ornate-jeweled scabbard. To my surprise, her saddle pommel had a leather thong attached, which held a small crossbow.

"I didn't know Your *Altesse* knew how to use a crossbow," I said as we galloped through the open portcullis.

"Both *mon frère* and *mari* taught me and I am quite accurate, for I strike the dummy-shaped man's heart each time from horseback."

As we completed the downhill road from her *château*, a large crowd of village subjects stopped doing their daily chores and lined up on each side of the road. As her big white horse pranced down the road through the village, each of her subjects bowed, then waved, and followed up with a loud cheer after she passed by them. It was obvious to all present, her subjects adored Helena.

We followed the Rio Jiloca for about a quarter of a league, when to my surprise, I noticed more royal *chevaliers* and a retinue of numerous courtier wagons following us.

"I thought this afternoon it was just you and me touring your vineyards." I felt somewhat disappointed.

"Grand Master Gilbért wanted to start back to Zaragozza before sundown, instead of leaving early tomorrow morning. He fears the weather might turn bad and tomorrow is Saint Lazarus's feast day, which means the cold winds will start to increase this time of year. Yet, I know he has other motives for leaving than the cierzo winds. I suspect he wants to stay one step ahead of de Tournay and Cardinal Folquet's arrest warrant. In addition, he desires to protect you, and the holy words of the copied *Sangraal* book, and keep your unknown traitor off guard."

Once again, Helena's observation was right, but would we have enough time to visit her vineyard before darkness? "Will we have sufficient time to see your entire vineyard?" I asked.

"*Oui*, we'll see part of it late this afternoon and the rest tomorrow," she said, leaving me confused.

"Where will we stay tonight and did the grand master tell you of his shortcut route?" I queried.

"I can't say, but he might stay overnight at a *monasterio* near the vineyards, and this will give us an opportunity to start out early tomorrow and tour the remaining vineyards."

She was right, this made a lot of sense, and this would give us some much-needed rest before returning to Zaragozza. Without thinking, I reached back and opened one of my saddlebags. My fingertips stroked the ornate carved cover, thus reassuring myself that it was still there. Slowly, we followed a seldom-used trail heading northeast. My momentary concern disappeared as

Helena's captivating gaze garnered my attention until interrupted by Sergeant de Hoult.

"Three riders coming!" he shouted.

All heads turned toward the west, with the sun's rays obscuring any detail of the riders. Instinctively came the *grinding* sounds of our swords coming out of their scabbards. A *clicking* noise, near me, quickly forced me to turn back in my saddle and seek out the sound. There, I witnessed Helena's hands holding a cocked crossbow ready to challenge any threat. Sergeant de Hoult was the first to spur his horse and he raced toward the unknown riders. His fellow Templar *frères* followed him with a thunderous gallop toward the same indistinguishable riders. The bright sun still prevented me from knowing if the riders were friend or foe. However, Sergeant de Hoult's horse slowed to an easy gait as he drew near. The rest of his fellow warrior-*moines* mimicked his pace as they surrounded the three riders. Then in an instant, they all turned their horses and galloped toward us. After just a moment, appeared Grand Master Gilbért, Muhammad, and Chaplain Jeremiah racing their lather-covered horses in our direction. Shortly thereafter, Grand Master Gilbért reined in his steed.

"Helena, did you know they were coming?"

"*Oui*, I knew. Grand Master Gilbért was afraid you might be captured for ransom or tortured."

I assumed his change of plans were purposely done to keep our spy off guard and make sure I didn't commit an indiscretion with the *marquésa*.

"Lord Robert, you didn't think we would miss the vineyard visit tonight?" he asked with a grin. "My fellow *frères* know a lot about *vino* making and are interested in seeing *Marquésa* Helena's outstanding vines. Besides, her *altesse* has invited us to a wine tasting at a *monasterio* near Cariñena tonight, after which we can discuss our scouting report in detail."

"*Très bien, mon ami*, your challenging conversation will keep my mind from threatening thoughts, especially now knowing you'll protect my back."

"Lord Robert, I fear it's not only your back that needs protecting but also your front." He smiled at Helena and me, letting us know he understood what was evolving between us.

We followed the riverbank trail for another quarter of a league until the Rio Jiloca became quite shallow; there we turned and followed it in a northern direction. The shallow river twisted and turned on its journey like a snake crawling on the ground, with portions of it wide and deep. The color of the surrounding ground changed from a light brown to a rusty-colored pebbled texture, with *montagnes* growing closer to our destination.

The winds grew colder as the cloudy afternoon continued, forcing us to pull our cowls over our heads. Helena did the same, enclosing her rosy-colored cheeks with her fur-trimmed hood.

In front of us, some distance away was a small village, which lay on a flat clear plain that butted up against the *montagnes.* To the southwest of the village stood an *église* and priory or a *monasterio* as the Iberians called it.

"Lord Roberto, you seemed vexed," Helena said.

"*Oui*, I am confused, especially since you and Grand Master Gilbért are the sole two people who are familiar with these rough unknown trails, if they're indeed trails and not deer paths."

"I was sworn to secrecy by Grand Master Gilbért not to divulge our route. Everybody knew the possible destination, but not the departure time or trails. If you study the plain before you, it's called the Campo de Cariñena and the soil is rusty-colored and well-drained. The dry summer heat, followed by winter cold winds, and the expertise of the *bon moines*, help produce the finest *vin* in all Christendom. As you start to see to your right, there's my army of grapevines."

To my surprise, the whole plain suddenly appeared as a stationary army of men waiting for their *roi* to give the order to attack. The closer we rode toward the priory, the vineyards seemed to never end.

"Our harvest time was finished two months ago, and the greater portion of our *vin* is ready to ship," she said, pointing in the direction of the *église.* "Do you see that *église* tower in the distance?"

"*Oui,*" I replied, wondering why it wasn't located in the village.

"There's a priory attached to the *église* and close to the vineyard fields. This is where my subjects work with the *moines* to help grow and ship the wine. We should arrive there before nightfall and you will see my *vin* presses, which are unsurpassed in all Iberia."

Her happy smile reflected the immense pride she had for her vineyard as we continued on our way. Row after row of endless cut grapevines surrounded us with their gnarled wooden-trunked stems. As usual, Muhammad had disappeared a while ago, only to reappear from a small ravine, covered with grape trunks. His Saracen tongue was now quite familiar to me as he reported to Grand Master Gilbért. He stated the priory road didn't have any of the cardinal's men waiting in ambush. Our military leader then ordered Sergeant de Hoult ahead to tell the *frères* that the Poor-Soldiers of Christ and their *alteza*, *Princesa* Helena, were arriving with her retinue. Promptly, the sergeant spurred his horse, then quickly galloped over the next ravine and disappeared.

Our caravan of courtiers, *chevaliers*, and soldiers rumbled on at a turtle's pace until after half a league we arrived at the small priory. The priory *église* was of Romanesque design and recently built by the appearance of the new red-tiled roof. The cloister was small, reflecting the few members who had newly joined this priory. However, its columns and vaulted ceilings reflected the many richly decorated saints' and disciples' faces carved throughout the buildings, *église,* and surrounding walls. To start this religious colony, it appeared a great amount of gold helped build the *monastère*.

Quickly, all the squires dismounted and then rushed to assist the *chevaliers*, *mademoiselles* from their coaches, and any royalty who needed assistance. Directly in front of the entranceway, two white-robed *moines* met us and directed our tired retinue to the nearest lavatorium and rere-dorter.

"Lord Robert, I would like you to meet Prior Etienne," *Abad* Miguel said, as the grape-stained, white-robed prior gave me the sign of the cross. "He is a *bon ami* of mine. He and I have known each other for several years."

"*Pax*, *Frère* Miguel and *Seigneur* Robert. *Bienvenu* to our humble house of God. I see you have brought our royal benefactor, her *altesse*, the *Princesse* Helena, and the Poor-Soldiers of Christ." Prior Etienne smiled at Helena.

"*Bonjour*, Prior Etienne. It's always a pleasure to see you," Helena said with a gleam in her eyes. "Did our last shipment of *vin* satisfactory arrive in England for *Roi* Richard's courtiers?"

"*Oui*, Your *Altesse*, and as you well know he isn't there to enjoy it. Our Lord and Savior has called him to the Levant to rescue the land of our Christ and Savior. In addition, his *frère*, Prince Jean, has ordered another thirty barrels for his own personal consumption."

"*Bon*, when will that be?" Helena lightly clapped her hands.

The casks are already shipped and should arrive by the feast day of Saint Stephen," Prior Etienne replied.

"Excellent, holy prior, but please forgive me, for I failed to introduce you to Grand Master Gilbért de Érail and his chaplain, *Abbé* Jeremiah de Compostela." Helena flushed with embarrassment.

"It's a pleasure and honor to meet the great warrior-*moine* and his savant chaplain. I have heard many remarkable stories of your bravery in the Levant, Grand Master Gilbért. And *Père* Jeremiah, it's well-known throughout Iberia your depth of religious history. Please, *frères*, follow me and I will show you to your quarters." The prior pointed toward a narrow stone corridor.

"*Merci beaucoup*, Prior Etienne," Grand Master Gilbért replied. "I am sure some of those stories are highly exaggerated or not true, at least the ones about me." Gilbért gave him a slight grin.

"You're too modest, Your Excellency. *Abad* Miguel has kept me informed on his former pupil and God tells me you and your companions are elected to do His will."

As I listened to their exchange, my curiosity surged about the smoothness of the prior's Gaulish tongue. His inflections were like mine, yet slightly different, prompting me to inquire where he was raised.

CHAPTER VIII

"Prior, where were you raised and what *abbaye* did you enter?" I asked, anxious to hear his answer.

"I grew up in the Champagne region and entered Clairvaux *Abbaye* as a postulant. Herbs and plants have always fascinated me, and my *père* encouraged me to study them. He worked in our *seigneur's* vineyard, and I helped him with the grapes. So, when it came time to acquire my final vows, *Père Supérieure* Bernard asked me to oversee the *abbaye* vineyards."

"Do you mean the *Santo* Bernard?" I asked, quite surprised he knew the *santo moine.*

"*Oui,* that's correct, and that's why our accents are similar, however, we haven't resided here long. *Roi* Alfonso the Second and *Princesse* Helena asked me to come to their kingdom and help with their nascent *vino* production. We Cistercians like to obtain God's forgotten land and make it into a place to praise Him. We use prayer and hard work to accomplish this, they're our garden tools."

"We don't mean to keep you from your important work," I stated, "but we can find our way to our quarters just fine."

"Our *Opus Dei* includes more than the making of *vin, Seigneur* Robert de Borron. As *Santo* Matthew wrote, 'All guests who present themselves are to be welcomed as Christ,' for He said, 'I was a stranger and you welcomed me.'"

We continued to follow the prior down the narrow corridor that led to a large open dorter with numerous straw-filled beds. Along one wall were several small open windows, which faced a small cloister garth.

"Our accommodations are quite plain, but I know the *frères* of the Temple and *Abad* Miguel will understand the sparse sleeping quarters. Pardon me for now, but I must bid you adieu, for I need to attend to the needs of *Princesse* Helena's courtiers. I am afraid they'll expect a little more attention. I have enjoyed meeting all of you and hope to see you off tomorrow. *Pax vobiscum* and *bonsoir, mon* fellow poor *frères* in Christ."

Quickly, we sought out our beds and placed next to each what little clothing we brought with us from Helena's *château*. I didn't dare store my saddlebag with my spare clothing but kept the *Sangraal* book slung over my shoulder as we moved toward the lavatorium. Upon reaching the lavatorium, we washed our faces and hands with cold water. Afterward, we used the soft towels to clean and dry ourselves before leaving, but just as I finished an unknown *moine* approached me holding a note.

"*Seigneur Baron* de Borron, the *Princesse* Helena wanted me to give you this note." He handed me the missive.

"*Merci beaucoup, mon frère*." I reached for the note from the white-robed *moine*, however, he didn't leave. "Is there anything else she wants?"

"*Oui*, she told me to wait for a reply."

Quickly, my fingers broke the royal red seal, but her rose-vanilla scented note momentarily distracted me from reading it. After my nostrils pulled in its pleasant fragrance, I read its contents.

"Tell *Princesse* Helena to expect me soon," I stated to the nameless *moine*, knowing she was anxious to leave for her vineyards before the early December sundown.

"*Très bien, Seigneur* de Borron, I will tell her *altesse* immediately."

Quickly, he turned around and left, his white robe flaring from a cold draft coming in through an open window.

I informed Grand Master Gilbért where I would be, to which he gave a hesitant nod of approval.

"Here, grab my spyglass, so you can see any trouble before it arrives. In addition, it will aid you in observing *Princesse* Helena's vineyard." He shook his head. "Be careful, *mon ami*, I will see you at Compline when you return."

I met Helena in the cloister grounds, where she had already mounted her big Andalusian horse. One of her gloved hands held her horse's reins, while the other held the reins to my horse.

"Quickly, Roberto, mount your horse so we can leave, for we have less than a quarter of the day's light left." She handed me my reins.

Right away, I leaped on my horse and spurred her as we raced through the priory entrance. Once reaching the road, a freezing wind blew across my face, which forced me to raise my white hood to block the stinging cold. The sky was void of any afternoon clouds, letting our vision see toward the *montagnes* and in all directions. We were all alone, just the two of us riding over the *crunchy* sounding frozen reddish soil. To our left were the snow-capped *montagnes,* and directly in front of us lay the Campo de Cariñena, forming a rolling plateau with rusty-colored soil. Breaking through the soil were sprouting evenly spaced gnarled-shaped grapevines. As we galloped past, each leafless trunk seemed to march toward Zaragozza. Periodically, we would come across clustered groves of small trees nestled in the ravines.

"What are those small trees growing in orderly rows at the bottom of each ravine?" I asked, not knowing their nature. Instantly, Helena reined in her horse to reply to my question.

"We call them *almendro* trees. They bear an oval-shaped nut, which we make a sweet dessert called *turrón*. When Advent is over, we will share this treat together." She smiled. "Your people would call this nut fruit *amande*, and some people say its shape is sacred, representing the external halo of baby Jesus sitting on his *mère's* lap, *Santo* Mary. The Italians call this narrow oval shape the mandorla and I embarrassed to say, they believe it resembles a woman's private body part."

Helena paused here to regain her composure, yet a slight smile came across her mouth along with her entire crimson face blending in with her red cheeks. Her eyes gazed down at the ground before she continued as if carefully choosing her next words.

"It's the shape we see when we first come into this troubled world, interspersed with short periods of happiness. Birth and our soul's realization begin here through this narrow oval-shaped design and my intuition tells me this will be another clue to your discovery of the next *Sangraal* parchments. It's serendipitous we stopped here, and you asked me about my trees, for my heart tells me the nut's shape is a key. One additional thought, its oval shape also resembles a fish shape without a tail. This reoccurring fish symbol seems to permeate throughout the New Testament and many of its chapters speak of fish and fishermen."

Helena said nothing else, only the buffeting wind broke our silence. We each sat in our saddles contemplating what she had just revealed. Her intuition was correct and so was her insight, yet what surprised me was her depth of thinking. To me, she sounded similar to an Old Testament prophetess, but her words had suddenly made me visualize in my mind's eye an old Celtic symbol. It hadn't occurred to me until now that two intersecting circles formed a fish design. Did this symbol have anything to do with our Lord's visit to the Celtic Isles?

"Roberto, what do you think this land before us will become in eight hundred years?"

"Why do you ask such a question and what makes you wonder about eight hundred years from now?" I knew she had indeed visualized an answer and I would soon hear it.

"I see giant villages without fortresses, little warfare, many wooden barrels of *vino*, happy people, and wide roads made out of smooth slabs of rock with strange racing carriages on them, yet stranger still, they have no horses attached." She had a distant stare as she looked over the land.

"Your prophecy, or I should say your imaginative prediction, is your future legacy. You and your *moines* have started with this barren land and turned it into an excellent *vino*-growing region. It's something future generations will inherit with the financial accomplishments you first started here. Forgive me for being pragmatic to your question, but eight hundred years from now, we will still have the same fears, hates, loves, and longings. Humankind is a flawed creature and only our continued faith in the Trinity can improve our lot in life. I pray some men and women will see there's a need to advance our civilization and stamp out ignorance, especially ignorance." As I gazed toward her for another comment, her rosy-cheeked face became solemn.

"Roberto, I am falling in love with you!" she exclaimed, her gray-blue eyes searching mine for a reply.

She left me speechless, and I didn't know how to answer. My eyes stared down at the reddish soil, thinking my mind would find the right words to say, but only the buffeting wind replied. Some days ago, my heart told me this moment might happen, yet I pushed it from thoughts. My feelings for her were the same, however, my loneliness had forced me into this moment of temptation.

"Helena, I feel the same as you do. If under any other circumstances, I would want you as my *amant*, but my mortal soul is now at stake, along with the *Sangraal* quest. Let us not fall victim to our loneliness and passions, for I truly *amour mon épouse* and two young *fils*, which they all depend on me. In addition, our Lord and Savior and His intercessor, Mary Magdaleine, have chosen me to seek out Saint Joseph's hallowed parchments. It's a responsibility I must seek to its completion, even if they don't exist or remain lost. Since I left *Château* Borron, the past weeks with you have made happy. Let's not have our emotional and physical attractions for each other interfere with our special relationship. I want to honor your intelligence, honesty, farsightedness, and kindness." I reached for her gloved hands and squeezed both. Our eyes then met, but all I noticed were eyes of disappointment and the familiar loneliness I had seen before.

"*Bien sûr mon affectueux* Robert, are we to be close *amis* and nothing more?" She stared at the frozen ground.

"*Contraire,* Helena, however, consider us as *amants* of similar ideas, close *amis,* and two kindred spirits who God has chosen for us to meet. The troubadours call this *cortez amores,* without the *fin amor,*" I tried to explain, but it didn't put the gleam back into her eyes. Instead, she turned her horse around with a pinch-faced gaze and galloped back toward the Cistercian priory. Quickly, my horse caught up with hers and I tried to start a conversation about her vineyards, the ancient Celts who settled in this area, and her beloved *moines.* However, she added little to the conversation and just stared toward the snow-capped *montagnes,* without facing me.

The winter sun hurriedly dropped behind the *montagnes* as we neared the priory; making me wonder how soon Saint Lazarus's Feast Day would arrive. If close, our Christ's Mass was soon. Suddenly, my vision caught the glint of metal from a distant hillock, however, I saw no rider and the metal reflection seemed stationary. Quickly, I stopped, reached for the spyglass, and then held it in steady fashion to focus on the glaring ray of light.

"Roberto, is there trouble?" Helena asked, finally addressing me.

"*Non,* it's just Muhammad Nur Adin shadowing us." I focused the spyglass on a riderless horse, which belonged to Muhammad. It seemed I didn't have any cloister garth privacy and was incapable of protecting myself or anybody else. Anger tightened my jaw, leaving me wanting to tell Grand Master Gilbért of my displeasure.

"Roberto, before we arrive at the priory, I want you to know that I respect what you said earlier about our special relationship. I wouldn't want to put you in a compromising situation. I understand your loyalty to your family, but this still doesn't change my affection for you, however, my mind tells me not to cause you angst. Please, Roberto, try to understand a lonely woman, that's all I ask."

Once again, silence prevailed until we reached the torch-lit cloister garth, where Sergeant de Hoult greeted us as we dismounted.

"Lord Robert, his Excellency Grand Master Gilbért would like to speak to you before the office of Compline."

"Tell him to expect me right away." I hoped I would have sufficient time to clean up. Why did he want to speak to me?

The office of Compline wouldn't arrive for a while.

I told Helena to meet me in the *moine's* parlor after Compline, to which she agreed.

Right away, I cleaned myself and then hurried to the prior's cell to meet Grand Master Gilbért. The smallness of the monastery made it easy to travel about. I arrived at the partially opened door.

"Please enter, *mon ami,*" Grand Master Gilbért said, "and then close the door. In addition, please bolt it too, for I have something quite sensitive to tell you. First, tell me, did you enjoy your brisk ride to the vineyards?" He glanced at the occupant, Prior Etienne.

"*Oui,*" I replied. "Yet, darkness shortened our journey, leaving several hillocks still to visit."

Was Grand Master Gilbért wanting me to divulge our personal conversations or just his concern for our safety? I put his question out of my mind and instead surveyed the prior's spartan room. Directly in front of me lay a straw-filled mattress on the stone floor. Next to the head of the mattress stood a low table, and on the wall above the bed hung a small wooden cross.

I turned back to him. "What's the urgency to see me?"

Right away, Grand Master Gilbért's face drained of its color before he started to reply.

"I have just received some disquieting news. Marshal Poncho Dìaz de Vivar has received word from our *frères* in Toledo that the Brethren of Purity is trailing us."

"That's the same cabal first mentioned by Commander de Polignac, then later by *Frère* Carlos!" I exclaimed, fearing somebody had heard me.

"*Oui*, however, the information I just received says they aren't just pursuing us but are after a new unnamed victim."

"Does Marshal de Vivar know where they might hide?"

"*Non, mon ami*, however, we should leave for Zaragozza before daybreak. I will alert *Princesse* Helena and explain our urgent need to return to Zaragozza along with my men. In addition, she'll know you're leaving with me too, and Helena will follow you back to the Aljafería Palace." He turned to Prior Etienne. "Not a word of this conversation should leave this room. Do you swear not to tell anybody what I have just said before God and His *Fils*, our Lord and Savior, Jesus the Christ?"

"*Oui,* I do swear," Prior Etienne quickly answered. "And in addition to the Holy Spirit, the saints who came before me, and all the angels in heaven."

Gilbért turned back to me. "After I leave, why don't you ask Prior Etienne if he is familiar with any of the drawings you have collected on our quest? Maybe he will reveal some new insight into what the drawing means."

The humble prior's forehead raised upward, letting me know his curiosity had just piqued. My warrior *ami* had brought all the drawings to the prior's sparse cell. Now duty called and he handed me the protected drawings, said his adieu to Prior Etienne, and quickly turned to leave.

"So, Lord Robert, you have some drawings to show me? I pray I can help you in some way, yet I am just a humble Cistercian *moine* and a servant of God. Prayer and hard work I know best, however, let me peruse your drawings."

I withdrew the drawings out of the leather tubes Grand Master Gilbért had left, unrolled them, and handed them to Prior Etienne. To my surprise, the prior's hazel-colored eyes grew quite large with amazement.

"I have seen these wheels, angels, and the five-pointed star somewhere in Toledo," he stated, leaving my hands shaking in anticipation of his remembrance. His studied moment of silence seemed to last forever.

"Ah!" he exclaimed. "Now I remember, there's a Grecian statue of a half-naked woman in the older section of Toledo. The locals say this statue predates Christianity. It was there long before the Visigoths and Moors conquered Toledo and my fellow *frères* tell me it harkens back to the Iberian Celts, who were good allies of the ancient Greek shipping merchants."

"Yet, if it predates Christianity, how will that help our Christian pilgrimage?" I inquired, still not wanting to tell the prior all the facts of our quest. "What does she have to do with these drawings?"

"First of all, she was called Hebe by the ancient Greeks and cupbearer to the Greek gods and goddesses. Each day she would serve them nectar, then ambrosia on their heavenly thrones at Mount Olympus. Her parents were Zeus and Hera, who gave her the power to restore youth in anybody she so desired. They received a second chance to relive their youth, yet some people called her Juventas for obvious reasons. In ancient Greece, she is depicted holding a cup or chalice in one hand, thus the statue in Toledo goes by the name cupbearer. Not far from her pointed cup-filled palm are the drawing symbols. They're small stone-carved blocks removed from some long-forgotten building, now used as steppingstones following the direction of her outreached arm. That's all I can remember, *mon fils;* age has clouded my memory."

It didn't seem urgent to come here, but more urgent to continue our quest as soon as possible. A tight feeling welled up in my chest to leave at once, yet we had to gather some pertinent information for our quest.

CHAPTER IX

Once again, I was stupefied in how each preceding clue was now falling in place; letting our dreams and hopes become closer to reality. I couldn't wait to tell Grand Master Gilbért the good news.

"Just a couple of other things, *mon fils*," Prior Etienne stated. "Since ancient times the city of Toledo has harbored many people's faiths, both pagan and the three faiths of Abraham. Remember, its sacred spots are one foundation built upon another. What you seek may reveal itself between one of these foundations."

"*Merci beaucoup*, Prior Etienne, for this revealing clue."

"*Dominus vobiscum*, Lord Robert, and *merci* for once again making my royal benefactor, her *Altesse* Helena happy. I haven't seen her this excited since our martyred prince, her *mari, Don* Pedro Bernardo, was alive."

We then both crossed ourselves, making me realize how obvious our affections were to each other. My conundrum with Helena had grown each day we were in the company of each other. Her intelligence and self-confidence in dealing with men, along with her gorgeous beauty repeatedly drew me near her like sips of sweet wine. The prior hadn't chided or warned me not to see her, yet his final words seemed to complement our relationship. This left me with a feeling of guilt and obfuscation, yet I knew I had to stay focused on my family and our quest. However, my emotions seemed saddled with numerous different emotional riders galloping in various directions.

"Prior Etienne, please pardon me, for I must see Grand Master Gilbért and tell him what you said about our quest to Toledo." I reached for the door latches.

Quickly, I left the prior's cell and darted down the narrow corridor searching for Grand Master Gilbért's whereabouts. Just as my feet approached the cloister garth entrance, there was Gilbért entering.

"Ah, just the person I want to see," he said, stopping his conversation with Muhammad.

"First, before you speak, there's something urgent I must tell you, which was just revealed to me." I told him Prior Etienne had recognized the symbols in the drawings, which the Greek Hebe statue in Toledo's Christian quarter pointed toward our symbols. Only a weak smile of approval came over his face, leading me to believe my new information wasn't as important as I first thought.

"That's good news, *mon ami*, and I am happy, but what does the statue represent?"

Quickly, I explained the significance of the Greek and Roman deities and how this clue fits into our *Sangraal* quest. However, he still didn't seem that impressed.

"I am afraid to douse your fire of enthusiasm with water, but Muhammad believes tomorrow we'll face an ambush on our way back to Zaragozza. He just told me he senses the possible threat of our so-called Brethren of Purity. It's the same uneasiness that knotted his stomach right before the unknown killers murdered his family. In addition, he thinks these might be the same killers that murdered *Frère* Gabriel."

"How can this be?" I retorted to Gilbért's bad news while noticing Muhammad's head nodding in agreement. "I thought he was robbed and left for dead by bandits?"

"Don't forget, Lord Robert, he wasn't just a poor *moine* working for God, but a messenger of truth on his way to deliver my missive to the Holy *Père* in Rome. I hoped he would expose the atavistic nature of Cardinal Folquet, but God willed otherwise. However, what I don't understand is that the cardinal has sufficient men to trail us and capture you and the *Sangraal* parchments. Why hire a shadowy group of unknown men to follow us and increase an already intricate web of conspiracy? There must be additional motives other than you and the *Sangraal* parchments that we are missing." Gilbért rubbed his gray-tinged dark beard.

A squeezing angst circled around my chest, as Gilbért revealed this new revelation, causing me to want to leave for Toledo right away. The new increased urgency left both my palms sweating and my mouth dry.

"Sharpen your sword tonight, *mon ami*, I fear what tomorrow brings or the days thereafter."

"How long do you think we'll stay in Zaragozza before we leave for Toledo?" I inquired, anxious to follow up on our latest clue.

"Let's proceed to the quiet of the *moine's* graveyard and there we can further discuss this matter." Gilbért pointed toward a small open green space next to the priory *église.*

We strolled toward the few small mounds of unmarked *moine* graves and stopped in a small windy corner.

"If everything works as planned," Gilbért said, "we'll leave right after the feast day of Saint Stephen."

"Why not sooner?"

"*Roi* Alfonso wants us to stay longer. Before we left for *Princesse* Helena's vineyards, he told me in private he was sending a military escort and his ambassador to Rome. He wants me to give a sworn deposition before his archbishop about what has happened to us and what I know about Cardinal Folquet. In addition, his *altesse* wants to verify my testimony with him before his ambassador departs for Rome.

"Lord Robert, it's better to have no obstacles before us as we seek out the next possible set of *Sangraal* parchments. Moreover, let's enjoy the holy days ahead of us, the hospitality the *roi* will provide, and the safety of Aljafería."

He was right, yet my whole body remained tightened for combat. In addition, a sense of dread came over me, knowing we would remain in Zaragozza for several days past the Christ's Mass. I was left with a sense of impending doom upon hearing of our delay, but Gilbért must have noticed my melancholy.

"Cheer up, *mon ami*. It will give you time to update your travel journal, write your *épouse*, and enjoy the pleasant company of the *Marquésa* Helena." He grinned knowingly.

Quickly my melancholy turned to anger, realizing how patronizing he sounded to me. Was it my pent-up frustrations causing me to react to his grin? I didn't know, yet I had to let him know how I felt.

"I don't want you to have me followed anymore by Muhammad," I demanded while feeling my increased pulse *thumping* along my temples. "I have proved myself in combat and you have trusted me with your secret strategies, however, you treat me as an inexperienced squire. Part of our quest and my destiny was ordained by God and His Son, Jesus the Christ."

"You are right, Lord Robert, and please forgive me. Nevertheless, don't forget what the old Cathar hermit told you in the Pyrénées *Montagnes* cave. We are the tip of the spear and guardian of lé *Sangraal*. God wills it for us to protect the parchments of Saint Joseph de Arimathea's book. *Mon ami*, you are the mouthpiece of God and His Son to translate His will to us lowly mortal men and women. Each of us has a responsibility to one another to carry out our quest and tell what Saint Joseph has written for present and future generations. *Mon ami*, trust my judgment in these matters; besides, I must spend some time seeing that my arrest warrant is revoked. Only *Roi* Alfonso and the grand master of our entire order, the newly elected Robert de Sablé, have enough influence with the Holy *Père* to accomplish this. Unbeknownst to you, until now, I have ordered Chaplain Jeremiah and *Abad* Miguel to travel to Toledo before us. They'll take with them our drawings, the updated information on our quest, and use all of this to seek out our trusted local scholars who will help us."

"Why can't I travel with them?" I hastily protested.

"I want you here with me, so if *Marquésa* Helena reveals any additional information, and she will only reveal it to you, this information could further protect us or hasten our quest for the sacred parchments. I know you have proven yourself as a seasoned warrior of God, but I can't jeopardize your divine talents and risk your capture. If you stay, I promise to honor your request and not have Muhammad follow you anymore."

"*Merci*," I replied, believing what he had just said.

"Let's obtain some sleep," Gilbért said, as we slowly ambled from the solemn windy graveyard.

Quickly, I dashed to the parlor as Grand Master Gilbért headed toward the small *église* for Compline before retiring. Upon reaching the diminutive parlor, I observed Helena's eyes staring into her *vino* cup, with her fingertips rubbing around its rim. Her fixed gaze indicated she was in deep thought about something, letting me enter the room unseen. As I approached closer, my motions made her glance up.

"Roberto, I am glad you came. I was afraid after our late afternoon ride you wouldn't want to speak to me again. Once again, I must apologize for my foolishness, for I acted like a pubescent girl at court. Do you still forgive me?" Her bluish-gray eyes searched mine for confirmation.

"*Oui,* Helena, and again I know how you feel, but we must use caution. Even close *amis* between men and women has its risks." I grabbed her warm hands and stared into her eyes. "*Merci beaucoup*, for helping me on our holy quest. What you have revealed has drawn us closer to our final triumph." She let go of my hand and poured me a cup of her fine *vin*, after which she placed it into my partially closed hand.

"Let's salute to a successful, but safe, quest in obtaining the next *Sangraal* parchments."

Our solid gold cups *clinked* with a uniform resonance.

"I wish I could travel with you to Toledo and help you search for the new parchments. I haven't visited the *roi* of Castile, my nephew, in several months. It's silly of me to even think of such a thing, but Roberto, promise me two things. First, you won't undertake any unnecessary risks, and second, promise to write me what the sacred parchments say."

"*Oui*, I will if God so wills it."

We drank another cup of *vino*, while she explained her lineage to the *roi* of Castile. After she consumed two additional cups of *vino*, her mind still stayed alert in telling me many stories about her late *père's* family. Because I was exhausted and knew the effect the *vino* would have, I refrained from any additional *vino* and just sat there partially hearing the latest information about her nephew. Finally, I squeezed her hand and bowed to kiss it before departing.

"*Bonsoir*, Helena, I must leave, for we have an early start tomorrow."

Several hours later, the weak gray morning light, coupled with the noise from the *moine's* soft *thumping* sandals aroused my senses. Quickly, I dressed, then rushed to the lavatorium, where I washed my face, hands, and after finishing, prepared to leave. One of the squires had sharpened my sword, another helped me with my chain mail and then saddled my horse, leaving me some extra time to leisurely stroll to the *église* for Prime and mass. The morning orange dun-colored sky quickly filled with dark clouds as I approached the *église*, however, after glancing up, I observed the red-tiled *église* roof glistening with ice. Apparently, during the night, my sound sleep had prevented me from hearing the sleet pelt the several priory roofs. The small nave quickly filled with all the courtiers, *chevaliers*, *moines*, and warrior-*moines*, leaving me little room to find a spot to pray. Without hesitation, we said our Glory Bes, *Pater Nosters*, and several psalms, with my angst increasing by the moment because of my urgency to leave. What seemed like an eternity, the mass ceremony droned on with Chaplain Jeremiah finally giving the benediction. Prior Etienne followed with a final blessing and then we departed to our waiting horses and carriages.

"Lord Robert de Borron, please wait, for I have some final words to tell you before you leave," Prior Etienne announced, as he hastened toward me before I mounted my horse. I stopped with one boot in my stirrup, turned toward his presence, and waited for him to continue.

"What you seek you will find, for God and His Son have told me so. He's guiding you on every twist in the roads and every bend in the rivers. Fear no adversary, for the Holy Trinity is protecting you from all human foes and Satan's army. *Pax vobiscum, mon fils.*" The elderly prior's hazel eyes stared into mine.

"*Au revoir*, Prior Etienne, and *merci beaucoup* for your hospitality and precious information."

I finished mounting my horse, turned him toward the entrance to leave, and observed the humble prior giving his final blessing to Helena as I galloped through the gate.

Once upon the open road to Zaragozza, the sleet returned with its icy pellets *plinking* against our scabbards, helms, and chain mail, which quickly covered our entire bodies with a thin layer of glistening ice. The sleet continued all day until we reached the outskirts of Zaragozza at sundown, at which time I said a prayer thanking God for our safe return and from the cardinal's men.

Our large entourage of followers snaked their way along the old Roman wall until we reached a crumbled Roman sentry building, which led to the main ancient stone gate to the city.

A short time later, we reached the bridge to the *Palacio* Aljafería and oh, what a welcome sight to see and hear the *flapping* sound of fiery torches positioned on each side of the main entrance. Directly above us, along the ramparts were palace guards who peeked out behind each merlon. Instantly, they shouted for the palace squires to come, while another guard ordered the gatekeeper to open the gate. Within an instant, we spurred our horses forward, while behind us the wooden carriages rumbled along the bridge's wooden planks. Quickly, an army of young squires helped our exhausted bodies to dismount and aid the courtiers.

I left the small bailey area and proceeded to my room. My nose caught the scent of roasted nuts as I opened my door, yet the first thing I noticed and felt was the *crackling* fire coming from my room's ornate stone fireplace. Then, my nose further drew me to a steaming pitcher. To one side of the pitcher stood a solitary clay cup and it too had steam dancing above its rim. Right away, my cold hands reached for the dark-brown liquid-filled cup and drew into my nostrils the nutty aroma of its smell. I sipped a small portion of the *café* and felt the hot liquid slowly slide down my throat. Instantly, my stomach was sufficiently warm, the cold skin on my frozen body beckoned me to sit in the large ladderback-armed chair. It stood directly in front of the fireplace, but at a proper distance to quickly warm me, yet not overheat my body. Just as I became sufficiently warm, there came a loud *thumping* sound on my door.

"Lord Robert de Borron, you're requested to come to *Marquésa* Helena's royal chambers now," came the sonorous voice of the royal chamberlain, Rodrigo.

Right away, I put my clay cup on a buffet table and crossed to open the door. Quickly, I unlocked it, opened the heavy wooden oak door, and spied Rodrigo waiting for a reply. It seemed the man grew bigger every time I met him, for as I glanced down to his open hands, they appeared the size of two great helms. He would only need one hand for a large two-handed sword, I thought.

"Tell Your *Altesse*, I'll arrive as soon as I am presentable; it shouldn't be long."

"*Si*, I'll tell her." He then left as I shut the door. Yet, I still heard his heavy stomping boots for some distance after closing my door, however, what was it about his eyes that seemed familiar?

CHAPTER X

With one large gulp, I downed my *café* or *qahwa* brew and then crossed my room to rose-scented towels and several washing bowls. After removing my chain mail coif, I started my ablutions, after which I viewed, draped across my bed, a clean white, red-splayed cross surcoat and mantle. Quickly, I donned my fresh clothes while pondering the urgency for Helena to see me. I knew both of us were exhausted from our icy ride, so why couldn't her meeting wait until tomorrow? After finishing, I hid my precious parchments inside the ticking of my bed, smoothed the covers, and proceeded to leave. Carefully, I locked my door, and lightly stepped into the hallway corridor.

As I ambled to Helena's royal chambers, many thoughts and conjectures entered my mind, yet one kept creeping back. What was the relationship between Helena and her chamberlain, Rodrigo? He appeared more than a member of her royal staff. However, I do remember her saying he was raised in her *père's* royal court and each were about the same age.

Just as I was about to knock on her door, Rodrigo appeared from inside, and held the door open for me to enter.

"Lord de Borron, I hope you have a pleasant evening with our *altesse* after your arduous trip." He walked out and shut the door.

"I see you refreshed yourself and had some of the Moor's special dark brown brew," Helena stated, as I entered her sitting quarters. "Please Roberto, come and have a seat with me on my pillowed settee. I will pour you another cup of *qahwa*."

Helena was dressed in a long flowing white chemise, with her dark reddish-brown hair draped down her back. It appeared she was preparing for bed, yet her demeanor seemed quite alert. As she moved toward the steaming silver decanter, the candlelight revealed every detail of her naked body behind her chemise gown. Her breasts were large, but not pendulous, her hips and her thighs proportionally matched Helena's height. As she finished pouring the *café*, she turned, and then faced me with her bare feet slightly apart. Helena's dark triangle-shaped hair of womanhood revealed itself as a small protruding mound against her thinly veiled gown. Had she invited me here to seduce me? I hoped not.

"Roberto, I know you are wondering why I have asked you here to tonight after our tiring return, but an important message was delivered to me today. It's disquieting news and I am afraid it concerns you and your quest." Her brow creased in consternation. "My spies in Toledo have gathered some dire information, which concerns your potential death and stopping your sacred search for the new parchments."

"It's already been put at risk," I stated. "Why would this information be any different?"

"My sources say these men aren't the cardinal's *chevaliers* and they don't fear death."

"Did your sources divulge who they were and who sent them?"

"*Non*, they didn't know their names or who sent them but they are called by what they do. They use concealment or dissimulation, which they said was called *taqiyya,* meaning they have the ability to appear and disappear without you realizing their presence."

"That's hard to believe," I replied, doubting the capabilities of this shadowy group, yet the same information was conveyed to me by *Frère* Carlos and Muhammad. "How accurate is this information?"

"Quite accurate. It's from local Moors living in Toledo all their lives. In addition, I pay them well and their past information hasn't failed me yet. I am so afraid for you and Grand Master Gilbért. Furthermore, my sources said there are possibly additional people who may come under their knife. I beg you, please tell your Saracen *ami* what I just told you. Maybe he can travel to Toledo, by himself, and search for these men." A tear rolled down one of her cheeks.

"*Merci*, for your concern. The information corroborates what we have already heard, however, my destiny was unknowingly determined by God at my birth. Recently, in a vision, the holy Mary Magdaleine informed me of my quest. I can't defy God's predestination for me, yet I think it's a *bon* idea for Muhammad to leave for Toledo first. He could mingle better with the local Moor community and use his great observation skills to help make our quest quicker." I hoped this would appease her concerns, yet it didn't. Her eyes now focused on mine moving back and forth, which pleaded for me not to travel to Toledo. She spoke not another word but then bowed her head with disappointment. Every muscle in my being wanted to squeeze her thinly veiled naked body. I could feel the heat of passion coming from her and knew at once I had to leave.

"It's time for me to leave, for dawn will come too soon."

"I know tomorrow you will have something planned for us."

I rose from the settee. My eyes broke contact with hers and I focused them on the door latches. However, she too jumped up and met me at the door, then grabbed my hand.

"Roberto, please think seriously about not traveling to Toledo. You may be wrong about your destiny." Her firm breasts brushed against my surcoat. I shook my head no, and finally, she released her firm grip from my right hand. I opened my door.

"*Bonsoir*, Roberto, I'll see you tomorrow and sleep well tonight."

I left Helena's chambers with numerous sets of emotions, from heightened fears of the elusive image of the Brethren of Purity. I now knew their terror was real, along with Helena's intoxicating beauty and the possible prevention of me not completing our sacred quest.

Upon turning down a corridor to my room, the hairs on my neck rose, alerting me that someone or something was stalking me. Slowly, my hand moved toward the pommel of my sword, which I grasped. I stopped, hugged my back against the rough moist stones, and eased down the stone hallway. The old Moorish palace had hundreds of alcoves for someone or something to hide and observe. I widened my eyes trying to see the least noticeable features, but alas, to no avail, there was nothing visible. With a creeping motion and sword drawn, I reached my room without incident. I placed my key into the lock and gradually turned it, until I heard a muffled *clank.* I then pressed on the ornately carved door.

As I closed the door behind me, I faced the dark room with my sword raised. I secured the latches and then crept toward the first nearby candle. There, next to the candle, were sufficient lighting straws. Slowly, I grabbed one and then strolled toward the dying embers of the fireplace. The straw stem ignited, letting me light several candles next to the fireplace. Right away, my room started to glow a flickering yellow, thus exposing every shadowy feature. Quickly, I surveyed my room, and then resheathed my sword with relief, leaving me to check on our *Sangraal* book.

When I had returned, I moved our holy book and hid it, along with the drawings, in an inglenook covered with wood. Upon approaching the ornate-carved stone fireplace, I held my breath and silently said a prayer to myself, hoping this wouldn't be a repeat of the stolen *Sangraal* parchments at Huesca. Slowly, I pushed the split wood from the inglenook base, opened the door, further clearing small sticks of sapwood from a shelf, which hid a loose panel. My trembling hands pried the wooden panel loose and searched for our leather-bound tome.

PART TWO

The Cave

CHAPTER XI

Cave at Arimathea

Anno Domini 37

"Yoseph," came his sister's voice, which jarred him out of his worrisome thoughts.

"I pray we leave here right away," Enygeus continued. "My baby son and I feel like trapped animals in a cave. My brother, please hold me, for I am scared. How can a man be this evil? Why is Barabbas taunting us? We haven't done anything to him."

"I wish I could answer your questions, but he slit the throat of that donkey to instill fear in us." He tightly embraced her. "I trust in *El Shaddai.* He will protect us no matter what happens. Enygeus, fear is one of the Evil One's many tools to ensnare us. Ever since Adam and Eve, this terrible *malach's* strength and guile have increased and we must have faith in our *Maishiach.* As soon as I finish my parchments on the current ministry, we will leave for the coast; probably in about two *Shabbats.*"

"But Yoseph, I implore you to leave . . . sooner. This monster wants to harm my baby. Please. I beg you to reconsider." She weakly pounded her fists against his chest.

He knew his sister was right, but their new faith was at stake, and he was its mortal leader. It was his responsibility, as their rabbi, to constantly encourage this new faith. In addition, to let each follower know the road ahead had many pitfalls. Suddenly, a thought entered Yoseph's mind. Philip knew the coastline well, with Caesarea his place of birth, and he was well acquainted with many sailors. He could send him ahead, with Hebron, Enygeus, and baby Enoch. Along the way to Yoffa, they could preach Yeshua's *kodesh* words, still leaving him time to finish his parchment.

"My sister, I don't want you to think I am not concerned for our safety, especially little Enoch's, however, I am now responsible for our entire band of Yeshua's followers and Yeshua's *kodesh* words. Today, I will discuss this matter with Hebron and Philip for you to leave with them for the coast. If they agree, we'll leave today. We must be circumspect with our decision-making so that all our teachings from Yeshua will penetrate the people's hearts. Each one of us can impart something they've heard or know about our nephew. It's my divine obligation to write these former moments, letting us pass this written legacy down to others after we are no longer of this world."

"Thank you, Yoseph, I couldn't ask for a better brother." His sister smiled. "Let me know what the details are, and I will follow them."

He squeezed her waist, until her trembling stopped, and she ceased crying. After which, Enygeus broke their tight embrace and excused herself to nurse young Enoch.

"Again, thank you, my brother," she said, still smiling, and then left.

Standing there ruminating in Yoseph's mind about what he just said, this prompted him to think it best to speak to Hebron and Philip right now and not wait until tomorrow. Both men were guarding the camels, with Hebron periodically circling the camp for an intruder or intruders. He caught him and Philip together and moved toward the braying camels.

"Yoseph, your furrowed brow shows me you're ready to tell us something," Hebron said, seeing his worried demeanor.

"Yes, you are right, and it concerns Enygeus. She's scared for baby Enoch's life, and if we stay here one day longer, she says he could be murdered or any of us put to the dagger. If we stay on the move, this will lessen the chances of this happening. Therefore, I want you to lead the others on to Yoffa and then meet me there. If I need you sooner, I will send for you. My second set of sacred scrolls are almost finished, and maybe after two *Shabbats,* you'll see me. It's important to our ministry that future generations have a completed record of our *Maishiach's kodesh* word."

"Rabbi, I want to stay with you!" Philip demanded.

"I planned on having you travel with the others to help arrange ship's passage to Egypt. I don't know how long our ministry will last in our homeland, but under the new terrible circumstances, we must now prepare our travel arrangements. Your contacts with the seamen are important to us, which if we must leave in a hurry will aid us."

"However, I must tell you, Yoseph, that Yohanan and I have dreamt each night, where our *Maishiach* speaks to us. He told me last night to stay with you and help finish the scrolls. You can't deny what Yeshua wants and besides, Hebron knows many of the same sailors I know. In addition, his authority is quite respected by the merchant captains."

He was right, there was no denying *Maishiach's* unknowing wisdom.

"You are right, Philip. Whom am I to refute our *Maishiach*? Both your dreams are important. You can stay, however, discuss with Hebron about your trusted contacts."

Hebron and Philip left to tell the others what Yoseph had just said, which was shortly followed by his fellow teachers gathering their blankets and clothes. Then all his family and friends embraced him and said farewell. Strangely, he felt no sorrow in seeing their small band of teachers disappear behind a large group of broken boulders. However, at times his emotions seemed stunned of feeling, leaving him to believe his imprisonment had left lasting consequences. Yet, hope and faith prompted him, no matter what happened, to meet his family and teachers at the appointed time.

Yoseph and Philip left Lydda that afternoon and traveled off the main road back toward Arimathea and their former cave home. They didn't observe anybody stalking their movements, but not having Hebron with them, he wasn't certain. The path back was uneventful until they encountered a dust storm, which forced them back on the main road. The gritty dust hindered their visibility, yet at the same time helped obscure them from evil eyes.

They reached their former cave home just before sunset, right as the dust storm cleared. Then they started a fire from some scattered dry wood. Shortly thereafter, the *crackling* sound from the newly lit campfire echoed off the walls of the cave entrance. Philip repeatedly fed it with additional wood. The old camp seemed so empty without the ever-present dashing about of Zechariah flailing his staff at an imaginary enemy and little Enoch crying for his mother's milk. However, the stillness and bright fire helped prepare Yoseph for a night of writing. He hoped to update his hidden manuscript and finish both his sets.

Philip handed him a warm bowl of barley soup. "Yoseph, my mind is confused about why you wanted to return to the cave. I understand the reason Yohanan wanted to accompany you, for he's returning to *Yerushalayim* and Yeshua's *amma*. Yet, why is it necessary to finish your parchments at the cave?"

"I want to hide them in this cave," he replied, raising his voice with some irritation. He sighed. "Please forgive me, my friend, that was fear and frustration coming from my lips. So many questions have left me quite overwhelmed. Let me explain; as you well know, our *Adonai* has asked me to write about His life and teachings. The more I preserve His logos in these trying times, the better mankind will prepare for His glorious return. I am an old man, and anything can happen to me and these original parchments," Yoseph hoped his explanation would assuage Philip's question.

"But Rabbi, why hide them? Nobody will know of our *Maishiach's* life and teachings if you bury them."

"You are wrong, my friend," he replied with a kinder voice. "By swearing to these words in our teachings, my hidden parchments are a foundation for future generations to know. I am not naïve to believe our teachings will remain the same down through the ages. There will be people who will change what Yeshua taught and what I have written. One day, a man will discover my buried parchments, just like the ones I hid at the *kodesh* Temple Mount. My secret here I give to you for you and your future generations to keep. When the time is right, another will know of what I have written here."

"Yoseph, thank you for trusting me." Philip gave Yoseph a large embrace. "I see now, the time you spent in prison, you must have prayed unceasingly and thought of your future ministry."

"That's true, but Yeshua and His *malachs* visited me and gave me back His *kodesh* cup. This helped sustain me and tempered my loneliness the entire time I spent in that horrible filth hole."

"I didn't know Yeshua and His *malachs* came to you. How did they appear?" Philip's eyes lit up.

"They first appeared as misty golden orbs of light, with all three taking human shapes in front of a solid stone wall. Both *malachs* placed all our sacred supper items in front of me, including our beloved *kodesh* cup, which Yeshua held, and gently placed it in my palms. Shortly thereafter, the two *malachs* melted back into the stone wall and left no sign of their presence. Yeshua departed a short time later, disappearing through my locked wooden prison door."

"Rabbi Yoseph, what did our *Maishiach* say to you before He left?"

"Mainly about our future ministry, and that we would build a new *Yerushalayim.* He didn't specifically say where but did tell me his *Abba's* house would often change down through the ages."

"Yeshua always spoke in riddles, leaving it up to us to find out His meanings," Philip said with a slight chuckle. "He was constantly challenging us to obtain a higher sense of learning, but right now I am tired, and his hidden meanings will have to wait until tomorrow. It's just as He told us during the night of His arrest; the spirit is willing, but the flesh is weak. Good night, Yoseph. We can further discuss this in the morning." Philip headed for a spot near the *crackling* fire.

Yoseph left his sleepy companion, grabbed a rag torch at the cave entrance, and entered the cave's interior. He placed his torch in a shelf of loose rocks near the opening, sat down against a moist wall, and hoped to commence finishing his parchments. The *hissing* sound of the torch drew his eyes to its orange-colored flame and for a short while his tired eyes stayed focused on the dancing flame, only to soon fall fast asleep.

"Behold the Lamb of *Elohim*, who takes away the sins of the world," came the familiar ethereal voice of Yeshua. Was His voice coming from a dream or was He here present with him in the cave? However, the voice began to radiate a bright golden *kabod* centered in Yoseph's mind's eye, while snuffing out his burning torch as Yeshua's diaphanous glowing form replaced it.

"Yoseph, my beloved uncle, I come to you tonight to tell you of your destiny. This destiny isn't totally yours, but also that of your fellow teachers. You will build my new house on the Glass Isle within sight of the mound the people of the oak forest worship. Travel to the land of the young king who gave you the small tin casket. There you will find my New *Yerushalayim*."

To the right side of Yeshua, a new ball of yellow light commenced forming.

"Behold the sword of my *Abba*!" Yeshua's voice roared in Yoseph's head. "And this is His sword-bearer who brandishes both His sword and judgment scales. Fear him not, for he protects you and your teachers, just as I do. The mount at the Glass Isle will henceforth go by the name of Mikhael. Woe to your enemies, for he will smite them with my *Abba*'s sword."

Yeshua's voice ceased, and the golden orbs disappeared. Someone shook his shoulder.

"Rabbi, you were dreaming," Philip said. "And I heard your incoherent mumblings coming from the cave. Are you troubled?"

"Yes, however, I believe I just had a fitful dream, yet it seemed so real. Philip, it was a prophecy from our *Maishiach*, who told me we'll build His First temple, where we'll speak of His *kodesh* words."

"Where will this be?"

"We're to build our *Maishiach's* house in the land the Romans call Britannia. It's where you wanted to visit several years ago when we first met at my olive garden." Yoseph grinned as Philip's mouth gaped open. He grinned once more and then left.

Slowly, Yoseph emerged from his cold stone bed and ambled toward the morning daylight radiating through the cave entrance. Once past the opening, Yoseph heard *thumping* footsteps and viewed Philip scurrying to meet him.

"Yoseph, there's somebody approaching on camels." Philip's voice sounded frantic.

"They are coming from the east." He gestured behind him, indicating several riders.

"Yoseph, what shall we do?" Philip inquired, adding his concern.

A dust cloud surrounded whoever they were, making it impossible for him to see them, as Yoseph's tired eyes focused toward the *Yerushalayim* road. Was it the feared Nazarene hater from Tarsus or their stalker with an accomplice?

CHAPTER XII

"Fear not, Philip," Yoseph replied, as his hands reached for his writing satchel and the covered *kodesh* cup. "I don't believe it's our evil stalker. He is too much of a coward to confront us face to face." He felt the warmth of the cup on his palm.

"Hold your ground, my fellow brethren, for our *Maishiach's* cup will shield us."

Then out of the enormous ball of dust came a familiar voice.

"Yoseph! Yoseph of Arimathea! It's your good friend, Eli, coming to give you some horrible news."

There was no mistaking it was Eli's recognizable booming voice, yet his greetings had a dolorous tone. Both camels came to an abrupt stop, spilling their dust trail into their eyes and noses. Yoseph owed a great debt to Eli for harboring and helping him in *Yerushalayim* after his imprisonment. Eli's son, Eliyah, was the first to dismount, after forcing his camel on its knees. Eli followed, with his camel braying its spittle on Philip, who was holding the camel's reins.

Both Eli and Eliyah acknowledged Philip with a weak *shalom*, after which they approached Yoseph.

"My friend, thanks be to *El Shaddai*, I found you here. I was afraid you had left." Eli's voice quivered. "Yoseph, Isaiah was murdered!"

"How is this possible?" Yoseph didn't want to believe what he had just said about Eli's son.

His terrible news tightened Yoseph's jaw and stomach with overwhelming grief. However, thanks to his new faith, his mind was clear and told him to embrace Eli and Eliyah in their time of need. Both men's tears washed over his face, as they repeatedly sobbed how they missed Isaiah.

"Tell me what transpired, my good friends." Yoseph directed them toward the early morning fire.

"I found him behind our courtyard with several dagger wounds in his back. He apparently was feeding our camels before retiring for the night, when the attacker lunged at him from behind. There was a written note beside him . . ." Eli paused to clear his throat. "Yoseph, it was written in my own son's blood."

Eli's face drew up in the contorted manner of a man tortured with pain and guilt, yet he found some inner strength to continue speaking.

"The note stated, 'This is what will happen to anybody who continues to help Yoseph of Arimathea and his family.'"

A sob escaped from the depth of Yoseph's soul. He took Eli's hands. "My heart grieves for your loss, my good friend, and I wish Hebron and I were there to help him." Yoseph didn't know what else to say.

Guilt was creeping in, almost luring Yoseph into its downward spiral of blame. He had to keep focused on their ministry and fellow teachers yet stay alert to the evil surrounding the people he loved.

"When did your righteous son die?" Yoseph inquired, hoping to glean something important from Eli's distraught mind. Also at the same time, praying to himself he could focus him away from his sorrowful state of mind.

"It has been nine sundowns since his death. After *Shiva* was over, I was on the road to Arimathea to find you. My friend, you and your family are in grave danger. This mad man means to carry out what he wrote in my son's blood."

"We believe he's already here, lurking in these hills, waiting for the right moment to attack you and your family. After replenishing our water bags, Eliyah and I will leave and return to *Yerushalayim.* I don't think he'll harm us anymore, for he has satiated his blood lust from my family." Eli stared at the ground. "Besides, Eliyah and I are sufficiently armed for what this animal may try next. In addition, we have promised each other not to be alone at any one moment."

Both men gathered back their mantles, which exposed two large swords, then slowly lowered their hands, and tightly gripped the hilts. Thrust down, behind their tunic belts, were two curved daggers, which were more weapons than he knew them to carry.

"Master Eli, this evil being is a coward," Philip added. "He's like a leopard stalking its prey. It uses the cover of darkness and stealth to its cowardly advantage. He won't attack face to face in daylight, which is how all evil survives."

"We've already seen the evil of this demon who threatens to kill my sister's son. Enygeus, Hebron, and the rest of our teachers have left for the port of Yoffa for their protection. I am to meet them after burying my finished parchments about our *Maishiach's* life and teachings. Tomorrow will see its completion; at which time I'll seal them in a large clay jar and bury them in this cave for future generations to read. Eli and Eliyah, remember this place and tell my nephew's brothers and sisters of my writings. When I am no longer of this world, my parchments will become the edifice of my nephew's legacy. Eli, I know this doesn't ease your sorrow, yet one day Isaiah and you will stroll side by side in *El Shaddai's* kingdom. Hurry back to *Yerushalayim* and seek out the house of Yohanan Marcus; there you will find comfort from your grief. Tell him I sent you and he will keep you and Eliyah safe. You'll have no need for your daggers and sword; the spirit of *El Shaddai* resides in his home.

"Yoseph, I see your confidence is led by *El Shaddai*, but my faith isn't as great. I still fear for my other son and his children and there may be an accomplice with this monster. Convince me to have faith in what you say, for now our swords and daggers are our only protection."

"My friend, let me show you the power and magnificence of my resurrected nephew, Yeshua." Yoseph strolled toward his writing satchel. Carefully, he reached into the sack and gently pulled out the cup of their *Maishiach.* Immediately, the yellow-white *buzzing* rays from the cup caused him and his son to raise their hands to shield their eyes, along with the rest of them.

"Behold the *brit chadashah* of our *Maishiach* who takes away the sins of the world!" Yoseph exclaimed, with a voice of authority. "Eli and Eliyah, what you now see and hear, let the others know, for His *kodesh* light will permanently blind your enemies."

Instantly, each fell to their knees and covered their eyes.

"Rabbi, is this an illusion?" Eliyah asked.

"No, my son, it is rays of light from Yeshua's heart. He came from the light and now will light your way. Follow His light and He will protect both of you."

"Yoseph," Eli said. "I am so glad we came here, not just to warn you, but now to show my son and me your faith. Your *kodesh* cup has given us reassurance of protection and comfort from sorrow. Your nephew and *El Shaddai* have truly blessed you and your fellow teachers. Is there anything you need before we depart for *Yerushalayim*?"

"Yes, we're in need of renting a ship. After we finish our ministry in Yoffa, we plan on traveling farther to preach about our *Adonai*, Yeshua's words. I have already requested so much from you, and I now feel guilty for asking once more."

"Yoseph, my friend, I would give you my last denarius if it would help your new faith and now mine. Let me write you a letter of credit to give to a man in Yoffa, whose name is Hiram. I think you know him and where he resides." Eli pulled a piece of parchment out of his tunic. Quickly, he asked for one of Yoseph's writing quills, grabbed it, dunked it several times in the clay inkpot Yoseph furnished him, and used Philip's back to write on.

"Yes, I remember the man, for he's an excellent sailor and business merchant. Why don't you and your son come with us to Yoffa?" Yoseph asked, hoping their company would lessen their sorrow. "Besides, there's strength in numbers and we have the *kodesh* cup to shield us. In addition, your trusty camels are superb guards, while we sleep at night."

"Well . . ." Eli stared toward his son for confirmation and quickly Eliyah nodded his approval. "You're right, my friend, and this will give me some time to choose an excellent ossuary for Isaiah. I buried him in a sepulcher close to your old tomb, where your nephew resurrected himself. I wish your nephew could bring him back to life, Eliyah and I miss him so much."

"Yes, Rabbi, a part of me died with Isaiah the night that vicious animal murdered my brother," Eliyah commented, his face flushed red.

"My wisdom and faith haven't sufficiently developed to answer why these things happen and how to reverse or stop terrible happenings. I am a new teacher of Yeshua's words and still trying to comprehend His infinite wisdom. In due course, He'll reveal all to my fellow teachers and me, for we have faith in Him and know our destiny is in His hands. Right now, both of you can't see His path ahead for you and my feeble explanation doesn't massage your deep pain, but have faith, my friends." Yoseph hoped in some small way both dolorous men would see Yeshua's ever-present healing light.

"You're right, Yoseph," Eli replied, and once again, Eliyah nodded in agreement.

The rest of the day, Yoseph finished completing his scrolls and just as the sun slid down one side of a distant mountain peak, he prepared the clay ewer to seal the parchments. Philip helped prepare a straw and the wet clay mixture to seal the large container. Carefully, Yoseph placed the scrolls in the clay ewer, placed some straw on top of each roll, after which he placed the moist clay over the opening. At the back of the cave, Philip had dug a perfect length hole, with sufficient depth to cover the clay jar. Slowly, Yoseph ambled toward the narrow opening, stooped down, and placed it at the bottom of the hole. Both Philip and Eli helped him cover it and then they lightly tamped the soil down with the palms of their hands. Yoseph said a silent prayer to himself, praying that one day a righteous person would discover its words and meaning. He had memories from his children playing in this cave many summers ago.

The next morning, they were back on the road to Yoffa. The sky lacked any floating clouds and visibility was excellent in both directions, yet the small hairs on Yoseph's neck told him someone or something was observing them. When the road ahead reached a tall rise, it let him observe the sandy flat soil in all directions.

"Rabbi, I feel somebody is following us, yet I haven't seen anything that would answer my fears, but someone or something is spying on us."

"Yes, Philip, I feel the same." Yoseph swallowed his fear. He felt quite relieved that Yohanan's return trip from Yoffa would have Eli and Eliyah accompanying him back to *Yerushalayim.* Yohanan and Yeshua were quite close to each other, and Yoseph believed Yohanan thought of Yeshua as his big brother. Yohanan never complained, he was always thinking of others, and spoke with concern about their lives. Yoseph could see his clear ebony-colored eyes, which reflected a deep sense of understanding and a far greater maturity for such a young man. Yoseph's niece, Miriam, was quite fortunate to have him care for her, especially knowing the empathy and understanding he could give her.

Quickly, they glanced up and heard a piercing cry from a black-tipped winged white seagull, which indicated the sea was close. Yoseph estimated another half league before the coast would appear, which still left them with some daylight to reach the port.

"We're close to the sea," Philip stated, as he pointed skyward toward a shrieking flock of birds heading west. "Yoffa is near, Rabbi."

"Do you think there's enough daylight to preach when we arrive?"

"Yes, Philip, and there's an old established synagogue in town if my memory is correct. We may encounter another confrontation similar to the one in Lydda." He thought it best to prepare their teachers for the worst.

The road ahead increased in elevation until they came to a short flat plateau, which overlooked the distant harbor.

Yoffa, the city proper, perched itself on one of the stair-step rungs of land, which led to the harbor and sea. The city was a terminus for several trade routes to the Mediterranean and other ports west. Its advantageous large bay gave it both the distinction of docking large seaworthy vessels as well as coastal boats.

Under the dark clouds, below the sea horizon, jutted dark spear-shaped masts of many ships, which seemed captive to a narrow finger-shaped harbor. Bigger ships had to offload their cargo from this narrow rocky inlet of land and have the shallow draft boats navigate their contents through the boulder-strewn shore. From their advantage point, they could see blue-colored wisps of smoke coming from the numerous forges, which dotted the city's boundaries. Snaking down the narrow-shaped roads were numerous heavy-laden donkey carts shining with multicolored fruits. The same scene repeated itself with carts heading the opposite direction toward *Yerushalayim* and points east. The chatter of business conversations, the metal *pinging* of the forges, and the ever-present sound of creaking wagon wheels created a cacophony of sounds that rose to their ears, obliterating the crashing roar of the sea waves.

"Yoseph," Philip spoke, bringing Yoseph out of his sea gaze and memories of dealing with the Yoffa merchants.

"Yes, what is it you want to say?"

"Wasn't this the town where our King Solomon had his cedar wood for the Temple delivered from King Hiram of Tyre?"

"You're correct, my friend, but what made you ask this now?" His question seemed unrelated to their travels, but hadn't their *Maishiach* ordained him to build another temple, and in the land of what the Romans called *Britannia*? Yeshua did tell him, "My *Abba's* house would have other Temples before I return again."

"Philip, hurry into town and see if you can find Hebron and Alein Yosephe," he said.

"No, Rabbi Yoseph, let Eliyah travel there instead," Eli suddenly said, before Philip could answer. "I have some old contacts in town who ask few questions. They will secure our lodgings and you and your teachers' appearances will be unnoticed."

"Excellent idea, my friend. We'll wait here until your son returns."

The others nodded in agreement.

"Eliyah, ask if they're possibly staying at the house of a woman called Dorcas, that's her Greek name, or she is also called Tabitha. She's the widow of an old client of mine and Hebron knows her. I used to sell her and her husband bolts of cloth. I still believe she is a dressmaker." Right away, Eliyah nodded, then strolled toward the direction of town and quickly disappeared behind the bluff overlook.

They sat on a grass-covered knoll, as Yoseph tasted the salty sea breezes filtering down into his lungs, which cleared away the thick dust of the desert. In the distance, his eyes delighted in feasting on the bluish-green sea, which contrasted with the multi-colored sails of the harbor ships. It appeared each seagoing vessel had bought numerous bolts of Eli's cloth to trim their sails. On one side of the quay, the color red festooned the ship's masts, only to be interrupted with sails colored with blue and black stripes. Yoseph's mind wandered, wondering what effect their *Maishiach's* words would have on the people of Yoffa.

A brief time later, Eliyah appeared on the grassy knoll, revealing a toothy grin.

"Master Yoseph, I mean Rabbi, your family and fellow teachers are indeed staying at the home of Tabitha. They're quartered in several upper rooms and Alein said to come after sundown, so we wouldn't be noticed. In addition, I met a man who said you helped save his life some years ago, along with your brother-in-law and Nicodemus."

"You must mean Shimon of Cyrene. Yes, it was during *Pesach* when the tetrarch, Herod Antipas, and his wife, the evil Herodias, were in *Yerushalayim.* The same year of our *Maishiach's* crucifixion and my imprisonment." Yoseph wondered how quickly those years had disappeared. Yet, at the time, it didn't seem so.

"Rabbi, he thought you were dead and was told nobody survived the Sanhedrin prison. You are a miracle, he said, and that *El Shaddai's* light has kept you alive these many years. He's anxious to see you when you arrive."

"Shimon is a good man. Nicodemus told me how he and his sons helped my nephew with his wooden cross. I owe him and his sons a great debt, but I don't have any monetary wealth to give him, only the final mortal words of our *Maishiach,* which all the gold in the Roman Empire couldn't buy from me."

Everyone nodded in agreement.

"Where is he staying?" Yoseph asked.

"Somewhere along the quay wharf. He said that he would depart in two days, traveling back to Cyrene to see his grandchildren. In addition, he told me to tell you his captain's name is Hiram and his ship's name is *King Solomon.* Those are two names you won't forget, Rabbi Yoseph."

"Yes, you're quite correct." He suddenly felt quite anxious to see his old friend.

"Besides the notable name, Rabbi, the boat is quite distinguishable from the others. The ship is larger than many and has a swan's head on its bow, and the sails are bright red. I am told she is the fastest fully loaded ship in the entire sea and makes excellent time between Yoffa and Alexandria."

"Eliyah, thank you for bringing me this information, for tomorrow we will seek out Shimon and his Captain Hiram, but for now let's sleep before nightfall."

CHAPTER XIII

The steady roar of the crashing waves and gentle sea breeze quickly lulled Yoseph's companions to sleep, but not him. Once more, Yeshua's words hummed in his head about building a new *Yerushalayim*. The wise ones with the names of King Solomon, King Hiram, and Hiram Abiff galloped through his mind like horses leading them toward their destiny. The divine hands of *El Shaddai* and His Son were directing them to their final house of ministry in *Yudah*.

At last, the sea swallowed the yolk-colored sun, yet they waited until three stars appeared before they left. Each of them lit an oil-filled lantern and ambled down a narrow path leading to the seaport. A cool salty smelling breeze buffeted his face as a golden glow emanated from quay torches and the town lamps. What a pleasant sight to see the town lights shimmer across the sea surface and melt into the distant horizon. In addition, the steady *whoosh* of the sea waves lured Yoseph toward them. Their sounds pulled on his senses as if he was one of Odysseus's sailors enchanted by the female singing Sirens. Eliyah's sudden knock on Tabitha's wooden door broke Yoseph's trance-like state. Slowly, the brine-covered door opened, exposing a small white-haired woman peeking out a narrow-slit opening.

"It's Eliyah ben Eli," he whispered into the narrow opening. "I spoke to you today about Rabbi Yoseph and his family."

"Please come in, Master Eliyah, I am so sorry for the extra caution, but the last several days somebody has lurked around my house. It was a human shadow following me during the day and shuffling sandals at night around my bedroom window. This wasn't the imagination of a lonely widow woman. But enough of my ramblings. Have the rest of your companions enter too." Tabitha motioned with her small, gnarled fingers.

They entered the well-lit room filled with many glowing oil lamps. She wore well-tailored clothes, though still wearing a dark mourning robe and black matching shawl. Under her dark veil, small sprigs of white hair protruded around her forehead.

"Rabbi, your fellow teachers and family are waiting for you in my upper rooms." She pointed to narrow stone steps leading upward through the ceiling. "Hurry, they're anxious to see you. I'll follow right behind you."

At once, they trudged up the narrow roll of steps, which opened onto a large landing. There they met Yoseph's family and fellow teachers.

"Yoseph, I am so glad you arrived safely," Hebron said, as he embraced Yoseph and Philip. Quickly, Yosa, Alein, Enygeus, Yohanan, Nicodemus, Yohanan Marcus, Clotho, and Georgeus did the same.

"Praise be to *El Shaddai* and His Son!" shouted Yoseph's sister. The rest of his fellow companions gathered around him and said the same praise.

"Yoseph," Hebron continued. "Truly, our *Adonai* and *Maishiach,* along with His army of *malachs* have protected you, Philip, Eliyah, and Eli on the road to Yoffa. Now let's give praise by saying the *Ashrei* for your safe return."

Without delay, they raised their arms upward as Hebron recited the psalm.

"We extol you, *Eloheinu* and *Melech*, and bless your name forever and ever. Every day we bless you and praise your name forever and ever. Great is *Adonai* and greatly to be praised; His greatness is unsearchable." Hebron continued with the rest of the psalm as Yoseph's eyes surveyed the upper rooms. It reminded him of another set of upper rooms numerous springs ago, yet each of these corners held purple, red, and green bolts of cloth.

He feared for this woman's safety for they posed quite a danger to her and her son, yet she risked her life to accommodate them. She seemed a righteous woman, seeing her say the words to the *Ashrei* with tightly closed eyes of reverence while nodding every so often when they gave praise to *El Shaddai*.

"Our *Adonai* protects all who love Him, but all the wicked He will destroy. Our mouths will speak the praise of *Adonai*, and all our flesh will bless His *kodesh* name forever and ever. Amen." Hebron finished, just as Tabitha left and quickly trotted down the stairs. A fleeting time later, she returned, carrying a large plate of dates, nuts, quail eggs, pomegranates, and lamb stew. Hebron rushed to her aid, as she reached the landing, to keep her from spilling the large plate.

"Tabitha, how did you prepare so much food in such a brief time?" Yoseph inquired, anxious to hear her answer.

"I know, Rabbi, you think this was a miracle, but it wasn't, for I must confess. Your family and fellow teachers helped me prepare this food earlier. Besides, I like having big meals for travelers. My son is a ship's captain and tells me his passengers think I am a great cook. Before they leave for distant lands, they come here for their departing meal and try to pay me, but I refuse. Some are so insistent, they even leave their mites hidden around my house. I donate their money to the synagogue, where it's used to feed and clothe the poor."

"Indeed, Tabitha, *El Shaddai* has shined His face upon you. He has made your heart kind to others, and we are here to tell you of a man sent by *El Shaddai* with more kindness than you can imagine. Tomorrow evening you'll hear the words of His Son and the glory He gave," Tabitha twisted her head to one side, fixed her solemn eyes on mine as she served the steaming lamb's stew.

"Rabbi, some of your teachers have told me about the *kodesh* man who was crucified by the Romans. Travelers from *Yerushalayim* say after three days the man escaped from a sealed tomb and ascended into the sky. I don't know if they're telling the truth, but their stories are all the same. Yes, I would like to hear about this man who made lame beggars walk and blind men see."

"Did you say your son is a ship's captain?"

"Yes, his name is Hiram, and his ship is named after *Melech* Solomon. As a young boy, my late husband taught him to become a good seafarer. Hiram acquired his *abba's* business and succeeded quite well, which I knew he would. He's a righteous man and gives to the synagogue the majority of his ship's earning. In addition, he sees after me, to which I give thanks to *El Shaddai* daily. However, I wish he would find a wife and give me some grandchildren. Right now, he's preparing his ship to leave for Alexandria. I have already sent him some stew, just before you arrived, otherwise he would be here."

Yoseph sat there contemplating what she had just said, realizing their *Maishiach* was guiding them to this sailor. Hiram's name, Tabitha a widow woman, the name of the ship, all this was prophesied to him. However, his angst asked him, what terror would he bring upon this righteous family? After they finished their lamb stew, Tabitha prepared them sleeping pallets and placed them throughout the upper two rooms. Sleep came fast and Yoseph's aching body quickly embraced it, yet their unknown stalker was the last thought on his mind.

The warm rays of the sun came upon Yoseph as a silent reminder to wake up and start for the quay. A morning meal awaited the sleepy band of teachers. A large table was prepared with figs, sticky honey cakes, and pomegranates stacked in the shape of a pyramid. Quickly, he finished his wooden plate of food, waited until Alein Yoseph, Hebron, and Eli's son had eaten their meals. They thanked Tabitha for her food and then proceeded to leave in search of Shimon of Cyrene and Hiram.

The sun glistened on the rippling sea as they traveled toward the quay, and the salty smelling air assaulted Yoseph's senses, which awakened his alertness. Finally, they reached a flat stone landing that overlooked a long narrow set of stone steps carved into the steep rocky hillside. The narrow steep treads let one person down at a time, thus leaving no room to stumble and certain death. Once reaching the end of the steps, Yoseph said a quick prayer of thanks and focused his attention on the quay. There—at the northern end of the wharf, where the quay pointed like a long finger into the sea—was quite an impressive ship. It was larger than the rest and carried two large red sails.

"That's Hiram's merchant boat," Eliyah said, pointing toward the boat he had spied.

It was one of the largest merchant ships Yoseph had seen in his many years traveling at sea. The jib sail displayed tangles of rigging, numerous pulleys, and the stern of the ship was in the shape of a large white-necked swan. The top of its head rose to half the length of the mainmast. On its deck were two men, one of whom was older than the other. The white-haired man seemed familiar, but at their current distance, he couldn't determine. Then he heard the older man shout his name.

"Master Yoseph, it's true, you're still alive!" the man exclaimed. He didn't wave back, fearful of whom he might be. "Don't you recognize me? It's Shimon of Cyrene."

Yoseph immediately waved back and shouted, "Yes, my friend." Quickly, they boarded a small skiff and rolled toward the docked ship. Once they roped the small boat to the outer wharf, Shimon and the young man helped them out of the skiff.

Yoseph hugged Shimon. "I should have known you couldn't stay below as a passenger and sit idly by while others worked. It's so good to see you once more." After finishing their embrace, he hugged Alein Yoseph, Eliyah, and Hebron.

"Master Yoseph, I was told you died in prison along with your good friend, Master Nicodemus. When I first saw you, I thought I was seeing a wraith, but your big brother-in-law was with you, and then I knew you weren't dead."

"The summers have been kind to you, my friend." He appeared not to have aged any since Yoseph last saw him before his nephew's last supper.

"I hear you have grandchildren. Is that true?"

"Yes, it's true and that's whom I am sailing to visit. It's my oldest son's children, but enough of my chatter. Tell me how you survived all these years."

"Our *Adonai* sustained me in Yoseph ben Caiaphas's *sheol* hole of a prison. In addition, Nicodemus is alive and with me here in Yoffa. By the grace of *El Shaddai*, after four summers in prison, I was released. Caiaphas is no longer the head of the Sanhedrin, yet I still believe he's promoting his nefarious ways. Who is this handsome young man standing next to you?" Yoseph thought it might be Tabitha's son.

"Hiram, this is Master Yoseph of Arimathea. His big brother-in-law, Hebron, and Master Nicodemus saved my life four summers ago. Herod Antipas and his evil wife almost trampled me to death with their slave-driven carriage. Master Yoseph's family and good friend, Nicodemus, tricked Herodias into thinking I would be imprisoned by the Sanhedrin."

"It is an honor to meet you, Captain Hiram. We are staying with your *amma,* and she said how proud she is of you." They embraced. "Let me introduce you to my son and brother-in-law. And no offense, Shimon, but Nicodemus and I would prefer you not to call us master. There is only one Master in our eyes, and He is Yeshua, our *Maishiach*."

"So, is it true what they say about your late nephew?" Shimon asked, his expression begging for answers.

"Yes," Yoseph said while searching the dock for staring faces. "But I would prefer to answer any further questions at Tabitha's home, maybe over one of her excellent meals."

After finishing their pleasantries, Eli gave a superb testimony of Hiram's sea captain skills, which prompted Yoseph to ask the astute sailor where he was sailing besides the port of Alexandria.

"How did you know I was sailing to other ports?" he asked with wide-eyed disbelief.

"Your ship is only at half draft and you're preparing to leave soon. Your noted sea experience, owner of a large ship, and a plentiful crew could only mean other port destinations to fill up your ship's hole."

He looked at Yoseph admiringly. "Indeed, you're quite right. I am heading first to Caesarea to load some purple dye and olive oil. You said you're not a master of anything, however, I disagree. I hear the voice of a merchant who has had many years of sea experience. Would you be the wealthy merchant my *abba* spoke of many years ago? He told me about a man who sailed to the isle of the Celts and the ends of the earth for mining tin for the Romans. Are you that man?"

"What you say is true, and yes, I did know your *abba*, but I am no longer a tin merchant. My *kavanah* has changed; I am now a teacher of our *Maishiach's* words, along with my fellow teachers of his way."

It was near the end of the second watch of the morning when Hiram finished telling him about his *abba's* seafaring experiences, he then invited them to his mother's midday meal.

"You don't have to ask me but once," Hebron said, as they quickly stepped into the skiff and cast off for the treacherous steps to Tabitha's house.

After descending the high embankment, Yoseph's nostrils caught the herbal smell of tarragon and thyme, wafting its way from the direction of Tabitha's house. As he reached the front door, the overwhelming smell of roasted poultry caused his mouth to water with hunger.

"Hiram, I see you have met our new guests," his *amma* said, greeting us with a pleasant smile.

"Yes, and Rabbi Yoseph once knew my *abba*. Now I remember *abba* said he was quite righteous in his business dealings with him. Rabbi, I feel it's an honor to have you and your teachers in our house."

"Thank you for the compliment, but I would rather you judge me and the teachers on what we have to say in the next several days, but for now I would rather honor your *amma* by eating some of her delicious food."

They both laughed, as Hiram led the way up the steps to his *amma's* tantalizing smell of roasted fowl.

"Help yourselves, my friends," Tabitha said, handing out wooden bowls. "Don't worry about proper manners; please feel as if my home is your home."

Yoseph felt good to enjoy a well-cooked meal and fine hospitality inside a home, rather than in the desert and a damp musty cave. His prison confinement had left him longing for human companionship, which he had received from Eli and his fellow teachers, but now they were moving from a persistent phantom evil threat. This left him both physically and mentally drained.

"Rabbi, please tell me more about this *kodesh* man," Tabitha said.

"Yes, Rabbi Yoseph," Hiram said. "At the quay you said you would once we were inside my *amma's* house. Will you speak of him?"

Yoseph smiled at each of them. "He is the long-awaited *Maishiach* foretold by our ancient prophets. He'll give you peace and eternal salvation."

Tabitha looked doubtful. "I have heard this before. Yet these so-called *maishiachs* repeat themselves as the seasons change. Why is he any different from the others?"

"He is the Son of *El Shaddai* and has come to remove your sins and give you spiritual immortality, my friends." Yoseph gazed into their eyes.

"What you say sounds like blasphemy, Rabbi," the widow said softly. "How can this be possible?"

"In addition," Hiram said, "I have heard some of his followers believe in cannibalism, eating flesh and drinking blood, and they say He makes the dead come alive. I am confused. Rabbi, can you explain?"

"Tonight, you will see His divine glory with the sacred supper we'll prepare. Each one of you will feel His loving presence and your innermost being will rapture with His invisible touch. Have faith, my friends, all our fellow teachers have seen and felt His divine love."

The quiet whispers of approval and head-nodding confirmations came from all the teachers in the upper rooms.

Hiram said he would wait until tonight, before believing in this *kodesh* man. "I am a practical man, but I do know there're things above and below the sea I can't explain. If it's true what you say, and I am not saying you and your teachers are liars, but at times strongly believing in something causes you to see things that aren't there." He stood up. "It's time for me to return to my ship. Until tonight, Rabbi Yoseph."

They all nodded to him as he moved toward the landing, there he then trotted down the steps.

Yoseph turned to Shimon.

"Shimon, let me express my belated thanks for helping my nephew in his final hours. If I were still a wealthy man, my entire wealth would be yours. What you and your sons performed on that black day was a courageous act. With the Roman Empire's whims of execution, you might have been upon another cross. To this day, guilt still hides in my body for not being there."

"Please, Rabbi, don't feel guilty. You were concerned about the safety of your immediate family. In addition, you had prepared an escape plan several days before his execution. Besides, Hebron picked me up from the clutches of Herodias and you nursed me well. The least I could do was to carry your nephew's cross."

"But Shimon, you are my immediate family too!" Yoseph exclaimed.

"Your nephew knew in advance what his fate would be, long before you found out. Use your new faith to exorcise this demon from yourself and do not let its guilt slow your ministry."

He was right, Yoseph's guilt would only be a hindrance to his teachings, and he couldn't let his fellow teachers down.

"Still, I would like to give you something that can't be measured in gold talents. Tonight, along with the *kodesh* supper, you will hear the *kodesh* words spoken by my nephew, our *Maishiach,* before His death and resurrection. He still speaks to me when we honor Him with our supper. This is the only thing He and I have to give, my friend."

"Rabbi Yoseph, you don't have to give me anything, however, I feel I can't extinguish your burning desire to make me your student. I never regarded myself becoming a teacher, but deep inside me I am starting to feel the calling of a rabbi."

The rest of Yoseph's day was hectic, especially with the preparations of their *kodesh* supper. Several times during the remaining daylight, his ears caught the sounds of darting footsteps. Each time he glanced out an upper window to see who it might be, he spied a long moving bent shadow between homes, causing the hairs on the back of his neck to rise. Finally, Tabitha started lighting all the oil lamps, signaling that suppertime was near. The last oil lamp she lit was on a long table where he sat.

"Rabbi, I must admit the anticipation is overwhelming me. Observe my hands, they are shaking," she said, as her trembling hands tried lighting the last oil lamp.

Philip chose the *kodesh* supper participants and had them gathered at the foot of the stairs. Hiram hadn't returned and Tabitha voiced her concerns as she sat down next to Yoseph. The procession began with the soft scuffling of sandals coming up the steps. Once their heads reached above the landing, there was a tingling excitement in what their hands held. Each procession member seemed to float through the opening to the upper room, with their hands carefully placing each *kodesh* object on the table in front of Yoseph. Tabitha, with an open mouth, intently observed each object as one of their teachers set it before her. The *kodesh* cup was the last to come through the landing opening, with Miriam holding it. The entire room radiated a golden hue and the cup's interior shaft of yellow-white light forced everybody to bow their heads. With eyes closed, Miriam slowly placed the cup of the *Maishiach* in front of Yoseph.

"Rabbi!" Tabitha shouted, "the light is burning my eyes. Please remove it, I am not worthy to be here!" She shielded her eyes with both palms.

"Yes, you're worthy, my friend." Yoseph patted her hand, as they quietly observed the sword, lamp, cup, spear, and paten that lay before them.

Suddenly, a dreadful moan came from outside Tabitha's home, stopping the silent ceremony.

CHAPTER XIV

"Help! Help! Who will help the *almanah's* son?" came a bloodcurdling cry from Hiram's voice. Hebron jumped up, and then quickly scrambled down the stairs followed by Alein Yoseph. Tabitha's owl-sized shaped eyes shined with fear as she gripped Yoseph's arm for strength. Did their stalker find another victim? His stomach tightened from angst. Yoseph stood to go downstairs.

"Yoseph, come and help us!" Hebron shouted from below. "It's Hiram, and he has numerous stab wounds. Come quick; I fear he is dying."

Yoseph rushed toward the steps, hearing Tabitha's bloodcurdling shrieks. Her bone-chilling sounds caused him to stumble on the top step before reaching the ground floor. Quickly, he regained his footing and continued scrambling down the steps to reach the front door. Once outside, he perceived the dark outlines of two men standing, one holding a sword faced him, while the other bent over Hiram's body.

"Yoseph, his heart has stopped beating," cried Alein Yosephe. Hebron held his sword ready to strike, as they picked up the blood-sticky body. Carefully they backed into Tabitha's house, while Hebron followed, swinging his sword back and forth to cover their retreat. Once inside, the door was barred by Philip, as Miriam and Yosa secured the window openings with wooden shutters. The lamp quickly revealed the extent of the dagger wounds on chest and stomach, which appeared mortal. Slowly, they lowered him to the floor as Tabitha rushed to hold him. Once she saw the horrific wounds, she stopped, let out a low guttural moan, and started ripping at her clothes.

"Rabbi, please help me," she sobbed. "He is . . . my only son. I am a faithful pious woman, please speak to *El Shaddai* and your *Maishiach* for me. I beg you!" She sobbed louder. "Make me believe how powerful your *Maishiach* is and save my son. Whatever you tell me I'll accept as true." Tabitha was now at Yoseph's feet with her cheeks covered with glistening tears, yanking his shawl.

"Miriam, grab the *kodesh* cup," Yoseph demanded, as he fell to his knees to pray.

"Tabitha, stop crying and pray with me." She did. "Do you believe in Yeshua the *Maishiach*, who died for your sins?" Yoseph firmly asked. "In addition, do you believe he arose from the dead and is the Son of *El Shaddai*? Lastly, do you believe in the *kodesh* Spirit in this room who will help save your son and will you become a teacher of our new faith?"

She answered positively to all his questions as the angst in her face melted away. Miriam handed Yoseph the warm *kodesh* cup, which then, to his surprise, slipped through his grasp and floated over Hiram's body, radiating back and forth its golden-white light. After which the entire room burst into a sweet-smelling golden hue. Yet, just as fast as it illuminated the room with its *buzzing* sound of golden white light, the cup's light vanished. The room became quiet as a tomb until a whistling wind came through the door threshold and buffeted the floor. Yoseph gazed at Hiram's pale white face. He noticed a rosy color moving up each side of his neck, which quickly flushed his cheeks, and then, he coughed several times. His eyes twittered several times, after which widened and stared into Yoseph's.

"What happened?" Hiram asked. "The last thing I remember was a dark shadow pointing a long dagger at my chest, then several burning pains, followed by darkness. Yet, the strangest thing happened next, I glimpsed a small golden light coming from what seemed like the end of a cave. After that, your face appeared."

Tabitha grabbed his face and kissed every feature, then tightly cradled it in her bosom praising Yeshua and *El Shaddai.*

"You must have been attacked by our evil stalker," Yoseph said. "You were close to death, but *El Shaddai* has delivered you from death's grip." He grabbed his chest and stomach, feeling for the puncture holes, but all he found were five torn sticky holes in his shawl. Still not convinced, he ripped his shawl and tunic off, exposing five pink-colored scars. Staring down, his mouth gaped open with disbelief.

"How can this be, *amma*?" he said, searching his *amma's* red-rimmed eyes.

"I too don't understand, my son."

Hiram slowly stood.

"You should ask Rabbi Yoseph, he possesses a great miraculous cup, which brought you back to life."

"Rabbi, am I to believe you saved my life?"

"No, it wasn't me or the cup, but your *amma's* faith in *El Shaddai* and His Son, our *Maishiach*," Yoseph firmly answered. "They and the *kodesh* spirit worked through me and the cup, prompted by your *amma's* new beliefs. I am just a humble teacher and nothing more, my friend."

"I have heard tell of the *Maishiach* you're speaking of. You must tell me more."

Hiram staggered over into Hebron's embrace.

After Hebron helped him to a chair to steady his body, Yoseph spoke. "When you have sufficiently regained your strength, we'll help you up the steps, and you and your *amma* will further see the divine miracles of the *Maishiach's* last supper cup."

After they seated themselves, once again their *kodesh* procession commenced, with Hiram covering his eyes from the cup's blinding light. The cup and paten overflowed with its never-ending wine and thin loaves of bread. This left their newfound followers amazed with smiles of euphoria. After their *Adonai's* supper was finished and the recession ended, Hiram spoke.

"Is this the same *kodesh* man I have heard speak of at the Port of Caesarea? If so, is He the one you constantly refer to as your *Adonai* and *Maishiach*?"

"Yes, to both your questions," Yoseph answered.

"The sailors there said He was a powerful healer of the sick."

"He still is, as you can now testify to others."

"However, I thought the Roman soldiers and the high priest had Him crucified. Is this not true?"

"Yes, He was crucified, but the *Ruach ha-kodesh* snatched him from death, for He is right here with us in this room."

"But Rabbi, I don't see Him. Is He one of the faces in this room I don't know?"

"No, He isn't, Captain Hiram," answered Yoseph's fellow teacher, Thomas. "Once I doubted just like you, but my Master, Yeshua, our *Maishiach* admonished me for having little faith. He told me it was far greater to believe He still existed after His resurrection, than witness the scourge marks on His body and then believe. Faith can't be measured with a ruler, my friend, or with your eyes."

"Rabbi, can you explain more about your *kodesh* cup and what the other *kodesh* objects represent?" Tabitha asked. "Don't leave out any small details."

"The *kodesh* cup was given to me by our *Maishiach* at the last *Pesach* we had with Him, right before His crucifixion. The day He was crucified, I stood in front of His cross, where my hands urged me to collect His blood and sweat. Each time the cup became replete with His blood, it would suddenly disappear. When thrown in prison, He and two *malachs* came to me presenting these wonderful precious gifts, which you now see in front of you."

"How did He and the *malachs* pass through stone walls to appear inside your prison cell?" Hiram asked.

"The same way He departed from my burial sepulcher," Yoseph answered. "I am just a mortal man, and I don't have the depth of understanding of the Son of *El Shaddai.* I still have much to learn, my friend, and so do you.

"The *kodesh* cup and bread paten sustained me with food until I was released. My cup was never empty of wine and the paten always had bread. The lamp helped me to write my gospel and gave me insight into how my new *kavanah* would lead me. Hiram and Tabitha, as you can see and taste, our *Maishiach's* body has turned into wine and bread for your spiritual sustenance. The sword represents Yohanan the Baptizer, who led the way and foretold the coming of our *Maishiach.* Herod Antipas used this sword to cut off the Baptizer's head and fulfill Yohanan's ministry. This sword won't harm another person and if used for a future evil purpose, the blade will shatter. The blood-tipped spear, which pierced the side of our *Maishiach,* represents our ministry's suffering and destiny.

"All these precious *kodesh* objects have the power to heal, quench our spiritual thirst, fill our bellies with knowledgeable answers, shield us from our enemies, and destroy those who wish to harm us. However, they simply acquire their *kodesh* power through those who believe in our *Maishiach* and *El Shaddai.* They're now our new battle standards to lead the *Maishiach's* teachers into this troubled world that needs our help."

"Rabbi Yoseph has spoken well," Philip said. "I was a beginning follower of our *Maishiach*, and before that time, a follower of Yohanan the Baptizer. Yeshua once told me, 'Where two or three are gathered in His name, there I will be.' In addition, he told His fellow disciples, 'I am the light that shines on everyone and the all.' He said, 'Everything comes forth from Me and it comes into Me. Split a piece of wood,' He told us, 'and I will be there. Turn over a stone and there you will find Me.' He was the sacrificial lamb on the altar of *Elohim* and his blood spilled out for the extinguishment of our sins. He further told me, 'Blessed are those who abide in the beginning, for they will know the end and won't taste death.' We now start his truthful vine of wisdom, and this is one of the reasons we are here in Yoffa, to teach his way."

"Yes, this is true," Miriam of Magdala commented. "Thank you, Philip, for your testimony. Yet, both of you must have the wisdom of snakes and the countenance of peaceful doves. Let no one deceive both of you about our *Maishiach*. He too told me, 'Many will come and say they are me, but follow your heart and what your fellow teachers say.' Now you must go forth and give testimony on what has happened here and speak of His kingdom."

"Where does He say His kingdom reigns?" Tabitha inquired.

"Awaken from your sleep, my brother and sister," Miriam said with a stoic face of seriousness. "His kingdom reigns inside your hearts. The Son of Man dwells inside both of you. The vision of a pure heart is the motive of his mercy."

"Miriam, tell me more what His kingdom is like," Hiram said, his dark eyes flashing.

"It's like a small seed when it falls upon the rich soil of the earth. There it becomes the great Tree of Life, and the birds of the sky come to rest."

"Each of my fellow teachers are now blessed with skills our *Maishiach* has given them," Yoseph affirmed. "These spiritual gifts will help further our ministry in helping the less fortunate or widen the eyes and strengthen the ears for those who will now see and hear our words and know our good intentions. I, Yoseph, who now sits with you, accepted the responsibility to see after the *Maishiach's amma* and write down the teachings of our *Adonai*. Miriam, sitting next to me, is my spiritual confidant and she has dreams, in which our *Maishiach* speaks to her and still tells her of his secret teachings. Thomas, standing behind me, gives testimony on how he once doubted Yeshua's existence after His crucifixion and burial. Yohanan Marcus, standing there with the leather satchel over his shoulder, uses his keen insight to observe our *Maishiach's* human traits and writes about them on parchment. My good friend Nicodemus, sitting on the other side of me, preaches about his salvation and how he was born again into a new faith."

Tabitha's and Hiram's mouths gaped with wonder, yet their eyes were still searching for more about Yeshua's ministry. The evening was still early, so each of our fellow teachers had time to speak in more detail about what our *Maishiach* individually taught them.

"We know we have a difficult job to do, trying to change the ways of the priests of *Moshe* over the last thousand summers. The numerous priestly laws have pushed down our people with the weight of the great pyramid blocks. To lift this burden, it will require all the strength and faith of our teachers, but I know we will accomplish this task. Our ancestors' numerous burdensome laws are habits of religious conduct and fears. The Gentiles would be easier to accept our words, however, many believe in nothing, still leaving us with a challenge."

They spoke long into the night, receiving an affirmation from both in their new faith and a promise they would preach the words of our *Maishiach*. As the sun rose, Yoseph fell asleep with satisfaction knowing Yeshua's blessed words and miracles had converted two new members to their nascent faith.

Later that morning, Hiram left for final preparations to sail to Caesarea and later to Alexandria. Physically, he jumped up from his pallet and acted as if he hadn't died. Quickly, he grabbed some goat cheese and crusty bread and his smiling serene face glanced back at Yoseph. Yoseph said a prayer to himself, giving thanks to *Elohim* and *Maishiach* for the miracle of the *kodesh* cup.

"Yoseph," Philip spoke, just as he finished his prayer, "what do you think about me sailing to Caesarea? In addition, our band of teachers could visit with me in the homes and synagogues and preach of Yeshua's way. I must confess, Rabbi, I long to see my family and four daughters. They're staying with my father-in-law there, and he doesn't approve of my preaching."

"It's an excellent idea, my friend, assuming the rest of our teachers agree, and Hiram doesn't ask to be paid," Yoseph replied, thinking the idea had already entered his mind.

"Yoseph, I never told you this, but my oldest daughter foretold we would meet. She once said I would travel with a rich man to many strange ports and lands. That's why numerous summers ago I was so intrigued with you when we first met at Gethsemane."

"It appears your daughter was born with a veil over her face given to her by *El Shaddai*. Philip, this is another sign from above guiding our ministry to its predetermined destiny."

They spoke more about what Philip had heard from their *Maishiach* and what He said about suffering in the world. Yeshua told Philip that if each person grew closer to the downtrodden, the sick, and the dying, that person would grow closer to Him and His *Abba.* Yoseph knew his nephew had taught them well and they would become apostles to the known world.

CHAPTER XV

Later in the day, they gathered in the upper rooms and his fellow teachers decided they would sail to Caesarea first and, after sufficient time to preach their ministry, they would continue to Alexandria. This would leave Yohanan the writer time to finish his ministry in Yoffa before he returned to *Yerushalayim* and Yoseph's niece, Miriam.

"Yoseph, we must leave before the tide goes out, otherwise it will delay my shipments," Hiram said. "Are all you prepared to leave before the end of the fourth watch?"

They responded with a resounding "Yes!" followed by the murmuring sounds of excitement. They then each said their thanks and good-byes to Tabitha, Eli, and his son, Eliyah. Yoseph felt a great sadness in his heart, knowing he would never see Eli again. He had sheltered Yoseph from his enemies, given him transportation and food, and lost one of his sons to be Yoseph's friend.

"Eli, I can't thank you enough for the sacrifices you endured to help me and my family. It's a debt that I can't ever repay, even if I were again a rich man. I'll miss you, my friend." Yoseph embraced him with tears trickling down his cheeks. Each member of his family joined him in his embrace with their tears staining his headscarf and tunic.

"Yoseph, you have shown me and my sons how our souls want to seek the divine in all of us. Yeshua, our *Maishiach,* suffered and gave up His mortal body so His spirit could join with *El Shaddai.* We must strive for this same union; I know this now, my friend. Your debt with me was paid the first day we became friends. Now good-bye and may *El Shaddai* and His Son always protect you, your family, and fellow teachers."

Yoseph gave the same tearful embrace to Tabitha and Yohanan the writer, then he departed out the front entrance into the dusk of the evening. Carefully they strolled back down the treacherous carved stone steps to the seashore, where Hiram asked several of his fellow captains to furnish them with some skiffs to roll toward the quay. Hebron and Yoseph were the last to enter the remaining skiff, but Hebron grabbed Yoseph's arm and spoke.

"Yoseph, that man in the red-colored hooded shawl is following us. I noticed him against the torch light as I started down the steps to the shore. Before that, he came out of a narrow alleyway and crept alongside the houses. Let me confront him now before we depart. I will expose his cowardly ways in front of everybody."

Captain Hiram shouted at them.

"Hurry, my friends, the tide is quickly receding, and our last boat will be stranded on a sandbar. The others are already on the ship."

Yoseph glanced at Hebron. "I feel as you do, but whomever it is, maybe they won't follow us. Let's hurry, our ministry is waiting." They jumped into the boat, grabbed the oars, and rowed toward the quay dock. As they departed, Hebron's gaze never left the man's image onshore.

Hiram's ship had already started raising its red sails to leave when their skiff's bow thudded against the wharf. If any of our fellow teachers wanted to change their minds about leaving, it was now too late. As they climbed onto the wharf, Yoseph glanced back one last time and surveyed the cliffs, realizing the Sanhedrin tribunal had banished him forever. It was just a fleeting thought; still thinking he was with his family, friends, and fellow teachers, knowing well, wherever he taught would now be his home.

Quickly, they climbed down on the ship's wooden deck, hearing the anchor chain *clank* against the ship, the wharf lines were thrown back, *thumping* on the quay dock, and then the ship slowly drifted toward the open sea. The steady wind caught the sails, propelling the ship forward with its bow slicing through the foaming waves. Just as they cleared the quay rocks, Hebron shouted.

"Yoseph, see toward the end of the quay dock! There's the same man waving a sword and dagger." He pointed toward the stern of the ship. At the end of the wharf stood the red-hooded man, his face partially covered with a red scarf while holding a large sword and dagger in each hand. He continued to brandish them until the quay melted into the horizon. Was he their stalker, Hiram's stabber, and Isaiah's murderer? Would he follow them to Caesarea? Would Yoseph ever see the completion of his dream of a new *Yerushalayim* built on a Glass Isle, while shadowed by a *kodesh malach* mount? Slowly, Yoseph's hand reached into his satchel and clutched the warm metal of the cup of the *Maishiach*, which filled his heart with confidence.

PART THREE

War Dog

CHAPTER XVI

Zaragozza
December
Anno Domini 1190

My fingertips touched the bound tome, prompting me to say a prayer of thanks, yet I was distracted by a scraping sound outside my door. Quickly, I replaced the panel and firewood and proceeded to investigate. On the tips of my toes, my body crept toward the door. Once there, my ears heard light breathing, causing me to quietly withdraw my sword and then place it up against the door.

"I know you're there!" I shouted followed by silence. Was this our stealth stalker or somebody else? After a short while, there was no more breathing, just continued silence. Then I reluctantly decided to retire, while keeping both my sword and dagger unsheathed. I laid them along the side of my bed and if the spy tried to break in, both my sword and dagger were ready to strike.

The next morning's daylight didn't arrive too soon. From my bed, I glanced over to see my door wasn't disturbed, however, before dressing, a pounding knock startled me. Suddenly,

Chamberlain Rodrigo's resounding voice announced his presence in the hallway.

"Our royal *altesse* requests your presence to help plan the birthday feast of our Christ Child. She wants you to pray with her at the cathedral. Meet her first in her chambers, she has other matters to speak to you about." Then I heard his *thumping* feet leave. Quickly, I dressed, while thinking how fast the Christ's Mass now approached. The copying and the quest for the next holy book seemed to make the days and months disappear like an early morning mist. However, I wondered why the insistence for us to pray together? Did she want me there to reaffirm her faith or something else first in her chamber?

Cautiously, I closed my door, locked it, gazed down both sides of the stone corridor, and gripped the pommel of my sword. I searched out all the shadows and side corridors and strained to hear the smallest sound. I moved like a stalking cat until I reached Helena's chamber door, knocked, and announced my presence. Instantly, she unbolted her door and asked me to enter.

"I am so glad you came right away. Please sit here next to me." She pointed to the bed. I hesitated at first, but her smile drew me to sit next to her. "Roberto, would you accompany me tomorrow to the San Salvador *Église* or as the locals call it La Seo?" She slipped her warm fingertips into mine resting on my lap. "It's quite important to me and let me explain why. I have had terrible nightmares the last several nights telling me of my death. I know this sounds foolish, but I feel Jesus is calling me to His kingdom." Tears started to roll down her cheeks.

"Put that nonsense out of your mind," I retorted. "And *oui*, I will accompany you to the cathedral tomorrow. Dreams are usually silly and meaningless; besides, you're protected by the best fighters on the entire Iberian Peninsula. Now cheer up and anticipate tomorrow's religious service and the royal banquet thereafter." She gently kissed me on my cheek and said *merci beaucoup* for agreeing to escort her. I thought it was time to leave and bid her adieu. I left her chambers sensing a foreboding of events to come. Was her premonition part of my feeling or was it the unseen stalker among us? Could her dream and this phantom person be connected?

The rest of the day, I practiced my swordsmanship with several young squires, testing my reflexes against their youthful quickness. My experience of actual combat and quickness of thinking stayed ahead of their lightning-like moves until I defeated a total of twelve of them. Then, I decided to retire and refresh myself with some *qahwa* back in my room. As I approached my entrance door, the hairs on the back of my neck raised straight up. The well-lit stone corridor made every stone block visible, but I still felt a presence. I even searched overhead, expecting some giant spider lurking above me, but grinned at myself upon unlocking my door. Quickly, I stopped inside and bolted the door, my sudden apprehension making me seem like a captive of my room. I drank two cups of the hot brown elixir, which prompted me to update my personal journal. Afterward, I reached for some loose parchment, whereupon I listed the clues both *Frère* Carlos and Helena had divulged. Praying that by organizing the sequence of the sigil drawings, ancient tome information, and Chaplain Jeremiah's knowledge might lead us to a more specific location of the next *Sangraal* parchments. However, halfway through my effort, there came a knock at my door.

"Lord Robert, it's me, Grand Master Gilbért, I need to speak to you."

"I'll be right there." Quickly, I jumped up from my writing table and hurried to the door. The bolt latches *clanked* away their release and he quickly thrust into the room with one single movement.

"We are now under a constant surveillance, *mon ami*," Grand Master Gilbért said, without saying *bonjour*.

"*Oui*, I know, but by how many or who are they?"

"Muhammad says he too is shadowed and believes they're Muslim men from the Outremer. He says their purpose is to kill us or capture you and murder Muhammad or me. Muhammad further said that he is sent by the cardinal or somebody else. Their first objective is to steal the *Sangraal* tome and follow us to the next *Sangraal* parchments. However, there may be another motive, yet it isn't clear to him. Before leaving to see you, his last comment was quite strange. He wants you to seek out a large black dog, for what reason he didn't say. I know this sounds strange, however, I have never questioned his judgment."

"The dog may be an omen to our phantom enemies," I replied. "We could use its greater sense of smell and hearing to track down our specter or specters. Yet, this doesn't give us much time to seek out such a canine, especially if we are leaving after the feast day of Saint Stephen. In addition, *Roi* Alfonso's banquet will last several days, which will require our presence. This leaves only one unanswered question. How does Muhammad know these men are from the Outremer?"

"All he said was they weren't Christian crusaders. He surmised they were Saracens, like himself. Their dissimulation behavior was similar to what he has experienced in Levant. I must agree with him, though I still believe there's a traitor among us."

"Could the Brethren of Purity be our phantom stalkers? Others have spoken about them and what few descriptions we have from them indicate such."

"*Oui,* but what greatly concerns me is the different types of machinations that are swirling around us. Quickly, seek out Chaplain Jeremiah and *Frère* Miguel. Both men have raised dogs as pets and used them to track and hunt. Tell them what Muhammad told me and I pray this black dog will help us. Once you find one, bring him back here before the Christ's Mass so we can start his training. Later, we'll ask Muhammad why he wants a black-colored dog now. I will lock up your room after you leave, fear not for the *Sangraal* tome is secure." Grand Master Gilbért motioned me toward the door.

I left my room feeling both fear and curiosity, still not seeing the true importance of a black dog. A short time later, my hand raised to knock on Chaplain Jeremiah's door, yet paused to hear the familiar voice of *Abad* Miguel inside. I knocked and announced my presence, which followed his creaking door being opened.

"It's good to see you, Lord Robert, please come in and join us. *Abad* Miguel and I were discussing our trip to Toledo," Chaplain

Jeremiah said, as he pointed at a chair to sit.

"I am fortunate that both of you are here together, for Grand Master Gilbért and Muhammad have a chore for the three of us." They both gave me a questioning gaze. "He and Muhammad want us to search for a large black dog. We must find one today and have it trained to track our unseen followers before we leave for Toledo. Would either of you know where we might find such a dog?"

"Knowing the grand master and Muhammad quite well," *Abad* Miguel said, "their reasons aren't entirely for tracking and the animal's keen senses, but another reason. Both the Christian and Muslim faithful still cling to their superstitions. Some of us as Christians believe that a black cat can bring evil, and it's the same thing with the followers of Islam in a black dog."

"*Oui,*" Chaplain Jeremiah added." And Muhammad wants to use the fear of the dog against our enemies. I suspect he knows we're being shadowed by Moors or Saracens and wants to use a black dog to keep them at a distance."

"However, what about de Tournay? He doesn't fear man or beast." I still felt he was our true nemesis.

"*Oui*, what you say is probably correct, but like the poisonous spider with eight legs. The more legs our enemy has, the quicker it can kill you. In addition, this new enemy can blend in with its surroundings."

Frère Miguel was right, showing us the wisdom and foresight of a learned *père supérieure.*

"I think I know where we can find such a dog," Chaplain Jeremiah announced. "There's a small fighting ring near the Zuda Tower. It's hidden by the old Roman walls. Let's go now."

We left the Aljafería Palace through the main gate and stepped on the frosty creaking drawbridge, after which we rushed down the road toward the Zuda Tower. It was difficult to keep up with Chaplain Jeremiah as his long legs set the pace, leaving *Abad* Miguel and me hurrying to keep up. We jumped off the road and traveled along a horse path, which *crunched* with ice under our boots. Up ahead loomed the Zuda Tower with smoke circling above it.

"My *amigos*, we'll travel on this side of the Roman wall until we arrive at the tower," Chaplain Jeremiah stated.

"Over a thousand years ago, Caesar Augusta had our town named after him and his soldiers built this now broken wall, which once surrounded the city. From here, you can see the Cathedral del San Salvador or as the locals call it La Seo, which was built over the old temple to Caesar Augustus. Tonight, the late Christ's Mass will be performed here at this cathedral."

The path drew us closer to the Rio Elbro and a chilly wind gusted from the river. This forced me to pull my white cowl over my head and braced my chin downward to lessen the frigid air from striking my face. A short distance away, the Roman wall appeared in its entirety and rose solidly some distance upward.

"Observe, this wall was left complete!" Chaplain Jeremiah shouted above the buffeting sound of the wind. "Soon, around this bend, we'll see an opening in the wall. The wall is thick and tall along this section, but the majority of it was torn down and the stones used in the surrounding buildings."

Then I noted loose stones scattered about, varying in size to the length and width of a man's height or in some instances the size of an ox.

"*Parada*!" shouted an unseen voice as we approached the bend in the wall. Slowly, from behind the opened wall emerged a black-hooded man with a large, white-splayed cross attached to his black tunic and mantle. Quickly, he marched to us with his hand resting on the pommel of his broad sword.

"*Pax vobiscum,* my fellow *hermano,*" said Chaplain Jeremiah. "We are soldiers of the Temple and men from the center of the earth. We mean you no ill will and we're on our way to rescue one of God's creatures. I know your Chaplain Carlos quite well and if you have any questions, please give him my name. I am Chaplain Jeremiah de Compostela, and I hope you'll let us pass."

The Hospitallers' guard stared at the three of us in silence, but especially me. He noticed my hand slowly move to the pommel of my sheathed sword.

"Wait here and I will indeed check with Chaplain Carlos," he finally replied.

Quickly, he departed backward on the path ahead, while facing us and his hand still on his sword pommel. He finally turned away just as it started to sleet. To our good fortune, he returned quickly, just as my chain mail gloves started to freeze.

"You may proceed, but don't come near the Zuda Tower, our order is having a convent."

Hurriedly, we traveled around the wall's bent path and approached some stone steps, which lead down toward the Rio Elbro. Carefully, the three of us trod down the icy covered steps and then approached a large stone ruin. Behind the ruin appeared the remnants of a Roman forum, where I heard a bestial sound, which I couldn't comprehend. Moreover, the noises emanated a ghastly bellowing and snorting sound. This followed with growling, barking, and then the piercing *whimper* of a wounded dog. As we approached one of the many broken stone entrances, I heard shouting men's voices, followed by an approving cheer. At the end of the elevated forum, I counted eight men at one end of a neck-level stone corral. When we jumped down to their level, all eight heads turned with wide-eyed expressions of surprise. Quickly, they grabbed their shiny silver coins and hurried from the corral. It was apparent they feared the men of the Temple and were pursuing an illegal interest, for they vanished from sight. We couldn't yet see what they had observed, but the snorting, bellowing, and the wounded *whimper* of a dog, still lingered in the sleet-saturated air.

Once we approached the large stone circular enclosure, a large white bull, with blood-tipped horns, and a bloody dripping nose appeared, pawing its front hooves in the muddy soil. Both nostrils flared with a steady stream of chilly air emanating from its nose. The bull prepared to charge at something near the end of the corral where we had stopped. I gazed over the stone ledge and spotted a large bleeding black dog, with a long bushy tail, lying on its side. The animal's right hind leg was oozing blood from a large puncture wound.

"Lord Robert, keep the bull at bay while I rescue this poor creature!" shouted Chaplain Jeremiah.

I leaped over the stone block fence, circled toward the bull to draw its attention to me, as I hugged the wall in case I had to exit. Both my arms rose in the air, with my voice shouting at the same time. Slowly, his sinewy neck turned, and his large dark-brown eyes focused on me, as Chaplain Jeremiah, aided by *Abad* Miguel, lifted the dog over the stone wall. His snorting and hooves now pointed in my direction, which left me frozen with fear. Suddenly, his thunderous gallop came toward me. The bull's lowered head, with its bloody horns, now raced straight toward me.

"Lord Robert, leap over the wall now!" screamed *Abad* Miguel. His shout broke my trance, which forced me to leap over the icy wall. On the other side, my body struck the frozen ground, only to hear a scraping thud against the stone blocks. Slowly, I raised myself, felt for any broken bones, which I didn't have, and observed the enormous white bull continue to butt its horns against the wall.

"We have the dog over the wall," came the excited voice of *Abad* Miguel. "Did you sustain any injuries, Lord Robert?"

"I am fine."

"Let's pray the dog isn't mortally wounded," voiced Chaplain Jeremiah. "We need to find a quick way to transport him to Muhammad and his medicines."

I surveyed our surroundings. There, next to the Hospitallers' entrance, I noticed a tied horse attached to a cart. Quickly, I hurried across the old Roman forum, and then carefully climbed up the steps. Once back on the path, it was just a short distance to the entrance and the horse. With my icy hands, the knot didn't want to untie, thus forcing me to cut it with my dagger. I threw the cut rope onto the cart, and then quickly climbed into the seat, and with one movement of my right hand, I lashed the horse onward.

Now, I had two problems, how to maneuver the cart down to the corral and pass the Hospitallers' sentry guarding the door to their secret convent. As the horse raced ahead, I observed a side road that circled in the direction of the river, but it was close to the Zuda Tower. Quickly, I pulled the reins to my left, just as the Hospitallers' guard shouted something in his native language. To my relief, the road led directly toward the stone corral. The guard started to chase after me with his sword drawn, but stopped, and then raced toward the Zuda Tower to alert his fellow *hermanos.*

CHAPTER XVII

Within what seemed several heartbeats, I met both holy men and our bleeding black dog. "Hurry and load him into the cart. The entire Hospitallers' commandery will arrive soon. This is their cart!" Gingerly, they loaded him on the cart's bed of straw, and then both men jumped in. I cracked the reins and off the horse galloped toward the Aljafería Palace.

"I see the frigid wind and sleet hasn't slowed your quickness, Lord Robert," *Abad* Miguel said. "In addition, you stole the *chevaliers* of Saint John's good horse and cart, but God will forgive you this time." He grinned. "Was that the first time you confronted a large fighting bull in an arena?"

"*Oui*, I mean *si*." I knew this was another trial in my search for the *Sangraal* parchment, and then I prayed that the parchments still existed.

"Chaplain Jeremiah, how did you know where to search for this dog and that his color would be black?" I inquired.

"Since Roman times, bullbaiting has occurred along the Rio Elbro. The ancient Roman citizens, who settled here, often enjoyed seeing different animals pitted against each other. I guess they enjoyed it to settle their blood lust and gambling habits. It doesn't appear the local citizens have changed much from our earlier conquerors. I come down here frequently with several *santo caballeros* and collect alms for the poor. The gamblers gladly give up their purses when they see the men of the Temple. Occasionally, I just come by myself and rescue the wounded dogs, yet I enjoy doing both." The young chaplain's smile was identical to his scar-faced *père*. "You asked how I knew the dog's color would be black. It's particular to this fighting breed; most of them are black."

We reached the palace in quick order and hurried to seek out Muhammad, however, *Abad* Miguel couldn't find him and said it was time for his midday *salats* or prayers. Soon though, we met him, as he was leaving the palace mosque. I recapped our rescue of the dog, and then the four of us rushed back to the cart tied to the stable fence slats. Slowly, Muhammad approached the bleeding animal, yet he seemed reluctant to touch the dog. He gave both *Abad* Miguel and Chaplain Jeremiah instructions on where to carry the dog. They lifted the animal from the cart, and with much circumspection, placed him on a large wooden storage box of horse feed. With the four of us surrounding the wounded animal, he became agitated and started snapping at our hands. The snapping and growling continued, even as we stepped away from him, but Muhammad started speaking softly to him in his native tongue and the dog quieted. It never ceased to amaze me the power this prince had over animals.

"Lord Robert," Muhammad said quietly, "help Chaplain Jeremiah tie the dog's muzzle and feet with some soft strips of cloth. Be careful not to make any quick moves or raise your voice until we have him tied."

After completing our task, he instructed *Abad* Miguel to help him clean the wounds, and with the stalking movements of a cat, Muhammad slowly approached his horse. There, he reached into one of the saddlebags and quickly pulled out several vials, which appeared comparable to the medicines we used at the mountain cabin. He gave the vials to *Abad* Miguel, who grabbed one of them and then applied the thick brown liquid to several gaping wounds. The dog's large round dark eyes focused on the *abad's* fingers and then gave out a low guttural growl. Slowly, he rubbed the ointment around and into each gaping inflamed fur opening. The animal reacted with several sharp *whimpers* of pain and started thrashing its paws at *Abad* Miguel. Muhammad reached for the other vial of white liquid, which *Abad* Miguel had placed near his feet. Carefully, he uncorked the liquid, and then slowly moved toward the dog's large muzzle as Chaplain Jeremiah gently pulled back the dog's gums, exposing his four incredibly long canine teeth. Slowly, Muhammad poured the thin milky like liquid between its huge teeth. It was the same liquid Muhammad called opium, which we used for our grievous pain at Gavarnie. Both men slightly loosened the ties around the black dog's muzzle and poured the remaining liquid into his mouth. Softly, Muhammad rubbed the animal's exposed throat, and the canine swallowed the elixir. Instantly, the animal's eyelids drooped, its tongue stopped moving, and all four paws relaxed. A brief time later, a light whistling sound came from the dog's big nose, he was now asleep.

"Muhammad, why did you refuse to touch this black-colored dog?" I asked as Chaplain Jeremiah started stitching up the animal's numerous wounds. "In addition, will he live?" He didn't answer any of my questions right away but slowly strolled back to his saddlebags. His silence didn't bode well. After putting the empty vials into his saddlebags, he turned and spoke.

"*Oui, mon ami*, he will probably survive if *Allah* wills it. He has given him to us for protection against the evil forces who seek us out. I will train the dog, along with Chaplain Jeremiah's help, to find the *Ikhwān aṣ-Ṣafāʾ*, or as you call them, the Brethren of Purity. They have many names, such as the *Hashishiyya, Fida'is, Nizari Ismailis,* and the Summoners. They're infamous for their use of *taqiyya,* which means concealment, dissimulation, or caution. They can appear and disappear using many disguises and some even say they can change into different animals. I later found out the *café* vendor was one of them after he disappeared from me tracking him. In addition, the man you glimpsed at Huesca, with the red-colored turban and boots, he too was a *Hashishiyya.* Many of these spiritually trained killers appear as house servants, especially as ordinary Moorish merchants, Saracen guards, and people you can trust. Their leader, or frequently called the *Mahdi,* is Rashid Al-Din Sinan, others call him Sheik el Djebel or the Old Man of the *Montagne*. His principal *château* is on a tall *montagne* near where His Excellency Gilbért's men—Sergeants de Hoult and de Béziers—were serving in the Levant. His *royaume* encompasses the Norsiri *montagnes* in the Latin principality of Antioch. His two strongholds are Masyaf and Al-Kahf. From these two *châteaus*, Rashid Al-Din Sinan sends out his *Fida'is* to do his bidding. He declared *fatwas* on both the great Salah Al-Din and my family. He wanted our land, which he said was his, but we rightfully claimed it since the time of our Prophet Muhammad ibn Abdullah, may blessings and peace be upon him."

Muhammad's face seemed frozen like a stone statue and his saddened ebony-colored eyes locked with a dolorous past vision. His silence made me uncomfortable and surprised. Here was a man of deep introspection and a past life that few knew, yet my uneasiness disappeared knowing he trusted me with his new revelations. Finally, his stoic expression broke like the ice on a pond as he continued to speak.

"*Mon ami,* he will continue to send his Summoners until I am dead, yet I don't think I am the sole object of his evil intentions. I believe he has entered into an agreement with someone of power to steal the holy book about *Issa* or Jesus, your Christ, and may peace and blessings be upon Him. You may not know this, but *Issa* in my faith is one of the Five Messengers of Firm Resolve. They were the prophets, Noah, *Ibrahim*, *Musa*, *Issa,* and lastly Muhammad. Muhammad was the final seal of the prophets, may blessings and peace be upon them."

"Judgment Day is only two finger widths away in time and *Issa* and the *Mahdi* or guided ones will be there to destroy the *Dajjal* or evil being. Cardinal Folquet, I believe, has entered into an agreement with Rashid Al-Din Sinan to capture or destroy the words of *Issa* and murder me.

"*Mon ami*, Rashid Al-Din Sinan's killers are quite adept in hand-to-hand fighting, and they don't fear death. You won't see his *Fida'is* until they kill you, which it's important to know, for they carry several concealed poison-tipped daggers. In addition, they wear three suits of steel at all times, but their mail isn't made of metal. Their first suit is blind obedience to the Old Man of the *Montagne,* second is occultation, and the third is their poison-tipped daggers, which the poison has no cure. These *Hashishiyya* haven't any equal when it comes to fighting with daggers. This is one of the reasons we now have a large black dog. In my culture, a large black dog is an evil *jinn* and when one appears people leave in fear."

"What is a *jinn*?" I asked, not familiar with the word.

"It's a spirit created out of smokeless fire, which can be helpful or evil, depending on the form it takes. He's similar too, for the People of the Book, your people, who believe a black cat is a bad omen. Yet, this isn't the main reason we need him. I have some of the deadly poison in a vial that the *Hashishiyya* use on their dagger tips, which I intend to train the dog to smell and recognize. No matter how well they disguise themselves, he will detect their presence well in advance. It will be difficult for me to work closely with him after he regains his strength, unless *Allah* wills it."

Abad Miguel's knowledge and great wisdom were right about the dog's purpose, which after Muhammad's detailed explanation made me feel a little more secure from harm. Chaplain Jeremiah sent one of the palace guards to fetch Sergeants de Hoult and de Béziers to bring the bull back to the palace and have it slaughtered. The cooked bull's meat would be highly prized for the *roi's* banquet after our Christ's Mass. *Abad* Miguel quickly left to meet the archbishop and help prepare for the late-night high mass. I stayed behind to continue aiding Muhammad with our injured canine *ami*. I gazed at our Saracen's smooth swarthy face and close-cropped beard, thinking he still exuded mystery, yet now I felt confident he trusted me with some of his past life's events.

"Lord Muhammad, tell me more about your faith and the prophet you are named after."

"What do you want to know about my beliefs and our prophet?" he asked, placing bandages next to our still snoring black dog.

"I detect there's some kind of schism in your faith."

"*Oui*, that's true, *mon ami.* The Old Man of the *Montagne* believes his line started with a man called Ali, who was the prophet's first cousin and married one of the prophet's daughters, Fatima. Rashid Al-Din Sinan claims he is a direct descendant of Ali's family. His followers called themselves Shiites or the followers of Ali. Ali stated that our most merciful prophet passed on secret *nass* or knowledge to him and Fatima. The Shiite line calls their religious leaders Imams, which, so they say, *Allah* has divinely appointed. This secret knowledge was given to them, and it's said they can read the hidden meaning of the *Qur'an*.

"In addition, the Shiite line has two separate groups. One states that there were seven *Mahdis* and Rashid Al-Din Sinan believes the seventh *Mahdi,* or as he calls him the riser, will soon come out of hiding. At that time, the seventh and final *Mahdi* will establish justice in the world, overthrow the Sunni line, and establish a final seventh era of human history. Others of the Shiite belief contend there were twelve *Mahdis*, which the twelfth is in hiding too. However, I belong to the Sunni line, which means the consensus of the people. It started after our merciful prophet appointed his close student, Abu Bakr, to be his successor and *khalifa* over all submitters of the faith. To my faith, both Shia lines are unacceptable, and my people call them *malahidas* or heretics. The Old Man of the *Montagne* twists the teachings of Muhammad, our most merciful prophet, to his own ends. Sheik el Djebel and his *Fida'is* are evil men, who are addicted to greed, power, and obedience. The *Qur'an,* in one of its *surahs,* says a religious bond that goes beyond tribal bonds, ethnic heritage, or rulers of *royaumes* should unite us. This is what I believe, *Rasul* Robert."

"Later, we must speak more of this matter," I said, still amazed with Muhammad's openness. "Before I leave, one other question. You just call me *Rasul* Robert, instead of Lord Robert. What does that title mean?"

"You are guided by *Allah*, *Alhamdulillah,* and specially chosen to seek out the holy words of the Prophet *Issa.* Wherever your *dawah* or call leads us, only *Allah* and His most merciful wisdom knows. It's apparent to me, at the time of your birth, your *qadar* or destiny was set. *Allah*, praise be to Him, has predestined your quest, *mon ami.*"

I left Muhammad to care for our newfound weapon, while still wondering why his holy book mentioned my Lord and Savior. What additional knowledge would our Saracen prince further divulge to me?

Reaching my room, a faint *rustling* sound came from its interior, causing me to pause before unlocking the door. With my left hand, I reached into my surplice belt and grabbed my room key and then my sword hand quietly withdrew the blade from its scabbard. Slowly, I placed my key into the door lock and adroitly turned its innards a quarter of a turn. Slowly, the door quietly opened, revealing Helena sitting on my bed. Quickly, I lowered my sword with relief and spoke.

"How did you gain entry into my room?" I asked with an angry high-pitched voice. "The door was locked before I left."

"Roberto, your memory is correct, yet you forget; I am a *princesse* and *marquise* in *Roi* Alfonso's *royaume.* Besides, I am here to give you a gift for *Nochebuena.*" Her dimpled smile melted my anger. Her ability to speak glibly between languages still surprised me. From behind her back, one arm brought forth a precious ornate tubular leather case. There were red and green-colored precious stones encrusted on its round lid, along with glinting gold filigree designs circling the lower half of the leather case. However, what caught my eye, and to my astonishment, were the repetitive designs of the seal found at the cave near the *monasterio* San Juan de la Peña.

"It's a gift from me, Roberto. I had it made so you could store your journal letters, drawings, and *santo* manuscripts, which I know you will find in Toledo."

"I don't know what to say; I am speechless. It's both exquisite and practical, but . . . I don't have a gift for you." I felt embarrassed and ecstatic at the same time.

"Do you remember several nights ago, when we were traveling through my vineyards and witnessed the many lit bonfires?"

"*Oui*, and I have meant to ask you about them, however, many things on my mind were distracting me."

"They're called *hogueras,* and we light the fires on the shortest day of the year. It's an ancient Iberian custom, which is supposed to protect our people from illness and bring good luck in the coming new year. As you rode with me, I knew the fires would protect us and I could go forward with my life and seek out the new year's good pleasures. No matter what happens to us, Roberto, our Lord and Savior is pushing us forward to do His pleasure and giving us His *santo* grace in return. Your presence with me is the best gift you could give me. To this, I say *merci beaucoup* and *Nochebuena.*"

We both peered into each other's eyes and searched for a loving agreement that couldn't be, our stare only broken by a small tear rolling down Helena's cheek. I followed the teardrop until it dripped onto the back of her hand. Slowly, I lowered my head, grabbed her hand, kissed the top of it, whereupon my lips tasted her salty tear. It was the only form of appreciation I could express as my racing heart desired to do more.

I heard her sharp intake of breath, and then she pulled her hand away and placed it on her lap. "After we return from the cathedral, the *roi* will lead us into the banquet hall to break our fast. His feast after Christ's Mass is the largest in the *royaume*; not even the *roi* of England could put on a better feast. I'll leave now and have Esperanza help me prepare for tonight's *santo* service and feast. *Adios,* for now, Roberto. Later, we'll meet after Vespers in the courtyard. I hope you'll enjoy my gift and always remember me by it."

Slowly, she walked toward the door, hesitated to leave, and strolled back toward me. Then she paused in front of me before leaving, where the warmth of her body brushed against mine, after which she left me with the cold wind of her exit.

The early morning December light was still dim and the bells for the divine office of Terce had just started *clanging*. I told myself I must speak to Grand Master Gilbért after Terce to see if he had any new evidence on our traitor. I grabbed my room door handle, pulled open the door and then slowly eased out my head and searched both ways down the dark corridor. Anger and frustration came over me knowing everywhere I traveled in the palace; some cowardly person could jump out and threaten my life. I longed for this shadowy person to meet me outside in open combat, so I could kill him and put an end to his nefarious ways. The constant nagging fear for our safety, the potential theft of the *Sangraal* book, and the many suspicions about traitors, shape-shifters, de Tournay, and the cardinal's machinations made my teeth clench with rage.

"*Buenos días, mi amigo.* Did you sleep well last night?" *Abad* Miguel asked as I entered the *chapelle* for Terce.

"*Oui*, I did and *merci* for your concern," I replied.

Between the *Pater Nosters* and psalm readings, my mind wandered back to my *château* in Burgundy. My mind's eye could see the small round faces of Henri and Brian racing across my green lawn with my arms in prayer wanting to hold them. Oh, how I missed my *fils* and Marie. The guilt of not writing to my family and my feelings for Helena overwhelmed me, while not realizing the office of Terce was finished.

"Lord Robert, we must leave," came the quiet voice of Grand Master Gilbért. "Did I not let you finish your prayers?"

"*Non*," I answered. "My mind was thinking of my family and how I missed them."

"I understand your angst and appreciate what you have done for me but stay the course and don't forget that God has a higher purpose for you," Grand Master Gilbért guided me in the direction of the old palace mosque. There, once again, we met Muhammad coming from prayer or *salat* as he called it.

"How is our canine *ami* healing, Lord Muhammad?" I asked entering the horseshoe-shaped entrance.

"Fine. He should start training while you celebrate the birth of *Issa*." A smile softened his stoic face.

The late morning sun poured in through the many ornate stone-carved windows circling the dome above. As my eyes gazed farther upward, to my surprise, the dome base had eight sides, with the dome ceiling center, likewise, carved in the large shape of an octagon. Within that design were two perfectly square-shaped boxes, forming an eight-pointed star. Inside the star design were two more octagon-shaped designs, with one larger than the other. At the supporting base of the mosque's dome was a large band of Arabic script.

"Observe, another clue," I said, pointing toward the top of the dome. "Notice the eight sides that support the dome and the numerous carved octagon-patterned designs in the ceiling. It's a signpost, *mes amis*, that we're on the right path to discover the next set of *Sangraal* parchments."

"*Si*, you're right, Lord Robert," *Abad* Miguel said. "It's a sign from God." He crossed himself.

"Muhammad, what does the Moorish script say on the eight-sided bands at the base of the dome?"

"It's the ninety-nine holy names we call *Allah* when we pray. That is why I carry the *tasbih*." He lightly touched a long string of brown-colored wooden beads tucked into his tunic belt. He used those same beads when we buried Squire Hughes in the Pyrénées *Montages*.

"Its purpose is similar to the *Pater Noster* beads you use when you pray to *Allah* and *Issa*. May peace and blessings be upon *Issa* and our beloved Prophet Muhammad. *Allah* wants to remind us life is sacred and protect that which He has given us. We use our beads as a reminder to praise Him for giving us such a precious life." He looked at each of us and smiled. "Now I must return to the stables and see our new injured companion. I want him as a strong amulet against the *Fida'is*, when we meet them."

He quickly left through one of the black and white-striped topped horseshoe openings and disappeared.

"Grand Master Gilbért, do you have any more thoughts about our traitor's identity?" I asked, hoping he would now know.

"Let's return to your room," he said in a hushed voice as his eyes stared around the numerous stone columns of the mosque. "I can divulge more information there."

CHAPTER XVIII

Hurriedly, we headed in the direction of my room, only stopping when we approached the entrance door. Before I unlocked the door, he stared down both sides of the corridor to possibly hear or see someone or something. I entered first, quickly followed by him, however, he hesitated to close the door but popped his head out once more for a final glance. Still whispering, after I locked the door, Grand Master Gilbért quietly revealed what he wanted me to hear.

"I am positive it's one of my . . . sergeants, but I yet don't know which one."

"How can this be?"

"*Oui*, it's hard to believe. Especially, on several occasions knowing they both saved my life. However, a traitor in our order must be severely punished. Yet, something tells me one of them didn't betray me for money, for I sense a hidden reason we don't see." Grand Master Gilbért glanced out one of my windows.

"What shall we do?" I insisted while thinking he was right about an unseen reason.

"Nothing, *mon ami*," came his unexpected answer. "We have nothing else to seek out in Zaragozza. All clues still point to a hidden manuscript in Toledo. Our enemies are expecting us to lead them there to it and kill all of us after you translate the new *Sangraal* parchments. When we arrive there, I will set a trap to expose the traitor. Now let's retire and hopefully rest before tonight's holy service and later feast."

"Wait, who told you positive it's one of the sergeants?"

"It was the *marquésa*." He grabbed the door to leave. "She pays her source quite well, even better than the cardinal. *Au revoir*, *mon ami*, see you tonight, we'll gather by the *chapelle* to proceed to the *cathédrale*."

One of his hands shook as he closed the door behind him; letting me know the *marquésa's* revelation had dented his iron nerves. Her latest information left me woozy with unanswered thoughts.

"*Mère de Dieu*!" I shouted as I realized the increasing spiderweb of deceit further tightened its hold on us, leaving me not wanting to gaze into their traitorous eyes. It didn't seem possible either man could lead us to slaughter; especially after all the spilled blood and suffering we had shared together. However, Helena's sources of information were amazing and even the mighty Poor-Soldiers of Christ were deficient compared to her information.

Once more, I perused my hiding place for the *Sangraal* book, praying as always it would be there in its usual concealed place. Finally, after seeing it, I commenced writing to my *épouse*.

> *Mon cheri, I am sorry I haven't written to you sooner, but we are constantly in the saddle riding from one place to the next. However, we're nearer to fulfilling our holy quest.*
>
> *I am staying at the royal palace of the roi of Aragón. It's a combination palace and Moorish fortress called Aljafería. The roi's royaume is quite exotic and unlike our provincial village at Borron. I pray you, Henri, and Brian are all well and your frère is protecting all of you from harm. Tell Henri and Brian they would like to meet the Saracen prince, Muhammad Nur Adin I am traveling with, for he can do amazing things with horses.*

I continued writing until the late December sun fell behind the old tower, at which time I concluded my letter, telling *mon épouse* to always stay near her *frère* and keep our children close. Again, I told her I was sorry for my negligence in not writing and I would improve my timeliness when we arrived at the next temporary location. Finally, I told her *mon coeur* ached for her embrace.

Quickly, I folded the papers in four sections, reached for a lit candle, and used it to melt some sealing wax on the final fold. Carefully, I pressed my family crest ring onto the red wax, removed it, blew on it to harden, and tucked the letter into my surplice. Suddenly, my nerves were startled with a heavy pounding fist on my door followed by a resonant voice.

"*Don* Roberto, it's time to process to La Seo," came the voice of Rodrigo, Helena's chamberlain.

"Tell her I will be there in a *momento*." I combed my hair, put on a clean mantle, and left for the procession.

The palace courtyard was teeming with various ranks of royalty, with both secular and religious orders of *chevaliers*, all of them scurrying to find their proper place in the procession. As I squeezed my way to the *chapelle* entrance, I could see many throngs of horse riders and carriages blocking the entrance. The din of voices made it difficult to communicate, leaving it troublesome for individuals to find one another and their proper place in line. The sergeants and *chevaliers* of the Temple appeared at the rear of the procession, along with the sergeants and *chevaliers* of the Hospitallers of Saint John. I was thankful Chaplain Jeremiah had returned their horse and cart. Many of the heavy clothed courtiers and royalty were starting to coalesce near the front along with the gold-brocaded robes of the secular clergy. As I twisted my neck in several different directions, I failed to see Helena, which caused me some concern. This was only for a moment when suddenly there came a loud cheer from the crowd of onlookers. With many waving hands, the large retinue of holy night people pointed toward their *Marquésa* Helena galloping through the crowd on her large white stallion.

"Lord Robert," she shouted above the noisy crowd, as her big horse trotted toward me. "Please come and let us ride together."

"I haven't saddled my horse," I replied, only to turn around and see Chaplain Jeremiah smiling as he handed the reins to my horse. Quickly, I mounted, but she grabbed the bridle to my horse.

"Roberto, let's ride with the men of the Temple on the way to the cathedral." Both of our horses pranced alongside each other. Immediately, the entire procession of heads turned in our direction as we joined the *frères* of the Temple.

"Roberto, please ignore the prying eyes of the courtiers. The bishop will snare their attention when he blesses the procession."

We joined the men of the Temple, along with Chaplain Jeremiah on foot, then the Hospitaller's chaplain of Saint John. In union, they exhorted the words, "*In nomine Patris et Filii et Spiritus Sancti*," and the procession surged forward. Then, both chaplains started once more chanting, while each swung a jingling smoke-filled thurible. Slowly, the sweet pine-scented incense drifted through the cold night air floating above our heads as the other *abbés* blessed their part of the procession. Suddenly, the procession crowd started chanting where we rode, with the chaplains saying, "*Dominus firmamentum meum*," or the Lord is my strength. Every courtier, *chevalier*, noble, and warrior-*moine* joined the chant. Their voices rolled forward like a thunderous wave crashing toward shore. Their shuffling feet slowly snaked their way along the old Roman wall.

"Roberto, did I tell you that my late *mari* and I were married in the *Cathédrale* San Salvador?" Helena asked during a pause in the chanting.

"*Non*," I answered.

"It's the greatest ornate designed *église* in Zaragozza in the *Mudéjar* style, though parts are Roman built. The *cathédrale* isn't complete, for it was originally a mosque until *Anno Domini* 1140 when Christian builders renovated it. *Roi* Alfonso has decreed all royal celebrations and major religious functions have their beginnings here. When he dies, he wants his oldest *fils* enthroned here too."

"How old is his eldest *fils*?" I asked, thinking of my *fils*, Brian.

"He is fourteen years old and young *Don* Pedro favors his *mère*.

You'll see him later tonight at the banquet feast." The chanting resumed and, once again, the *abbés* and chaplains shouted their Roman words for all to hear, "*Paravi lucernam Christo meo,*" or I have prepared a lamp for my Christ. Without notice, we stopped proceeding, as a flicker of light, where the bishop stood, increased in brightness.

"Roberto, observe closely what will happen," Helena said, keeping me in suspense.

Gradually, the glimmer of torchlight moved toward us like a radiating-colored stream of water. Since Helena's conversation had made me oblivious to my surroundings, I hadn't noticed that each member of the procession carried an unlit torch.

"When the torchlight reaches us, Roberto, you'll see a wondrous sight." Her eyes reflected the oncoming flames. She was quite right, the golden glow that rose above us was spectacular and extremely spiritual. However, it now revealed the *cathédrale* structure in its entirety. Not a shadow remained or an unseen hidden corner. The structure didn't impress me with its two narrow towers at the entrance and, in addition, facing to my left was one large square tower, which was Moorish in design. There were the ubiquitous horseshoe-shaped openings on each side near the top, which I suspect was once a minaret. From my seat in the saddle, I observed a cloistered enclosure that lay behind the tower. The *cathédrale* roof was of wood and the smaller interior buildings had red clay tiles for their roofs. A long narrow nave bisected the lopsided square main structure. The entire grounds reminded me of an ancient Roman villa or fortress.

As we approached the main entrance, there appeared the typical tympanum with Old Testament scenes carved into the stone. Both of us dismounted, trying to avoid the newly chisel-shaped stones ready for some unknown placement. The numerous large stones made it difficult for the procession to enter the *cathédrale,* yet fortunately, the bishop, *abbés*, and chaplains directed the wide line of worshippers forward in an orderly fashion. The front of the structure, facing around the small cylinder-shaped towers, revealed black and blue checker-shaped embedded tiles. These alternated, every so often, with crescent-shaped white moons. I surmised the large plain cut stone blocks came from the old Roman walls, making it quicker to build the *cathédrale*.

Now it was time for us to enter, yet the entrance didn't have a narthex, forcing us right into the nave. Instantly, my nose caught the smell of pined-scented cut wood, then mold, followed by stone-chiseled dust. There was one lancet-shaped window over the chancel and choir, with several uncompleted windows in each of the several *chapelles*. The large apse held numerous completed stained-glass windows, however, what caught my eye were the ornately carved column capitals. Each one had beastly tongued animals, Greek centaurs, and a multitude of loping deer. Toward the choir were various painted statues of apostles. Some were standing by themselves, while others were bas-relief into the checkered Jacqués designed walls. The altar, the main *chapelle*, and along each wall aisle were huge white burning candles augmented with some of the torches brought into the *cathédrale*.

"Roberto," Helena whispered. "I know our *cathédrale* isn't as grand as those in your native country, but San Salvador is less than fifty years old, and the threat of hostile Moors has made its completion difficult."

"*Oui*, I understand," I said as we found our place in the nave near the altar. "Yet I know *Roi* Alfonso and his royal progeny will make your *église* the finest edifice on the entire peninsula." We watched as the bishop seated himself in his marble-built throne.

"Bishop *Don* Ramón de Castellazuelo will be officiating this evening," Helena said. "You do remember him from the first banquet *Roi* Alfonso gave when you arrived?"

"*Oui*, yet I don't think the bishop approves of Grand Master Gilbért and the men of the Temple."

"That is so, *mon ami*, but it's a political game the *roi* must play for the warrior-*moines* to help protect his *royaume* and to satisfy the *Santo Mère Église*."

Before the midnight Christ's Mass started, all who desired came forward and proceeded to one of the finished *chapelles* to pray for the dead. The monastic orders prayed first for the departed, with the choir chanting the "Magnificat," after which a final preces was given. Lastly, they slowly returned to their former positions in the nave, letting the nobles and courtiers proceed toward the numerous *chapelles*. There, we grabbed a single burning taper and lit as many candles as possible for our deceased relatives, friends, and loved ones not of this earth. Each *chapelle's* dark shadows disappeared with warm glowing lights flickering throughout the *cathédrale*. I knelt on the damp stones and prayed for my *mère, père,* and a baby *soeur* who had died before me. Yet, I lingered a little longer in prayer for our recently martyred squire, Hughes de Montbard. In addition, the suicide of the young Cathar girl, and even the evil misguided men I killed in combat.

Suddenly, there arose the soft droning words of a common prayer.

"Oh God, our *Père,* Creator of all the living, we entrust to Your gentle care all those departed we have loved or have fallen in combat, who have gone before us and have gone to their rest in the hope of rising again. *Santo* Mary, Mother of God, pray for us sinners, now and at the time of our death. Amen."

After finishing my prayers, I crossed myself, and then quickly rose, with Helena's warm hand slipping into mine and squeezing it tight. Yet, she still knelt and continued praying, counting her dark purple chaplet beads, and reciting her Glory Bes and *Pater Nosters*. As the crowds started moving back to their former positions in the nave, Helena quit praying, crossed herself, and stared into my eyes. The sadness in her eyes seemed to search my soul for help, yet I couldn't give her the *amour* and physical closeness she so desired. Even a *princesse*, from a great *royaume,* couldn't purchase happiness, no matter the amount of gold and jewels she owned. Oh, how my *coeur* ached for her.

The archbishop started his homily about Jesus the Christ's birth and how eventually His Second Coming would herald Judgment Day. His sermon was powerful and to the point, but my mind didn't digest his words in its entirety. The homily was pushed out of my mind's eyes with images of Brian's and Henri's faces, *mon épouse*, and a *crackling* fire in my great hall. As I gazed up, staring at the barrel-vaulted ceiling above me, I closed my eyes and perceived my humble church at Borron. There I was with my family celebrating the Christ's birthday mass, along with the villagers and serfs.

As the archbishop finished his homily, my eyes flashed toward a young peasant woman strolling toward the chancel altar carrying an infant. Once reaching there, she carefully lowered her baby into a manger in front of the altar steps. Slowly, she knelt and began to pray. This wasn't a Christ's Mass custom in my native home, but nevertheless, it was spiritually exhilarating.

CHAPTER XIX

"Roberto," Helena whispered as she placed her full lips next to my ear. "I would give all my wealth to trade places with that peasant woman. She watched the woman at the altar. "Only to hold my own baby in my arms." Tears of angst rolled down her cheeks.

"Helena, you're a striking woman and still young enough to bear children. In addition, you're intelligent, not easily intimidated, and have wealth to use wisely. Fate has a way of giving us what we don't want and then tests our resolve, or giving us what we desire, and we still want more. What little free will we have, we must use it wisely," I whispered into her ear while breathing in her rose-vanilla scented fragrance. Once again, she squeezed my hand as her bluish-gray eyes met mine.

"*Merci beaucoup*, Roberto, for giving me such confidence and wisdom. They are the greatest gifts to give me for the memory of Christ's birth."

When the mass ended and the benediction completed, we started our procession out of the *église*, with each of us holding a small white lit candle. There wasn't a need for torches as the many burning candles combined to form one gigantic source of light. Quickly, our squires returned with our horses, then helped us mount as Helena and I clutched our glowing candles. The long *cathédrale* service and the hungry anticipation of the *roi's* banquet made me oblivious to the wintry night air. This night and the coming day, I anticipated with excitement, knowing good company surrounded me and realizing how close we were to possibly finding the next set of holy parchments.

Suddenly, the mass of human bodies surged forward toward the Aljafería Palace, followed by a quiet shuffling of feet, the creaking of carriage wheels, and the rhythmic prancing of horse hooves. It was an amazing sight to see as if some giant flaming millipede was winding its way searching for an unknown safe destination. The flickering flames cast our ambling human shadows on each large building and the remaining Roman walls we passed until we reached the palace drawbridge. There, the *roi's* guards slowly raised the portcullis and we started proceeding into the courtyard. After we crowded into the ornate interior of the palace, once again, we lined ourselves to enter the great banquet hall according to our proper station. The palace's lord high chamberlain, Rodrigo, and his assistants guided us to our appropriate seats. The bull-necked Rodrigo continued to shout commands to his assistants above the clamor of the courtiers' and nobles' voices, only stopping when everybody sat down.

To my surprise, once again they seated me between Helena and the *roi's épouse*, *Reina* Sancha.

"*Mon Seigneur Baron* Robert, did you enjoy our *Nochebuena* service and our Christ's Mass tonight?" the *reina* asked. "I am positive our customs are quite different from your native land."

"*Si*, or *oui*," I replied in both languages. "There isn't a nativity scene near our chancel altars, even in the large *cathédrales*. If there are decorations, it's usually holly, evergreens, and mistletoe hung in our homes. Our *églises* are barren of Advent decorations, except for the Advent candles. Though, I must admit, your candles are quite large in thickness compared to our narrow tapers."

"Lord Robert," Helena formally stated. "My favorite Advent candle is the purple-colored one, representing God's *amour* for us by sending His only *Fils* to save us. My second favorite is the large, white-colored candle representing the radiant white light and spotless nature of the Lamb of God. His white light always shines for us, so we never travel in darkness."

Just then, the archbishop stood to do the blessing. After he prayed to God for the bounty of our food, he gave thanks to our *Père* for giving us His *Fils,* which prompted us to make the sign of the cross. This was the signal for the servants to rush in with their large round steaming trays of food. The first course was a nut treat covered with a sticky nougat coating.

"What is this first course?" I inquired.

"It's what we call *turrón* and tastes well with some of my first-course *vinos,*" Helena answered. "Do you remember just outside my *château*, the small bare trees planted between my rows of vineyards?"

"*Oui,*" I replied. "You called them *almendro* trees. A nut you use in cooking cakes and candies."

"Try it," Helena coaxed.

She threw one in her open mouth, slowly chewed on it, and after swallowing, she licked her sticky fingertips. I too did the same with the sticky sweet concoction that melted in my mouth, after which we drank several sips of *vino.*

"It's delicious!" I exclaimed while enjoying several more bites and then washing down the sweet taste with more *vino.*

"This dish is nothing, compared to the marzipan," Helena said, "which we'll serve last. Oh, Roberto! Here comes the steaming cooked partridges covered with mushrooms. Can you smell the thyme and oregano?"

The servants placed several salvers of the small spicy-smelling fowl in front of us.

"*Oui,*" I replied to her question. "But what's this white cheese alongside the trencher of yeasty smelling bread?"

"It's called *queso Manchego*, or ewe's milk made *fromage* in your native tongue, which has an aged taste similar to your Roquefort *fromage*. It's *très bien* and tastes well with another of my *vinos* from *mon Château* Maluenda."

Salver after salver sat before us with pieces of roasted lamb, pork, seafood, and venison. I was so famished after Advent fasting, each entrée didn't seem sufficient. Muhammad gave me his sizable portion of pork because his faith wouldn't let him eat it. I devoured it in a wolf-like manner, only occasionally glancing up to see if Helena and *Reina* Sancha were observing my uncouth eating. Yet, to my surprise, everybody around me was eating at the same ravenous pace. Not a word was spoken, only the sound of dishes *clinking*, meat knives scraping against metal plates, and the low murmur of satiated royalty and nobles.

After finishing the main courses, the marzipan-designed pastries that Helena had spoken about earlier were set before us. Each serving tray was replete with colorful-shaped camels, magi, shepherds, lambs, and stable animals, with the main salver bearing the baby Jesus and holy family. Each pastry had a sweet creamy-colored icing that quickly dissolved in my mouth making me want more of the designed holy characters. The pastries never seemed to cease and along with washing them down with various cups of *vino*, they forced me to loosen my sword belt.

"Lord Robert, did you have enough to eat?" *Reina* Sancha asked with a smile.

"*Oui*, I am quite full of your delicious cuisine, which should last me until Three *Rois* Day. Maybe even until Candlemas." I laughed. "Please tell me there isn't any more food."

"Lord Robert, that's the last of the courses, only your cup will still be filled, and fruit served if you so desire," *Reina* Sancha said.

"*Merci beaucoup*, Your *Altesse*. Both you and *Roi* Alfonso serve an excellent feast." I nodded my head to her.

"Are you still leaving after the feast day of Saint Stephen for Toledo?" *Reina* Sancha asked as she motioned for one of her servants to refill my cup.

"*Oui*, I am afraid so. My time in your *royaume* has been quite enjoyable and interesting. I can say the food, *vino*, and your family has immensely raised my spirits."

Quickly, *Reina* Sancha glanced at Helena and smiled, acknowledging to the both of us she knew of our close relationship.

"Even the evil *bâtard* de Tournay didn't spoil my good time in your court," I stated.

"*Oui*, one day soon that *diable* will come to a worse end than what he gave those poor souls he butchered," retorted the angry voice of Helena. "Last night I had a fitful dream and in it was a murky figure of a man brandishing a large two-handed sword. No matter how hard I focused on him, I couldn't recognize his darkened face. Suddenly, Marcel de Tournay appeared, he too didn't see the shadowy appearing man. De Tournay was facing another man with his sword and dagger held high. This second man too I couldn't see, only a misty outline of his body. Marcel's evil grin flashed at the second man, and he started speaking, however, de Tournay's lips moved, but no words came from them. Suddenly, he turned, faced the unseen first man, and his evil grin changed to one of horror. A huge silvery blade sliced through his sword arm, with blood spurting from the clean-cut stump. Once more, the huge sword was instantly raised and then came its sideways swing, at which time my dream ended."

"Helena, I hope your fitful dream is fulfilled," I said. "It would make my quest easier to complete. Yet, more important, it would withdraw the threat to my family. Nobody I know would shed a tear for his terrible demise, even the cardinal. He would just obtain another miscreant to do his evil deeds." I felt hot anger surge inside me. "If your good premonition comes true, I suspect the murky executioner was Grand Master Gilbért wielding his sharp Damascus-made sword."

"I don't think so," stated Helena.

"If not him, it must be me," I said feeling the heat of anger on my face.

"*Non*, it wasn't you, the murky shape was larger in size. Whoever this executioner might be, Marcel de Tournay won't suffer enough."

"*Oui*, I agree," *Reina* Sancha said. "However, his punishment on earth will be pale in comparison with the fires of hell and *El*

Diablo will never let him rest from pain. *El Diablo* has set a fishing snare with three of the cardinal sins: lust, greed, and pride. There's no escaping *Satanás's* soul settlement."

She was right, but while on earth, a *Diablo*-trained killer was a powerful foe for any man to face. Quickly, I said a prayer to myself for the realization of her good portent.

Suddenly, my thoughts were interrupted by a loud *rumbling* noise. *Roi* Alfonso had risen, followed by all the nobles and courtiers. The entire banquet hall stood, leaving me the last to rise as he raised his huge silver chalice.

"I, *Roi* Alfonso the Second, *roi* of all Aragón, Catalonia, and count of Barcelona and Provence, hereby propose a toast to our esteemed visitors. To the Grand Master of Iberia Gilbért de Érail, his Poor-Soldiers of Christ; the Emir Muhammad Nur Adin from the Levant; to our *bon ami* from Northern Burgundy *Seigneur Baron* Robert de Borron, *chevalier* and troubadour; and lastly to my great wise advisor and beloved teacher, *Abad* Miguel de Huesca, *merci beaucoup*. Great *salud* to all of you, may you always have my protection."

It made me both proud and safe that the *roi* had given us a toast, for we needed all the secular protection we could obtain. Standing next to the *roi* was his *fils*, who indeed did favor his *mère*. His skin color was a golden light brown, slightly darker than his *père*, yet their straight hair matched, and their body frames were similar in stockiness. Prince *Don* Pedro held his cup in a like manner to his *père*. I prayed for the *Royaume* of Aragón, with the young *fils* reigning long, fairly, and firmly as his *père*.

The early morning light was fast approaching and Archbishop *Don* Ramón de Castellazuelo concluded our feast with a benediction. Thereafter, he reminded us of the remaining masses occurring in the up-and-coming holy weeks ahead. At the conclusion of our feast, he sained us, followed by the high lord chamberlain, *Don* Rodrigo, directing us out of the banquet hall in noisy, but orderly fashion.

"Lord Robert . . . please meet me today after the holy office of Nones," Helena whispered. Her soft voice tickled my ear. "Come to my quarters, for I have several gifts to give you before you leave."

"*Oui,* I'll be there, but you don't have to give me a gift," I whispered back while smelling her sweet-scented neck. "Your wonderful company is the best gift you have indeed given me. I don't think anything can exceed your gift of presence with me these last several weeks."

"You're quite kind, Roberto, and your *épouse* is quite fortunate to have you as her mate." She released her arm from mine. "*Buenas noches*, Roberto."

She left to continue to her room as the long holy day, excessive eating, and a certain amount of anxiety left me exhausted. My stride back to my quarters seemed quite slow the closer I came to the entrance door. As I reached for my key to unlock it, suddenly a dark shadow darted into a small unlit passageway. Instantly, my hand slid to the hilt of my sword, pulled it from my scabbard, and raised it to my shoulder.

"May the peace and mercy of *Allah* be upon you, *mon ami,*" came the disembodied voice of Muhammad Nur Adin.

"Please, don't frighten me anymore. I am quite nervous already," I admonished him. "Give me a fair warning before you shadow me again." Slowly, with the movements of a cat, he slipped into view below one of the lit iron torch holders.

"Pilgrim, by frightening you, your senses will become honed like a sharp sword. I fear the next several days our lives will be in mortal danger," my Saracen *ami* stated.

"Why would this be any different from previous days we've faced?"

"It's what your followers of *Christo* . . . call a pre . . . monition."

"Shouldn't reason explain our concerns about an unseen foe?" I countered, hoping to sound pragmatic, yet realizing I was fooling myself.

"I would trust revelation before reasoning any day, *mon ami.* However, both together and used wisely let you have the ability to predict events in the future. While you were in your *église* and at the *roi's* banquet, I was working with our dog. I detect he senses some unseen intruder, for he is no longer *whimpering* with pain but emitting a guttural growl as if someone or something is spying on us. You and Chaplain Jeremiah have chosen wisely a quick learner and an animal with keen senses, which makes him easy to train.

"The next several days you won't see me, however, still listen for me. It's important you're always alert. I won't leave the palace but search for my face in everyone you see. Anyone of us who fears *Allah's* judgment is now a target for murder or capture before we depart for *Tolati-tola*. Now sleep, *mon ami*. If you desire my presence, slip a missive under my door, then expect me soon after." He slowly stepped back into the darkness.

Quickly, I grabbed his knotty forearm and stopped him. "How will I know it's you and not our foe?"

"I will give you a signal only known to you." He once again melted back into the darkness.

Immediately, I unlocked my door, quickly entered, locked it behind me, and without hesitation checked the bound pages of the *Sangraal* tome. Once more, to my relief, it was still in its undisturbed hiding place. After securing it once again, I collapsed on my bed and didn't remember falling asleep. However, what seemed like only moments later, came the loud pounding of *Don* Rodrigo's fist.

"It's Christ's birthday and we'll leave soon for the *cathédrale*," he announced like a noisy hammered nail into my head. "Meet us in the courtyard near the *chapelle*." His booming voice seemed to bounce from every stone in my room.

The *cathédrale* mass consumed the first part of the morning, thereafter, I returned to my room anticipating a light midday meal. Before entering, I drew my sword in one hand and my room key in the other, heeding Muhammad's words of caution.

CHAPTER XX

Once inside, I hurriedly latched all the locking bolts, then my nose caught the scent of yeasty smelling fresh-baked bread. Upon turning around, there on my writing table lay a salver of *queso Manchego* and a dome-shaped loaf of crusty bread. Beside the salver was a glass crystal carafe of *vino*, which was strange to see, for glass crystal in my native land was quite rare. This light meal suited me perfectly, which would give me the strength to update my personal journal.

Time slipped by quickly while reminiscing on parchment about my quest, the dangers I faced, the new people I met, and the strange lands encountered. Just as my small inkpot drew low, came a softer knock on my door than usual.

"Lord Robert, it's me, Chaplain Jeremiah. Would you come with me to see how well Muhammad is training our dog?"

Cautiously, I unbolted the door and viewed the tall chaplain.

"I met him in the hallway. He requested me to lead you to the stables."

"Why now on our Savior's birthday?" I locked my door and then proceeded toward the stables.

"He wants you to give the dog a name so he can train him quicker. In addition, I believe his medicine and soothing voice has helped revitalize our new war dog. You know the magic he can do with animals. In addition, after the holy office of Matins, Grand Master Gilbért desires a meeting there."

"Who will attend this meeting?" We strolled down the steps to the courtyard.

"Just you, me, Muhammad, and *Abad* Miguel."

Before reaching the stables, the pungent smell of hay and straw caught my nose and drew me in its direction. Once there, Muhammad was standing among the horses, but our dog wasn't in sight.

"Where's the dog?" I asked, before greeting Muhammad in his customary bow.

"He's right here, *mon ami.* Don't you see him?"

"*Non.*" I strained my eyes for his black fur.

"See not with your eyes but try to sense his presence. He's here and quite close."

This was a test for me, as well as our new canine *ami,* and I hoped the dog and I would pass. Suddenly, the hairs on the back of my neck rose, which quickly alerted me of some presence, followed by some inner voice telling me to glance upward. Directly above me, crouching on the wooden edge of the hayloft was the big black dog ready to pounce. He hadn't barked or growled or wagged his tail. He stood there silently like a black canine statue and didn't even pant. He had learned well the art of stealth from the Saracen master himself.

"To train a person or animal for *taqiyya* or concealment and stealth can increase your powers against your enemy many folds," Muhammad stated.

"*Oui*, you are correct, *mon ami.* I shouldn't have thought any less of a wise emir from the Levant."

"What name shall we give the dog, *mes amis*?" Muhammad glanced at each of us.

"Lord Robert, you are the writer and *trouvère* and should name the animal," Chaplain Jeremiah said.

"Then it's *Noir Ombre,*" I said, with a sudden inspiration. "That's what I will call him. He will be like a black shadow to our enemies, always present, yet unseen, black as night, and quick to pounce on his prey."

Both my companions nodded in agreement to the *nom de*

guerre I had given our new canine scout and soldier. Muhammad further demonstrated his training skills by having *Noir Ombre* retrieve a dropped sword and crossbow. Amazingly, the Saracen prince accomplished this feat with hand signals and much praise. However, he didn't work the animal too long, knowing just when to let the dog rest and recuperate.

Both Chaplain Jeremiah and I left Muhammad to change the healing dog's bandages and hurried to the *chapelle* to meet Grand Master Gilbért and the office of Matins.

"How's our injured warrior progressing?" Grand Master Gilbért asked, meeting us at the *chapelle* door.

"Quite well," I answered.

"Will he be strong enough to travel tomorrow on Saint Stephen's Day? We need to leave as soon as possible. We are quite behind on our schedule for Toledo."

"*Oui*," I replied. "Muhammad has already trained him with hand signals to do several things. I suspect he will be fit enough to travel with us to Toledo."

"I knew Muhammad could treat the poor animal with his great medicine, yet his possible fear of a black dog could have been a deterrent. However, I now realize this wasn't a problem; now let's proceed into the *chapelle* and pray." We followed Grand Master Gilbért as he led the way.

After the office was over, I returned to my room and repeated the same cautious routine of opening my room door. Oh, how I wished to confront this phantom stalker in combat. Once in my room and the door secured, I had some spare time to continue writing in my journal. My personal journal had become a safe harbor for my emotional angst and gave me some daily relief, yet there was always some type of conflict, be it constant traveling on horseback, combat, or natural elements to confront. However, I was grateful for what little personal time I had to myself and didn't dwell on any other thoughts, using my time wisely.

After a goodly period of time, there came the pounding on my door from the oversized fist of *Don* Rodrigo.

"Lord Roberto, the *marquésa* wishes your presence in her chambers."

With much wariness, I unlocked my door, crept out into the dark corridor, while Rodrigo guarded my back, and I then locked my door. Moreover, before leaving, I shook the door handle to make sure the rim lock held. Slowly, we both strolled down the dank corridor toward Helena's room, while I hoped Muhammad was somewhere in the shadows. Halfway to Helena's quarters, I caught a brief whispered word, which came from a dark side corridor. "Brian," came the name of my *fils*, however, Rodrigo didn't hear it, but continued, with his ears distracted by his noisy *thumping* boots. A sigh of relief came over my body as we approached Helena's door. Muhammad uttered Brian's name one last time, just as Rodrigo raised his huge fist to pound on the door.

"It's your Lord Chamberlain Rodrigo, Your *Alteza.* I have Lord Roberto with me as you commanded."

From behind the large oak door came the soft voice of Helena, followed by another women's laughter.

"Please enter, Lord Robert," Helena commanded.

Rodrigo, with his broom-sized hand, reached for the door handle and pushed the door open, after which he stepped aside. To my surprise, standing in the room was *Roi* Alfonso and Grand Master Gilbért standing between Helena and Esperanza.

"Greetings Your Most Christian *Majesté* Alfonso, Your *Altesse* Helena, Dame Esperanza, and Grand Master Gilbért de Érail," I said, bowing before the royalty present.

"Lord Robert de Borron, you can remove that gawking expression from your face," Grand Master Gilbért said with a crooked smile.

"*Oui*, please drink a cup of *Marquésa* Helena's *bon vino,*" the *roi* said, pointing to five filled cups.

As Esperanza handed out the cups, I glanced at Grand Master Gilbért's face, which instantly changed from his scar-faced grin to a dour expression as we sat down.

"*Marquésa* Helena has just given me some recent news on the whereabouts of Marcel de Tournay's hidden camp," Grand Master

Gilbért said. "I will let the *marquésa* explain and show you the map she has drawn."

"De Tournay has moved his base camp from Tauste to Alagón, which is about three to four leagues from Zaragozza. In addition, my sources say he has sent for reinforcements, however, they won't reach him until the new year of our Lord and Savior. This map I had made shows his exact location." Her long slender fingers moved across the map lying on the table. "He's quartered in a small mud-brick structure, a stable I believe, which is on the southeast corner of the village. You can see its location marked in red ink." She pointed to the spot.

Slowly, I bent my body closer to see the exact mark.

"Now is the time to strike and cut off the viper's head," she said. "He'll be quite sluggish after our Lord's birthday and slow to react. De Tournay will be in his snake hole not expecting us to pull him out."

To my surprise, her face became cherry red, and her left hand slammed on the table next to me. Coming from Helena, this was quite an unusual display of anger and vengeful satisfaction, which left me amazed.

"Indeed, this is God-sent information, yet our evil foe is similar to putting a withering poison serpent into a cloth sack. Unless you clamp down on its head, he is still able to strike a fatal bite," I stated to our fellow group of hunters.

"*Oui*, Lord Robert de Borron is right," Gilbért added. "However, Prince Muhammad and my men of the Temple will set a snare. I will call up all my men, except two, and ride by night to Alagón and set our trap. Nowhere will he be able to slither out of his hole and escape." The grand master glanced at the *roi*.

"When do you plan on springing this trap, my *amigos*?" *Roi* Alfonso asked, a satisfying grin on his reddish-brown beard.

"My men will arrive at midnight on Saint John's feast day, and then wait for my signal to carry out our overdue justice." Grand Master Gilbért reassured his old *ami*.

"Then it's settled," said the *roi*. "You have my full support. Once he is captured, and I want him brought back here, and I will have him tortured to implicate the cardinal and anyone else in the curia." Quickly, the *roi* rose, followed by the rest of us in the room and said his final words.

"May the *Santos* Miguel and Jorge give you and your swords the strength to fight our enemies." Rodrigo opened the door for his liege lord.

"Lord Robert," said Grand Master Gilbért, "meet me in the *chapelle* tomorrow at Matins, we'll prepare to seek out de Tournay."

"*Oui*, this is a ride I greatly anticipate, which will give me utmost satisfaction," I replied. "*Bonsoir, mon ami.*" Rodrigo closed the door behind Grand Master Gilbért and spoke.

"Your *Alteza*," inquired Rodrigo. "Do you need me for anything else?"

"*Non*, Lord Chamberlain, and I wish not to be disturbed. Please lock the door when you leave."

"As you wish, Your *Alteza*." Immediately, he opened the door, entered the dark corridor, and then shut it. After which a loud *clank* came from the lock.

"Roberto, please accept this map and obtain some rest, for tomorrow that *bâtard* de Tournay's evil machination will cease."

She handed me the rolled-up parchment map while caressing my hand then slowly released her hold.

"Roberto, let me fetch your gift before you depart, and you can carry it back to your room." She gracefully moved to a large carved wooden chest, then opened the lid and pulled out an ornate appliquéd cloth sack.

"Here are some oranges, which I hope will remind you of me. In addition, I have prepared some marzipan cakes for your dangerous journey. Also there's a letter of recommendation from me to my young nephew, the *roi* of Castile, Alfonso the Noble, as his subjects call him. He's my half-*frère's fils* and with my letter, he'll do anything to help you. However, I wouldn't speak specifically about your purpose in his *royaume*. Tell him you're on a scholastic journey to seek out God's spiritual glory. Only say, you're there to meet Isaac the Blind and obtain his spiritual guidance. The *chevaliers* of Saint John have the *roi's* ear and they could interfere with your quest. Keep your quest secret at all times, *mon ami.*"

She handed me the soft silk sack, pausing to squeeze my hand as she put it in my palm.

"Come to my quarters after the office of Nones tomorrow. It's the feast day of Saint Stephen and we can discuss some more about the scholarly city of Toledo. There won't be a royal guest this time, just you and me. *Bonsoir, mon trouvère chéri.*"

She then stood on her tiptoes and kissed me on my cheek, while one hand released her grip off my shoulder and the other slid down my arm to grip my hand. I longed for her breasts to stay close to my chest, but she pulled away as she led me to her door. Her jewel-encrusted fingers reached for the door latches, slid back each one of them, and paused once more. Then she pressed her chest against mine, as I squeezed out the partially opened door, speaking a final affirmation of our next meeting.

"Roberto, don't forget, we have a meeting tomorrow after the office of Nones." Then the door closed, and the locking bolts made their *clanking* sounds.

I crept out into the corridor, hoping I wouldn't make any noise. Each of my footfalls stepped softly while praying I would move undetected and fool our unknown stalker or stalkers. A short distance from Helena's door, I heard my *fils'* name whispered, which reassured me Muhammad was somewhere protecting my back. Upon reaching my room door, I glanced over each of my shoulders before entering, and then quickly unlocked the door. I sat down on my large wooden chair and reached for my previous unfinished cup of *vino*. Before putting the garnet-colored liquid to my lips, I stared into the cup, thinking about our hard-fought entry into Zaragozza at the beginning of Advent.

The old Celts believed that if you gaze long enough into a pool of liquid, you could see the future. Their priests called this scrying, but I didn't want to see any images in my cup, for they would certainly be nefarious in nature. Therefore, I just gulped the liquid and forced my mind to banish any troublesome thoughts. It felt good to do nothing or think of nothing.

Later that evening, I continued working on my journal, while organizing my clues to the next possible location of the *Sangraal* parchments. After emptying my second cup of *vino*, I stopped, closed my journal, and slowly stumbled toward my bed.

"Lord Robert," came the familiar voice of Grand Master Gilbért. Next came his pounding fist. "Wake up, *mon ami*. We have a busy day ahead."

"*Oui*, I am coming!" I shouted as I stumbled out of bed. My hands reached for the locking bolts, unlatched them, and then quickly opened the door. Swiftly he entered with his usual cat-like movements, wearing a new white mantle and surcoat.

"Would you like some of *Marquésa* Helena's orange-colored juice?" I inquired, not knowing if he had broken his fast.

"*Oui*, that sounds *bon*."

I found a clean cup, then poured the sweet-sour tasting liquid into it and held out the goblet for him. Quickly, he swallowed the juice.

"As soon as you dress," he said, "we are to meet Muhammad, *Abad* Miguel, and Chaplain Jeremiah in the mosque."

Quickly, I threw on my clothes, chain mail, buckled my sword belt, and then slipped into my boots.

"I am ready; let's leave." We left my room, followed by me locking the door.

We reached the mosque horseshoe-shaped entrance just as *Abad* Miguel and Chaplain Jeremiah arrived. Quietly, we stood by while Muhammad finished his morning prayers. Once finished, he rose, and then strolled toward us, pausing outside the entrance to put on his boots.

"*Salaam alaikum, mes amis*. What news do we have today?" he asked.

"None so far," replied Grand Master Gilbért.

"Your Excellency," Muhammad said. "I have already prepared the supplies for our horses and replenished the quarrels for our crossbows. Tomorrow, when we leave for Alagón, we'll only have to saddle our horses."

To my left and down a side corridor from the mosque came a sudden growl. Was it *Noir Ombre*? As I strolled over to see, the growling continued, until he glimpsed me smile, then came a low whine, followed by his wagging black tail. Slowly, I walked over to him, placed my palm on his furry head, and then rubbed it. Instantly, the huge dog rolled over wanting me to rub his belly. There were still some small red streaks shooting outward from where Muhammad had stitched up his wounds.

"Will *Noir Ombre* be well enough to accompany us tomorrow night?" I asked Muhammad, as the dog licked my hand.

"*Non*, he will need several more days of rest and care, however, he should be fit when we leave for *Tolati-tola.* Yet again, last night he sensed some unseen danger, for he continued growling during the night. I don't think it was pain from his bullfighting injuries."

"What are you trying to tell us?" Grand Master Gilbért asked, staring at the rest of us.

"He indeed knows we're being observed by smelling some kind of evil presence. I too sense the same *taqiyya* and my fears tell me it's ready to strike. In addition, my inner voice says it's one of the guardians sent by the Old Man of the *Montagne*. One or more of them are here to kill us, just like the ones who murdered my entire family. May *Allah* guide my sword hand to avenge my dead family's honor," Muhammad had a steely sounding edge to his voice, which caused a shiver to creep down my back.

"How many of them do you think are here at Aljafería?" I asked, wondering if there was more than one.

"I can't give you a firm total," our Saracen *ami* replied. "It could be twelve or any number above that figure. When our canine *ami* is finally well, I'll use him to track them down before they attack."

I didn't want to hear the top end of the number, knowing twelve killers could attack us at once or unseen, one at a time. It was at that moment I wondered how Grand Master Gilbért had still fooled both Sergeants Jacque de Hoult and Guy de Béziers about our secret meetings and plans.

"Do you think both of your sergeants suspect anything we've planned?" I asked, knowing now was the time to shield our activities.

CHAPTER XXI

"Bon question, *mon ami.* I have a plan, which should protect us from any messages arriving for de Tournay or Cardinal Folquet. *Abad* Miguel and Chaplain Jeremiah, I want both of you to leave for Toledo today." Both holy men nodded in agreement, yet his *fils* had a slight expression of surprise.

"Both sergeants will travel with you for further protection, so they think, however, the rest of us will have an excuse to stay. I will tell them the *roi* and the *archbishop* wants us to stay and help set up a *laus perennis* or perpetual choir of prayer for his deceased *mère*, *Reine* Petronilla. Our order has donated a large amount of gold to help maintain the choir in her memory."

"It sounds like a good ruse, yet will Muhammad be scouting for us?" inquired Chaplain Jeremiah.

"*Non*," answered his *père*. "He'll stay behind and continue nursing our newest fighting member to good health. Some more of my men will travel with both of you, so as not to seem out of the ordinary. I've sent a sealed message to the commander at San Servando telling him to expect you. You're our well-protected decoy, which should keep the unknown traitor off guard, including de Tournay. Any unusual activity you see from either sergeant, inform me promptly by messenger."

We each left the mosque separately and cautiously sauntered a circuitous route back to our rooms. All the whispering, meeting in secret, and constant glancing over my shoulders left my palms and forehead drenched with sweat. I unlocked my door, entered, then sat down on my bed and started ruminating about our forthcoming battle with de Tournay. My emotions seemed mixed, greatly desiring revenge, yet knowing justice was really in God's hands. His fate for me was His design and not my own. I was His seeker and redactor put upon His earthly domain, yet I knew nothing about de Tournay's personal life, other than he was the cardinal's seneschal. What motivated this man to rape an innocent young girl, who died by suicide, then kill poor villagers, our Romany protectors, and murder a holy man? Was it all for money, power, lust, or all three? It shouldn't have made any difference, for all were mortal sins and hell's fires would soon be his new home. However, for some unexplainable nagging reason, my conscious mind wanted an answer. Maybe Helena could shed some light on my conundrum, however, I wasn't to meet her for a while. In the meantime, I needed to breathe some fresh air, while hoping to clear my head of confusion.

I unbolted my door and proceeded to enter the corridor, unexpectedly seeing a palace guard posted outside the door. My legs jumped back against the cool corridor stone wall ready to defend myself with my hand on the pommel of my sword. He gave me a crooked smile and I in turned acknowledged him as I locked my door. Why was there a guard posted at my door? Was there some new threat, which had just transpired? His protection of me was in need of an answer from Grand Master Gilbért. I nodded my *au revoir* to the guard, but my sweaty palms seemed to betray my sense of security After proceeding down several dark corridors, I met Muhammad as he slowly came from behind a stone column.

"*Salaam alaikum*, Lord Robert," came his soft voice. "You appear as if you're in deep thought. Are you thinking about your family?"

"*Non*, but *merci* for asking. Do you have time to speak, *mon ami*?" I hoped he might explain the guard at my door and give me some further background about de Tournay.

"*Oui*, I was just coming to ask you to follow me to the stables and see another demonstration of our canine soldier."

When we reached the stables, a long black wagging tail and a panting smile greeted us. Muhammad's mystic touch had removed *Noir Ombre's* stitches early, which reflected a new feistiness and some weight gain.

"You have done an excellent job nursing him back to health," I said to Muhammad. "Will he be ready to travel to Toledo after Saint John's feast day?" And do you think he is ready to seek out the men of the Brethren of Purity?"

"*Oui*, let me give you a demonstration."

Muhammad said something to the dog in his native tongue, which *Noir Ombre* then stared into his eyes with his ears raised. After just a slight motion of Muhammad's arm, *Noir Ombre* raced to the back of the stable and leaped at a straw scarecrow holding a wooden-shaped knife. Immediately, the dog ripped off the straw wrist and shredded it with his teeth, then started gnawing at the wooden dagger.

"This is quite impressive, *mon ami*," I stated with a sense of pride. "However, will he understand my language?"

"*Oui*, but I am not through yet." Muhammad motioned for *Noir Ombre* to come forward.

Once again, his hand directed the dog to move to my left side. *Noir Ombre's* black and pink-colored tongue licked my hand and then stared up at me with his glistening ebony-colored eyes.

"He knows both hand signals and each of our native tongues, but hand signals have more stealth against our enemies."

Suddenly, our canine soldier emitted a guttural growl and his black tail stiffened. Directly in front of us, a helmeted man appeared, wearing a heavy padded aketon covered with chain mail. I reached for my sword, but Muhammad stopped me with his hand.

"Motion for *Noir Ombre*," he said. "Point toward the man with your hand, he will then attack this intruder."

I bent down, stared into the canine's eyes, and thrust my arm forward. His paws didn't seem to touch the ground as he lunged forward, barking and snarling. He jumped at the unknown attacker at full force, knocking the man backward, yet the attacker jumped up and started swinging his broad sword at the circling canine warrior. Each time the attacker thrust his sword toward *Noir Ombre*, the animal would quickly dodge the blade tip and then circle the man in the opposite direction. Muhammad shouted a word at the dog in his native tongue and immediately *Noir Ombre* froze his movements. The second command brought our warrior canine to sit next to Muhammad, at which time he handed him a chunk of red meat. Then to my surprise, a familiar voice came from the unknown attacker.

"Lord Robert, it's me, Chaplain Jeremiah. Fear not, *mon ami*, this was a practice drill." He pulled off his great helm.

I then realized the practice drill was a prank played on me to show the effectiveness of our new warrior *ami*. I slid my partially drawn sword back into my scabbard and then reached out my hand to rub *Noir Ombre's* head. Both men were smiling at me, which even included my wagging-tailed *ami*.

"Well, the joke is on me," I stated. "I came here to discuss with Muhammad about Marcel de Tournay but saw what our new four-legged warrior-*moine* could do to our enemies. I am quite impressed, *mes amis*. Both of you have done an excellent job in quickly rehabilitating him. However, now that I have both of you here, what can you tell me about the evil *bâtard* Marcel de Tournay's personal history?"

"Why do you want to know?" Muhammad answered first with a question.

"I want to know if he has any *frères* who might seek revenge on my family when I kill him. I don't fear for myself, but I fear the torture and death his family may bring upon mine."

"I understand quite well your angst, but I know nothing of his evil past. I am sorry, I can't tell you more about this damned *chevalier.*"

"Lord Robert, I know some information about him, yet it may be of little value," Chaplain Jeremiah added. "He serves as the cardinal's chief bodyguard, and some say he is one of the cardinal's many *bâtard* children by different women. His home is in Toulouse, and he often accompanies the cardinal to Rome. The rumors say he has murdered and will murder anybody who stands in the cardinal's way, even including his own *mère*. You shouldn't worry yourself about this evil man; God will protect your family. Besides, Grand Master Gilbért has told me your *épouse's frère* is the greatest fighting *chevalier* in all Christendom."

"*Merci*, Chaplain. I appreciate your words of comfort. I'll return to the palace. Maybe the *Marquésa* will know even more information." A moist cold nose nuzzled my palm. Both my hands responded by rubbing his furry head and muzzle, then I quickly departed as Muhammad continued giving our canine *ami* commands. It was now time to meet the *marquésa*, and I hurriedly strolled through the columned courtyard toward her room.

Just outside her quarters stood another palace guard, yet at first glance, he didn't resemble the previous palace guard in both appearance and recognition. His uniform seemed different, however, I couldn't be certain. My mind made a mental note to discuss this with Grand Master Gilbért when I met him next. Suddenly, the door opened, and Helena greeted me.

"Roberto, please come in. I have been expecting you."

"How did you know I would be standing there before you opened the door? I might have been one of de Tournay's men or worse," I asked and admonished her simultaneously.

"Do you always greet a *princesse* with a question and not *bonjour*?" Helena smiled.

"*Non*, but I fear for your safety. It's apparent with these additional guards outside our rooms, there's now a greater threat to all of us. In addition, why is the guard outside your room wearing a different uniform than the one next to my door?" I asked.

"To answer your first question, I recognized the *thumping* of your boots. The second question about the guards outside our rooms has an explanation. *Roi* Alfonso believes there's an imminent threat to one of us. He thinks there's the possibility of our abduction and then being held for ransom. Third, my guard's uniform reflects his higher rank and shows he has been in the *roi's* service for many years."

"Please forgive me for not addressing you properly, but my mind was on the guard's uniform and your safety."

"*Merci* for your concern, *mon ami*, now let me show you what I have." She handed me a rolled parchment and a silver chalice replete with *vino.*

I unrolled the parchment and perused its contents. "I have seen these symbols before!" My index finger pressed down hard on the same symbol that first appeared on the black onyx signet ring at Vézelay.

"Helena, this symbol was on a ring finger of a dismembered arm I witnessed at Vézelay several months ago. An outnumbered dead Templar *moine* had hacked it off before dying in combat. He sacrificed his life in delivering the note to me from Grand Master Gilbért. Where did you obtain this parchment?"

"My *mari* sent these drawings to me before he died at Hattin. His accompanying note said he obtained this parchment from a Byzantine *moine* who had traveled to Persia. Supposedly, these symbols predate the Muslim prophet, Muhammad. The ancient Babylonians said the crescent moon was the lamp of heaven. It was one of their many gods and the eagle symbol represented a secret lair or fortress of some important Imam or leader ruling in that region. In addition, the *moine* told my *mari* the people of this great ancient Persian Empire went by the name *Sassanian.* I knew I wouldn't see you after Saint Stephen's Day and thought these symbols might be important to your quest. Can you read the ancient writing under the symbols, Roberto?" She pointed her slender finger at the words.

"*Oui*, it says on this line the symbols represent a secret group of winged men who can drop from the sky and attack their enemies. The words further state you'll never hear or see them until it's too late."

This new revelation wasn't welcome information, and the so-called "winged men" were the Brethren of Purity. It was now obvious to me these were the murderers of the Templar messenger and *Moine* Gabriel.

"Why did you keep this parchment?" I asked Helena.

"You know how important any information is to me and what it might later reveal. In addition, the more we conversed, this came into my mind. I am sorry our talks have interfered with your quest. Was this useful, *mon cheri*?

"*Oui*, quite useful," I replied, as she gave me a kiss on my mouth, and I slowly pulled away.

"Our Lord and Savior said we must give of ourselves before we can receive His goodness. This parchment is another gift from me, Roberto. Please always remember me, for our lives are so fleeting," Her breasts pressed against my chest, as she gave me another kiss on my lips.

"Roberto, will you see me before you pursue de Tournay?"

"*Non*, but your kindness has so touched my heart. You will always remind me of the exciting time I had with you." I stooped over to kiss Helena.

Then reluctantly, I left the room, while praying her soft lips wouldn't force me to return. The corridor was dark and strangely the guard was gone. Was Muhammad still guarding my back? My ears strained to hear a familiar word only known to me, yet none came. My mind was so mentally exhausted, I didn't care if he was there or not, but I hurried to my room, quickly unlocked my door, disrobed, and fell on my bed asleep.

CHAPTER XXII

"In the middle of the night, I heard my *épouse's* voice call me to hold her. My mind first thought I was dreaming, however, the warmth of her naked body radiated against my loins. Hesitantly, my fingers reached for her breast, with my fingertips slowly surrounding her rock-hard nipples.

"Roberto, it's Helena," she said to my sudden surprise. "Please don't move away, for I *amant* you so much."

As her soft fingertips moved toward my thighs, a dark shadow moved along the side of my bed. Helena at once stopped her hand near my hipbone, turned herself toward the shadow's direction, and then partially raised her body. Immediately, I heard a *thump*, followed by a guttural scream from Helena. Right away, she fell on my chest as the dark shadow leaped toward a narrow window. Immediately, I felt the cold jutting steel pommel of a dagger pressing against my chest. Slowly, my mind reacted as if a mace stunned me, nothing made any sense. How and who had entered my room? Was this Helena lying next to me? I didn't want to believe any of it, but my ears heard a feeble rasping voice.

"Roberto, tell me . . . you *amant* me," came Helena's gasping voice.

Surprisingly, the dark phantom hesitated at the window, which prompted me to leap naked from my bed and grab my sword. Just as I raised it to strike, he grabbed hold of a rope secured with an iron spike, then leaped out the window and disappeared. Quickly, I stuck my head out the window, glanced up, then down the *château* walls, and finally to each side. I observed nothing but darkness and a crescent-shaped moon hanging in the night sky. It was as if this dark being had flown away. I ran toward the fireplace, grabbed a wooden ember, and then lit a candle next to my bed. To my horror, the light revealed her pale naked body with a protruding dagger hilt between her breasts.

"God damn you," I cursed while pounding my fists on the cold stone floor. "Why did you let this happen?" I screamed at God repeatedly until nothing came from my throat. Then a voice, as if speaking from inside a deep cave penetrated my ears.

"Robert, what has happened? Let me in at once," came the muffled voice of Grand Master Gilbért. "You have awakened the entire palace."

"The Devil himself has visited me tonight!" I cried out. "You don't want to know what has happened!"

Suddenly, the wood of the door splintered. Quickly it swung open, followed by Muhammad and Grand Master Gilbért entering my room holding two huge iron maces.

"Lord Robert, why is the *marquésa* lying naked in your room?" Grand Master Gilbért asked. "How did she enter your room? Wasn't it locked? Did you let her in?"

"*Non*! *Mère de Dieu,* I don't know!" I exclaimed. "Maybe she had a key and locked herself in. What have I brought upon these innocent people? It's my entire fault and this dagger was meant for me. Thus, I am to blame for a trail of murdered God-fearing people, which now their violent deaths are burned on my eternal soul. To hell with the *Sangraal* parchments and to hell with you, Grand Master Gilbért. We're chasing after some diaphanous parchments and not facts. I won't let my *fils* and *épouse* be murdered by these phantom killers!"

Suddenly, my face stung from a heavy backhanded blow.

"Lord Robert, calm down!" Grand Master Gilbért's booming

voice shouted. "Did you see who did this evil act?"

"*Non* . . . its movements weren't capable of a mortal man and its image was a black mirage." I tried to marshal my thoughts. "Please cover her naked body." Carefully, Grand Master Gilbért and Muhammad began wrapping her body with my bedsheets, yet before covering her body, Muhammad paused and meticulously examined the dagger hilt.

"This wicked act was done by the Brethren of Purity and one of its *Fida'is*," Muhammad stated after his observation. "Grand Master Gilbért and I will quickly remove her body to her quarters before the palace guards arrive and there it will appear she was murdered in her sleep."

"*Oui,* I agree with Muhammad and besides, she and her spy sources were quite close to exposing this man or men and their many nefarious purposes. Helena was the main purpose of his attack, *mon ami*, but I am not saying he or they won't try to capture or kill anyone from our small band of warriors. If he wanted to kill you tonight, you wouldn't be alive speaking to us. Now put on your clothes and stay here in your room until we return. In addition, barricade both your door and window and under no circumstances leave this room. Tomorrow, I'll tell the *roi* the killer attacked you too, but you chased the murderer away. We'll leave now and place Helena's body in her chambers. Shortly, Muhammad and I'll return and guard your door until dawn." Muhammad had already picked up the *marquésa's* body and left.

After both left, I pushed several pieces of heavy furniture against my door and then a large cabinet against my tapestry-draped window. I couldn't return to sleep and lay on my blood-soaked mattress. So, I sat in one of my wooden chairs and stared at the dying embers of the fireplace. Quickly, my lugubrious demeanor changed, with a sudden surge of angry hot blood pumping through my veins. A raging sense of revenge clenched my entire body, yet my new enemy was like smoke above a fire. My sword was useless against it, but not against de Tournay. I definitely could focus my hatred at him and then immediately kill the *bâtard*, while not waiting several days. Each muscle in my body tightened like taut ropes and my restless palm ached once again to grab my sword. Yet suddenly a quiet voice blocked my further anger.

"Roberto, please use reason and not revenge to fulfill justice for my death."

To my confusion, it was Helena's voice and it emanated from some unseen location in my room. My anger melted as fast as the hot dripping candle wax from the light in my room. However, a more sinister cold feeling of emotionless planning replaced it. To efficiently kill an evil cunning man, I had to discipline my thoughts, so I could see to its completion. Suddenly and with a giddy sensation, I felt my lips curl, while thinking now I was the wolf after its prey.

The next day the *roi* found the missing guards, who obviously had been lured away, but he hung them anyway. He was to convene a court of inquiry into Helena's death. The dolorous news had traveled fast and the whole city of Zaragozza was in mourning. Everywhere I gazed, citizens, nobles, and courtiers were draping black cloths on the palace, their homes, and the merchant shops. All the members of the court dressed in black, constantly reminding me of my personal task ahead. Helena's funeral mass was planned for five days after the feast day of Saint Stephen, which postponed the secret attack on de Tournay's lair. It meant the *bâtard* would have more reinforcements and daily spy reports said he wasn't leaving, but Grand Master Gilbért and *Roi* Alfonso didn't care. The inquiry would begin the day after the funeral, which was perfect timing for me. The many up-and-coming court inquiries were an excellent cover for me to leave the palace undetected. De Tournay's death would culminate with vindication for the deaths of Gabriel, the nameless Cathar girl, Hughes's painful demise, the beheaded Romany *roi*, and my beloved Helena. However, a faint voice told me to continue my God-given quest and not seek retribution. My vengeance overpowered this thought.

Helena's funeral would occur in the Seo *Cathédrale* the next day. Just a few days earlier we were standing next to each other celebrating Christ's Mass. My entire body refused to return there and see her dead body, but fate deemed otherwise. *Roi* Alfonso had sent numerous messengers to all the realms of Iberia proclaiming the day of the funeral. The word of death always travels fast. Every Christian warrior-*moine* order was present, displaying a field of black, white, and red-colored surplices throughout the sanctuary. Even several large contingents of multicolored dressed Moorish nobles with black and white-turbaned hats. As I proceeded to the standing knot of Aragón courtiers, my eyes gazed down on the still exquisite but shrunken body of the kind woman who had pulled on my heart and mind. Pausing in front of her bier, my legs started to buckle, followed by dryness in my mouth and a faint sensation encompassed my head. Staring at her eternal slumber, I prayed she would awaken, reach up, touch my cheek, and say, "Roberto, all will be well," but it didn't happen. Instead, I crossed myself, said a quick prayer, and touched her cold hard cheek, causing my tears to drop on her body. It was now over and the beginning of justice and retribution. Her nephew, the *roi* of Toledo came along with his court. The *roi* and his retinue gave me frowns of suspicion. I felt they blamed me for her death.

After the requiem mass, I waited two days, while Grand Master Gilbért and *Roi* Alfonso made their final attack preparations. I told them my stomach burned with bile and I was too sick to attend their war council. All my efforts and thoughts now focused on how to leave Aljafería unseen. The *roi* had ordered his guard, on the threat of punishment by death, not to let anyone in or out of the palace without his personal consent.

My plan was to leave when the guards were changed at the ringing of the midnight bell. I found out through Sergeant Jacque de Hoult, the Templar commander from Toledo was leaving at that time to stop a bandit threat on the road to Toledo. This gave me the perfect opportunity to sneak out with them as a cowl-covered Templar *chevalier*. In addition, I overheard a palace guard say the *roi* had already given permission for them to leave.

Just as the midnight bell rang, followed by the changing of the guard, my foot stepped into the stirrup of my horse. Slowly, I fell in behind the last, white-mantled *chevalier* and galloped across the wooden bridge leading from the palace. Quickly, we reached the dark outskirts of Zaragozza, and my gauntlet-covered hands gently pulled back on my reins. Quietly, I drifted back from the main body of Templar *chevaliers,* while momentarily stopping for them to disappear into the ink-black night. After which I pulled my horse's head in a westerly direction and then swiftly spurred her flanks. She lunged forward with a startled gallop and headed down another pitch-black road. She repeatedly snorted into the freezing wind as my spurs edged her faster. Each *thumping* gallop of her hooves quickened my resolve to deliver justice to de Tournay. As her speed increased, my horse's *clopping* hooves resembled imaginary sounds of me slicing Marcel's body with my sword.

I rode until just before dawn, only stopping once to rest my horse, and then galloped off the main road and followed a deer trail to Alagón.

About midday, I stopped once more in a secluded copse of trees to rest my horse and ate some cheese I'd packed. After eating my fill, I became groggy for sleep, however, to stop it, I sharpened my sword with a palm-sized sharpening stone, then watered my horse in a hidden stream. I checked Helena's map for the last leg of my trip to Alagón and then mounted my horse. Darkness would be my shield to enter the village. From my map, I remembered a hidden approach to the village. It was a steep bank, which led down to a small tree-lined river.

As I continued my ride, a small river appeared heading in the direction of Alagón. The bank on my left side steadily moved higher until the adjacent plateau disappeared, just as the sun slid below the horizon in front of me. Shortly thereafter, a half-moon appeared, giving me just enough light to follow the bank and still not be seen.

Unexpectedly, my nose caught the smell of burning wood, which prompted me to stop, and then dismount, followed by me quietly tying my horse to a sycamore tree. I crawled up the bank and once reaching the crest of the bank, there appeared a glowing lit mud hut that caught my attention. Was this the small house where de Tournay planned his evil machinations? Slowly, I withdrew my sword from its scabbard and positioned it on the damp clay soil. With my other hand, I reached for my dagger and did the same. Creeping on my elbows and knees, I slowly approached the dark side of the mud house. Inside, I heard noise coming from its interior. Possibly and to my hope there weren't any other *chevaliers*.

Suddenly, a man with his back to me exited the entrance door and ambled away from the hut. He paused, gazed up at the stars, and then started urinating on the frost-covered grass. After finishing, he turned, faced in my direction, and to my instant gratification, it was de Tournay alone. Carefully, I rose in the darkness, however, De Tournay turned his head in the direction of my noise, but he turned and started to dash toward his hut. That's when I jumped from my hiding place and blocked the path to his front entrance.

"You're now facing the divine justice of Saint Michael's sword!" I screamed as a sudden bug-eyed expression of surprise came across his face. My furtive plan had momentarily surprised him, but he quickly recovered his icy composure, expressing a crooked sneer.

"So, we meet once more, Lord de Borron. You're truly a determined pilgrim. I commend your fortitude, which will make killing you so much better, so prepare to die." He ran toward me and swung his sword toward my shoulder, but I parried the downward blow and thrust forward with my dagger, aiming at his ribs. He sidestepped my lunge, catching me off balance while raising his sword for another downward blow. Quickly, I sprung upright like a released mangonel weapon and deflected this blow. Swinging to his side, once again I thrust my dagger to his side. Then suddenly, like an unexpected dream, his head separated from his shoulders. My face felt his warm salty tasting blood splatter across my face and lips, now telling me this wasn't a dream. My senses were still in disbelief as his head bounced once on the ground, after which it rolled toward my feet until it stopped at the tips of my boots. De Tournay's face stared up at me frozen with his ever-present twisted evil grin. His headless body lay near the mud hut doorway with blood still pulsating out of his neck stump. I stood there in a state of bewilderment, not knowing if I had struck the fatal blow and didn't realize it, but my answer came quickly.

CHAPTER XXIII

"Lord Robert de Borron," came a raspy familiar voice out of the darkness. "I overheard your conversation with Sergeant Jacque de Hoult and followed you . . . until I found a quicker route," he gasped. "I couldn't let you steal my revenge for my *hermana's* death."

The voice still didn't reveal itself, but a huge dark outline of a man appeared. I then realized it was the lord high chamberlain, Rodrigo. Out of the darkness staggered his gigantic form holding a dripping blood-red sword. Rodrigo's neck, back, and chest were penetrated with a total of eight crossbow quarrels, making him seem like a ghastly dying porcupine. Apparently, he killed a guard inside the hut after he was struck by his quarrels.

"I loved my younger *hermana* with all my being and . . . made a vow at an early age neither man nor beast would ever harm her . . ." He collapsed to the ground. Both of his ham-sized hands motioned for me to draw closer.

Quickly, I rushed to comfort him, bent down, and then with each of my hands carefully raised his head as he tried to speak.

"Lord Robert . . . Helena loved you dearly and I know you felt the same in your heart. Please tell me this is so before I die."

Rodrigo's brown teary-filled eyes waited for my reply.

"*Si*, it's true, my *amigo*."

He didn't speak anymore, yet he had enough strength to give me a final smile and then gasped his last breath. Finally, Rodrigo's hand released his sword and it fell to his side.

He had killed de Tournay and one of his men, leaving me wanting in receiving my justice. However, that night I buried him in a shallow grave with my helmet as a shovel at Alagón. Later, *Roi* Alfonso would reinter him at Zaragozza as a martyr and hero with full royal honors.

I didn't arrive back at Zaragozza until almost daybreak. Slowly, I trotted my horse through the portcullis as the sun was sinking behind the palace's lone square-shaped tower.

"Lord Roberto de Borron, you seem tired!" shouted one of the palace sergeant guards.

"*Si*, my *amigo*, more than you realize," I replied, slowly dismounting from my horse.

I strolled to my room, unlocked my repaired door, and then entered. Yet, I didn't check to see if the *Sangraal* tome was still secure. At this moment, I didn't care if someone had stolen it, for my concern and enthusiasm had vanished. There was a crucifix above my bed, which instantly drew me toward it. Promptly, I fell on my knees and prayed. My prayers continued until I had completed ninety-nine *Pater Nosters*. After which I fell asleep, accompanied by the same reoccurring dream for the rest of the night and early morning. It was an image of de Tournay's head flying through the dark night.

A loud pounding at my door suddenly jarred my groggy head. At first, I thought it was Rodrigo.

"Where have you been, Lord Robert?" reverberated the loud voice of Grand Master Gilbért. "*Roi* Alfonso's men have searched the entire fortress for you. I was just about to send Muhammad to check the roads."

"Grand Master Gilbért, please wait until I let you in, for I have some news of de Tournay's demise." Instantly, there was silence behind the door as I unbolted all the latches, then I quickly opened it. He entered with his dark eyes as round as walnuts.

"He's dead, you say?"

"*Oui*, he was killed by Lord Chamberlain Rodrigo," I replied. I then recounted my travel, travails, and surprising information.

He remained silent and frozen in one spot.

"You need to send your men to retrieve his head and put it on the tip of one of their lances," I said.

"I will have my men present the head to the *roi*. In addition, Rodrigo's body will return to Zaragozza with full religious honors. It's a surprise to me that the lord high chamberlain was *Marquésa* Helena's *frère*. To my knowledge, not even court gossip knew of this relationship, but the *marquésa* was excellent at keeping secrets. Now, let's convey this good news to the *roi*."

Right away, I locked the door, and followed him to the *roi's* chamber, whereupon I repeated to the *roi* about de Tournay's overdue demise. However, we agreed de Tournay was just a small evil puppet guided by a greater evil, Cardinal Folquet. We knew his tentacles of power were everywhere and cutting off one didn't kill the beast.

Roi Alfonso seemed quite pleased how de Tournay died, yet like me, he wished he could have personally executed the evil *bâtard*.

"Grand Master Gilbért, I want to accompany your men to Alagón and help retrieve Rodrigo's body and carry de Tournay's head on a spear to every village in my *royaume*. It's the least I can do to avenge both their deaths. When you arrive in Toledo, tell the *roi* of Castile I'll send him de Tournay's head in a wooden box when I return. In addition, convey to him how we'll miss Helena's kind heart and tell him her memory will live with us forever. When I complete my tour, I will immediately leave and travel to Rome to see the *Santo Padre*. Folquet has seen his last days as a *principe* of the *santo iglesia*.

I gave *Roi* Alfonso a final bow of respect, and then said *au revoir*, and praised him for his hospitality. Quickly, I left his secret chambers, while Grand Master Gilbért stayed behind to discuss with the *roi* what to say to the Holy *Père*. From the inner sanctum of the palace, I hurried to my room. As I approached my door, Esperanza met me there.

"*Mon Seigneur Baron* Robert, please wait before you step inside your room," she said, with her eyes red-rimmed. She handed me a small, sealed missive.

"*Marquésa* Helena wanted me to give you this note before you left. She couldn't bear to hand it to you in person. I guess now it doesn't make any different, yet what it says explains why she wanted you to have it if she had lived."

Without warning, she stood on the tips of her shoes and gave me a long gentle kiss on my right cheek, followed by her *au revoir.*

"*Vaya con Dios,* Roberto," she said, slowly turning to leave with tears streaming down her cheeks. My eyes stayed on her movements until she disappeared down a dark side corridor. What would she do now that she wasn't a lady-in-waiting for a *princesse*?

I entered my room, and then latched the bolts behind me, then I broke Helena's royal seal on her note while seating myself along one of my long writing tables.

> *Dear Roberto,*
>
> *By the time you read this message, you will be leaving the Aljafería Palace. I pray for your safety and hope you find the next set of holy Sangraal parchments. You are a gifted man with many artistic talents and our Lord and Savior favors you. Please forgive a lonely widow for her earthly desires and affection for you. My heart will always be with you throughout all eternity. Mon chéri, please don't forget me.*
>
> *Helena*

Both anger and sorrow welled up inside me after reading her note, but I had experienced so much sorrow and hatred on my quest. At once, tears streamed down my face. My heart told me we would meet again in another lifetime. At that very moment, a voice called my name, which stopped my bawling. It was Mary Magdaleine speaking to me once more. Oh, how I now needed her counsel.

"Robert, remember what Yeshua said while being nailed to the cross, '*Abba*, forgive them, for they do not know what they do.' Heed our Savior's words to finish your quest. Hatred and anger are a double-edged sword that will cut down both your body and mind."

Her voice vanished as quickly as it had entered, followed by a loud pounding fist on my door. I tucked the note into my surcoat and heard Grand Master Gilbért speak.

"Lord Robert, it's almost time to leave. Please let me in."

I jumped up from my chair, raced to the door, and then unlatched it. He cautiously entered with his usual cat-like movements.

"We leave before dawn breaks. Have your horse and the *Sangraal* book ready to ride right after the divine office of Matins. You're the sole person who knows of our departure time."

"But how will the others know when to leave?" I was confused.

"They'll be surprised and that's what I want. It's sixty-seven leagues to Toledo and it will be at least ten days to reach there. You see to awakening Muhammad and our dog, while I'll roust the sergeants, which should keep them off guard. Secrecy and our unexpected departure will give us some protection."

Grand Master Gilbért abruptly finished, turned, grabbed the door handle, and then exited the room. After he left, I sensed his angst. Oh, how I longed to see my *épouse* and *fils*, yet Mary Magdaleine's recent words still echoed in my mind, reminding of my God-appointed destiny.

I received little sleep during the night and had no trouble hearing the morning *chapelle* bells, causing me to arrive ahead of the others for Matins. However, like me, Grand Master Gilbért was ahead of the rest of his men.

"Did you sleep well?" he asked.

"*Non*," I replied.

"Me too. I worried all night, wondering which one of my sergeants was the traitor." He glanced over his shoulder to see if they were approaching. "I pondered the whole night what our betrayer's motives are. Neither one of them has ever disobeyed my orders or given me any doubt of their loyalty. Yet, I fear the cardinal may have threatened their families."

As we proceeded into the *chapelle*, our fearless leader's drooped head reflected disappointment. This was the first time I noticed the grand master in such a melancholy mood.

After Matins, we met in the large columned courtyard. His pinch-faced expression and gloomy demeanor prompted me to speak my mind.

"Why don't you have both men arrested and detain them until our quest is over?" I asked.

"Lord Robert, that sounds easy to do, but I am using each one of them as bait to catch the cardinal and anyone else associated with him. Besides, how do I not know both men are spies? The cardinal is a cunning and evil man, which has considerable power over the Curia and the Holy *Père*. It will require more than a large sword to cut through his thick evil web and permanently destroy it. I want to lay as many snares as possible to finish him off."

Without warning, his chain-mailed fist slammed against one of the palace's many ornate-topped columns. His new behavior instantly reversed itself, which gave me a heady brew of confidence.

At that moment, *Roi* Alfonso approached us. Along with the *roi*, Muhammad and *Abad* Miguel brought our riding horses and the big Andalusians packed with supplies and weapons. Darting toward me was *Noir Ombre* wagging his tail and happily barking to see me. He stopped in front of my horse and sat, waiting for me to give him a command, which I motioned with my right hand, by moving it behind me, causing him to rise, and then he trotted behind me, while I waved my left hand for him to stop, forcing him to sit alongside me. He followed all the hand commands perfectly that Muhammad had taught me, warranting a vigorous rub on his big head.

"Let's mount," came the now confident voice of Grand Master Gilbért. "We must reach the Rio Jiloca before nightfall." Our warrior leader put one foot in the stirrup.

"Lord Roberto," *Roi* Alfonso said. "Rest assured I'll do everything I can by using my royal power to obtain justice against Cardinal Folquet. You just concentrate on your God-given quest to seek out the next set of *Sangraal* parchments. I swear before our Creator to see to the cardinal's arrest." He then gave me a large embrace.

"*Merci beaucoup,* Your *Altesse,* and I would like to say your hospitality was beyond belief. One day, after God is finished with me, I will return to your *royaume,* and we'll reminisce about old times. So, until we meet again, *au revoir, mon ami.*"

"*Si,* and now *vaya con Dios,* my *amigo.*"

I mounted my horse to leave. Quickly, we galloped out of the great Aljafería Palace, crossing the long wooden bridge with Muhammad and *Noir Ombre* racing ahead. I glanced one last time at the Moorish *château,* thinking my stay there was part pleasant, yet filled with anguish. However, Helena's dimpled smile image caused me to remember the pleasant part as we galloped down the road toward Toledo.

"Lord Robert, you seem in serious thought," Grand Master Gilbért said, as his horse trotted alongside mine. "Are you still melancholy about *Marquésa* Helena's death?"

"*Oui,* I still see myself responsible for her untimely death. Tonight, I would like to speak to you in private once the camp is completed."

We said nothing more to each other, until Muhammad returned with a scouting report, after which we stopped, dismounted, and gathered around to discuss it. He said three leagues in front of us and behind was clear of any travelers or *chevaliers,* making it safe to camp for the night. Quickly, we cooled down our horses. Afterward, we gathered some dry limbs for a cooking fire. Muhammad didn't eat anything, but immediately grabbed his bedroll and prepared for sleep. Later, he would repeat his scouting patrol in the same territory, while one of us slept. I was to relieve Grand Master Gilbért from his sentry duty late in the night, which would give me time to discuss my personal concerns with him.

After a hasty meal of dried rabbit meat, I fell asleep but was quickly awakened by one of our horses emanating a nervous *whinnying* sound. Immediately, I jumped up, drew my sword, and silently crept toward the tied horses to investigate. Once near the picket rope, a sudden black image moved toward me, yet it was only a stray cow, which gave me a much-needed laugh. Gazing up at the moon, surrounded by its ink-colored sky, the stars told me it was time to relieve Grand Master

Gilbért. As I rounded a group of large boulders, which hid our camp, a cold north wind struck my face just as I caught the dark silhouette of the grand master.

"I see you are here to relieve me. Now you can tell me what you wanted to discuss."

"You spoke earlier today about using both sergeants as bait to snare Cardinal Folquet. How are you going to accomplish this and catch the right sergeant who is our spy?" I sat down next to him.

"The cardinal's evil nature, particularly his greed for power and hubris, will cause him to use all the political tools of his office to bear down on us like the heel of his boot. The more power and control he obtains, the more his evil pride grows. Yet, by doing so, he leaves more implicating documentation, dead bodies, tortured victims, and a standing army of enemies."

"Why not use the evidence of his many mistresses and *bâtard* children? Shouldn't that be sufficient evidence to remove him from office?"

"*Non*, they are easily bought off or just suddenly disappear. We must catch him doing one of his evil acts and pray we have willing living witnesses to testify against him. *Mon coeur* tells me he is using others as an advantage to manipulate one of my sergeants. Confidently, my trap in due time will tell us. Now Lord Robert, let me leave you and obtain some much-needed sleep, for we have a long ride ahead of us tomorrow."

"*Merci*, for answering my questions, I hope you sleep well." He stood to leave and slowly strolled along a row of boulders until he disappeared behind a huge rock. Thus, leaving me to count the stars on my watch and ponder what he had just told me. His explanation made sense in drawing the cardinal into a trap, but we were all part of the bait too in capturing the cardinal.

Without warning, to my right came the soft trotting sound of someone or something rushing toward me. I tried to focus my eyes on a moving object, yet all I observed was the dark horizon. It wasn't the cow this time, for the footfalls were distinctively different in sound. Was this the Brethren of Purity attacking us with their poison-tipped daggers, while planning to murder us in our sleep?

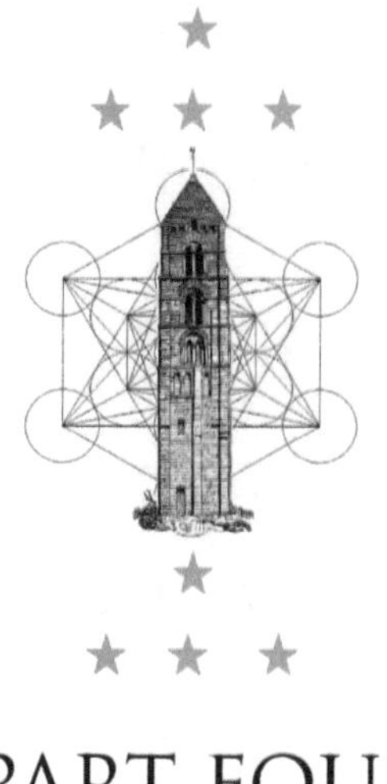

PART FOUR

Metatron and Star Tower

CHAPTER XXIV

Toledo

January

Anno Domini 1191

I started to alert Grand Master Gilbért but stopped when I felt the *thumping* of a tail against my chassis. It was *Noir Ombre,* invisible by the dark hair on his body, however, his muzzle pushed my palm upward wanting me to recognize him. Suddenly, all my tense knot-like muscles relaxed, followed by a sense of relief on my nerves.

"Pilgrim, you're fortunate that your throat wasn't slit," came the familiar disembodied voice of Muhammad. "You must move constantly if you're on sentry duty, *mon ami.*" Slowly, he materialized like a dark wraith in the ink-black night. His silent creeping movements appeared to make his footsteps float across the frosty ground.

"We have nothing to fear from the cardinal's men because they're no more since Marcel de Tournay received his just reward. That *Shaytan jinn* now has a new home in hell's fire, but I sense a greater threat that is close by. This threat is like a nest of hidden coiled serpents in the bushes. They will kill you before you know it." He shook his head. "Now, I am retiring, while *Noir Ombre* keeps you company on your watch. Trust his senses, *mon ami*, for he can see and hear beyond mortal man's narrow reality."

Slowly, he turned from me and silently melted back into the darkness of the night. Both *Noir Ombre* and I moved constantly during the remaining night, partly out of the fear of an ambush and partly from the cold night air. Later, Grand Master Gilbért relieved me, immediately I assumed his place at the campfire, and quickly fell asleep.

It didn't seem I had slept at all when Muhammad nudged me to awaken early the next day. My sleepy eyes focused on a red-streaked sky as I mounted to the leave camp.

We headed in a southwestern direction, chased by the sun, but our travels became even slower when we encountered several heavy rainstorms. Now the road became the consistency of rye dough, which slowed our ride to a crawl.

Suddenly, on the slate-gray horizon appeared Muhammad galloping toward us, with his horse's back hooves kicking up large clods of mud as he approached.

"There's a scouting party of *dāwiyyas* or warrior-*moines* a league in front of us, leaving just a day's ride to *Tolati-tola*," Muhammad shouted while pulling on his reins to stop. "In addition, the road behind us is clear of travelers." He fell in alongside us.

The rainstorm stopped just as we reached the Rio Tagus, still leaving dark granite-colored clouds above us. From the river back, we followed a road for about a half a league, until we spotted a large four-towered fortress perched atop a tall hillock. The low-lying clouds seemed to skim across the crenels the closer we approached the town. It was a perfect place to build a fortress. The fortress and town sat on a high cliff-faced peninsula of land surrounded by both a stone wall and the Rio Tagus. A high curtain wall of stone protected the back landside.

"Where's the *Château* San Servando?" I asked while gazing down the river and wondering where I would rest tonight.

"It's on the other side of that arched Roman bridge," answered Grand Master Gilbért, pointing to an ornate bridge, which spanned the Rio Tagus.

My eyes fixated toward the far end of the bridge that terminated on the same bank cliff that we were traveling. The bridge road forked coming off the bridge, with our road continuing; the other rose a steep distance to a finger of land that overlooked the bridge approach on both sides of the river. There above the river and viewing the town of Toledo was the square-shaped *Château* San Servando. It was quite apparent to the naked eye; the fortress protected the bridge approaching the town.

"Toledo appears as if it's burning." I gazed at a blue haze of smoke surrounding the whole town.

"*Oui*, it's the steel ovens and forges spouting forth their smoke," Grand Master Gilbért said. "It's where we obtained our fine fighting swords. In addition, less than a hundred years ago, El Cid conquered this town or as he's rightly called, *Don* Rodrigo Diaz de Vivar, and *Roi* Alfonso VI. After the *Reconquista*, it became the Christian capitol of all Iberia.

"*Abad* Miguel and Chaplain Jeremiah will be waiting for us at the San Servando fortress, and I hope they have discovered some new clues in finding the next set of holy parchments."

Slowly, we followed the rim road until we came to the Puente de Alcántara bridge entrance, as our warrior leader called it, and from there we headed uphill a short distance. San Servando wasn't as impressive as the Calatayud fortress, but maybe a quarter of its size. However, its compact structure and many crenellations made it appear as a gigantic square stone with a royal crown. It seemed impossible to me; no hostile army could continue across the bridge without coming under fire of the fortress. The fortress road and *château* had an excellent view in all directions of the town of Toledo. In addition, the opposite high riverbank would make it difficult for an attacking army by boats to storm up its sides and overrun the town.

"What is that large perfectly square-shaped fortress in the center of the town?" I asked Grand Master Gilbért.

"It's the royal fortress of El Alcazar, and eventually we will travel there to pay homage to *Roi* Alfonso VIII, nephew to the martyred *Marquésa* Helena, may God bless her soul." We both crossed ourselves.

I wasn't anticipating meeting him, for he and his courtiers were at his aunt's funeral and court gossip said they hated me. *Roi* Alfonso VIII de Castile thought I was responsible for both Helena's and Rodrigo's deaths.

In the distance, coming out of the portcullis, galloped Chaplain Jeremiah, and *Abad* Miguel, escorted by eight *chevalier* Templars.

"Hail, *Su Excelencia*!" shouted his *fils,* as he pulled up the reins to his trotting horse. "It appears you made it to Toledo without any problems, *si*?"

"*Oui*, and do you have some good news leading us to the next set of parchments?" his *père* asked.

"*Si*, we'll discuss this matter after the both of you are settled in the fortress," the young chaplain said, leaving me in suspense.

"*Abad* Miguel, I hope you're well after the long trip from Zaragozza." I knew the physical and mental strain he had endured.

"God has given me the faith to persevere and *gracias* for asking." He gave me a toothy grin.

The escort of *chevaliers* joined behind us in quick order as Grand Master Gilbért led the way up the steep path to the Templar fortress. The small *château* walls and sparse towers bristled with arbalest holes strategically placed to rain down arrows in all directions. The keep was U-shaped and appeared later after the completion of the fortress. The main gate entrance, which had the same ubiquitous horseshoe-shaped designed arch, which most buildings possessed in Iberia, overlooked the river, bridge, and town. As we approached the arched entrance, there appeared a second interior entrance with the same shaped arch, where a bevy of squires raced from carrying box-shaped steps for us to dismount. Somewhere inside the fortress, I heard the droning sound of voices coming from some unseen interior *chapelle*.

"Lord Robert, please follow me to your cell," Chaplain Jeremiah said, as he started climbing up the musty smelling set of stone steps. Upon reaching a short narrow corridor, we strolled down it, until we stopped in front of a small wooden door. This door too had the same pattée cross design carved into its surface as the many other Poor-Soldiers of Christ monasteries.

"I am sorry your room isn't up to the same standards as the *Château* Maluenda or the Aljafería Palace, but don't forget we're poor warriors of Christ and your cell is better than our communal sleeping quarters." Chaplain Jeremiah grabbed his large ring of keys attached to his sash, found the proper one, and proceeded to unlock the cell door.

We entered the small room. "Please sit down, Lord Robert." The young chaplain pointed to what seemed similar to a child-sized wooden bed. He then bolted the door, then sat on a small three-legged stool. "*Abad* Miguel should arrive shortly," he continued.

Just then, there came a gentle knock on the door. "It's me, *Abad* Miguel."

Chaplain Jeremiah jumped up from his stool, reached for one of the sliding bolts, unlocked the door, and then let him into the room.

"Well, I see we're all here to discuss the possible whereabouts of the next *Sangraal* parchments," *Abad* Miguel said with a mischievous wink from his eye.

"*Si*, Your Excellency," replied Chaplain Jeremiah. "Lord Robert, I will let *Abad* Miguel inform you about our forthcoming meeting."

"Lord Robert, we have arranged a meeting tomorrow with two of the greatest scholars in both Gaul and Iberia. One is a *Judio* and the other is a Moor. The Moor is here in secret to confer with his *compadre* and fellow scholar, the Almohad Caliph Yaqub al-Mansur. His court jurists have banned him from all of Iberia and if captured he is facing execution. We are quite fortunate to have them here at the same time, while we're searching for the *santo* parchments."

"What are their names?" I inquired.

"The Moor is called Averroes or occasionally Ibn Rushd. The *Judio's* name is Yitzhak the Blind or Rabbi Yitzhak Saggi Nehor, which means of much light. Both men are polymaths in numerous books of knowledge. Some say Rabbi Yitzhak possesses a mysterious book, which tells of supernatural powers."

Suddenly, an unexpected knock emanated from my door.

"Let me in now," came the urgent voice of Grand Master Gilbért. "Lord Robert, I've some serious news to tell you. Hurry and unbolt the door."

His *fils* was standing close to the door and quickly reached for the bolt and slid it back. Grand Master Gilbért thrust himself into the room, bearing a furrowed brow, and hurriedly acknowledged us.

"Lord Robert, I have just heard some terrible information. *Roi* Alfonso VIII has given you only two days to rest and then you must leave. He and his court still hold you responsible for his Aunt Helena's death. I swore to him, may God forgive me, you are a *chevalier* of Christ and in my custody. This only gives us two days to find the next set of holy parchments before we must leave. We can't waste one moment in our search for those blessed words. At first light, have Chaplain Jeremiah, *Abad* Miguel, and Muhammad arrange for you to meet the holy men who may help us. If we can't conclude our quest in two days, your arrest and execution are possible. My influence here is untenable, for the *roi* doesn't favor our order, but only that of the *chevaliers* of Saint John of the Hospitallers." I noticed a slight twitch coming from one of his eyelids.

"So, our entire quest for Saint Joseph's additional parchments, if they still exist, is predicated on the information of two heretics?" I asked, a lump forming in my throat.

"*Oui*, I am afraid so, *mon ami*. This is what it has come down to in risking our lives, yet don't despair. In two days, we'll leave immediately and attempt the search at another time."

I didn't like the sound of his answer, however, after the many dangers we had faced and survived, I had to trust him. Quickly, he left as fast as he came into the room, leaving me with *Noir Ombre*.

An inner voice told me to leave Toledo now. Yet, to my surprise, *Noir Ombre* traipsed over to my side and licked my hand, possibly sensing my distress.

"Lord Robert, *Abad* Miguel and I will see you at dawn," Chaplain Jeremiah said. "Let *Noir Ombre* assuage your apprehensions; dogs sense our troubles more than we realize. Good rest and the morning daylight will increase your insight in what to ask these scholarly men." He patted *Noir Ombre's* head. "I must leave now; may our Lord and Savior calm your angst. *Bonsoir*, Lord Robert, we'll see you tomorrow."

Noir Ombre did calm me with his presence, for sleep came quickly and so did dawn. Once again, a pounding fist on my cell door shook my slumber.

"Lord Robert, are you ready to leave?" asked Chaplain Jeremiah with an anxious high-pitched voice.

"*Oui*, let me put on my chain mail coif and sword," I replied. Slowly, I ambled to my door and unlatched the bolt. To my surprise, he was holding a steaming bowl of *qahwa.*

"I thought you might want this before meeting our religious scholars," the young chaplain announced.

"*Merci beaucoup*, you did anticipate my desire for the magic elixir, but let me wash my face before we leave." I moved toward a flagon of water and towels. Quickly, I splashed the chilly water on my face, which instantly forced my mind to sweep the clouds of sleep from my thoughts. With only two sips of the brew, my mind was now ready to interact with our forthcoming savants.

"I'm ready," I stated. Yet, before leaving, I secured our *Sangraal* codex behind a loose-mortared stone in my cell. Upon reaching the bailey area, our horses were ready to ride. There saddled were *Abad* Miguel and Muhammad ready to meet us.

"Lord Robert, did you sleep well while *Noir Ombre* kept you safe?" the *abad* asked.

"*Oui*, and see, he's racing ahead of us," I said, as *Noir Ombre* started barking for us to leave.

We galloped out of the bailey area with *Noir Ombre* leading us onto the descending fortress road. Quickly, we reached the main rim road and then crossed through the tower command post of the ancient Roman bridge. The new year sky was a clear azure color and the water current was swiftly gurgling past as we made our way up the hill road toward Toledo. While passing the town wall, the acrid smell of the many blacksmith shops and foundries attacked my nostrils. We followed Chaplain Jeremiah through numerous narrow uphill streets until we came to a small sandstone building next to an old Moorish mosque. Surrounding the mosque were several prosperous merchant shops starting their day with customers wanting the best foods or merchandise.

"Lord Robert, we'll dismount here," Chaplain Jeremiah said. "Let's hide the horses and tell *Noir Ombre* to stay in those trees behind the building next to the old mosque. After tying your horse, follow me, but don't let the *chevaliers* of Saint John see us enter the adjacent building next to the former mosque. The mosque is now a Christian *chapelle* called the Mezquita del Cristo de la Luz and guarded by the Hospitallers. Stay behind the tree line."

Quietly, we dismounted, tied our horses, and Muhammad gave a hand signal for *Noir Ombre* to stay. Slowly, we crept forward, while hunched over, using the copse of large trees to hide behind. The weak light of dawn gave us some additional cover to conceal our movements, yet there was just enough light for me to notice the unusual architecture of the small mosque. Its shape was a perfect square, except for the rear of the building, which apparently had an apse added after the Christian conquest of Toledo. The front part of the structure or entrances had the ever-present horseshoe-shaped arches, of which there were three. However, what further drew my attention were two things. The front façade, over the arches, had six fish-shaped designs carved into the upper half of the building. On the flat roof stood a square-shaped tiled dome, which at one time was a minaret as Muhammad called the structure.

Chaplain Jeremiah knocked on the large iron-edged door, and we waited a while before it opened. Standing in front of us stood a young boy about eight years old. His feet were bare, and he wore a loose stripe-colored caftan with his head topped in a white-colored round hat.

"They're here!" the young boy shouted. "Two *dāwiyyas* or warrior *hermanos*, a Christian *santo* man, and a dark-skinned one wearing a huge *jambiya* dagger. One of the *dāwiyya* may be the *rasul* you told me to look out for." The boy glanced back into the dark interior of the building. Shortly thereafter, a wise-appearing older man came forth.

"*Salaam alaikum.* Please come into my humble *madrasa.* I am Averroes or as some call me Ibn Rushd. Please enter and partake of our hospitality and don't pay attention to my noisy *nieto.* It's not often he gazes upon a Saracen emir from the Levant and a *señor* from Northern Burgundy."

The Moor was elegantly dressed in a green silk robe with his large white turban giving him the air of a scholar. In his right hand, bearing clean-trimmed nails, he held some unknown scholarly text. He was about my height and had a close-cut piebald-colored beard. Quietly, he led us into the dark interior of the building, where all the walls had wooden shelves replete with books. Several long trestle-shaped tables were stacked with more books than I had time to count, and at the end of the row of tables, a dimly lit man sat in a high back wooden chair.

CHAPTER XXV

"Grand *Mufti* Ibn Rushd," Muhammad said, as he bowed before the old *ulama* or scholar. "It is an honor you have invited us here and to be in your presence."

"*Gracias* for the compliment, Emir Muhammad, but let me introduce my esteemed colleague and fellow *ulama*, Rabbi Yitzhak Saggi Nehor."

The small man rose from his seat while supporting himself with a long wooden staff. He appeared a little older than I did, yet he stared at us with a fixed gaze. Both of his eyes were a solid milky-white color and absent of any pupils. He was obviously blind, yet he knew where we stood in the dark room.

"It's a pleasure to meet so many *caballeros* from afar, but which one of you is the *señor* from Northern Burgundy?" the shawl-draped *Judio* asked.

"I am *Señor* Robert de Borron," I answered.

"*Si*, you're the one wearing the sacred hamsa, my *amigo*," the rabbi stated to my disbelief. How did a blind man know I was wearing it, for even if he could see the hamsa, it lay hidden under my chain mail?

"Please sit next to me, my *amigo*, for you were expected before Chaplain Jeremiah and *Abad* Miguel spoke to us."

"*Si*, *Allah* has willed it, and it's your *qadar* or destiny, *Señor* Robert de Borron," Averroes added.

"You can see that I am blind, but don't let my physical condition prevent you from seeking my counsel. *El Shaddai* has blessed my other senses to see many different dimensions of life. My mind's eye can still see, and that is how I knew you were wearing the sacred talisman. Is this not true, *Señor* Robert?"

"*Oui*, or I mean *si*," I quickly answered.

"*Si*, indeed, you are protected from the evil eye, and I sense I am in the presence of a *rasul* or *navi* sent for an important duty," Averroes commented.

"The amulet about your neck harkens back to the time of *Moshe*. *Moshe's* sister, Miriam, received it by the hand of *El Shaddai*. However, my colleague says it was given to Fatima, the prophet's daughter," the rabbi stated and gave a slight grin.

"May peace blessings be upon them," Averroes said. "And the five fingers represent the five pillars of Islam or, as our Shiite *hermanos* would say, the first five patriarchs of Islam, which they call the Five People of the Cloak."

"I disagree with my Muslim *hermano;* it represents the first five books of our Torah or *Moshe's* law. In addition, it signifies *heh*, the fifth letter of the Hebrew alphabet. *Heh* is one of the many names my people call *El Shaddai*. However, my *amigo*, you didn't come here to hear two flawed mortal men of the Creator argue."

Once again, the number five or *penta* was spoken with a connection to God. And it stupefied me that a blind rabbi and a grand *mufti*, as Muhammad called him, sensed what was hidden around my neck.

"*Abbé* Jeremiah told us," Averroes stated, "that you seek the light of *Issa* or as your People of the Book call Him, Jesus, may peace and blessings be upon Him. It's important to have the light first before you can understand the words for the mortal flesh. In your book about creation, *Allah* said let there be light; and there was light. Moreover, *Allah* saw that the light was good; and *Allah* separated the light from the darkness. You must have this light to see the hidden meaning of *Allah*, or *El Shaddai*, as my *amigo* calls his Almighty. He has placed hidden meaning in the *Qur'an*, which my faith calls bāṭin, and as well for the Torah, which certain mortals may find. However, you need the divine tools of *Issa* or Muhammad, may peace and blessings be upon them, to seek out these hidden meanings."

"*Si*," *Abad* Miguel added. "If you think you can understand God's mysteries, it's not from God. Saint Augustine's divine insight knew this."

Averroes nodded. "Your *wali taqi* Juan, or Saint Juan, said it best, 'In the beginning was the Word and the Word was with *Allah*, and the Word was *Allah*.'"

"*Si*, Averroes is correct," Yitzhak said. "Symbols, numbers, and your mind's eye will help peel back *El Shaddai's* occult meanings. *Señor* Roberto, I see you have the light of understanding given to you by the Prophet Jesus, but not His spiritual view of understanding. I detect your heart is bound with revenge, yet you're struggling with trying to unbind it with forgiveness. You must quickly embrace this forgiveness for your enemies, otherwise, revenge and hatred will interfere with your quest for the hidden words you seek. A heart chained with hatred, *El Shaddai* won't enter. My colleague once said that Plato stated, 'to understand all, is to forgive all.'"

"*Oui*, Yitzhak is right," Chaplain Jeremiah added. "For Saint Paul also said, 'It's love that matters the greatest of all, and the loving heart is dearer to God than the wisest of wise sayings.'"

"Of those who seek the holy parchments you desire, many are ill-prepared to face the divine light of *El Shaddai*, though his *Shekhinah* is no further than our own spirit. However, there are many paths the mind's eye comprehends, but only one leads to the true path and it's our gift to show you the right one," Yitzhak Saggi Nehor said.

"Several months ago, a man named Guiot de Provins started his search for the correct path but failed to complete his quest. His attempt left him crippled and later he joined a cloister as a Cluniac *hermano*. He, like you, was a troubadour and a writer of letters. Beware, my *amigo*, what we'll show you is like Jacob's ladder. It's man's ascent to a higher level of consciousness to reach the cosmic

Tree of Life and be in the presence of *El Shaddai*. Enoch, Jacob, Moses, Yeshua, and Muhammad all saw this celestial ladder. It can lead the earthly righteous and faithful to the kingdom of heaven. Man doesn't need eyes to see in climbing this *kodesh* ladder. How many times have you searched for something, and it was right before you? You will develop your inner vision to expand your soul's sight. You must reach deep into yourself for the *nous* and use it for your *kodesh* quest. However, my *amigo*, each rung you climb may be fraught with danger."

"*Si*, my blind friend, Rabbi Yitzhak, is right in warning you, for my Sufi brethren would say you are on a spiritual journey or *lataif* to regain the divine knowledge lost by Adam. You seek what Adam lost, my *amigo*, to eat the fruit from the Tree of Life," Averroes said with a dour frown.

This new news was upsetting, with a lump sensation forming in my throat. To me, it seemed incredulous the religious advice I heard, especially coming from two infidels helping me find the hidden parchments of a Christian apostle. However, who was I to judge these two scholarly men? I was just a rural nobleman and *trouvère*.

"*Señor* Roberto, you're like the seventh patriarch from Adam, Enoch, who was given *kodesh* books by a *malach* or an angel called Uriel," the blind cleric said in a soothing voice. "Enoch first comprehended the Tree of Life when he traversed the heavens with *El Shaddai*. Some prophets say he is the *padre* of mathematics and astronomy. Furthermore, I believe the more we understand mathematics, the nearer we come to *El Shaddai*. In addition, Enoch left his sacred books of knowledge and prophecy for his great-grandson, Noah, to use in building the ark. Yet, I believe the *Malachs* Uriel, Gabriel, and Miguel gave Enoch even greater insight and prophecy. He divulged to us mortals an excellent communication device called the *Kabbalah*, which is one of several ways to seek out the infinite wisdom of *El Shaddai*. The *Kabbalah* is what we will show you how to use."

"The Patriarch Enoch is called Idris by my people," Averroes added. "May peace and blessings be upon him. In the *Qur'an, surah* 19, verses 56–57, it says he was exalted by *Allah* to a high station in life. In addition, ancient scholars have written he was the prophet for philosophers and the first man to use pen and ink."

"But what is this *Kabbalah*?" I asked, feeling quite relaxed in their presence.

"Later we'll explain, but first we'll speak some more about sacred numbers before preparing you for the *Kabbalah*," Yitzhak answered. "As your Christian saint, Isidore from Seville, said, 'Remove numbers from all things and everything in the universe perishes.' It's quite apparent to you there's a significance in the numbers five and eight. The Greek stoic philosopher Boethius said, 'Numbers can guide the human from perceptible things to the invisible truth in *El Shaddai*, thus the material to the immaterial. You must fully use these sacred numbers to reach a higher level of consciousness to obtain the *santo* parchments you seek. *Abad* Miguel has shown me copies of the symbolic drawings you have received, which my fellow colleague and I have reviewed. *Señor* de Borron, they are quite impressive; your powerful sources of information are spiritual in nature. Yet, this information has come together by a divine hand. As Prophet Isaiah wrote, 'Symbols tell a story, but you must have the key first,' however, just not the numbers by themselves, but numbers in symbolic geometric shapes. According to Plato and Pythagoras, the art of passing divine wisdom is through geometric forms as symbols. In Pythagoras's Greek school of geometry, the pentagram star sheds its five points of light on the initiate. We believe you must seek out your *santo* parchments by a five, six, seven, or eight-pointed star illuminating from above the parchments' hidden place. Especially, a five or eight-pointed star shining on the line of King David." The rabbi gave me a weak smile.

"*Si*, there's the pseudepigraphical work of the legendary Testament of Solomon, which says *Rey Sulymon* was given a ring by the Archangel Miguel," Averroes said. "On that ring was a pentagram star and the wondrous name of *Allah*. The ring lets him command both evil and good *jinns* to cut and lift the enormous stones in helping build the great Temple of *Sulymon.* The old Celts of Iberia called this sigil the Druid's Foot. I believe the pentagram star is more than a signpost but will indicate what is asked from the writer of the ancient parchments you seek." What he said confirmed what Jesus the Christ asked of Saint Joseph de Arimathea.

"Two other points I might add," Rabbi Yitzhak interjected. "The pentagram star, at one time was found carved on the walls of Jerusalem representing the symbol of the city of Jerusalem. In addition, some say this was the shape of the star over the manger when your *Maishiach,* Jesus, was born.

"In our *santo* order of the Poor-*Caballeros* of *Christo*," Chaplain Jeremiah added, "the pentagram star represents infinity, connectivity, and oneness too. Also an early Christian symbol representing Jesus the Christ."

"The polygon shapes—tetragon, pentagon, hexagon, heptagon, and octagon—I see as keys to unlock the door to end your quest," Rabbi Yitzhak said. "Now will start your meditative training to understand the seventy-two names of *El Shaddai*, preparing you for the thirty-two paths of the *Kabbalah*."

Suddenly, a high-pitched scream echoed from the back of the *madrasa*, followed by the rapid scampering of feet.

"*Abuelo*! *Abuelo*! *Abuelo*! There's an evil *jinn* hiding in the trees behind our *madrasa*," Averroes's *petit-fils* exclaimed. "He has large, pointed teeth and big black eyes!"

"We didn't mean to scare your *petit-fils*, but the canine belongs to us," I replied in my native tongue, which both scholars understood. "He is a trained war dog and traveling with us on our quest."

Averroes rose from his seat, excused himself, and proceeded into the dark interior of the *madrasa*, as he called the building. Shortly, he returned holding a large soup bone.

"Ali, carry this bone to the black dog, and fear not, for he won't hurt you," Averroes said to his excited *petit-fils*. Quickly, Ali raced off holding the large bone.

"Ali has a lot to learn about fear, and I know it's difficult to overcome fear, but if you don't defeat it, that fear, or fears, will become the master of you. However, good preparation, knowledge, and understanding can help alleviate the fears that control us."

Averroes was right; pertinent information and good preparation for your fears were more powerful than the strongest army. Surrounded by these God-fearing and intelligent men gave me reassurance of the value of their important tenets.

"Now let's return to the main purpose of your visit, *Señor* Robert de Borron," Rabbi Yitzhak said.

"*Abad* Miguel and Chaplain Jeremiah have both told me your spiritual knowledge is far greater than most of my students. They say you have divinely received the ability to read and understand the languages of Aramaic, Hebrew, Latin, Greek, and other languages from the ancient Far Eastern realms. However, there is more to these languages than reading them and having a mortal's understanding of them. Our mortal bodies see only in three dimensions, but there are additional dimensions hiding from our feeble mortal sight. The Hebrew alphabet has twenty-two letters as you well know, and number values assigned to each. I assume you didn't know the letters had value?"

"*Oui*, you're correct," I answered. "Yet, Saint Joseph alludes to what you just said in some of his writings."

Slowly, the blind cleric reached into a strapped satchel, which hung on the arm of his chair, then pulled out two rolled parchments and a cloth covering. The cloth covering had white and ivory-colored stripes woven into it, along with fringe at its edges. It appeared similar to a religious head covering. In addition, he placed several small, black-colored square-shaped boxes, made from leather with straps attached, on the table. One of the boxes was like what he wore on his forehead. His milky-white eyes gazed at me as if he wasn't blind. Then I saw the sightless eyes in my head as if searching for my soul.

CHAPTER XXVI

"What I am about to say and show you, no ordinary Gentile has ever seen, heard, or performed this *kodesh* ceremony. *El Shaddai* has sent you to seek out powerful spiritual knowledge and convey his words to the elect, but first, you must know about *Moshe*. When the Pharaoh Ramses the Second's army pursued the ancient Israelites, *Moshe* received the seventy-two secret names of *El Shaddai. Moshe* used these seventy-two triads of letters to part the Red Sea."

Carefully, he unrolled one scroll and alongside it he placed the white wool shawl with its four corners of fringe. At each corner of the parchment, he placed four small lapis lazuli stones. In the center of the document was a large, almost square-shaped drawn box. The box-shaped design revealed a grid design drawn in its interior, with three Hebrew letters written in each section of the grid. I counted a total of seventy-two triad letter sets. Without much effort, the triad sets of letters were easy for my mind to pronounce, yet before finishing each set, Rabbi Yitzhak interrupted my thoughts.

"Please place the leather box and prayer shawl upon your head, and here are two more for your arm and hand, *Señor* de Borron. The *kodesh* shawl will help you meditate and heighten your senses to be one with *El Shaddai*. The leather boxes have sacred passages from the Torah. During your meditation, you'll feel pulled toward an inner sense of divine emanations. A deep sensation of comfort will come over you, followed by mental healing, which will reveal the hidden answers that you are seeking."

Reverently, the blind rabbi tied the leather straps around my head, hand, and arm. Lastly, he placed the prayer shawl around my head. He then unrolled the second parchment and placed a second set of jeweled stones, which were citrines. The design on this document was like nothing I had seen before. There were ten spheres, with twenty-two interconnecting lines. Three of the straight lines formed columns, with the left penetrating three of the spheres, the center column penetrating through four spheres, and the right penetrating three spheres.

"The *Kabbalah* means to receive, and now, *Señor* de Borron, you'll see what few men have seen." Rabbi Yitzhak traced the lines with his fingertips. "The *Kabbalah* is a guide to the paths that leads to the presence of *El Shaddai*, which moves upward with numerous sets of steps into heavenly halls assisted by angels. The halls are filled with long descriptions of how to make the safe journey up through the Tree of Life. It requires the elect to know the seventy-two names of *El Shaddai* and to overcome the demons along the way. Sammael and his minions will bring forth every fear, doubt, and uncertainty in your life. Before you reach the *kodesh* light, your religious resolve will come under attack. Each path corresponds to the named letters of the Hebrew alphabet, which have equivalent numerical values. The three top spheres or *sefirot* go by individual names. The first is *Keter*, meaning crown; the second is *Hokhmah*, meaning wisdom; and the third is *Binah*, meaning understanding. Then followed by *Hesed*, meaning loving-kindness; *Gevurah*, meaning law or judgment; *Tiferet*, meaning beauty; *Netzach*, meaning victory; *Hod*, meaning splendor; *Yesod*, meaning foundation; and lastly *Malchut*, meaning sovereignty. Each of these spheres has an archangel guarding a *sefirah*. The lowest sphere is the *Malchut;* it's guarded by the Archangel Uriel, occasionally called Sandalphon. The next *sefirah* is the *Yesod*, guarded by the Archangel Gabriel;

it represents foundation. Next is the *sefirah Hod,* guarded by the Archangel Mikael or Jophiel and this *sefirah* represents splendor. The next *sefirah* is *Netzach* guarded by Archangel Haniel, which represents victory or *El Shaddai's* will. Next, comes the *sefirah Tiferet,* guarded by Archangel Raphael; it represents beauty. Next is the *sefirah Gevurah,* guarded by Archangel Chamuel, and it represents strength or *kodesh* judgment. Coming next is the *sefirah Hesed,* guarded by the Archangel Zadkiel; it represents loving-kindness. *Binah* is the next *sefirah* and is guarded by Archangel Tzaphkiel; it represents understanding. The next to the last *sefirah* is *Chokmah,* and it's guarded by the Archangel Raziel; it represents wisdom. Finally, the last *sefirah* is *Keter,* or the crown, guarded by the Metatron. It's the first and highest order of the angels or the *kodesh* Fiery One of Enlightenment. It's said this *malach* helps hold up the throne of *El Shaddai.*"

"How will these holy diagrams help me seek out the next *Sangraal* parchments?" I asked of the blind rabbi.

"You will proceed upstairs and meditate on the names of *El Shaddai* and trace the paths through each sphere. If you're worthy, each angel will let you pass toward the radiant light above you. Once reaching the final sphere, *Keter*, all will reveal the location of the *kodesh* parchments. Accept these drawings and follow the stairs to the upper room of this *madrasa.* There is a table and a small oil lamp there and you must sit down and concentrate on these drawings. If your mind wanders, beware of the demons; Ashmedai, Kafkefoni, Taninniver, Sammael, and especially Lilith, Sammael's mate. Each has its own power to lead you down a path of destruction. Don't deny these steps, they must be followed even though they are quite repetitive and laborious. If you don't, I can't vouch for your later mental stability. Always repeat the seventy-two names of *El Shaddai* when they approach. They will vanish when you say one of the seventy-two names of *El Shaddai.* Each archangel will let you pass when you recite one of the *kodesh* One's many names. You aren't to eat or drink anything in the upper room. Once you find what you seek, return here, and divulge what you have seen and heard. Now, leave at once and start, for the path upward is long and arduous." Rabbi Yitzhak handed me the rolled-up scrolls.

As I rose from my seat, mixed emotions of fear and exhilaration slowly crept throughout my body. The stone steps were located at the rear of the building, where little light penetrated that part of the *madrasa.* A cold drafty breeze followed me as I trudged up the steep steps. Once reaching a small landing, I spied a small narrow table and chair, with the table illuminated by a brass oil lamp. Upon closer inspection, eight semiprecious stones lay in a group on the table. Once seating myself, I could see they were similar to the stones downstairs. Carefully, I placed the eight stones at each corner of my unrolled parchments and began reciting the seventy-two names of *El Shaddai.* The prayer shawl and *tefillin* helped focus my vision on both diagrams, which left me oblivious to my surroundings. At the bottom of the *Kabbalah* diagram were numerous ancient Aramaic sentences. One was some unnamed quote: "*El Shaddai* encompasses all there was, is, and will be." The other appeared directed toward me, for it said, "It's not *El Shaddai* who changes, but the ability to perceive *El Shaddai* that changes." The last lines were a protection prayer, which said, "May Mikael be at my right hand and Gabriel at my left, before me Uriel and behind me Raphael and above my head the divine presence of *El Shaddai.*"

Suddenly, my body seemed to be pulled upward, with a heavy tugging sensation starting at my head. Hurriedly, I commenced repeating the Hebrew names of *El Shaddai*, hoping this feeling would stop, but it didn't. In fact, it became worse, with my body rising toward the ceiling. Suddenly, and to my horror, I gazed down on myself, still seated in the dimly lit room. However, to my incredulous understanding, I could hear my voice repeating the names of *El Shaddai* and see my fingertips following the *Kabbalah's* paths on the diagram. Yet, my body propelled toward a distance set of spiraling stairs, which my boots touched before I could clearly see where the stairs led. With each step, my boots seemed filled with lead ingots. My breath labored, but the quicker and the more resolute I said the names of *El Shaddai*, the faster my steps became. Once reaching the first landing, I spied an iron gate, where suddenly a human-shaped apparition appeared holding a large leather-bound book in one hand and emitting a blue-tipped flame from the palm of its other hand. Its face glowed a brilliant white and spoke to me, saying he was Uriel. However, his lips didn't move, yet his voice sounded in my head.

"Is this what you seek, human?" it asked. Then the pages of the book opened, revealing the design of the mosque next to us. A second page mysteriously flipped forward showing geometric star-shaped designs with many arches supported by columns. The third page was then revealed, and, to my surprise, a drawing of me excavating something from a stone floor surrounded by the same columns. Instantly, the gate swung open, and another set of stone steps quickly appeared before me. Each set of steps had had a single Hebrew letter written on each tread. Once more, an angelic being met me by an iron gate, this time holding a radiating chalice. It reached out to hand me the blazing cup, but quickly it rose from the angel's hands and perched high above its head out of my reach.

"I am the cupbearer called Gabriel, or Hermes the Greek humans once called me," the angelic being announced. "Pilgrim, you must travel deep into the earth's foundation to obtain this blessed cup. Only the most righteous will see its mysteries. Behold! At my feet you see the sacred cup's companions."

Its long glowing arm pointed toward its sandals, where a silver-tipped spear, sword, and paten appeared. The same items that were mentioned in Saint Joseph de Arimathea's *Sangraal* parchments. They too rose in the air alongside the cup and emitted a searing light, which forced me to turn away. And then appeared an image of a headless stone statue holding a small cup in one hand. The human-like statue wore a Roman or Greek-style dress. Was this vision the same signpost that the Cistercian *abbé* spoke of at the *abbaye* of Campo de Cariñena? Next came the creaking sound of the gate opening, letting me know I could enter, after which my body was whisked away to the next set of lettered steps. Once again, my boots felt heavy, yet my mouth continued to recite the seventy-two names of *El Shaddai.* At the top of the steps, I entered a long hallway; at the back of the far hall appeared a radiating light. As I drew nearer to the light, I could see bodiless arms reaching out to grab me. My hands pushed them away and I continued onward.

"Soldier of *El Shaddai*, come forward," a booming voice announced. "You're in the great hall of *Hod* and my name is Mikael. Hurry closer so I can see you."

As I drew nearer, the apparition's one hand held a scale, while the other held a fiery, orange-colored sword, which it brandished above its glowing head. The entire being's body glowed from its plate armor. Once more, this ethereal creature spoke to me with its thoughts.

"Poor-Soldier of Christ, for the King of Glory, you will defend your quest at all costs, even if it means your family is in harm's way." It lowered its sword.

I spied words engraved on the fuller, which said, "He who is as *El Shaddai.*" My ever-present litany of the seventy-two names forced it to open the gate so I could pass. Yet, as I was instructed by, behind Mikael a dark moving specter appeared. The black image grew larger as I approached the next set of steps with its dark and fetid-smelling body starting to materialize in front of me. Its hair was a writhing nest of long-fanged snakes.

"Human, I am Ashmedai," the sulfur-smelling beast said. "I am here to give you the entire wealth of your earthly world. Honor me and it will be all yours."

Behind the demon was an entire room filled with glistening gold and silver coins. In addition, all four walls were encrusted with precious sparkling jewels. I knew this was but an illusion, for the mind-boggling wealth disappeared as I stepped my boot on the next stone tread. Once entering the next great hall, the angelic being spoke into mind.

"Human creature, you're now in the hall of *Netzach* and I am the *Malach* Haniel," it said, gazing at me through the iron bars. "I foresee victory is within your grasp, pilgrim, but don't let fear dissuade you." It pointed upward to an ever-greater beam of light. The barred iron gate flew open, and I rushed toward the next set of steps. Once reaching the next hall, a misty-shaped being spoke out the name of the hall.

"Defender of the *Maishiach*, you're now entering the gorgeous hall of the *Tiferet,* and I am the *Malach* Raphael. Here you will view and taste my sparkling walls." It was correct, for my diaphanous body floated back and forth through the ceiling, all four walls, and the floor, leaving me quivering with ecstasy while alleviating all my past sadness. The gate didn't open this time for me to enter, but my transparent body floated through the iron bars and left. Once stepping on the next stone tread, my body became solid. Then I caught sight of a black shadow in front of me.

"My name is Kafkefoni, and I am here to slowly disembowel you," it stated to my horror.

The horrid beast had a huge, pointed beak, which it snapped repeatedly seeking to fulfill its desire. I reached for my sword, but it wasn't there. My body froze in dread as the demon creature crept toward me. Once more, I recited God's protection prayer, causing the hideous bird-like beast to disappear.

Midway up the next long set of steps, there appeared a ghastly crawling snake-like creature with scaly wings and its mouth exhaling flames.

"My name is Taninniver, I am the blind dragon of doubt. I have appeared to you many times and you didn't recognize me. My fiery hot breath will melt your resolve and I will become your master of indecision. However, my next two companions are more subtle than me, yet far more powerful."

As my boot stepped toward the next tread my hamsa amulet swung out from my chest and its power caused the scaly creature to vanish, leaving me with another stone stairway, which seemed to have no end. As I completed my long climb, a labored wheezing sound came from my chest, leaving my body like one human weighted lead ingot. At the end of the long hallway wasn't an angelic creature, but a six-winged Chimera, whose head changed from a human-like person to those of an eagle, ox, or lion. Yet, the greater fright was its multitude of moving eyes on each of its six snow-white wings. Was this a demon or an angel? Without warning, it began to speak, facing me with its human head.

"Seeker, you are now in the great hall of *Gevurah,* and I am called Chamuel, which causes you to burn with mental desire. Along with Mikael, we both seek justice and execute the Law. I see clearly the burning face of *El Shaddai*, which will uncover what you seek and more.

Slowly, the radiating being's hand held out a long, unrolled, brown-colored parchment, which had numerous unknown, white-colored symbols and odd formed letters.

"Observe the sigils of our nature," the burning-faced angel said. After which, the iron gate creaked opened and it exclaimed, "*Kodesh, kodesh, kodesh* is *El Shaddai*; the whole earth is full of His glory!"

Without hesitation, my soul shot forward to a set of steps with the Hebrew letter *kaph* written on each tread. The rays of light above me grew brighter, followed by a booming voice telling me what hall I had entered. My palms sweated with fear, hoping I hadn't missed any steps or words. I didn't want to lose my mind, but my mental capacity to think clearly was fading. A sense of approaching doom touched my entire body.

CHAPTER XXVII

"Behold the servant for the King of Glory! I am Zadkiel, the *malach* of loving-kindness and you have arrived at the hall called *Hesed*. Learn forgiveness and carry it with you always, no matter how evil your treatment. Revenge and hatred are the prince of evil's two swords, which will make him your master. For eons, the human creature hasn't embraced my light, yet your race of beings still seeks to kill one another. Leave here with a contrite heart and mind."

Instantly another set of spiral stone steps appeared, with the Hebrew letter *zain*. Slowly, I started trudging up the endless set of steps, however, a soft hand caressed the back of my neck stopping me. Immediately, my nostrils drew in the familiar sweet scent of rose-vanilla perfume.

"Roberto," the gentle voice announced. "It's me, Helena."

Quickly, I turned to see her naked body.

"Roberto, please come with me," she said, as a door mysteriously opened behind her. Helena then smiled, lifted her hand, and motioned for me to follow her.

"Depart, enchantress!" I shouted, but she moved closer, putting her arms around my neck while rubbing her naked body against mine. Quickly, I recited the angelic protection prayer as she pulled me toward the dark opening. Suddenly, she stopped and gave me a crooked smile. Then her lips curled, and Helena turned into a scaly horn-headed beast.

"I am Lilith!" she exclaimed, as her spittle burned my face. "My many naked minions will visit you at night when you least expect them." Immediately she disappeared, then my boots moved up the never-ending steps, until, suddenly, my body propelled forward toward a stone entrance embedded with glowing white pearls. There at the end of the hall, behind a golden gate, stood a human-shaped being radiating moving rays of brilliant blue lights.

"It's a pleasure to see such a lowly creature like you," it said. "Few of your kind have reached my hall of understanding," it said. "Maybe there's still hope for the human animal, but first, please come forward into my *Binah* hall of emanation. Let me see you closer so I can determine if you're the proper aspirant for understanding."

Instantly, my body floated forward, only stopping when I reached the barred gate, which glowed with sapphire stones.

"I am called Tzaphkiel, and yes, you pass my scrutiny for understanding." The voice sounded feminine. "To understand all is to love all." It opened its glowing gate.

Past this gate entrance, my body flew to the next set of steps bearing the Hebrew letter called *dalet.* Each set of steps and the new halls seemed easier to reach as I advanced toward an ever-increasing brilliant light. On each side of the spiral-shaped walls were drawings of ancient dressed women and long-bearded men. None I could recognize, yet two of the men's faces had symbols next to their cheeks. One of them was in the shape of a hemlock tree and the other a burning lantern. Farther on, another symbol appeared, like that of serpent-shaped staff and to the right, a long-bearded face, while on the other side of the image was a set of stone-shaped tablets. Was this the image of Moses?

As I slowly approached the entrance of the next great hall, my ears heard a booming sounding inner voice.

"Behold the favored creature of YHVH!" Then my mind became silent. Just before entering through the great hall, I observed the lintel opening had the carved words in Hebrew for the "Secrets of *El Shaddai.*" On each pillar, supporting the lintel, were book-shaped carvings. Below one book, I spied a carved naked man and woman darting out an unlocked gate with a flaming sword above it. One ancient book carving had a large chisel-designed ship floating in deep water directly below it. As my right boot reached for the last marked tread, it froze in a raised position, and I couldn't step any farther. Quickly, I recalled the next to last *sefira,* then vocally shouted the four Hebrew letters of its name. "*Hei, kaf, mem, hei!*" after which my feet moved forward. Once entering the great hall, I observed its walls contained symbols, numbers, and letters that were beyond comprehension. Suddenly, my mind heard the being speak again.

"My name is Raziel, and you have succeeded in reaching my hall of wisdom, called *Hokhmah.* You're just one of a few who has reached my great hall. For my gate is narrow and the road is hard that leads to the Tree of Life, and there are few who find it. You're here to seek out *El Shaddai's* secrets for your quest, which you have divinely earned." With one of its radiating hands, it plucked out a symbol from the stone wall of an unrecognizable *église* or possibly a mosque.

"Here's the destination you seek, but it won't be your final one. Search for the Magdala tower and to the eight-star women including their *mère*, there you will find the octagrammation of *El Shaddai.* In its depths, you will find His words.

"Eons ago, I visited your ancient race to find a wise human creature; but I didn't find any. After the great deluge, a few existed, however, not many have appeared since. You belong to this small chosen group and are now so honored. Your last set of steps and the great hall are now ahead, however, this will be your greatest trying challenge. Writer of the words, use your divine wisdom to tread lightly and dodge the net of evil."

His narrow gate of rubies opened, revealing another spiraling set of stone steps. On the first tread was the Hebrew letter *alef,* which could barely be seen from a pulsating shaft of light that forced me to squint. My feet stumbled several times against the risers as I made my way along the narrow spiral corridor. Once again, the corridor walls were replete with symbols, numbers, sets of numbers, and geometric designs. Not one spot of the stone walls lay barren of marks, yet the higher I climbed, the less I could see. The brilliant light was now so great, its rays forced my head downward, only seeing the Hebrew letter *alef.*

Suddenly, the harsh golden rays of light diminished, and I heard footsteps coming my way. For just a moment, I thought I heard both of *mon fils* giggling, accompanied by *mon épouse*'s voice admonishing them for laughing. Was this another evil snare? Yet, I heard her voice say my name.

"Robert, we have traveled far to visit you. My *frère* came with us for protection, so we can finally be with you." My nose caught the scent of her lavender perfume.

We embraced, with tears streaming down both our cheeks. Happiness now overwhelmed me, and my entire body shook with joy.

"Please let me gaze upon you," I said while glancing at my two *fils'* small glistening swords. Henri and Brian were a hand's length taller than I remember. "Where are you staying?"

"*Mon chéri*, we're staying at *Château* San Servando, with the Poor-*Chevaliers* de Christo," Marie said, with a slight smile. "Your *fils* want you to spend some time with you and so do I." She kissed me on my mouth. "Robert, come with me and stop this insane quest. I know a shortcut to leave this dark place; just follow me and your *fils*." Her hand reached for a door latch.

To my surprise, the door opened to a bright peaceful afternoon facing the riverbank that surrounded Toledo. One of my boots stepped over the threshold to leave, but as I glanced back for my *fils*, they each had crooked smiles. Right before my eyes, and to my horror, both had their swords drawn. Instantly, one of them grew into a horned scaly being, half-human and half reptile. The other, a full-grown man with his sword raised to strike me.

"I am Sammael, the prince of evil," the creature announced, "and the woman you see is my *princesse,* Lilith. The scaly being in front of you is one of our many *fils* and we must insist you leave here by this door."

Quickly, I turned my sword hilt to form a crucifix and recited the name of each angelic being I had encountered. In addition, I shouted the Hebrew Tetragrammaton for God, "Yud, hey, vav, hey!"

I stepped back onto the steps, understanding I almost allowed the demons to win, and slowly, all three evil shapeshifters and the door began to fade. My entire body dripped with sweat and both of my legs began to buckle toward the steps. Carefully, I sat down on the warm tread, bending my head down from the ever-increasing fiery shafts of light, and rested. I don't know how long I sat there, however, I feared climbing any higher. I begged my Lord and Savior to free me from this torment, but all I heard was silence.

After a short while, I thought I heard a voice. Was this an answer to my prayers? However, a sudden whiff of smoke entered my nostrils, which smelled similar to the *abbé's* frankincense-filled censer. The strong fragrance seemed to give me strength and confidence to continue on to the ever-steeper spiraling steps. Every tread in front of me had the Hebrew letter *alef* written on it, but to my surprise, suddenly each step seemed easier to climb. On each side of me was an uncountable number of geometric drawings. Some I recognized, however, several I didn't know or couldn't see for the brilliant light above me. Finally, I reached a great entrance, where the large lintel had a carved geometric design of six circles with six lines forming six vertices, which connected as diameters of each circle. The entire outer design formed a hexagram with a six-pointed star in its interior, followed by more interior geometric star figures. Directly below the geometric designs were the Hebrew letters *beit, tav*, and *dalet.* On each cubed-shaped pillar, supporting the lintel, were numerous cube designs.

"Mortal man, you're now in the great hall of the *Chayot Ha Kodesh*," a thundering voice announced. "My cohorts are noted for their enlightenment and are the bearers of *El Shaddai's* throne. Come closer so I can see you, for I was once human like you. Once my people called me Enoch ben Jared, and I was the great-grandfather of Noah. Now my name is Metatron."

Painfully, while trying to glance up and see his face, my eyes burned from his violet and golden-white colored aura. Finally, I could see two beams of light, which divulged his orange-colored burning eyes of smokeless fire. He sat on a cube-shaped throne and gazed at me through bars made of glowing tourmaline stones. He possessed no wings but surrounding his throne were hundreds of stacked sky-blue glowing books. Next to him was a large table with a sizable clay inkpot placed on it. Beside the pot lay a long narrow stylus. On the chest of his amber-colored tunic was an undecipherable circular sigil. At the foot of his throne were the Hebrew letters *mem*, *teit*, *dalet*, *vav*, and *nun*.

"I was the *shekinah* who led *Moshe* and his people out of the clutches of the pharaoh. In addition, I am the being who Ezekiel viewed measuring for the new Temple of Jerusalem. Heed that passage, for it's important in what you seek. *El Shaddai* has appointed me as crown prince and guardian of the *Etz Chaim* or Tree of Life. You can't travel any farther; few of your kind have reached this final pinnacle called *Keter* or last emanation. Earlier, you met my relative, Sandalphon, or as you called him, Eliyah. You have traveled from the beginning to the end as the King of Glory calls Himself."

Without warning, both of his palms erupted with columns of fire, reaching above his fiery white hair. Quickly, two burning rocks formed, one in each hand, which appeared as chunks of flaming carved ice. As the columns of fire dissipated, geometric-shaped crystal stones formed, still sparking from their formation.

"Behold the fruits from the Tree of Life!" shouted the ancient *malach*. "The Archangel Uriel first let me taste its fruit. In my right hand, I hold a cube; in the other is a dodecahedron. The dodecahedron's faces are in the shape of a pentagon and the cube has eight vertices. Here are your *penta* and *octa* the King of Glory spoke into the *kodesh* Yoseph's ear." Suddenly, a rainbow-colored glowing gate opened and pulled me into the throne room. "These are yours, writer of words. Guard them well, for they will help you see what numerous mortal men can't see. You seek the truth, yet beware, it's a merciless taskmaster and its meaning can be both bitter and sweet."

Both geometric-shaped crystals flew from his glowing palms, stopped at my eye level, hovered momentarily, and then slowly settled in each of my palms. Unexpectedly, my body fell like a large stone, hurling toward some unknown distant speck below me. I tumbled downward at a painful incredible speed as I focused on myself still sitting at the upstairs table. Abruptly, my descent slowed and then I drifted into my body. The next thing I knew, my head raised from the *Kabbalah* drawing. Quickly, I searched around the dim upstairs room and observed a lone burning lamp. It appeared I had fallen asleep and had a fitful dream, however, both my hands were squeezing two sparkling crystal objects. Gazing into my palms, they were the same geometric crystals the ethereal Metatron had given me.

"*Señor* Roberto," hollered the voice of Averroes. "Are you all right? I have prepared a meal for you and your compatriots. In addition, while you were upstairs more of your fellow warrior *hermanos* have arrived. Please come and join us for some food."

Quickly, I gathered up the *Kabbalah* chart, the seventy-two Hebrew names for God, and then carefully placed the crystals in my writing satchel. As I started down the steps to the *madrasa's* lower level, my mind told me there would be questions asked, but I wasn't about to tell all that I had seen and heard. Even if I did, nobody would believe me.

Grand Master Gilbért had arrived, along with Sergeants de Hoult and de Béziers as I entered the long library room.

"It's past the office of Nones. What did you learn? Please tell all of us. You have the white color of a frightened man who saw many spirits. Are you feeling all right?"

"*Oui*, I am fine," I lied, knowing how true his astute observation was. "I suspect I am pale from a lack of food. Maybe after I have some *vino*, my color will return."

"Please, Roberto, sit next to me," the blind cleric said. "I am curious to know what the Tree of Life told you?" Yitzhak reached for my hand. To my surprise, he squeezed it hard several times, as if he already knew what I had seen and heard. Young Ali poured me some *vino* and then proceeded to do the same for my Christian companions. He picked up a brass pitcher of aromatic smelling *qahwa* and poured some for Muhammad, pausing to gaze upon Muhammad's wide curved-shaped *jambiya* dagger and then he filled the small porcelain cups of his grandfather and Rabbi Yitzhak. Would my explanation make any sense? Would they think I had lost my mind? All eyes focused on me. However, the rabbi spoke first.

CHAPTER XXVIII

"The *Kabbalah* and the *kodesh* names of *El Shaddai* reveal things that most mortal men can't comprehend," Rabbi Yitzhak stated. "The *Kabbalah* identifies the link between the spiritual world and the physical world. The heavens above and the physical world below is potentially the bridge in between. Yet, there must be a point of correction or *tikkun* in man's destiny. Some call it free will, others call it divine intervention, however, it's the ability to receive *El Shaddai's* grace and love. *El Shaddai* doesn't exist for those who don't fully open their hearts to let Him enter. The *Kabbalah* tells us that our five senses perceive so little of reality, let alone the world above. Our conscious realm and unconscious realm increase as we embrace constant sharing with others."

"*Si*, my astute young colleague is right," Averroes affirmed his fellow scholar. "History and life aren't one dimensional, contrary to what historians would lead you to believe. Is there really a past, present, and future, or are we mired in the present? While still repeating the same mistakes, prejudices, and hatred, calling it something new and passing it off as the future? The higher levels of consciousness, which we may obtain, show us that our limitations, finalities, endings, restrictions, doubts, and death are all illusions.

"Study the gematria of the Greek and Hebrew alphabets. Here are examples of a sacred interaction between numbers and letters. Several thousand years ago, the prophets taught the elect gematria, and some say Idris or Enoch—may peace and blessing be upon him—gave us this sacred knowledge. Groups of numbers or values of numbers can divulge sacred words and passages in the Torah or the *Qur'an.* Every verse of the *Qur'an,* the Sufi masters say, conceals a minimum of seven hidden significations. Is spiritual and scientific knowledge that much different? The more the elect knows of each, the closer they become."

"Grand *Mufti* Averroes and Rabbi Yitzhak," said Muhammad. "I respect your scholarly knowledge and wisdom, but I was once a practical Saracen horse owner and seller from the Levant, as my *amis* call it, however, we quickly need answers to complete our quest. I know you are familiar with the *Ikhwān aṣ-Ṣafā'* or the Brethren of Purity, which seek to destroy us and steal the holy parchments."

"Emir Muhammad, they're like the wind," Averroes responded, "that blows through dark caves. It's not important where they hide or live, for the *Hashishiyya* and their adepts are like stunted trees, sprouting perverted philosophies, while ignorant to their potential growth. Only their flawed physical beings manifest their writings. However, I do realize their dangerous nature and am familiar with their leader, Sheik Rashid Al-Din Sinan, and his messianic beliefs. It's probably best for *Señor* Roberto to tell you what his vision told him." Once again, all eyes stared toward me.

"*Si*, I too at once would like to know," Grand Master Gilbért stated. "*Roi* Alfonso VIII has given you less than two days to remain in Toledo, or otherwise he will arrest you, and we don't have time to explain why."

"*Si*, I am already privy to the reason," Averroes said, "and my fellow scholar and I know it isn't true."

"My mind's eye has revealed two old mosques," the blind *Judio* cleric surprisingly announced, "which are now *iglesias* of the Prophet Yeshua. In addition, I see great sorrow in the heart of Emir Muhammad. His family once came under the daggers of the *Hashishiyya.*"

"*Si*, you're right, Rabbi, and I viewed myself digging into the stone floor of the Hospitaller's *chapelle* next to us, however, my vision didn't show anything about Emir Muhammad's family," I replied.

"Grand *Mufti* Averroes, could the parchments be there?" I asked. "In addition, the vision told me there's a large star on a tower nearby, which is attached to one of the *iglesias.*"

"First, the former ancient mosque was once named Mezquita Bab-al-Mardum and built over a former Visigoth *iglesia*," Averroes stated. "However, when *Rey* Alfonso VI of Castile reconquered Toledo, along with the great El Cid, El Cid's horse mysteriously bowed down before the mosque. A brief time later, construction workers found a bricked-in Christian altar, tore it down, and found a lit candle with a cross, which they claimed was a miracle. My *amigo*, it's up to you to fulfill your vision. The star tower you perceived is the *Iglesia* de Santiago del Arrabal, which is near the old Greek statue of Hebe, though her head is now missing. An ancient mosque once stood there until the Christians built an *iglesia* over it and some say you can see the constellation of the doves through its tower opening, especially this time of year. The locals say the tower is where the seven-star sisters live along with their *madre*, Pleione. The ancient Greeks, *Judios*, and my People of the House call this constellation Pleiades. Through my glass-windowed tube, I observe the star sisters each night."

"What's the significance of the constellation Pleiades to our quest?" I asked, trying to organize all the clues in my mind.

Averroes continued.

"One of the stars of the constellation is called Maia, the eldest and greatest beauty of all the sisters, however, what's more important, the old Greek mythology says she gave birth to Hermes the messenger. To all Muslims, he is similar to Jibril and the messenger to Muhammad, may peace and blessings be upon him. To your People of the Book, his name is Gabriel.

"Lord Roberto," Averroes said. "This represents your message or the signpost to the written words you seek. I can't tell you where your parchments might be hidden, but I suspect the mosque next to us will lead you to the correct location."

"There's just one problem," Grand Master Gilbért said. "The Mezquita del Cristo de la Luz is heavily guarded by the *chevaliers* of Saint John. It would make it impossible to sneak in."

"Maybe not," replied Averroes. "In the late evening, they change all the guards for new ones. Shortly thereafter, the new guards eat a light meal and drink some *vino*. The food and *vino* arrive a short time after their watch starts. One of their sergeants delivers it to them."

"Grand *Mufti* Averroes, if we could reach the food before it's delivered, I have a strong potion that will put them to sleep," Muhammad stated.

"That won't be a problem," Grand Master Gilbért said. "I am familiar with where their food is prepared. In addition, I know the location of their spare clothes. Muhammad, give me the sleeping potion and I will put it into their food, while dressed as one of them. That only leaves us wanting for digging tools and the specific location of the hidden information."

"I believe the sealed container will have the name of *Allah* written on its lid, which Muhammad can translate for you," Averroes said. "Search for the old *qiblah,* an arched-shaped niche pointing toward *Mekka*, though, possibly the Hospitallers bricked over it. Each vaulted ceiling has a geometric design. Seek the ones that are in the shape of a pentagon design or octagon. The mosque was once a perfect cube-shaped building. Keep your search in this area."

"In addition, I have some digging tools with me here at the *madrasa*," the grand *mufti* added. "There are several pry bars, shovels, and a pickaxe if needed."

Muhammad handed the sleeping potion to Grand Master Gilbért, and then he raced out of the building. The daylight was fading fast, creating long narrow shadows through the windows. If our military leader could accomplish his deception, we would be digging in the mosque soon.

"May I ask permission for my fellow companions to sleep here tonight?" Chaplain Jeremiah asked of his host. "I fear when we're finished, sleep will be needed. In addition, traveling at night in Toledo's cold dark narrow streets would put us in harm's way."

"*Si*, it's fine with me," Averroes replied. "Both my *nieto* and I will leave late tomorrow. *Señor* Roberto and I have similar problems. It's not safe for me to stay in Toledo too long. My fellow *ulamas* have always displeased somebody in power and the *rey* would like to ransom me to the *khalifa* in southern Iberia. I fear I have displeased him, and he wants me dead."

"How far is the *Iglesia* de Santiago del Arrabal from here?" I asked.

"Follow this road in front of the *mezquita* or mosque for a short distance and you'll see the Puerta de Valmardón," Yitzhak answered. "It's not far past there after which the great tower will lead you there."

Suddenly, the front door opened. My hand quickly reached for the hilt of my sword.

"It's done!" came the winded words of Grand Master Gilbért. "The ruse worked perfectly. They're none the wiser, yet the easiness of fooling them troubles me. Now let's wait until the sergeant arrives."

"Shortly after he arrives," Averroes said, "I'll send my *nieto* to see if they have fallen asleep. He won't attract any attention if any of them are still awake. In the last several days they have grown fond of him."

The apprehension of knowing our quest to Toledo was near closure tightened my stomach. Then Ali spotted the sergeant bringing the food.

"*Abuelo*, the sergeant has arrived," he whispered.

The grand *mufti* rose from his seat, and then ambled toward the dark interior of the *madrasa*, accompanied by Ali. A short while later, they returned, both holding digging tools.

"Hopefully, you will accomplish your tasks if *Allah* wills it," Averroes said, as both handed us their tools.

Once again, we waited until the *chevaliers* ate their food and the sergeant left, which to my surprise wasn't long. Young Ali darted out the front door while using a long stick to strike a leather-shaped ball. I viewed him playing with the ball in front of the *chapelle* while making several noisy sounds of glee. He then purposely whacked his ball inside the *chapelle*, darted after it, then disappeared inside. The wait for him to return seemed excruciatingly long. However, to my relief, he raced out of the mosque holding the ball in his hand.

Quickly, I opened the door as he bounded inside, out of breath.

"They're sound asleep, with all of them snoring!" he exclaimed. "Emir Muhammad's magic potion worked. He must give some of his magic liquid to my *abuelo*. He says I am never tired enough to sleep."

Chaplain Jeremiah, *Abad* Miguel, the two sergeants, and Grand Master Gilbért gathered up the digging tools. We left by the back entrance, where some trees and bushes hid our exit. We crept alongside the mosque, and I spied a side door. Above the door was a set of horseshoe-shaped windows with their arches radiating outward with alternating red and white stripes. Grand Master Gilbért entered first to see if they were still asleep. Shortly thereafter he returned, using his hands to direct us inward. I heard him whisper to Muhammad to place our canine warrior *ami* as a sentry at the front entrance. We entered the dimly lit *chapelle* stepping over several snoring, black-robed warrior-*moines*. With my boot, I nudged one, making sure he wouldn't wake up.

There were nine small individual vaulted ceilings, supported by numerous intertwined horseshoe-shaped arches resting on single columns. Each vault was perfectly square with a geometric design embedded in its ceiling. Everything in my recent vision was coming true, for in the center of the mosque was the small cubed-shaped cupola or minaret. Centered in the top of the vault was a perfect-shaped octagon figure and in its center, another small, shaped octagon design. A few remaining rays of blue-gray light cast its shadows on the floor stones. One ray of light bounced off a coin-sized pentagon-shaped symbol encased in one of the stones. The ray then traveled to the east-facing wall and struck a narrow-pointed alcove bearing an icon of Mary Magdaleine. I couldn't believe my eyes!

"Here's the spot the *Sangraal* parchments are buried!"

Muhammad rushed inside when he heard my loud exclamation.

"Lord Robert, keep your voice down," Grand Master Gilbért whispered. Quickly, we converged on the embedded pentagon-shaped object. However, we encountered a problem. Lying across the edge of the large floor stone was a sergeant of Saint John. He snored loudly, yet we had to move him some distance from where we were to dig. Both of our sergeants picked him up and moved him to the opposite wall next to another of his compatriots. Yet, to my horror, the sergeant began to mumble. Had the drug been enough? Would he alert the others? To my relief, he started snoring once more.

Immediately, Grand Master Gilbért used a thin flat pry bar to wedge in between the floor stone and its mortar. With the precision of slicing one of his enemies, quickly the square stone block loosened, while Muhammad used another longer pry bar to lift it out of its place.

"Let me grab another pry bar and help," I whispered, as my shaking hands picked up a still longer bar. Our ever-searching eyes betrayed our anticipation. Finally, it lifted out with a gritty-*grinding* sound, leaving us to stare into a small dark shaft.

"Sergeant de Hoult, bring one of the lit prayer candles now," Grand Master Gilbért ordered. Before the sergeant could hand the candle to his superior, I grabbed it and knelt. To my nervous surprise, the candle revealed a cube-shaped lead box. Quickly, I said a prayer of thanksgiving, and then I reached down and lifted the lead box from its almost five-hundred-year home. Carefully, I placed it on the cold stone floor, noticing the lid revealed some written Arabic calligraphy. Quickly, I rubbed off the dirt, revealing the swirling script. I smiled, not solely because the parchments might be there, but because my divine gift prevented me from reading the Saracen language. My prolonged smile caught the attention of Grand Master Gilbért.

"Why do you hesitate in opening the box?" he asked. "Is there something wrong?"

"*Non*, I can't read Muhammad's language. He'll have to translate it." I turned toward him to proceed.

"The Kufic script represents the *Basmala,* which means in the name of *Allah,* the Most Gracious, the Most Merciful. The writing says that Ahmad ibn Hadi had this mosque erected on another ancient mosque site using his own money and requesting a reward in paradise, for it was built for *Allah,* may He be praised.

"The smaller script announces it was completed with the aid of *Allah* under the direction of Musa ibn Ali, architect and *sa'ada,* and finished in the Muslim month of *Muharram* in the year 390 after the prophet's hegira to Medina."

Immediately, I reached for my dagger, slid it out of its small scabbard, and used the blade to pry the lid open. Its musty smelling interior further increased my anticipation, but it quickly ceased upon seeing a single parchment sheet, knowing this couldn't be the *Sangraal.* Carefully, I placed it under one of our candles and faint symbols and drawings emerged. To the right of the parchment was Saint Joseph's sigil; to the left were seven pentacle-shaped stars and a larger one above them. Directly below the eight total stars appeared a long narrow tower with Latin letters written at its base. However, the Latin words didn't make any sense, no matter how long I studied them.

"Can anyone tell me what these disarranged Latin letters ... mean?" I asked with a quivering voice.

"I suspect it's a Latin code used to conceal a clue from the local Moor population," Chaplain Jeremiah responded. "Let me come closer."

I handed him the single parchment, and his eyes widened as he perused its contents. My disillusionment weighed heavily on my mind as he continued studying the candlelit letters.

"*Si,* it's a Caesar cipher shift code!" he exclaimed. "I must admit, it's quite ingenious, and however, I know I can solve it."

Once again, my anticipation shot upward like an arrow, while hoping it might render us another clue.

"It's a left shift, three-letter cipher," Chaplain Jeremiah added. "Lord Robert, do you have pen and ink in your satchel?"

"*Oui,* or I mean *si.*" Quickly, I reached in my bag and grabbed a pen, ink, and a small piece of blank writing parchment. With my shaking hands, I handed the items to him.

"Remember, Lord Robert, there isn't any j, u, or w in Roman letters. I think with the accumulated information we have gained in the last two months, the next set of parchments is within our grasp," the young chaplain stated with a reassuring grin.

His writing hand glided across the parchment scrap as fast as gushing water, only occasionally stopping to evaluate what he'd written.

"I have it!" he exclaimed. "The code is broken; we must leave now." He quickly rolled up the piece of parchment. Immediately, he corked the inkwell, cleaned the pen tip on his boot, after which he dropped it all in my satchel. "Your Excellency, please place the lead box back into its hole, along with positioning the floor stone and the mortar pieces in their original position. We don't want the *chevaliers* of Saint John to know we were here. Let's hurry before they awaken, for we have little time." His long legs rushed toward the side entrance. Hurriedly, I jumped up then raced behind my *amis*, while wondering where we were heading.

"Can you tell me where we are going?" I asked.

Chaplain Jeremiah glanced back at me. "To the *Iglesia* de Santiago del Arrabal and Saint Joseph's *Sangraal* parchments!"

CHAPTER XXIX

We exited by the side entrance and quickly crept down a narrow street via Averroes's partially hidden *madrasa* following Grand Master Gilbért's lead. He carried our one lone torch, casting its dancing shadows on the clay walls of the surrounding buildings. *Noir Ombre* trotted ahead, sniffing, and then peeing on each corner of the numerous homes. Once, he stopped and growled at a man sleeping in a doorway, forcing us to reach for our swords. The man jumped up with a wide-eyed glance and rushed from the *chevaliers* of Christ.

As we approached the edge of town, I observed a large stone horseshoe-shaped arched gate guarded by a lone *rey's* guard.

"Who approaches the *Puerta* de Valmardón?" he demanded as we trudged uphill toward the gate.

"It's Grand Master Gilbért de Érail and the Poor-Soldiers of Christ. Let us pass or the *rey* will hear of your disobedience!" he shouted. Immediately, the guard raised the gate and let us enter. From the gate exit, we traveled a downhill road, which to my relief, on our right revealed the headless stone statue of Hebe holding a cup. Directly in front of us loomed a large square tower. It didn't seem connected to the small buildings surrounding it. Our flickering torch flame danced across its brick surface, exposing a total of eight narrow horseshoe-shaped open windows at the top of the tower, with two on each side.

"Lord Robert," Chaplain Jeremiah whispered, "you can now see the constellation Pleiades shining through the topmost windows. It appears this tower was once a minaret, which they were often used to observe the stars and keep track of the seasons."

The constellation hovered like fireflies hesitating to fly through the windows and into the tower interior. However, I knew ancient people called the constellation "the doves" and I prayed this was the Holy Spirit guiding us here tonight.

We quietly crept toward a curve-shaped entrance revealing a massive wooden door. Muhammad was the first to grab the large iron door handle while holding his scimitar in his left hand. He pushed on the door, and surprisingly it creaked inward. He entered and we quickly followed behind him. At first, the bell tower interior didn't reveal anything. The sole thing I noticed was a lone baptismal font in one corner. Its eight-sided bowl drew me toward it.

"Behold!" I exclaimed, not realizing my loud excitement. "There's a pentacle on the floor in front of the font." I pointed at the stone-carved star. I knew this was the location of the hidden parchments. Immediately I fell on my knees and then brushed the dirt off the star with my hands. My fingertips touched each angle portion of the star, yet I felt something below the star.

"Grand Master Gilbért, quickly bring the torch." He rushed forward as I bent over to focus my eyes on the dim light. There were two small marks side by side, which appeared as two small side branching one-limbed trees.

"What is this?" I inquired of my companions.

Muhammad was the first to speak.

"It's the numerical value of thirty-three written in my eastern heritage. However, I don't have any idea what it represents. I do know the pentacle signifies something magical in the night sky."

"Muhammad is right about the numerical value," Chaplain Jeremiah stated. "In addition, it was the age of our Lord and Savior when He was crucified. Furthermore, the pentacle was an earlier representation of the five wounds of Jesus."

Once again, the sacred number five appeared. Would this be

our final clue? I thought while reaching for the pry bar.

Grand Master Gilbért ordered Sergeant de Béziers to station himself as a guard at the tower entrance. Quickly, Muhammad and I started using our pry bars to gain an edge around the stone block with the chiseled symbols. It required some time before the grout loosened, giving us a place for our shovel blade to slide down the narrow slits. What seemed like half the night, the stone finally moved upward. After two good downward motions with our shovel handle the stone rose enough to slip the pry bars and my fingers underneath it.

"De Hoult," Grand Master Gilbért whispered, "grab that end."

Quickly, he knelt, slipped his hands under the heavy stone, and raised it up with a large grin. The rest of the surrounding stones came up with some effort, finally creating an opening sufficient for a man to stick his head and shoulders through.

"Give me the torch!" I shouted, not caring if anybody heard me. Slowly, I stooped forward to see inside the opening. Yet, before my eyes could see into the hole, my nose inhaled the smell of musty earth. The moist aroma, trapped for over four hundred years, spurred me on to complete my sacred task and see what was below. I said a quick prayer of thanks to God, Jesus, the Holy Spirit, and Saint Joseph of Arimathea. Right away, I spied a man's arm length narrow lead box.

"There's a lead box down here!" I shouted once more. "Muhammad, hold our torch so I can reach it, He grabbed the torch from me, and I stuck my arms and head into the opening. My fingertips touched the cool lead surface, and then I tried to lift it up, but to my disappointment, it wouldn't budge. Now my angst started coursing through my veins and my palms broke out with sweat. We didn't have much time left before the divine office of Prime and morning mass commenced.

"I can't lift it out. It's . . . stuck!" My nervous voice cracked.

"Let me try to lift it out," Grand Master Gilbért whispered.

Quickly, I withdrew myself from the opening, and then he slipped into the hole, followed by grunts, followed by his long legs thrashing about.

"Sweet Mary and Joseph!" his muffled voice exclaimed. "I don't understand why it won't move." Quickly, he raised his head out of the opening and spoke with a cherry-red face.

"We'll have to remove more stone."

"We don't have enough time," Chaplain Jeremiah said. "Mass will start soon."

"*Si*, or even sooner with the start of Prime," *Abad* Miguel added.

Now my heart started racing as time ended.

"Lord Robert, hurry and tell Sergeant de Béziers to come here immediately and help us remove more stones."

I rushed toward the entrance to retrieve him. Apparently, he heard my *thumping* boot steps and slid in front of the doorway.

"We need your help to remove some additional stones," I whispered. "I believe we've found the hidden second set of parchments. Come now."

We sped back to the opening, and I noticed more excavated stones. Beads of sweat trickled down the foreheads of each of my companions as I knelt to help *Abad* Miguel lift a stone block.

"I haven't done this much work since I repaired a *monasterio* wall at Huesca," *Abad* Miguel said with a pink-faced sheen.

The stones' *grinding* sounds, our grunting, and the constant *clanking* of the pry bars against the limestone blocks made a cacophony of sounds. I feared that at any moment somebody might hear our digging, which forced me to dig faster. Finally, the opening was sufficient in size for me. Because I was the smallest, I climbed inside the small undercroft.

Whoever had buried this narrow lead box, secured it with masonry grout on the stones surrounding it, thus permanently attaching the box. Instantly, I grabbed my pry bar, put it under one surrounding stone, and leveraged it upward. Suddenly, I heard a loud crack, and the stone fell away from the box. The second stone did the same, after which I put my pry bar under the lead box and used one of the broken stones to lift it out of its four-hundred-year-old bed.

"I have it!" I shouted. "Be ready for me to hand it to you."

However, before I lifted it up, I noticed some Kufic writing on the lid of the box. But Grand Master Gilbért's large hands grabbed the lead container from mine and disappeared, then another large hand appeared and reached down to pull me out of the small crypt.

"Lord Robert," Chaplain Jeremiah asked while grasping my wrists, "Do you see anything else of significance?"

"*Non*, but hurry and lift me out," I said. His strength catapulted me out of the opening with one swift jerk. Once standing on my feet, I witnessed Grand Master Gilbért studying the narrow lead box with our torch.

"Hurry Lord Robert, there's something you must see," he said with large round eyes.

As I approached the box, Muhammad stooped over it, while mouthing the written inscription.

"Lord Robert, it's written here: 'This contains the written relics of *Issa*.' May peace and blessings be upon him."

My excitement and anticipation shot down my spine with the quickness of a crossbow quarrel in flight. This final moment was what some of us had sacrificed our lives for, endured pain, and me numerous months absent from my family.

"Do you think the parchments are in the box?" Chaplain Jeremiah asked.

"*Oui*, why else would this unknown person trouble themselves to bury something worthless? Besides, if it were gold or jewels, there would be little of it stored in such a narrow box. Just think if you were one of the *khalifa's* scholars and realized how valuable this might be to ransom or use against the church. No different than Cardinal Folquet using it for his own greedy nefarious purposes," I stated.

"We must pray the *Arma Christi* is in this box voicing the words and secrets of our Savior," Chaplain Jeremiah said.

"Enough discussion, *mes amis*," I exclaimed. "Let me open it now!"

I used my Damascus made dagger, with much difficulty, and pried the lid off. It popped open and fell to the floor with a dull thud. Hesitantly, I reached my hand inside the box, to remove the musty smelling scrolls. Carefully, my fingertips caressed the tubular-shaped parchment roll.

"Muhammad, bring the torch closer so I can see," I said. I pulled the thick scroll out of its narrow casket with ease, revealing a large green wax seal.

"What does the seal represent?" I asked Muhammad. "What are these strange designs embedded in the seal?"

"It says it's the royal seal of the khalifa of Cordoba," he replied. Quickly, I used the pommel knob of my dagger and gingerly broke the seal. Once again, I hesitated from unrolling the scrolls, for fear of disappointment. Slowly, I unrolled the first sheet and started reading its contents.

"*Mère de Dieu*! Indeed, it's Saint Joseph's handwriting and the second set of his parchment. We need to leave now!" I glanced at Grand Master Gilbért. "We've finally found it," I carefully placed the thick set of scrolls into my writing satchel and prepared to depart.

"Lord Robert, check again the lead box to make sure we have obtained all of it."

Quickly, my fingertips searched the cool dark interior of the lead box, but nothing else touched my fingers, thus forcing me to throw the box back into its burial hole.

"Should we place the stones back where they were?" Sergeant de Hoult asked, glancing at his superior for an answer. *Did he purposely want to slow us down*?

"*Non*, we obtained what we came for, but you can scrape the markings from the lid, and throw it back into the undercroft."

Hurriedly, we gathered our tools and raced toward the entrance. A fleeting time later de Hoult came dashing out of the tower as we briskly stepped up the road toward the gate and guard. Once more, *Noir Ombre* trotted in front of us sniffing the road ahead.

"We made it out of the tower before the *moines* arrived," I said, with a giddiness overcoming me. "I feel as if I could fly back to the *madrasa* and *Château* San Servando, Grand Master Gilbért. Do you feel the same?"

"*Oui* and *non*," came his odd reply. "Not until we're back at the fortress will I enjoy our success. Empty towns in the early dawn hours are dangerous places."

He was right, yet my heart *thumped* faster, not from fear, but from the anticipation of departing for home. My quest was now complete, other than translating the parchments.

"Quiet," came the sudden word from Grand Master Gilbért.

Immediately, we stopped. He pointed toward the empty guard post at the Puerta de Valmardón gate. Quickly, he motioned toward the raised tail and frozen stance of *Noir Ombre*. He hand signaled for Muhammad and Sergeant de Hoult to creep forward and place themselves against each side of the entrance.

"Lord Robert," he whispered. "Grab *Noir Ombre* and move quietly through the entrance. I'll be behind you with Sergeant de Béziers."

Slinking forward, I slowly withdrew my broad sword, while carefully reaching with my other hand for *Noir Ombre's* spiked collar. Quickly, his head turned toward me and peered into my eyes as if wanting to know my instructions. We moved slowly through the dark gate entrance, my eyes searching every section of its interior. *Noir Ombre* gave out at a slight *whimper*, and then my nose caught the sweet smell of human blood.

"Over here," I whispered, as I pointed toward the other side of the entrance. There lay the guard in a pool of fresh billowing crimson blood. His head lay to one side of his body, near his wrist, with the stub of his neck still oozing blood. It appeared he didn't even have time to draw his sword, for it was still in its scabbard.

"Lord Robert, this man was killed by surprise," Grand Master Gilbért whispered. "Whomever it was used an extremely sharp sword. See how clean-cut the neck stump is," he stated while pointing toward the guard's headless body.

"*Oui*, that's true," Muhammad added. "Only a blade made in Damascus can cut this sharp."

"We must leave now for the fortress. This man's death doesn't bode well for us," Grand Master Gilbért said as he rubbed his beard.

Quickly, we trotted toward the *Château* San Servando, yet not hurried enough to attract attention. We traveled down several narrow side streets while avoiding the *madrasa* and the *chevaliers* of Saint John's mosque-*église*. Quickly, my giddiness vanished, replaced with a throat-swelling fear.

The coming slate-gray dawn gave us sufficient light to travel, and Muhammad quickly discarded our torch. However, the narrow streets, surrounded by tall buildings, and shadowy blind corners left me feeling I was fleeing through the bottom of a canyon.

Suddenly, and once again, *Noir Ombre* stopped with his tail raised straight up. Yet, this time he gave out a deep throaty growl.

"What does he see or hear?" I quietly asked Muhammad.

"Lord Robert, it's not what he perceives or hears, but what he smells," *mon* Saracen *ami* answered, as he slowly withdrew his long-curved scimitar.

"I don't smell, see, or hear anything." However, as soon as I said it, I was wrong, for in the misty morning distance was movement. Out of the mist appeared numerous hooded *moines* coming toward us around a spacious fountain. I counted a total of twelve, as they seemed to glide through the fog in our direction. Muhammad bent down and said some unrecognizable Saracen words into *Noir Ombre's* left ear. Immediately, his shiny black hair rose on his back and every muscle in his thick neck and chest rippled. Then, in less than a heartbeat's length, Muhammad screamed.

"*Hashishiyya*," and raced toward the *moines* with his scimitar and *jambiya* dagger raised. Why was he charging toward these defenseless *moines*? Then I knew why. The *moines* revealed the red tips of their *thumping* boots. It was the Brethren of Purity who charged toward us. Once again, on the rush, Muhammad shouted, "*Allahu Akbar, Allahu Akbar*!"

My companions followed right behind him loudly chanting, "*Non nobis Domine, non nobis, sed nomini tuo da gloriam*" with their swords and daggers drawn. I raced alongside Grand Master Gilbért, until I momentarily slowed down. When to my horror, one of the attacking *moines* charged toward me, clenching a dagger in his teeth, and in his remaining arm cradled a crossbow. This was one of the murderers from Vézelay. Immediately, my reflexes reacted, and I dodged into a recessed doorway just as the quarrel headed toward me.

CHAPTER XXX

It struck the edge of the stone entryway and fell to the ground, spraying chips of masonry into my eyes.

"Lord Robert, be careful! Their weapons are tipped in poison!" Grand Master Gilbért shouted, just as he cut through the leg of his first attacker. Chaplain Jeremiah picked up the man's dropped scimitar and cut off the sword hand of his attacker, causing blood to spurt onto his surcoat. Then my one-armed attacker threw down his crossbow and reached for his scimitar, then raised it to slice me as I came out of the doorway.

"Lord Robert, fear not," came the voice of *Abad* Miguel. "*Santo* Miguel is in my staff." He brought it down with a *thump* on the one-armed man's head. Stunted, he fell forward onto my sword with a strange glazy-eyed stare. However, his eyes didn't flutter from the beginnings of death but stayed focused on me in a frozen trance.

Another hooded man dashed toward me as I stood in the entranceway and lunged at my stomach with his dagger, and then raised his scimitar to strike. I deflected his dagger with mine and parried upward with my sword. He too had the same fixed stare in his eyes as I thrust my sword into his stomach. To my horror, he didn't fall but turned aside to attack *Abad* Miguel. Immediately, with my dagger I stabbed him in the neck, and then he turned back toward me and collapsed. His empty hand slid down my chain mail revealing the same eagle and crescent moon sigil ring that I buried at Vézelay.

A third hooded attacker rushed toward me as I pushed *Abad* Miguel away. This one slowly circled side to side in front of me waiting for an opening to thrust his poison weapons.

"Lord Robert!" Sergeant de Hoult shouted. "To your right, there's another man creeping alongside the house!"

These two men were working together, horribly reminiscent of the wolves from the Pyrénées *Montages*. Sergeant de Hoult threw his axe, while still fighting his attacker, which stuck into the back of the man's skull circling me. However, the attacker still moved closer until *Abad* Miguel used his staff to knock him off his feet.

It was terrifyingly obvious these men weren't easy to kill and didn't know pain. How could this happen? I jumped out of the entranceway, turned to face the man near the building while keeping some distance between us. He tore toward me with his dagger and sword held waist high. Suddenly, Chaplain Jeremiah hurried behind him holding a fallen scimitar and swung it similarly to a scythe at my attacker's lower leg, which flew off. Blood droplets splattered on my surcoat, while *Abad* Miguel knocked the weapon from his hand.

It seemed I was living in a nightmare. How many of these ungodly monsters were coming for me?

Suddenly, I heard a familiar groan of pain. It came from the staggering motions of Guy de Béziers.

"Have mercy on my damned soul," he cried out with a poison dagger protruding from his armpit. He took one additional step and slumped to the ground. Suddenly, I too staggered forward from a blow to the back of my head. My vision dimmed, then I felt my face strike the stone path. Quickly, a sharp pain revived me from my momentary blackness. I tasted salty blood on my lips, then flipped over as my hazy vision tried to focus on my wide-eyed killer. Struggling to raise myself, his knee pushed down on my chest, which forced me to gasp for air. He already had my writing satchel with the holy scrolls slung over his shoulder.

"Damn you to hell, heathen! You won't steal those scrolls," I screamed while thrashing my legs to rise. Once again to my terrible horror, it was the one-armed killer from Vézelay. He hadn't died!

"You have caused me enough trouble."

He put his dagger blade between his teeth, pressed the stump of his arm against my lower throat, grasped the cord around my neck, and yanked it upward. His eyes widened even greater when he viewed my hamsa amulet. This broke his concentration just long enough for me to gulp a breath and call out *Noir Ombre's* name. Our huge dark dog raced forward, snapping and drooling as he galloped toward me. The one-armed man glanced up, threw the amulet down, and this was the first time I observed fear in his eyes. His trance-like appearance vanished, replaced with rolling eyes of disbelief. *Noir Ombre* leaped toward his dagger hand and chomped his large teeth into his wrist. Both *Noir Ombre* and the attacker shook each other as the hooded man stood.

Blood from my forehead streamed into my eyes as I staggered upward. Barely, out of the corner of my left eye, sunlight reflecting off a raised scimitar blade. Was this my final demise with the *Sangraal* parchments snatched from my grasp? A cool breeze swept across my face and the killer's head flew from his shoulders as *Noir Ombre's* jaws still clenched the fallen dead man's wrist.

"Praise be to *Allah*, the Lord of the final Day of Judgment!" Muhammad shouted as he dropped his sword.

All the hooded *moines* were dead or mortally wounded. Several had stabbed themselves with their own poison and would soon die. Sergeant de Béziers lay motionless a short distance from me. I used my mantle to wipe the blood from my eyes and then viewed his lips slowly moving as I drew near to hear his gasping words.

"Grand Master Gilbért, Chaplain Jeremiah, and *Abad* Miguel, please forgive me for my traitorous acts . . ." he confessed. "*Abad* Miguel and Chaplain Jeremiah, please draw closer so you can hear my confession."

"*Si,*" both men replied.

"Cardinal Folquet holds my . . . family hostage. He threatened to kill them if I didn't spy for him. Please forgive my sins against

God. Grand Master Gilbért, help . . . rescue them."

These were his last words, followed by our kneeling Grand Master Gilbért whispering, "I will." Tears rolled down the cheeks of this fearless leader of the Army of Christ, and I knew he hated himself for thinking Guy de Béziers had totally betrayed us.

Quickly, Sergeant de Hoult reached for his body, and I helped put it on his shoulder and then grabbed my precious satchel. It was urgent for us to leave before anyone discovered what happened. Chaplain Jeremiah grabbed my writing satchel from me, and we headed toward *Château* San Servando. Each of us alternated in carrying Guy's body so we could maintain a steady pace. It was apparent we had killed and stopped all twelve killers, for not once did *Noir Ombre* alert us to any additional killers.

We reached the Puente de Alcantara bridge just as a few of Toledo's inhabitants strolled to the market. I placed my mantle over Guy's body, hoping we wouldn't attract any attention. Muhammad had returned to the *madrasa*, gathered our horses, returned the tools, and apparently found a shorter route back to the bridge. There we met him and placed Guy de Béziers's body over the back of one of our horses. Several Templar sergeants guarding the tower bridge signaled to the *château* fortress our forthcoming arrival. Quickly, we reached the top of the hill and then trotted through the open main gate.

"Lord Robert," Grand Master Gilbért said. "Help me carry his body into the bailey. Chaplain Jeremiah, follow us there to bless his body." We laid him on a low stone ledge and Chaplain Jeremiah raced toward the *chapelle* to retrieve his holy oil. He quickly returned, stooped over the body, and then made the glistening outline of a cross on Sergeant Guy's forehead. Grand Master Gilbért crossed himself, as did the rest of us present, except Muhammad. Once more, Muhammad reached for his prayer beads from his colored tunic belt and started fingering each. Sometime later, after silently mouthing his prayers, he spoke.

"This man was a *shaheed* for his prophet, *Issa*, may peace and blessings be upon them both." Then he turned and left.

Grand Master Gilbért dropped to his knees and repeatedly cursed Cardinal Folquet. Yet, I wondered if Cardinal Folquet was really the instigator of these Outremer killers.

I too left and strolled back to my quarters. Once I reached the splayed cross door, I unlocked it and entered. The humble bed beckoned me, after which I lay there thinking with troubling emotions. Sergeant Guy, another martyred soul, who was one of many I had experienced on my travels to Toledo. Who else would come under the cardinal's sword? I knew the evil man's ways had to cease, but I need not worry about that now, for my quest was over. Quickly, I would translate the new parchments, then return to Borron, and see my beloved family. Instantly, I fell asleep with their pleasant faces flashing before my eyes.

CHAPTER XXXI

Northwestern Iberia
January
Anno Domini 1191

Once more, my fellow Templars were on the road, but this time I would be traveling home. The town of Toledo was just a misty outline as I glanced over my horse's croup. Sadly, once again we were missing one of our fellow *frères*, Sergeant de Béziers. I did forgive him because of the dire circumstances his family was under. The steady *clopping* of our horses' hooves let my mind wander to my *château* at Borron. There I perceived both of my *fils'* faces with their brown and blue eyes dancing with their smiles.

"Lord Robert, you seem preoccupied in thought," Grand Master Gilbért said.

"*Oui*, you're correct. I was thinking of my *fils* and how soon I would see them. How far is it to our next destination?" Suddenly, our dark canine companion raced by me.

"Hold that question for a moment, for *Noir Ombre* has picked up the scent of something. Observe the hillock on our left; there's movement." He pointed to a distant copse of trees.

"I don't see anything. Would you hand me the spyglass?" He gave it to me just as *Noir Ombre* trotted up the hill road in front of us. I raised the leather tubular-shaped glass to my eye and observed a small cloud of dust.

"It appears someone or something stirred up some dust clouds, possibly locals or cattle. The hillock isn't dense with trees, so no possible ambush. What do you think, Muhammad?" I handed him the spyglass.

Muhammad observed the area for some time. "It is the *Hashishiyya* or Brethren of Purity who trails us. Those never ending damned *malahidas,* or as you call them heretics, won't stop until we kill them all. They use their drug-distorted beliefs to murder innocent victims as you already know. Observe! Our four-legged dark *jinn* is scratching the dirt where they stood with their horses." Muhammad handed me back the spyglass.

"Let's hurry and catch up with him before he chases after them." We spurred our horses' flanks and galloped toward the hillock.

After reaching the summit, Muhammad quickly shouted for our dog to stay. *Noir Ombre* gave out an anxious *whimper* and nervously shifted on his front paws.

"I count six sets of hoofprints, and they headed toward that small river at the bottom of this hill," Muhammad said. "They know we can track them with our dog, and they'll use the shallow rivers to throw off their scent."

I shook my head in disbelief. "I still can't believe there are any of them left!"

"In the Levant, Muhammad and I had some association with these silent killers," Grand Master Gilbért stated. "There are many and we only killed a handful of them. They work for the highest bidder, whether Christian or Muslim. Also the cardinal is paying them to track us. However, they're still after Muhammad and me for rescuing Muhammad in the Outremer. The cardinal wants the last set of *Sangraal* parchments too, if they still exist, and for you to translate them. They won't try to kill us in daylight but disguised and in darkness. Now, let's leave for Salamanca."

"How many days before we reach there?" I asked.

"Four to five days of hard riding, and some *montagnes* to cross before we arrive, but they shouldn't slow us down."

At sunset, we stopped in a dusty ravine and made camp for the night. Muhammad was the first to take the watch while perching himself on a rocky hilltop a short distant from our camp.

"We'll need to continue to Ponferrada and finally to Santiago de Compostela," Grand Master Gilbért informed us. "There I have some personal matters to address before we set sail for La Rochelle. Since you're not accompanying us to obtain the final parchment, it's tantamount that you discover its location," he stated.

Immediately, I reached for my saddlebag and found *Princesse* Helena's leather tube-shaped container and cautiously pulled out the fragile scrolls. With each scroll, my heart seemed to stop beating in remembrance of Helena and her deathly sacrifice. Quickly, I sat down near the smokeless fire and started copying what it said. *Noir Ombre* circled a couple of times near me and finally settled down next to my leg.

"Lord Robert, as soon as you figure out where Saint Joseph of Arimathea is traveling or his destination, please let me know," Chaplain Jeremiah stated as his fire shadow approached me.

"There is an excellent cathedral school in Salamanca that could help us find the final parchments. I know the provost there who could help us. I will slip off just before we reach the town outskirts and pray I'll succeed."

"If we do find anything definitive, I am still going home. When we reach La Rochelle, that's where we'll depart from one another. I *amour* each of you as true *fréres,* but *mon coeur* longs for Borron and my family. Please don't try to convince me otherwise. My determination is rooted tighter than an oak tree."

"Lord Robert, please forgive me. I know you want to—"

Suddenly, *Noir Ombre* gave out a low guttural growl and jumped up with his tail stiffened upward, with his eyes fixed, and with his entire body frozen, resembling a black canine statue. Slowly, his ears raised, and his black nose moved from side to side sniffing the air. Then came light footfalls, which stopped several times. When they started again, it was in the opposite direction. Our fellow canine soldier turned around with his gums bared and his large teeth snapping, followed by throat barking. Grand Master Gilbért unsheathed his sword and grabbed a large burning stick from our fire to see well. Quickly, I put the scrolls in my saddlebag. I too drew my sword, but then held tight to *Noir Ombre's* collar as he lunged forward. Promptly, I hit the ground as I heard the deadly *hissing* of a crossbow quarrel piercing the moonless night, followed by the high-pitched words, "*Allahu Akbar*," and a loud thud coming from the darkness. The night air drew deathly silent, followed by a human gurgling sound, a short distance from our camp. Once again, what seemed like endless stillness was followed with quiet footfalls from the north of the camp.

"It is me, Muhammad," spoke a welcome voice. "I just slit the throat of a *Hashishiyya*. He was sent to kill Grand Master Gilbért with his crossbow. We're quite fortunate not all of them came at us at once. Their killer instincts are strengthened by the darkness, *mes amis.* Apparently, he pledged to his master to go alone."

"May I see his hands?" I asked, wondering if our killer wore one of their tribal rings.

"*Oui,* Lord Robert. Follow me." He motioned to both Grand Master Gilbért and me.

We followed him just a short distance with *Noir Ombre* trotting ahead. As Grand Master Gilbért held his burning stick over the body, *Noir Ombre* sniffed the still billowing blood. Our killer's throat revealed a neatly cut gaping wound from ear to ear. The burning light reflected off the same golden crescent moon, and eagle symbols embedded in a black onyx stone ring. Identical to the one I observed at Vézelay many months ago.

"Is it the same ring?" Muhammad asked.

"*Oui*, I am sorry to say. I now believe these *Hashishiyya* are hiding everywhere we travel. Will they track me to my home in Borron?" I glanced at both Grand Master Gilbért and Muhammad as my stomach tightened.

"Possibly," Grand Master Gilbért replied. "The cardinal needs you to translate the writings and cipher the codes. He'll use any manner of persuasion to accomplish his evil task. Muhammad, Jacque de Hoult, and I are a fortress around you that he will try to destroy. So, going home doesn't assure you anything."

"Damn it to hell!" I shouted. "So, it doesn't make any difference if I translate these parchments or not?" I could feel my face flush with hot anger. "It appears that we must plan to kill the cardinal before I'll ever see *mon* family again." I couldn't believe I was saying this, which was a mortal sin, but I would rather burn in hell than not see my *épouse* and two *fils*.

"*Non*, you are wrong, *mon ami*. I am the one who is laying the trap so the monster will kill himself. I can't prevent you from going home, but I believe you would put your entire family in harm's way if you did. Lord Robert, what we're accomplishing is far greater than either of us can comprehend. All our salvations are at stake. We need to protect what the *Sangraal* parchment words are telling us and pray our Lord and Savior's words and teachings don't fall into evil hands. I believe still, in my heart, the cardinal's own malevolent web will snare him. That's all I have to say and now let's bury this vile killer, so you can complete your translations and solve the ciphers."

We hastily buried the *Hashishiyya* killer and thereafter I returned to my translating Saint Joseph of Arimathea's gospel. I noted several clues about where Saint Joseph and his small band were traveling. He had returned to his boyhood home of Arimathea searching for his family after being released from prison. There he reunited with his family, *amis,* and some of our Lord's disciples and apostles including Philip, Mary Magdaleine, John the Writer, Nicodemus, Martha, Lazarus, Thomas, John Mark, and Shimon the Zealot. From their cave, Joseph showed them the miraculous cup that Jesus the Christ had given him. During this time, the small band of followers learned the five hallows of the *Sangraal* procession. They all agreed to go out among the Gentiles and teach the words of their Savior and show the wonders of His cup.

He and Philip, before leaving, had several visions concerning the location of their Savior's church.

Finally, I came to where the parchments stated the possible location of the first Christian church. Swiftly, I jumped up with trembling hands and rushed to awaken Chaplain Jeremiah.

"*Abbé* Jeremiah, please wake up," I whispered while shaking him. Slowly, he rose and gazed at me with narrow fluttering eyes.

"Lord Robert, are we again under attack?"

"*Non*! I've discovered the country where Saint Joseph of Arimathea and his teachers are destined to reach. It is the Isle of Britannia or England where we will find the first Christian church."

"How do you know this?"

"The first parchments mentioned the Isle of the Celts several times. Don't you remember Saint Joseph's son giving his sister a silver-colored box he brought back from this isle? In addition, Saint Joseph's traveling with our Lord to Britannia in search of tin and meeting Pontius Pilate's father. The second thing he said, that a *roi* of those lands asked Saint Joseph and his son, Alein Josephe, to visit the Isle of Mist. Third, Saint Philip's name was mentioned about his interest in visiting the Britannia Isle at the Mount of Olives supper. Furthermore, remember our Lord's prophecy at the cave of Gethsemane about John the Baptizer's son starting a line of *rois* on the Britannia Isle."

"*Oui,* I remember all of that, but England is a big isle with many small isles. It would take a lifetime to search out this first Christian church and Saint Joseph's *Sangraal* parchments," Chaplain Jeremiah retorted. "You woke me up for old information?"

"*Non*, there are more new clues. Both Saint Joseph of Arimathea and Saint Philip had dreams that revealed additional information. In his second set of parchments, Saint Joseph had a dream or vision of our Lord with the Archangel Michael holding a sword and scales. Our Lord told him he would build His church on a misty glass-like isle alongside a tor or mount that's now named Saint Michael. Our Lord said this would be His *New Jerusalem* to build His first church. In addition, Saint Joseph revealed some troubling news too; he said he and his family were stalked by a killer and feared he might not survive our Lord's prophecy."

"Indeed, possibly this information gives us specific clues where Saint Joseph's church stands along with the third set of parchments. As I mentioned earlier, there is an excellent cathedral school in Salamanca. These new clues should help us determine a destination. Have you told these new findings to Grand Master Gilbért?"

"*Non.*"

Just then, I heard a second *hissing* sound come out of the darkness.

CHAPTER XXXII

"They are attacking us again!" I shouted, as I drew my sword and jumped out of the firelight. Grand Master Gilbért rushed toward the ink-black night, and Sergeant Jacque de Hoult followed him. We were suddenly stopped by a desperate, high-pitched *whinny* sound from a horse, followed by a loud *thump*.

"*Mère de Dieu*, I am hurt," gasped Chaplain Jeremiah after running toward the horse.

The quarrel bolt dangled from his red cross surcoat, as he stumbled backward. My eyes quickly adjusted to the dark. To my right raced four wraith-like dark objects. I heard a familiar guttural growl followed by sharp, high-pitched barking, then came Muhammad's voice, "*Allahu Akbar*." His black turbined head came out of the darkness.

"There was another killer partially hidden in the dirt. He had lain there before his accomplice attacked us. The soil and his secret herbs must have deceived *Noir Ombre's* nose," Muhammad said. "His poisonous quarrel did kill one of our pack horses, but I am afraid Chaplain Jeremiah is a victim of his second shot. As you can see, my axe found its mark on the back of his head."

Muhammad's battle-axe had exposed the killer's pinkish, gray-colored brain, but my immediate concern focused on the still body of Chaplain Jeremiah. Both Grand Master Gilbért and

I rushed to his unresponsive side and noticed his eyes closed. Carefully, I removed the poisonous quarrel tip and observed no blood as Grand Master Gilbért held a blazing torch over his body. I touched a hard metal object under his aketon. My fingertips traced the outline of a large metal cross with a sizeable indentation on it. I shook him several times that resulted in a slight moan, only to observe his eyes twittering before me.

"Chaplain Jeremiah, our Lord's cross protected your life tonight," Grand Master Gilbért said to his *fils*. "The side of your head hit a rock."

"However, he didn't protect your head," I stated as our chaplain's blood-tipped fingers came from his head.

"We need to leave here now!" Chaplain Jeremiah exclaimed as he staggered upward. "I must reach Salamanca as soon as possible. While unconscious, I dreamt more of their black-masked faces appearing to me. Let's ride tonight. Sitting or sleeping here, even with no campfire, will attract more of the killers. In addition, Lord Robert just divulged some new clues on the whereabouts of the third set of *Sangraal* parchments."

"Why didn't you tell me you found some definitive clues about our quest?" the Grand Master of Iberia asked.

"I just discovered this information right before the second attack. Besides, you were asleep, and our chaplain previously told me he knew a source in Salamanca who would help us with our quest."

"*Non* more discussion; let's leave immediately, Lord Robert."

Quickly, I saddled my horse along with my fellow companions then Muhammad led us forward with a hastily made *crackling* torch.

We rode all night and into the next morning, only stopping twice to water our horses. The western horizon became a milky red color as an approaching storm appeared in front of us.

"Grand Master Gilbért, how far is it until we reach the outskirts of Salamanca?" I asked.

"It's another three leagues by my estimation. There's a cave about a league from the town, and we can stay there for the night, if it's empty.

Muhammad, speak to our horses so they'll gallop faster!"

Muhammad shouted, "*Allahu Akbar*!" and our horses hurtled forward with incredible speed.

We reached the cave just as the storm came. It was God's providence we had made it before our torches became extinguished. The cave was unoccupied and large, letting us unpack our horses with ease. Sergeant Hoult immediately started a fire as I unsaddled my horse with aching arms and back. My tiredness had left me unable to steady myself, which caused me to collapse on my knees near the fire. Next, I only remembered putting my head against the earthy smell of the cave's dirt floor. Sometime during the night I awoke to the whispering sound of a human voice. I bolted straight up and reached for the hilt of my sword. I cautiously rose, after which I faintly heard my name. I stared toward Muhammad, who guarded the entrance, but he didn't acknowledge the whispering voice or me. Was I dreaming? However, the numerous past experiences with what I thought were dreams had become actual reality. With caution, I moved toward the raspy sounding whisper. Slowly, I removed my sword from its scabbard and crept toward the darkness. My eyes adjusted to the darkness to see a small flickering light farther ahead.

"Pilgrim, come forth," the faint voice demanded. "*Mon ami*, we meet once again, but this time you are older and wiser. There's still much before you to come and gaining wisdom and salvation have no bounds."

I recognized the voice as the mysterious *moine* from the Cathar cave in the foothills of the Pyrénées *Montagnes*. However, how did he know we would stop at this cave?

"You're the *moine* I met in the cave where the Cathars held their religious services, *non*?"

"*Oui*, and I see you are in good health," his dark-hooded face stated.

I still couldn't see the details of his face, for it seemed as dark as the interior of the cave. He held a candle in his bony hand and slowly reached toward a rock niche and placed the burning taper into it. His brown sleeve fell back exposing a thin, sinewy pale-skinned arm.

"The quest now before you contains doubt, betrayal, and your fellow companions' weaknesses. Your strong leadership will reflect your steady faith in our Creator and His *Fils*. The coming days won't be free of physical battle, but you now face greater enemies. The final battle will have minds filled with evil and indecision, and each has a strong chain mail. Your goal is near, pilgrim, but an enormous chasm still confronts you."

With his other bony arm, he slowly reached into his brown *moine's* habit and pulled out the same bronze glowing chalice from the cave at the foothills of the Pyrénées *Montagnes*. The blinding white light forced me to place my arm before my eyes. Squinting with both of my eyes to see, they ached with pain as they moved back and forth following the radiating beams of yellow and white lights.

"Pilgrim, at the right time you'll be able to see what this cup beholds. The cup of salvation will appear when you find the third and final set of parchments. Now I must go, for my journey is long, and my body is old."

"What is your name, *mon ami*?" I asked, hoping he would finally tell me.

However, all I heard was a reply of, "I am a guide."

I stood there troubled with confusion and uncertainty as the old *moine* disappeared back into the darkness of the cave. My salvation and responsibility to others depended on me to continue. That made my head throb as if a mace had just hit it.

The next day we were in the saddle before first light and after some distance we reached the outskirts of Salamanca and made camp. Abruptly, Chaplain Jeremiah left, leaving us wondering where in England this first *église* might be.

Toward dusk he returned and announced our final destination. It would be a town called Glastonbury, which was a holy isle town on a dried-up inland seabed in the southwestern part of England. An ancient codex at the college said that early Christian *pères* inhabited this isle shortly after a tin merchant converted the Druids to the way of our Lord and Savior.

"Will this definitive information change your mind about traveling with us to England?" Chaplain Jeremiah asked as he and his *père* sat down facing me around the *crackling* campfire.

"I have no choice, but to protect my faith and see that divine justice is served," I answered. "Besides, we know that the tin merchant was Saint Joseph of Arimathea."

"What choice do you not have, Lord Robert?" Grand Master Gilbért asked.

I explained my angst and the immediate need for justice for my faith, family, and late departed *amis*. Immediately, a large grin erupted across Grand Master Gilbért's face.

"Sweet Mary and Joseph, we now have a final objective for our third and final set of holy parchments. I am quite relieved to hear this *bon* news. When we get to our fortress at Ponferrada, I'll arrange for a ship to take us to the southern coast of England."

I didn't want to tell him about the *moine* in the cave and his warning, but I knew it was necessary.

"There's a warning," I said. "I just learned of it.

"What kind of sign?" Grand Master Gilbért inquired.

"At the back of the cave, I had another visit by the *moine*, whom I originally thought was a Cathar bishop. He called my name and once again showed me . . . a radiating bronze chalice. In addition, he prophesied a cryptic warning about our travels ahead. He said we would confront new enemies—that of our emotional weaknesses and demonic minions. These new enemies will bring out our soul's shortcomings, and they would thwart our quest. My leadership will help staunch these personal failings."

Immediately, everyone around the campfire gazed at each other. *Abad* Miguel sat there with a reticent face as the dancing campfire flames reflected in his eyes.

"Lord Robert, may I speak to you in private?" Chaplain Jeremiah asked.

"*Oui*," I replied as we moved from the campfire and strolled some distance from camp.

"I apologize for imparting this unwelcome news. The old

moine's predictions are quite accurate, and I can't explain how he knows where we travel."

"Lord Robert, you don't need to apologize. *Oui*, I am mad, and it will take a while for me to get over this bad revelation. However, I fear for our grand master's spiritual being. You were right about our new enemies of emotional nature. Sergeant Guy de Béziers's death and betrayal, along with Squire Hughes de Montbard's death, and Grand Master Gilbért's wounds have pushed our leader to the brink of spiritual and physical collapse. You don't see this, but I do. True, his reflexes have slowed, but his mind too isn't reacting as fast. Please don't tell the others, for I fear the prophecy will come true and *oui*, we'll need your strong leadership."

We ambled back to camp as Muhammad stood guard while the others tried to sleep. I strolled toward Muhammad as *Noir Ombre* trotted toward me. His wagging tail greeted me with his large pink tongue licking my hand. He was now the sole companion of our group I could trust. Was Grand Master Gilbért's *bâtard fils* right about his *père* or was this a trick to discredit him? Now it began, my numerous suspicions. However, I had to disapprove of these suspicions and not let mindless conjecture fill my head.

"*Rasul*, how do you feel?" Muhammad Nur Adin asked. "Your face reflects your thinking, and I see thousands of ants crawling inside your brain and none of them going in the same directions."

He was right, I did have a thousand ants in my head, and they were slowly starting to march in step.

"*Oui*, you're right, but I have a plan and you know I can't divulge it."

"That's true because *Allah* guides you. You're a *maymum* or blessed by Him and if He wills it, you will find your holy parchments and maybe more."

"Why do you say and maybe more?"

"I dreamt about the Prophet *Issa*. May peace and blessings be upon Him. Your *Issa* told me you'll find far greater glory in His name than written down by His holy witness, Yoseph of Arimathea."

"Did your dream say what that greater glory might be?" I asked.

"*Non*, but I suspect the Prophet *Issa* will surprise you."

It amazed me that the different faiths my journey had exposed me to now seemed connected in some strange way. My entire troubled quest was illuminating yet filled with more angst than I cared to know.

I decided to translate more words from Saint Joseph's second set of parchments before I obtained some sleep, yet I was apprehensive about what I might find about the stalker-killer called Barabbas. Now I read that Saint Joseph's family feared the unseen evil that surrounded them on the road to Yoppa. Later they would see what happened at the home of Tabitha or her other name of Dorcas, which was her Greek name. This killer hadn't only attacked her son and murdered him, but earlier murdered the son of Saint Joseph's *bon ami,* Eli, the cloth and camel merchant. Much earlier he slaughtered a donkey and smeared its blood on the baby of Saint Joseph's sister, Enygeus. Then left a message saying he would murder all of Saint Joseph's family and Jesus the Christ's apostles in their sleep. However, reading further, Saint Joseph mentioned several miracles of the *Sangraal* cup. Once, saving a dying baby's life and later resurrecting Tabitha's son, Hiram.

I rolled up Saint Joseph's parchments and bound them with some twine, then placed them in Helena's leather tube, which she gifted to me. I stretched out near the fire clutching the new leather-smelling container; thereafter falling asleep, knowing the *Sangraal* cup had relieved some poor soul's pain and suffering.

At dawn, we raced off toward the Tormes River and after one league came to a rushing whitecapped waterway.

"We can't cross here, it's too swift and deep," I announced.

"True, Lord Robert, but there's a ford another league west of here," replied Grand Master Gilbért. We traveled as fast as a gale wind and now stood before the shallow ford. We spurred our horses and galloped across it. Afterward, we headed toward our next destination, Zamora. Grand Master Gilbért said the town was fifteen leagues ahead and sat on a rocky plateau above the

Rio Douro. It began as an important outpost in the fierce fighting between Muslims and Christians between the seventh and eleventh centuries of our Lord and Savior.

"Lord Robert, did you know El Cid, or by his Iberian name Rodrigo Diaz de Vivar, became a *chevalier* at the *Iglesia* of Santiago de los *Caballeros*?" Chaplain Jeremiah asked.

"*Non*," I replied. Not caring as my mind tried to deduct methodically who our traitor might be. Who had the most to gain by risking their life to betray us? Was it Muhammad? He had his lands taken away and was only left with just a title. His faith didn't believe our Christ was both our Savior and Redeemer, and Christ didn't rise from the dead and sit on His throne next to God. He was my chief suspect for now, yet what about Sergeant Jacque de Hoult? He had always done his grand master's bidding and didn't receive any promotion for his faithful service. My next suspect was Chaplain Jeremiah and the many years spent away from his unacknowledged *père*. In addition, there was *Abad* Miguel. Why did he want to travel with us to England? A busy *monastère* called him to oversee it, which now lacked his blood *frère*. How would I investigate and find out their real motives without alarming them?

We camped near a large outcropping of rocks that protected us from the northwestern winds that now brought icy rain. There was no fire built tonight, and the slippery ground was so dark from no moon that even the fallen ice didn't glisten. I found a comfortable rock, if there was such a thing, and laid my head upon it to go to sleep before my designated watch time.

Sometime during the night, Muhammad shook me to rise and relieve his watch. In addition, *Noir Ombre* licked my face before I could raise one knee. I staggered upward, only to slip on the ice and fall on all fours. Once again, our canine warrior *ami* licked my face and then stood back with his large dark eyes staring at mine. His pulled-back gums and long dangling pink tongue seemed to be laughing at me or ready to play.

"Lord Robert, it seems *Noir Ombre* is laughing at your fall, and he's now ready for you to chase him," Muhammad said with a grin.

"It's *bon* both of you are laughing at my expense. It's seldom we get to smile on our quest and my canine *ami* has helped us do this. My clumsiness is now a tonic for our band of warriors, yet I pray this doesn't happen when we're under attack."

"What's all the commotion?" Grand Master Gilbért asked.

"Lord Robert was showing me some new sword moves he learned from our attack at Toledo," Muhammad said, a hint of a smile on his cheeks.

"Why is Lord Robert smiling and so is our canine *ami*?" he questioned Muhammad.

"Grand Master Gilbért, I wasn't showing Muhammad a new sword move but fell while rising from my sleep," I confessed.

We all chuckled, glad to have rare laughter

Grand Master Gilbért put his arm around me. "I must say, Lord Robert, you have an affinity for slipping. Maybe you should follow the moves of *Noir Ombre* instead of the *Hashishiyya* killers. He has two extra legs, which helps him stay upright."

"*Oui*, you're right, *mon ami*."

Grand Master Gilbért moved toward his saddled horse. "Let's move on to Zamora before daylight. I don't need any more sleep; besides there's a warm bed waiting for us at the *monastère*."

CHAPTER XXXIII

The road from Salamanca to Zamora was cold, yet uneventful. Winter still had its cold claw on us, and it was near the holy feast day of Saint Sebastian when we arrived in Zamora. It was like any other town I had visited. Situated high on a bluff overlooking a river or rio as the locals called it. A stone-walled fortress surrounded the town protecting its inhabitants. All the towns and all the fortresses seemed to appear the same. I had traveled for a total of four months and, like the poor martyred Saint Sebastian, my entire body stung like the many arrows inflicted upon him.

"Lord Robert," called out Grand Master Gilbért. "The *monastère* is to our left. Do you see the tower and dome of the cathedral?"

"*Oui*, it's different," I replied, but I didn't really care. The cathedral sat close to the Rio Duero and all I desired was rest. I told myself maybe some sleep would help me to reveal the new traitor.

"Grand Master Gilbért, when will we leave Zamora?" I asked.

"We won't be staying in Zamora. We'll head north from there to a Cistercian *monastère* called Santa María de Moreruela. It is six leagues from here and isolated from the prying eyes of Cardinal Folquet's spies. We can rest there and then it's a day-and-a-half's ride to the fortress of Ponferrada. From there on to Santiago de Compostela to arrange for our ship to England."

It appeared we wouldn't stop until nightfall. Oh, how I wanted to sleep. After slowly avoiding Zamora, we raced due north all day. Muhammad kept the horses trotting by shouting at them in his high-pitched commands.

We arrived there just as the sun hid behind the base of the apsidal. We were let in through the fortified walls by a white-habited *moine*. Just as we approached the front of the *iglesia*, the *abbé* greeted us.

"*Bonjour*, Grand Master Gilbért de Érail. It's great to see you once more," the dark-haired swarthy faced *prêtre* said.

"Same here, *bon ami*. *Abbé* André, how did you know we would stop here?"

"There is only one Iberian Poor-Soldier of Christ master who has a Saracen for a scout. He frightened all the other *frères* when they spotted him in the tree line. Have you journeyed well?"

"*Oui*, yet some bandits were foolish enough to try to stop us. Most of them met their untimely end. We hope you will let us stay here a couple of days and rest. My fellow *frères* are exhausted. We are headed to our fortress at Ponferrada."

Grand Master Gilbért chose his words carefully as his tone told me he was suspicious. He now questioned everyone and their inquiries. His lack of ease made my palms start to sweat. The traitor or traitors in our midst tightened my neck to solve this evil threat, which seemed to grow each day. Maybe I will have time in the next two days to solve this danger to our quest.

"*Frère* Gilbért, what did you do with that ancient book you brought back from the Levant? It raised the curiosity of all the *moines* at Clairvaux."

At first, Grand Master Gilbért didn't reply, but remained silent. I wondered what he would say. His hands twisted with each other and then he replied.

"I gave it to papal legate at our fortress at Montpellier. He wanted it so he could find somebody to divulge the ancient words. He hoped some scholar in Rome might be able to read it. I haven't heard a reply or seen it since the day I turned it over to the legate.

Now, my fellow *frères* and I would like to retire."

"*Oui*, I will have my drapier show you and your *chevalier* to our guest quarters. *Abad* Miguel can stay with me, and your sergeant can stay with the rest of *mon frères*. The Saracen can stay in the stable. I fear the other *moines* are terrified of him."

"*Oui*, he won't mind sleeping in the stable with his horse *amis*, and like him, I could sleep anywhere."

We followed the drapier to the guest quarters that overlooked the snake-coiled road to Ponferrada. The room's spacious size with its three beds beckoned me to go to sleep. Grand Master Gilbért's narrow eyes spoke of his tiredness too as we both fell on top of two of the beds, yet Grand Master Gilbért surprised me by speaking.

"Lord Robert, I suspect the *abbé* knew something of Saint Joseph de Arimathea's book at Clairvaux *Abbaye*. Don't forget how ornate the book appeared, which was completed at Clairvaux. André always followed me in his role as assistant *abbé*. Late one night, I hid the gospel under some loose altar stones. *Abbé* André prayed several times in front of these stones, not realizing the book lay hidden underneath. Several nights later I retrieved the book and then left for Montpellier. *Mon ami*, we must leave here tomorrow."

Grand Master Gilbért didn't say another word but fell fast asleep with a quiet whistling sound coming from his bed. The tone in his voice had reflected despair and frustration and reminded me that our leader's confidence no longer existed. It appeared that I must trudge farther in our quest and assume the leadership that he now lacked.

The next day we left, telling *Abbé* André that we were urgently needed at the fortress of Ponferrada. The long ride ahead gave me time to contemplate about our unknown traitor among us. I told myself that I had four suspects: one was Muhammad; the second was Sergeant Jacque de Hoult; the third was Chaplain Jeremiah, Gilbért's *fils*; and finally *Abad* Miguel. De Hoult never told me about his family or when he joined the order. Other than serving in the Levant with Grand Master Gilbért and his knowledge of the Arabic language, further information was sparse. Muhammad owed his life to the grand master, and Chaplain Jeremiah was a blood relation. This left *Abad* Miguel who helped raise Gilbért. I deduced that Sergeant Jacque must be the spy for Cardinal Folquet. However, it was left up to me to determine his motive, which I prayed wasn't the same as Sergeant Guy de Béziers. Holding one's family and ransoming their lives for information left me with a tight feeling in my chest. Maybe some indiscreet questions over the next several days would divulge some information.

During the ride to the Ponferrada fortress, I gathered my thoughts to set up some questions to ask Sergeant Jacque de Hoult. Carefully in my mind, I asked him my first question after trotting alongside him.

"Sergeant Jacque, do you have family nearby?"

"*Non mère* or *père*, just a living *soeur* and *frère*. My *soeur* is in a nunnery, I know not where. *Mon frère* is with our order in England. He has a trusted position at our temple in London. He educated himself to do bookkeeping and he manages our order's finances. I hope to see him if we travel to England. As children we worked at Temple Bruer in Lincolnshire, England. Most of my family died in one of the many plagues that swept that part of the country. The men of the Temple helped raise me until I became a Poor-Soldier of Christ. I long to see my *soeur*, but our order doesn't encourage us to fraternize with the female members of our family. She was sickly as a child and *mon* last surviving *soeur*. I still worry about her, even though she is safe in a nunnery. The rumors I have heard, say she might be living in the priory at Stixwould, which is situated in Lincolnshire, England."

His information didn't reveal any great revelations, other than his *frère* oversaw the order's financial records. Could his *frère* be used to discredit Grand Master Gilbért and implicate him in financial malfeasance?

As we got ready for sleep in a copse of trees, that just left one more day's full ride and we would rest for several days at Ponferrada. It seemed impossible, the leagues we had to travel.

"Grand Master Gilbért, I have two questions to ask you," I said with a whisper. "How will we arrive in Ponferrada in just a day?"

"*Seigneur* Robert, I remembered a shortcut we can take to reach Ponferrada. I need to rest and all of us need to rest. What was your second question?"

"Do you suspect the traitor is Sergeant Jacque de Hoult? I do, and he has a blood *frère* working at the London Temple."

"*Oui*, I know he works there. I don't want to discuss this now. I'll feel safer discussing this at our fortress. We'll speak of this later. Do you understand?" Gilbért replied with a narrow-eyed grimace. He then abruptly left me and prepared for sleep.

His sudden departure and response troubled me. He seemed to slip even deeper in his indecisions. I prayed he would improve after resting at the fortress.

PART FIVE

Ponferrada Cross

CHAPTER XXXIV

Ponferrada Fortress
Late January
Anno Domini 1191

The next day, we broke camp before sunrise and raced toward our shortcut to Ponferrada. We only rested to water the horses and ate some stale cheese as we hurried forth. We arrived just as the sun set behind some newly built round towers. The *château* was still under construction and perched on a tall hillock between two valleys and *montagne* ranges. We found a suitable place to cross the Sil Rio. Quietly, we approached the unfinished barbicans where several Poor-Soldiers of Christ ordered us to *detener*. Behind several merlons appeared two sergeants.

"It is *Su Excelencia* Grand Master Gilbért de Érail of Iberia. Please let me and my fellow *hermanos* in for the night."

We crossed a stone-arched bridge and entered through the barbican entrance. A tall dark-haired man rushed out of a heavy wooden door with large dark piercing eyes. He wore a clean white mantle with a matching surcoat. The large embroidered pattée crosses seemed to glow in the dusky light.

"Commander Juan Felipe, it is *bueno* to see you once more," Grand Master Gilbért announced.

"Si, *Su Excelencia*, it has been over a year. Please follow me to my commandery headquarters so we can discuss matters. I see a couple of new people with you this time."

Quickly, several squires rushed out and helped us with our horses. All around us was wooden scaffolding and one enormous wooden crane.

"*Perdón*, the *castillo* is a mess. We are expanding our headquarters for the many pilgrims on the way to Santiago," Commander Juan Felipe stated. "Please come into my quarters and sit down. Grand Master Gilbért, I received *Rey* Alfonso's message you would arrive here, but he didn't give a date. He stated it was an urgent matter."

"*Si*, it is important, but I can't divulge any more information. We need to prevail on your hospitality and rest our horses for several days. All I can tell you is my fellow *hermanos* and I need sailing transportation from A Coruña to La Rochelle. Can you arrange this with our fleet there?"

"*Si*, *Su Excelencia* Gilbért, and the admiral of the fleet is my *tio*. Just give me an estimated time of arrival and I will send one of my *caballeros* tomorrow to make the arrangements. The winter weather will break soon, and sailing will improve. When will you be leaving?"

There was a long pause before Grand Master Gilbért spoke. It appeared he was in a deep trance and not hearing the question asked of him. What was troubling our leader? His quick decisiveness had disappeared. I dreaded that his mind was failing, yet after what seemed an eternity, he replied.

"I estimate after two days of rest here and another four days to travel to Santiago de Compostela and then rest there for several days; followed by another five days to A Coruña. You are not to speak of this matter other than to your *caballero*. Now I must rest. Where will I sleep?"

Commander Juan Felipe pointed to his bed and immediately Grand Master Gilbért fell into his loaned straw bed.

I introduced myself and my fellow comrades to Commander Juan Felipe and *Abad* Miguel and Chaplain Jeremiah. He seemed to be an affable person and personally directed us to our quarters while Muhammad cooled down our horses.

Our guest quarters were sparse with bare wooden beds and a lone pattée cross-shaped window. The commander spoke to *Abad* Miguel in a hushed tone then left as the drapier arrived. The drapier placed clean sheets and pillowcases on the beds and stuffed additional straw in each pillow and mattress. After he left, I asked Chaplain Jeremiah what Commander Juan Felipe said.

"He wondered if his Grand Master Gilbért was sick, because of his distant and abrupt responses. He remembered him as a very decisive *caballero* and full of self-confidence. If we needed any additional help, he invited us to come to his quarters. He also said there are several maps and books in the *castillo chapelle* sacristy that might aid us in our travels. Among those books would be parchments to copy maps and information. I suggest we go there early tomorrow morning after we break our fast."

"*Oui*, I agree and we can chart our course to England and the shortest roads to Glastonbury *Abbaye*. Right now, all I want to do is sleep. My legs feel as if they have double chain mail, and my mind is empty of any initiative. Now that we have determined we will meet in the sacristy tomorrow, sleep beckons. *Bonne nuit*, *Frère* Jeremiah." Like Grand Master Gilbért, I fell upon my bed in a sole sleeping room, thinking that Sergeant Jacque de Hoult was our traitor and what must I do or say next to our leader.

A distant barnyard rooster awakened me with a beam of blinding sunlight coming through the pattée cross opening. I heard footsteps next to me and quickly noticed it was Sergeant Jacque de Hoult. My hand grasped for my dagger, but it wasn't there. I bolted out of bed and asked him what he wanted.

"*Seigneur* Robert, last night I partook in the liberty to remove your dagger, sword, and spurs. I hope you slept well. Besides, Chaplain Jeremiah wants you to meet him in the refectory to break your fast. I just finished and he gave me the message."

How many times had the sergeant entered my one-man room? A deep shiver crept down my back knowing he could have murdered me in my sleep. I buckled my dagger and sword, which last night were placed next to my bed.

"*Oui*, I slept quite sound. Maybe too sound." He kept staring at me as if he expected a confrontation. "Now I must leave and speak to Chaplain Jeremiah. Also I famished," which was a lie.

Slowly, I strolled out of the guest house and headed toward the refectory. One thing I didn't have was an appetite. Chaplain Jeremiah, still eating his bowl of gruel, glanced up and motioned for me to sit at his table. His eyes never met mine, but he finished his meal, got up, and then pointed toward the direction of sacristy. We both strolled out into the frosty morning air to see the sun break above the mountains surrounding us. The door to the *chapelle* was arch-shaped and thick. More of a barricade door ready for defense. The narthex had a side door, which led to an adjacent small building. Here we entered to reveal numerous altar items used in performing mass. Once again morning light streamed through another pattée cross-shaped window. Yet this time the room glowed an orange-red color from its stained-glass window. Along the sacristy wall I spied a wooden trestle table with numerous large books with quill pens, small clay ink pots, and several sheets of blank parchment paper. In the far-right corner hung the chaplain's vestments and stored in an open-faced cupboard were altar items for mass.

"*Seigneur* Robert, we must maintain a muffled voice while we peruse this material. Did you have something to say before we start? Your face and mouth seemed drawn."

"*Oui*, I believe Sergeant Jacque de Hoult is closely observing me and could murder me at the proper time. He was in my room last night and retrieved my sword and dagger. Lately, he has displayed the strange behavior of scrutinizing me more than normal."

"We'll discuss this matter later. Right now, let us use these resources while they are still available to us. Behold! Here is a red-colored leather-bound tome that has the word England written on the leather cover. Let's hope this book will have the information we seek."

Chaplain Jeremiah's large hands reached for the thick laden book and started fingering the pages. They emanated a *crinkling* sound as he perused the many parchment sheets. Suddenly he stopped. His index finger pointed to a drawing of a *moine,* with his tonsured haircut, writing on a large upright board. There was a signature below the page which read *Frère* Dunstan.

"I can't believe what I am seeing," retorted Chaplain Jeremiah. "This is the great saint who was the *abbé* of Glastonbury and fought the Devil there and harnessed him with Saint Dunstan's metal working iron tongs. Also there are written words by him."

I glanced in the direction of the section he was saying in Latin and translated it in my mind.

"'In this place at God's command the first neophytes of the catholic law discovered an ancient church, which we now call *Vetusta Ecclesia*, built by the Holy Spirit . . . consecrated to Christ and our most blessed Mother Mary. Here below is another picture of Saint Dunstan playing his harp while the Devil creeps through his doorway. When I studied in Paris, we discussed many times what he contributed to our Christian faith. He was a strict teacher of Saint Benedict's rule that led him and his fellow *moines* to rebuild and enlarge the *monastère* there in southwest England. He knew of the old church. *Seigneur* Robert, this is a signpost for us and the next *santo* parchments. Also there is another map showing a boat dock at Weymouth, England, and a road that leads to Glastonbury."

"What does the pattée cross mean near the left of the town of Shaftesbury?" My finger pointed to the small cross. "Is it a religious house?

"*Si,* or I mean *oui, Seigneur* Robert. I suspect it is a Templar house. We need to speak to Grand Master Gilbért about what we have found." His large hand flipped to another page, which revealed a treatise by a *moine* named Guillaume de Malmesbury. "It is called *De Antiquitate Glastoniensis Ecclesiae* or *On the Antiquity of Glastonbury.*" Silently his coal-black eyes flashed back and forth across the page.

"The *moine,* Guillaume de Malmesbury, visited at Glastonbury *Abbaye* during the years 1129 through 1140 and wrote and studied there. He dedicated his *On the Antiquity of Glastonbury* to the *abbaye* and bishop there by the name Henri de Blois. This *abbaye* and bishop held the office of papal legate and assumed the position of the most powerful religious man in England. He and *Frère* Guillaume became *bons amis.* I need to read this further before we leave for Santiago de Compostela. Give me until the office of Nones and I will let you know what it says. Let us leave now and meet back here at Nones. Does this sound satisfactory, *mon ami*?"

"*Oui*, and this will give me sufficient time to converse with Grand Master Gilbért." Which I hoped would reveal some answers or advice. We left the way we came but were stopped by the sight of Grand Master Gilbért on his knees slowly creeping toward the altar of the *chapelle.* My mind became numb with incredulity as I saw tears streaming down his cheeks. He was holding his chaplet beads and saying his Glory Bes. Gilbért didn't seem to notice us but continued advancing toward the altar. In front of him, on the altar, sat a jewel encrusted silver cross. It displayed two sets of horizontal arms and the arm tips displayed sapphires and emeralds. The center of the silver cross revealed a large ruby. About halfway down the vertical shaft two golden angels appeared. One on each side.

"Behold the true cross!" bellowed Grand Master Gilbért. "All are sinners before it, except the Holy One who hung on it. We must now kneel before it. Did you hear me, soldiers of Christ? Do it right now, I command."

Both Chaplain Jeremiah and I went down, crossing ourselves with a simultaneous thud. Slowly Gilbért crossed himself, and then rose and we followed. He bowed to the cross and afterward reached for it. Gilbért carefully grasped one of the angels and twisted it. What was he doing? Slowly, he rotated the angel to the right, which then forced the shank of the cross to open like a hinged door. Thus, displaying a dark piece of wood lying in a purple cloth. Once again, he shouted, "Behold the true cross of Jesus the Christ!" We both again went down on our knees a second time and crossed ourselves. Was this truly a piece of the crucifixion cross? It really didn't matter, for my whole body started trembling and a feeling of euphoria came over me. I felt as if I was lifted into the air and then drawn toward the cross. Once there, Grand Master Gilbért reached for the other angel and twisted it. A small door-like lid swung from the back of the cross, opposite the front, and a small scroll fell out. It was the length of my index finger and slowly it floated to the altar table. Immediately Grand Master Gilbért collapsed onto the altar step and remained unconscious. My shaking hand reached for the small parchment scroll, not wanting to touch the sained cross, and tucked it in my sword belt. A blinding golden light emerged from the wood along with a sweet-smelling fragrance. The small *chapelle* filled with hazy smoke as *Frère* Jeremiah attempted to close the front door lid of the cross. What appeared as an eternity of time, his hands closed both small doors. Then he screamed after noticing his smoldering fingers and raced toward the holy water font.

"Where did that cross come from?" shouted Chaplain Jeremiah.

I didn't know who he was asking, but I knew I didn't have an answer. After dunking both hands in the holy font, he wrapped both with religious stoles hung near the altar. I reached down and raised Grand Master Gilbért's head. His lips mumbled some unintelligent sounds and then he shook his head and opened his eyes.

"What happened . . . to me?" His voice sounded tired.

"You grabbed the cross and twisted both angels, which exposed the piece of wood inside it. That is when you fainted. I must know where that cross originated. You already knew its extreme holiness after barking orders for us to kneel and show profound respect."

Was his son mad because of his seared hands or something else? His crimson face indicated such as he placed his face near Gilbért's nose.

"Your Excellency, this is not your normal behavior. You are a cautious and respectful man. Rash moods and non-commonsense behavior are not in your bailiwick. Now tell me where this cross originated," Chaplain Jeremiah demanded.

A long pause came from Grand Master Gilbért.

"Its style told me that it was made somewhere in Britannia and perhaps one of our *chevaliers* brought a piece of the holy crucifixion cross back from the Outremer. I guess he had the gold cross made at his commandery in Britain. Our order moves holy artifacts around for safekeeping. The kings, bishops, and lords of Christendom desire these holy relics for their kingdoms and cathedrals."

"Yet, how did you know this specific wood came from our Lord's crucifixion?" his *fils* asked.

"I don't know! Its power spoke to me."

"Did you know there was a small hidden scroll inside the back section of the cross door that you opened upon twisting the second angel?"

"*Non*," came their collective responses.

"May I see it?" Chaplain Jeremiah asked.

Carefully, I reached inside my belt and retrieved the finger-sized scroll. My hands slowly unrolled it and then placed it on the altar table. All three of our heads moved closer to reveal its contents.

"It is a map," I announced. "But where?"

"See those three lions stacked on top of each other and the precise writing?" Chaplain Jeremiah asked. "A monastic precentor or scribe wrote this. The lions represent the Isle of Britain and the red lines heading north appear to be old Roman roads. The small red cross is an abbey at the top of the red lines near Hadrian's Wall. Is that large red cross Glastonbury *Abbaye* with the flaming towers and why are they burning?"

I suspected this map was hidden for a later retrieval, but by whom?

"Lord Robert," Chaplain Jeremiah said. "Let's return to the library cupboard. Pray we will discover additional clues."

We traveled back to the library and sacristy to retrieve the book. Once removing the book from the cupboard, the spine revealed the same designed cross that Grand Master Gilbért just grabbed.

"Behold the design of the cross." I said. "It's the same as the altar cross. The clues are leading us in the right direction. Hurry and search the pages, Chaplain Jeremiah."

His hands and finger continued where he last read. After perusing all but the last section, his finger stopped.

"Observe this drawing and the words under it." Our chaplain's face drained white with surprise. "The drawing shows the cathedral consumed in flames and the Latin writing says it is the *abbaye* Cathedral of Saints Peter and Paul located at Glastonbury, England. The year is *Anno Domini* 1187, the year of the fire. Apparently, our map was drawn after 1187, by a *moine* well-trained in the art of mapmaking. I fear our third set of scrolls may have perished in the flames. Pray this is not so. We must ask Commander Juan Felipe where and when this tome and holy cross arrived at his commandery."

"*Oui,* and we don't want to divulge any more information, outside of us three, about what we have found. Chaplain Jeremiah, you are a scholar and have supervised a scriptorium. I say you ask the commander about the book and the cross's provenance. This will create less suspicion in his mind if you inquire."

"Lord Robert, it will be done after Compline. I think we should leave earlier than we planned. We still have a great distance to travel before reaching Santiago de Compostela."

Just then I heard scurried footfalls and then they stopped. After a fleeting period of time, a bird whistling sound broke the silence.

"That is Muhammad . . . Nur Adin," Grand Master Gilbért feebly responded. "He wants to speak to us now."

Chaplain Jeremiah replaced the red tome in the cupboard, and we left the sacristy for the courtyard. Our leader stumbled several times before reaching the bailey area. There he seemed to regain his normal gait and began to speak in a coherent fashion.

"Muhammad, what do you have to report? It is not good news I surmise. Your signaling told me so."

"Your Excellency, the leader at the previous *abbaye* is following us with two other men. They are two days behind us. I think he must know something about your holy quest." Muhammad's dark eyes searched Grand Master Gilbért's face waiting for an answer.

"I suspected *Abbé* André might shadow us. He is one of the cardinal's spies. Once again, we must cut our visit short. Don't divulge to anybody, we'll leave before dawn tomorrow. First, I will check with Commander Juan Felipe to see if his man has left for our sailing arrangement and then I must rest. We have seven days of hard riding before we reach Santiago de Compostela and from there more days to A Coruña before we sail for England."

Abruptly, Grand Master Gilbért left and headed for his cell. Muhammad eyed me and then gazed at *Abbé* Jeremiah.

"His excellency seems troubled. I started noticing this after we left the cabin in the Pyrénées *Montagnes*. Do either one of you know what is going on? His old alertness is not there, and he is moving quite slow."

"I agree and I am sure *Abbé* Jeremiah agrees." He nodded his head in affirmation. "However," I said, "what shall we do? We have fifty leagues yet to travel. I might suggest we ask Commander Juan Felipe for additional *chevaliers*. They wouldn't draw any attention, for they always patrol this pilgrim road to Santiago de Compostela."

I sighed. "Then it is settled. I will ask the commander if he approves us going with his men tomorrow."

The walk to my room left me heavily laden with more responsibilities of Grand Master Gilbért's leadership duties. Once reaching my bed, my mind raced with many thoughts. Each one competing for my mind's dominance. I sat there and thought it best to return to the *chapelle* to search for some holy guidance.

The *chapelle* was empty when I entered through a side door. The holy cross was still there, but it didn't draw me forth. Instead, I went to my knees and started praying with my chaplet beads. Unexpectedly, a light formed at the base of the cross and its multicolored rays struck my face. The rays started forming a red-clothed woman.

"Robert," a voice emanated from the base of the cross clearly speaking my name. "Robert, we meet once more." By now her form was complete, yet the light or nimbus around her head still partially blinded me. Dimly I observed a small radiant, green-colored ointment jar held by her glowing hands. It was the jar Mary used at the tomb.

"Heed closely to what I have to say, for other men's lives are now your responsibility. Your holy quest is in more jeopardy than previous times. When you reach the cathedral of Santiago de Compostela, pray to my good friend and fellow apostle. He will give you strength and show you the way. Wear his scallop shell and it will protect you. All mortal men and women have free will, which the Devil knows how to manipulate. This also goes for the men closes to you. Satan comes in many disguises, as you well know. Robert, now contemplate on the Poor-Soldier of Christ, Gilbért de Érail, he needs all your prayers. I leave you now and know not when I will return, but call my name when your heart tells you."

Her voice ceased and her brilliant glow disappeared, leaving just the base of the empty cross. Afterward, I prayed for Grand Master Gilbért as Mary Magdalene had told me to, fearing the dire consequence of not doing so. I also prayed for my family and my health to be strong enough to face what might come. I then returned to my room.

Thereafter, it was about time for Compline, which I readied myself and attended. I used my spare time to write some entries into my journal before praying once again and eating my supper meal. My mind felt comparable to a lone caged bird; not able to escape the small prison to confide in others of my many predicaments. I spoke to the commander about our sailing arrangements and leaving early. Before I could say another word, he said his sergeant left early this morning to see about our ship and suggested we accompany his men the next morning on their routine patrol to Santiago de Compostela. He didn't question why we were leaving early other than he knew Grand Master Gilbért and his men must have important business ahead. I thanked him for his hospitality, and he said his drapier and armorer would furnish us with proper supplies.

Juan Felipe placed his hand on my shoulder. "Lord Robert, *vaya con Dios, mi amigo,* and serve our Savior's destiny He has for all of you."

Shortly thereafter, I searched out Muhammad and *Abbé* Jeremiah and they accompanied me to the bailey area of the Ponferrada fortress. There, with a hushed voice, I told them the good news.

"We'll leave at first light tomorrow, be ready. Expect the armorer and the drapier with weapon supplies and fresh food. *Abbé* Jeremiah, let *Abad* Miguel know of our early departure. I will notify Sergeant Jacque and Grand Master Gilbért."

CHAPTER XXXV

Before sunrise, we left the confines of the Ponferrada fortress with our additional Templar escort. It was easy to convince Grand Master Gilbért to leave early. He still seemed in a daze from our experience in the *chapelle*. For the first time in many days, I felt some relief from outside threats. The additional *chevaliers* and sergeants gave me time to observe Sergeant Jacque de Hoult. It now fell to me and Muhammad to prevent Sergeant Jacque from any further nefarious treason. I said a silent prayer to myself that I would meet this leadership challenge and continue with Saint Joseph of Arimathea's quest.

"Muhammad, I need to speak to you." Muhammad quickly turned his horse and came to our rear. "I need your trust and help," I whispered. "I want you to notice Sergeant Jacque, especially when I am asleep. I fear he'll thwart our quest. Your scout duties now entail just protecting our rear. This patrol knows these roads ahead and won't waste any time on arriving at Santiago de Compostela. Please get as much rest in your saddle as you're able. Also wake me at night if you see anything suspicious by Sergeant Jacque. It is important."

Nothing happened for the next three days. On the fourth day, once again I put on my daily scallop shell. After about a quarter of a league, we approached the outskirts of Santiago de Compostela.

Now I know what Saint Joseph of Arimathea experienced at Passover in Jerusalem. The road into the shrine appeared like a sea of bodies flowing into a small entrance. Rising above the entrance was a huge cathedral swallowing everybody into its interior. Our escort cleared the way once the shell-clad pilgrims ascertained the red-splayed crosses on our surcoats. We arrived a brief time later close to the crowded front entrance. The cathedral entrance was surrounded by a horseshoe-shaped line of food vendors, *vin* merchants, and booths of unknown origin. Several young *garçons* or *muchachos* hurried toward us offering to hold our horses' reins for a fee. I tossed them several coins and then we dismounted.

"It's *bon* to be here once more," Grand Master Gilbért said as he strolled toward the cathedral entrance. "Lord Robert, please let me show you the interior of the Church of Saint James the Greater."

Our leader strangely seemed like his old self as he motioned for me to follow him up the terraced steps toward the three tympanum entrances. How odd, I thought, after several days of observing his morose behavior.

"Chaplain Jeremiah and *Abad* Miguel, come with me to show Lord Robert Saint James the Greater's final resting place." Once again Grand Master Gilbért motioned with his hand for us to follow. His expression seemed to convey another past time and place.

"With the large crowds of pilgrims, it appears to be a holy day," he said as he bounded up the steps. "You will be amazed at the cathedral's gigantic swinging silver censer inside the transept. It is called the Botafumeiro, which means smoke expeller. I suspect they are starting to swing it right now."

His description left me a little confused. I had seen numerous censers before; why was this one any different? Once again, the red-splayed crosses on our surcoats let us push forward into the massive sea of bodies. The cathedral seemed like the size of a large hill. From the narthex to the apse, it was some shorter than Vézelay Abbey cathedral, yet the width and transept were beyond belief. The censer appeared as a medium-sized smoking bell. A long-knotted rope was attached to a circle eye hook with three silver chains adjoined to the hook and the chains then fastened to the censer. Everybody around me displayed their pilgrim mounted scallop shells and then suddenly eight men in red vestments appeared and grabbed the long dangling rope. They grasped it and started pulling on it.

"Note, Lord Robert, it is starting to swing," Grand Master Gilbért said.

This focused my eyes upward to reveal an eight-sided octagon-shaped lantern tower where a pulley mechanism was mounted. Here was another signpost with the holy number eight. Eight men to pull the censer and an eight-sided tower to hold it. To my amazement the bell-shaped Botafumeiro started swinging to both sides of the transept. The crowd of people gave out a collective "aha." The more I traveled on our quest, the more I was amazed with the strange customs and traditions of our hallowed quest. Each led us divinely forward.

"Grand Master Gilbért, where is the sepulchre of Santiago?"

He didn't answer at first, for his moving eyes were fixated on the ever-higher swinging Botafumeiro censer.

"Lord Robert, did you say something?"

"*Oui*, where is the tomb of Santiago?"

"It is the open doorway next to the high altar. We will go there right after the service. There are some stairs that lead down to the undercroft. You will see several stone sepulchres, with the largest stone tomb his."

He didn't say anymore, yet his eyes stayed fixed on the swinging censer. To me it was remarkable, but some force drew me to the underground Santiago sarcophagus. My feet and legs moved in an uncontrollable direction. I grabbed my legs to stop, but to no effect. I left immediately and headed toward the crypt stairs. A strong musty smell entered my nose as I ambled through a narrow corridor. At the end of the walkway were several kneeling benches with pilgrims praying. Numerous people kissed the stone tomb and continued praying.

Suddenly, a *buzzing* noise came to my ears. At first it was a muffed voice. I started to swoon but grabbed the side of a stone pillar.

"Pilgrim, what you seek is not here, yet I will direct you to your destination. It is a road or *el camino* different from mine. My *frère* John spoke of your journey in the holy gospel of Revelation."

"Who is this voice entering my mind?" I voiced with a whisper.

"I am titled by many names, but you earthly pilgrims call me Saint James the Greater, Santiago, Ya'akov, and one of the sons of thunder. Robert, you are one of Moses's descendants and a *kohen.* You are the new priest for the New Jerusalem, which Moses and my *frère* spoke of in the books of Exodus and Revelation. You must seek out the new square temple of God. Remember the Tent of Meeting builders and the First Jerusalem Temple's dimensions and numbers past, present, and the future. In that holy temple, you'll find everlasting wonders. You are the new Yoseph of Arimathea. It is not just the Christ cup you seek, but He will be there to guide you. The future is yours to see."

The voice stopped and I staggered forward toward the Santiago tomb and then kissed it. I steadied myself against the stone railing and ruminated about a square temple, the Tent of Meeting, and who would guide me. This voice didn't sound like any I'd heard before. No doubt his voice came from the tomb of Saint James the Greater. Who was *he* to guide me? A square *église* to find, and me a Hebrew priest seeing the future. I knew who the builders of the Ark of the Covenant, the Tabernacle, and the First Temple were. God guided Moses to instruct Bezalel and Oholiab to create the Jewish Tabernacle and Ark. The First Jewish Temple, God instructed King Solomon. Once again, more clues and no definite answers. It appeared I needed all the pieces of the enigma before I could solve our quest. Yet, me a priest, I couldn't believe it! I must consult with *Abbé* Jeremiah now. Hurriedly, I departed the undercroft and searched for him. The sole person I met was Grand Master

Gilbért. His eyes were still moving back and forth fixated on the Botafumeiro. Just as I gazed toward the narthex, *Abbé* Jeremiah headed toward the *cathédrale* entrance.

"*Abbé* Jeremiah, please wait. I have some great news to tell you. I just heard Santiago speak to me." He stood still and his eyes widened.

"*Seigneur* Robert, let us go outside where we can discuss this, because we don't know if there are spies about. Also I am thirsty and in need of some *vin*. Earlier, I observed a female *vin* merchant distributing *vin* to the pilgrims and I believe this will give us some privacy."

We walked out of the entrance and then strolled in the direction of the shop. A large tent covered a spacious seating area. We found a secluded spot in the back of the tent and waited to be served. A fleeting time later an attractive older woman with streaks of white in her black hair and ebony-colored eyes approached our table. She spoke to us in her Iberian dialect, and we gave her our order. I noticed she had a silver-colored Star of David necklace around her neck, but what really grabbed my attention was the shocking resemblance to *Abbé* Jeremiah.

"What is your name?" I asked.

"It is Joanna, and this shop belongs to me. My older *hermana* operated it many years ago before she died."

"Your name means God is gracious," replied *Abbé* Jeremiah.

"*Si*, and to you Gentiles, she was one of the myrrh bearers to your *Christo*."

"What was your *hermana's* name?" I asked.

"Her name was Deborah. Why do you ask? The *Caballeros* of *Christo* don't care about a *Juive mujer*."

Just as she completed her last word, Grand Master Gilbért entered the tent and spied our location. He strode toward us and then stopped to face Joanna.

"Deborah, is it you? *Si*, you are still alive after these many years."

To my stupefaction, Gilbért reached to hold her. His exhausted mind deceived him in thinking she didn't die.

Unexpectantly, Joanna screamed and then tried to race toward the tent opening. Gilbért and *Abbé* Jeremiah stopped her just as she reached the opening. She screamed again with an ear-piercing voice and lunged once more toward the opening. Grand Master Gilbért's grip tightened around her wrist. Yet, what distressed me the most were her dark eyes bulging out to the size of walnuts.

"Deborah, please let's converse. Now come back into the tent."

Grand Master Gilbért's soft voice didn't relieve her wide-eyed expression. Not until *Abbé* Jeremiah spoke to her in Hebrew and called her *Doh-dah* Joanna did she stop shaking and leaping forward. I presumed he addressed her as his *tante* in my native language. She gazed at his face and her hand caressed his chin and nose. She then realized it was her nephew, but Grand Master Gilbért kept calling her Deborah. She tried to tell him they were *soeurs*. He didn't stand for her reply.

"*Non*, *non*, you are Deborah. I am sure of it. This is our *fils*, Jeremiah. Can't you see he favors you?"

Grand Master Gilbért's scarred face contorted into begging lines of creases when she didn't reply to his question.

Abbé Jeremiah glared at his *père*. "You must stop this outburst of poor behavior. You are the grand master of this entire peninsula. I understand your misidentification, but she isn't Deborah; she is her *achoti* or sister in Hebrew.

"My *hermana* confined in me once saying she had a *hijo* by a Gentile man. She spoke little of this affair, but said she once loved him before she died. My parents acquired the baby to be raised by a rabbi and his *esposa*. I never met him again until now. I can't believe I have a good-looking nephew."

After she said these things, Grand Master Gilbért let his head fall forward. My heart ached for him. But I wondered at the coincidence of meeting *Abbé* Jeremiah's *achoti,* as he called her.

CHAPTER XXXVI

Joanna gained the initiative and spoke. "Grand Master Gilbért, peek at my left hand." His eyes ever so slowly rose as she pointed to her ring finger. "I am married and have four *niños*. My sister didn't have this red birthmark on the top of her right hand! I will take you and your *padre*, or I mean my nephew and your *hijo* to her grave. This may help ease your tormented mind and give you some peace. As you well know, the cemetery is just a short distance from here."

Chaplain Jeremiah grabbed his *père's* hand and helped raise him up. They moved toward the tent opening with shuffling feet and then disappeared. I didn't know what to do. Follow them or wait for *Abad* Miguel, Sergeant Jacque de Hoult, and Muhammad Nur Adin. I decided to wait and let Grand Master Gilbért have a private moment with his family. I prayed this might break him from his shell of illusions and shock him back to reality.

Just then, Muhammad entered the tent. "Where is Grand Master Gilbért? His horse is gone." I didn't know what to tell him. Months ago, I had sworn to Grand Master Gilbért not to divulge his secret in my writing or verbally until after his death.

"Does this have anything to do with his *fils* and deceased lover? If it is so, say no more for I know you are sworn to secrecy."

I didn't say anything but sat there and remained in silence. It was now left to me to assume the leadership role to continue our quest. Once again, I prayed I might meet this challenge and conqueror it.

The sun displayed long shadows from the *cathédrale* when both *Abad* Miguel and Sergeant Hoult returned from the inside of Santiago de Compostela. The sergeant asked me the same question that Muhammad asked.

"Where is Grand Master Gilbért and Chaplain Jeremiah? What is this place?"

"It is a *vin* and water tent for pilgrims. The proprietor will be back soon. She is helping Grand Master Gilbért with some provision arrangement. In the meantime, here are coins to go and buy some dried meats, eggs, and bread for our trip to A Coruña. We are staying overnight here and will start out before dawn for the northwest coast. Now hurry and complete your task before the shops close." They headed for the tent entrance, but *Abad* Miguel turned and gave me a wide-eyed stare of bewilderment. I knew in his mind he knew why his long-ago student was absent. Yet it seemed strange that *Abad* Miguel didn't seem concerned about his former student. My partial lie seemed to work, though I didn't like deceiving my fellow *amis*.

It wasn't until after dark that they returned with the dried meat and eggs. Grand Master Gilbért and his *fils* hadn't returned; leaving me to explain his continued absence.

"Your grand master still must busy. I am sure he will be here after we are asleep. Muhammad, you take the first watch, and I will follow you about midnight." We ate the meat and washed it down with the stored *vin* in the tent and left a few coins for Joanna. How would I assume the leadership for our quest if our leader never returned? I prayed for this not to happen.

During the night I was awakened by hushed voices from Muhammad and Grand Master Gilbért speaking in Muhammad's native tongue.

But not until I relieved Muhammad did I get my answer. He told me that our leader believed Joanna and they departed on *bon* terms. Anxiously waiting, my guard time seemed to never end. I wanted to speak to Grand Master Gilbért and observe his demeanor. I finally got my chance just before we saddled to leave. I watched Grand Master Gilbért leave a note and coins for Joanna's return and then approach me.

"Lord Robert, may we speak in private?"

"*Oui*, where?"

"Let us go to the side of the *cathédrale*."

I followed him to a dark location where no pilgrims slept. At first, he stared at the dark earth with silence.

"Lord Robert, I must apologize for my unusual behavior. Our holy quest for the parchments has taken its toll on me. I'll need your leadership in the coming days when we sail for England. I am not used to dealing with so many traitors in my midst at one time. Everything is fine with Joanna. I met her husband, and he is an exceedingly kind man. Chaplain Jeremiah feels the same about his new relatives as I do. The husband gave me a map for a shorter route to A Coruña and its seaport. Normally it's fifteen leagues from here and a good two-day ride. His secret shortcut would save us half a day or more."

Grand Master Gilbért seemed different, like his old self, but he had hidden too many problems in his old self and that persona failed him. Now I worried about him relapsing and identifying the traitor and both their next moves.

We galloped out of the *cathédrale* courtyard. The sky was clear, and the sunlight warmed our chain mail. Spring was edging closer; an extended sea voyage excited me. I hadn't stepped on a boat since my time with *bon* Remy the bargeman and his sons. How many months and leagues had this been?

"Lord Robert, what are you thinking about?" Chaplain Jeremiah asked as his horse trotted next to mine. "I can surmise it is traveling by sea. Have you been to England before our quest?"

"*Oui*, you are correct about sailing, but *non* about England. Only my ancestors traveled there fighting with Guillaume the Conqueror. I have some distant cousins who settled in England after the battle. Where they live, I know not and one hundred twenty-five years have elapsed. I suspect you are about to tell me you have traveled there."

"*Oui.* Grand Master Gilbért's *bon ami*, Guillaume, is the marshal to the English *Roi* Richard. I believe his *bon ami* will be the first earl of Pembroke soon. Guillaume ensured that I studied my letters at Oxford, located in the middle part of England. I hope to meet him once again in England."

Suddenly, *Abad* Miguel rode up alongside us and queried what we were discussing. After Chaplain Jeremiah repeated our conversation, Miguel made further inquiries.

"Who is this Guillaume the marshal? Gilbért hasn't spoken of him before. He must have the *roi's* ear and sounds quite powerful. I know *Roi* Richard is sailing toward the Levant and left his *frère*, John, in charge of administering the kingdom of England or is it the marshal who is handling things?"

Two factors struck my mind. First, why the sudden interest of *Abad* Miguel in who is ruling the English throne? Second, why didn't he come to the emotional aid of his former pupil and our leader? His new distant personality from Grand Master Gilbért and his interest in English politics caused my suspicious nature to creep into my mind. Did I have two traitors in my midst? I sat riding in my saddle ruminating about my predicament with serval squawking gulls flying overhead. My nostrils inhaled the salty driven wind as *Noir Ombre* barked at the gulls. His black shiny coat and scurrying legs pulled away my thoughts. Muhammad motioned for me to trot forward and join him, which I did.

"Lord Robert, my thoughts the past week tell me that something odd is happening. It is not about the *Hashishiyya* or the cardinal, but as if one of us is trying to disrupt our quest. I know you want to return to your *château* and family, and Grand Master Gilbért has lost his usual assertiveness. I have sworn on the *Qur'an* to follow Grand Master Gilbért anywhere. I owe my life to him, and he wants to help me to avenge the deaths of my family. We need to seek out the traitor as soon as possible. I am a Muslim and can't make accusations against a supposed Christian. Lord

Robert, you have few suspects to call out and they are all holy men. I know you suspect me. However, I have saved your life on numerous occasions, and I could have left you to die."

"*Non*, Muhammad, I don't believe you are a traitor and once more let me say *merci beaucoup* with all my soul. I will never forget your kindness."

Just then Grand Master Gilbért motioned for us to stop. We dismounted and strolled toward a nearby stream and watered our horses. Thereafter, we said the divine office of Nones while Muhammad said his *salats* or *Asr* afternoon prayers.

"Lord Robert, you and Chaplain Jeremiah will ride ahead and arrange our passage. I want us to leave on the first tide. Here is a note to the Templar admiral. It instructs him to obtain the fastest ship available. The two of you can make faster time without our pack animals. Search for the largest sail with a Templar cross. The port will be quite busy and has a dangerous reputation for cutthroats and robbers."

Grand Master Gilbért seemed to be improving in his disposition, but I needed to confirm my supposition with his *fils*. Now our ride alone would give me that opportunity to detect any possible traitorous information he might divulge. We both mounted our steeds and then galloped toward A Coruña.

"Chaplain Jeremiah, do have any thoughts on who is betraying us?"

"*Non*, Lord Robert, but I have surmised what they are seeking isn't just Saint Joseph's gospel. Cardinal Folquet knows there is something far greater than the parchments. *Oui*, they are earth changing in themselves, but their holy words are leading us to something we can't spiritually comprehend. The cardinal is power hungry. Remember the people he murdered that we have loved so dearly. This doesn't include his minions he has sent to kill us, and we had to kill them to further our holy quest. I know how worried your thoughts are for your family. The fear of your family's death under the cardinal's sword is a burden I can't imagine. I pray every night for you. His power has corrupted him in the eyes of God, but he seeks absolute power. Only Satan can give him this, and he must pay a price for his lust and hubris. That will be God's judgment price, and it will be far more horrible than his mind can grasp."

I glanced at his face, and it appeared like a man in a deep trance. A slight smile formed next to his lips but disappeared as his former stoic face returned. His demeanor stayed this way for some time until a large flock of gulls squawked overhead. The windy salt-smelling air and warm sun helped to sharpen my thoughts.

"Sorry, Lord Robert, for my silence. My mind sometimes sees blurry things and feels things that have yet to happen. Also my deep faith gives me these partial visions. You are not the only one whom God has given grace to see and hear things."

It was impossible this man was a traitor. I sensed we were both kindred spirits even when I first met him. This left me with three suspects: Muhammad, *Abad* Miguel, and Sergeant Jacque de Hoult. I believed finding out their motives would determine which one was guilty.

Close to sundown, we reached a tall promontory hill. Around us was the greenish-blue Atlantic Ocean. In the sky were funnels of white flying gulls. They appeared above the seashore and the small town in numbers I couldn't fathom. Going down the road and into the village, the gulls' squawking made communication impossible. The seaports were some distance away from the small town and all downhill. I observed various ships with colored sails of blue, red, and white. At the far end of the quay, I spied a large, splayed, red cross sail. The closer we were to the docks, the more it became quite crowded. Yet, each person in the crowd stared at us as we passed. As two mounted Templars, one a chaplain, the crowd issued forth a *buzzing* whisper of conversations.

"Lord Robert, there's our ship." Chaplain Jeremiah pointed in its direction.

The galley ship was a two-masted *tarida* with the name of Saint Michael written on the bow. The poop deck was long with two *château*-type housings at the stern and a smaller one at the bow. The ship appeared sleek and fast, yet what was most noticeable was the loud *whinnying* sound emanating from the belly of the ship.

We were to meet the Templar admiral and confirm our passage to England. A tall man with long dark hair and bushy beard greeted us at the gangplank. He wore a bicorn-shaped black *chapeau* with a red pattée cross affixed to one side. On top of the *chapeau* ridge were abundant white feathers. Covering his white, red cross surcoat was a black mantel with a crescent moon and several pentagram-shaped solid stars below the moon. He wore a curved-blade scabbard like Muhammad, but the pommel was quite unusual. It consisted of ivory and on top of the pommel I spied a skull and crossed-bone figure.

"Greetings, *frère chevaliers*, I have expected you. My name is Admiral Hidalgo de Fernando. Your mission sounds urgent. Grand Master Gilbért de Érail said he needed my services without delay. My nephew's note said you were traveling to England. *Si*, is this correct?"

"*Oui,* I mean *si*. Will we sail directly from here to England?" I asked.

"No, first we will stop at La Rochelle to deliver more horses for the crusaders. This is a valuable cargo and I fear we might face some pirates, but we Templars have faced stronger enemies. I see Grand Master Gilbért has brought along his chaplain. That means God's protection, and whether they are weather demons, sea demons, or land demons we are protected by the armor of God. When will Master Gilbért and the rest of your fellow *hermanos* arrive?"

"It will be before dawn. Is this satisfactory?"

"*Si*, the tide will just start receding and the winds will prevail for the sails. You may want to seek eating and sleeping accommodations in our small town. My ship is spacious, but the horse smells and the noise you will know all too soon. You should enjoy this last night on shore. It will be a long trip to England with several days spent in La Rochelle. I recommend the Bloody Bucket Inn. The food is excellent, and the beds are stuffed with feathers. Go to the end of the pier and bear left. It is the only two-story building on the path. I will see you at dawn. *Vaya con Dios, mis amigos.*"

We departed from the gangplank and headed down the wooden pier. Just as we turned around a small red building, two unknown Templar *chevaliers* darted out and stopped in front of us.

CHAPTER XXXVII

"*Hola*," a large thick-necked man addressed us. His right hand rested on the hilt of his sword and the other man the same, except he had a large dagger tucked into his belt.

"I see you and the *capellán* appear to be leaving tomorrow. Is this so?"

"It is none of your damn business," I replied and immediately drew my sword. So did Chaplain Jeremiah. "We answer to no earthly man, so get the hell out of our way!" I swung my blade to his shoulder. He deflected my blow just as his partner went after Chaplain Jeremiah. Jeremiah raised his sword over his head and aimed for the other *chevalier's* right arm. His blow was also blocked by the other man's dagger.

"The cardinal desires both of your presence, yet he said not to kill you, but he didn't say not to injure you sufficiently so you might comply," the large thick-necked man declared.

From out of nowhere, eight men appeared in the instant of an eye wink. It was as if they had dropped from the sky. How could this have happened? A large lump formed in my throat as I noticed the eight men wore black surcoats with the red-splayed pattée cross on their chests. They too unsheathed their swords and moved toward us.

"Pilgrim and *capellán* Templars," said a voice behind me, that I recognized as Admiral Hidalgo de Fernando.

"It appears you are in a predicament. Grand Master Gilbért, in his note, said he thought this might happen. I had you followed once both of you left my ship. Also my sailors, from our rigging, noticed these men approach you, and they are not Poor-Soldiers of Christ. I don't know who they are, but you know that answer."

He loudly addressed the attackers. "However, you attacked several of my fellow *frères*. You will pay for that with your lives." Without any fear or assistance, Hidalgo ran toward them.

The admiral charged into both men. One he decapitated with his curved sword, but the other was more cautious. The man used his dagger to feint a lunge and used his sword to sweep toward the admiral's head. The admiral ducked and his hand grabbed a long silver dagger out of his boot and thrust it upward into his enemy. The man's eyes froze from an unexpected dagger plunge under his ribcage. The hostage taker fell backward and collapsed. Blood gurgled from his moving lips as he tried to say something. The admiral leaned forward to hear, then he glanced at me.

"Admiral, what is he saying?" I asked.

He took a deep breath. "He's saying the cardinal has your *esposa* and two *hijos*."

The dying man's words smacked me like a well-swung mace. This wasn't true, I told myself. *Mon beau-frère*, *Comte* Gautiér de Montbéliard wouldn't let this happen. It was his *soeur* and two *neveux* he was protecting. I fell to my knees sobbing, then praying this wasn't so.

I called out to God that the cardinal didn't have them. "Surely dear Lord, this information isn't true. It must be a lie!" With tears rolling down my cheeks, I shook his dagger-stabbed body for more information, but he'd ceased to breathe. At once, I wanted to leave and help secure their rescue. With my right boot I started kicking the body, as if to awaken him. I lost count how many times I struck him, until Chaplain Jeremiah and Muhammad pulled me way. After calming down some, I expressed my appreciation.

"Admiral, *muchas gracias* for saving our lives," I said after shaking his strong hand.

"Admiral, my sentiment as well and I will pray for you each night on our voyage to England," Chaplain Jeremiah said.

"I'll see you both before dawn and have one of my sailors be on the lookout for Grand Master Gilbért. Also don't worry about this unfortunate mess. My men will take care of it. *Adios,* my *frères.*"

Right away we left for the inn. As we entered through the door, the overpowering smell of fish nauseated my stomach. I rushed back outside and vomited. The terrible news about my family and our unexpected attack left me sick with anxiety. The clearing of my stomach and the fresher air revived me, but my stomach remained as if it held a large worrying rock in its bottom. My fear told me to quit this foolish quest and leave.

"Lord Robert, are you well?" asked Chaplain Jeremiah.

"*Si,* let us go back inside." We then checked with the innkeeper, and he led us to our rooms. I opened my door, meandered in. There was a large fireplace, bed, and ample washing bowl.

"Is there anything you need before we retire? Like food, *vin,* or prayer."

"*Oui,* Chaplain Jeremiah, please pray with me for the safety of my *épouse* and my two *fils.*"

After we said our Glory Bes and *Pater Nosters,* we specifically prayed for my family. Our chant, in unison, helped some to relieve my angst. He left shortly after, and I reclined on the bed. Surprisingly, sleep came fast, but at a cost. A reoccurring nightmare came to me. I could see my *épouse*, Marie, and my two *fils*, Henri and Brian. All three were tied to chairs and a red long-sleeved arm held a dagger next to Marie's throat. I couldn't help them or wake up. My body was frozen like a stone sculpture. I tried to scream, but no noise came from my stationary lips. My mind wanted to break out of its stone head, yet there was nothing but silence. Suddenly a red-sleeved arm, holding a dagger came toward me. Its tip pierced my neck and then I woke up. Standing over me was Grand Master Gilbért and Muhammad with our war dog, *Noir Ombre,* licking my feet.

"I am so glad to see all of you. I was trapped in a nightmare while I was sleeping."

I gave them all the details of my fitful dream.

"Your *épouse* and *fils* weren't captured by the cardinal's men or the cardinal. I just received a report the other day, which said they were safe. No more of this cardinal nonsense, let's get ready and leave for La Rochelle."

Grand Master Gilbért seemed like his old self and took away my fears. I quickly dressed, washed my face, and put on my boots. We left the inn after I paid for our expenses, and we then hiked toward the ship. I loaded my horse, and the rest of my fellow *frères* did the same. *Noir Ombre* ran up the gangplank wagging his tail and stared back for me to follow. Afterward, five of the sailors pulled up the gangplank and the oarsmen started rowing away from the dock.

About three quarters away into the Ría da Coruña or bay, the wind caught the sails and the ship *Saint Michael* surged forward. The sea spray caught my face, helping me to wake up. Yet, a little voice in my head kept asking me what if Grand Master Gilbért was wrong about his new information? Doubt is a vicious animal and sometimes doesn't let go.

"Lord Robert, can you see the *Torre* de Hércules to your left?" Grand Master Gilbért asked. "It was once a great tower and lighthouse for sailors. The Romans built this tall building for their navy, which prevented them from crashing into the rocks."

"I must chat with you in private about some major issues."

"Lord Robert, let us go toward the forecastle. There are no sailors or our men there."

We climbed the steps to the upper deck as the waves roared against the bow. The noise and ocean splashes would conceal some of our conversation, but the shoreline had yet to disappear.

"I don't think these issues will surface until we reach land, but we need to discuss certain preventive measures. I believe Sergeant Jacque de Hoult is our spy."

There was a long pause before Grand Master Gilbért spoke, leaving me troubled. Did he know something I didn't know?

"What makes you suspect him instead of Muhammad, my *fils*, or *Abad* Miguel?"

"He is the only one we know little about. Also he has been in my personal belongings while I have been asleep. Do you remember what I told you last week about his *frère* and *soeur*? His *frère* is a bookkeeper at your temple in London and his *soeur* is a nun at a convent in England."

"*Non*, yet I haven't been in my right mind for several weeks. Lord Robert, once again please forgive me, for I owe you a large debt of thanks."

I refreshed his mind and continued my evidence of Sergeant Jacque's guilt. He listened closely and nodded various times in agreement.

"You mention preventive measures to block his spying. What specifically do you have in mind?"

"One, we take shifts scrutinizing his every move when we reach La Rochelle and England. He must not be out of our sight at all. Two, we need to tie him up once we reach England and have Muhammad guard him. However, I have another concern. It is me. I am not a Templar, but I am a *seigneur* from Northern Burgundy. Prince John of England may think I am spy for the *roi* of Gaul."

"Lord Robert, I know a *chevalier* of great importance who will help us if that happens."

Just then I happened to glance over to the port side of the ship and witnessed five men riding along the shoreline with raised swords. They were shouting something through the crashing waves.

"What is it?" Grand Master Gilbért asked, looking to see what caught my attention.

"I don't know. But I have a bad feeling about this."

PART SIX

The Storm

CHAPTER XXXVIII

Mediterranean Sea

Anno Domini 38

Yoseph's mind was still back at the Yoppa quay and the image of the red-hooded stranger. He prayed he wasn't their killer and stalker, but Yoseph knew better. His exile would be difficult, he thought, yet not at the risk of seeing his friends and family harmed. Enough blood was spilled and Yoseph wouldn't let this happen again.

The cool sea spray from the ship's bow felt good against his face as his brother-in-law approached. Hebron's pale face told Yoseph he was seasick.

"Yoseph, did Captain Hiram say when we would reach Caesarea?" he managed to ask.

"No, he didn't. If weather conditions remain well, I estimate we will arrive in a day and a half." Yoseph knew Hebron wasn't much of a seafarer and suddenly crept toward the ship's edge, bent over, and vomited into the sea.

"I must have eaten a large amount food while breaking our fast," he replied with a slight grin. Hebron then wiped his mouth on his sleeve.

"Yoseph, Enygeus wants to know where we are heading after leaving Caesarea."

"We'll then sail toward Alexandria, Egypt. Philip and I discussed this the last night before we left Yoppa. There are several large Jewish colonies residing in Alexandria. Besides, I know a man there by the name of Philo. In many of my past trips we discussed numerous things. He will be helpful in our new ministry about our *Maishiach's* teachings. Philip wants us to go to the Glass Isle or Albion from there. It is a long journey and will assess our faith and determination. It is our duty to spread the seeds of what Yeshua said and prophesied to us."

Yoseph thought his answer satisfied Hebron, which would help his sister's angst. Alexandria was a large city, and their band might blend in with the population. How long they would remain there, Yoseph didn't know, but he felt they should leave before the winter storms.

A day-and-a-half later their ship landed at the port of Caesarea. Captain Hiram docked at a quay that appeared manmade by the Romans. There were idolatrous statues of the Roman gods, frieze details all along the sides of the wharf, and much Roman-chiseled writing.

"Hiram, how long will it take to unload cargo?" Yoseph asked.

"The rest of the day and into the night, but we will leave tomorrow at first light. I must load the olive oil and wine amphoras to deliver to Alexandria."

Yoseph thought it best he leave Captain Hiram to his many duties and speak with his band of teachers. He stepped down the small steps to the below-deck compartments. Yoseph sniffed the sour smell of vomit. Numerous members of his band of teachers were recovering from seasickness.

"Gather around, my fellow brothers and sisters. Philip and I would like to discuss with you where we will be traveling beyond Alexandria. Philip, please tell them where we will dock next after Alexandria."

"Yoseph and I have discussed a coastal town between Hispania and Italia. It is a small city in Gaul with Hebrew merchants comparable to us. There is a large delta and river that empties into the Mediterranean Sea. The Romans call the town Massalia. The river there gives us an interior passageway to the interior of Gaul. Eventually we can travel from Gaul to Britannia, as the Romans call the island. Yoseph tells me he has land there to start a temple to our *Maishiach*. With Yoseph's permission, I might explain how to approach the new pupils of Yeshua's God-given words."

Yoseph nodded his support and Philip continued.

"Those who are not of our old faith will be simpler to convert. Their thoughts are not tainted with rules and many laws. We offer them hope, friendship, love, and everlasting salvation. No earthly person can stamp out their spirit. The familial love and the taste of our cup of salvation will quench their thirst. The holy cup procession will show to the world that we are sincere and our *Maishiach* will one day come again to lead us to the New Jerusalem."

Philip's words were far more revolutionary than Yoseph expected. Yet, Yeshua had brought out the wisdom and foresight of all in their band of apostles. They were all different in some way and could see through the thick cloud of the present into the future. Then Philip revealed something that Yoseph didn't know.

"I have four daughters who are prophetesses. The people in Caesarea shun them and fear their words and the sight of them. They augur the future around the people they meet. This has forced them to lead sheltered lives, which isn't of their choosing. They have no husbands or children. Their *amma* died some years ago and my sister has raised them. I will leave shortly to visit them, yet I will return before our ship sails. Yoseph, good-bye for now and look out for me at sunrise."

Philip left the boat, and strangely, Thomas followed him too. What that meant to Yoseph, he didn't know. Thomas hadn't let him know about leaving. Yoseph continued to speak to the apostles about his former merchant trips to the Isle of Britannia and its numerous smaller isles. He explained about their plaid clothing. Especially the men's plaid pants and bushy mustaches. That their kings wore golden torcs around their necks and jeweled brooches on their cloaks. They rode in chariots when they went to battle, and their women fought alongside the men. Every one of the Celts or *Keltoi*, as the Greeks called them, painted blue-colored woad on their faces, arms, and chests. Their Druid priests were quite powerful, and only they could stop a battle. Their initiates studied twenty years before becoming priests, and they were both male and female priests. Each priest specialized in law, music, prophecy, and philosophy, or all these subjects. They dress in a long white tunic and covered themselves with hooded white cloaks. Their belt buckles bore precious stones, and around their necks they wore plate necklaces of pure gold. The Druids spoke Greek, Latin, and some Hebrew. They believed in the immortality of the soul and did not fear death. That made them and their people fierce warriors. Their philosophies and intellect, they say, came from the stars and animals. The Druids conversed with the animals, and the animals divulged to them many secrets.

"Rabbi Yoseph, they say their priests practice human sacrifice and cannibalism," Lazarus asked.

"If their captured enemies don't submit to their conqueror's rule, then yes, they are burned in a large wicker basket shaped like a human. If they eat other humans, I have not heard or seen them do this. If we can obtain the approval of the Druids, we will be able to travel anywhere and teach the logia of our Savior Yeshua. Besides, we have the protection of King Arviragus, the king of the Silures tribe."

"Rabbi Yoseph, where do the Druids live?" Miriam of Magdala asked. "You have told me they travel all over the Isle of Britannia."

"I really don't have an answer to your question other than they dwell in oak *drunemetons* or sanctuaries, and they highly value mistletoe that grows on the oak branches. Also the hazel and holly trees are venerated too. Don't worry, my fellow apostles, Yeshua will be there to protect us and see to our missionary completion. Let us rest before we sail tomorrow. Hebron, you take the second watch, and I will take the first. I know the sailors will observe too, but we can't take any chances."

Yoseph sat there on the wooden deck and gazed at the stars. He thought about the scholar Philo and Hebrews now living in diaspora among the ancient Egyptians. He could relate to the prophet *Moshe* leaving there to then wander for years. Would his fate be the same? He prayed not, but how would he and his fellow apostles convert people of his old faith? The task seemed dauting, yet his immediate concern was their stalker. Had he followed them? Was he hiding in the dark night ready to kill them in their sleep? Yoseph worried not for himself, but for his fellow teachers.

Hebron relieved him when the moon was high in the dark sky. "Yoseph, have you observed anything strange or unusual?"

"No, so far nothing to question our safety. I have the holy cup and the rest of the grail processional items to keep me safe, yet I worry about the rest of you. I think we will lose several of our apostles before we reach our destination. Hebron, what do you think?"

"Yoseph, Yeshua has given each one of us a calling. Just as we have different personalities, His calling has affected us differently. Only Yeshua knows our final fate. I trust in His knowledge and judgment. Good night, Yoseph."

Yoseph proceeded to find a comfortable location on the ship. The deck was laden with human bodies, both sailors and their fellow teachers. He laid down at the stern of the ship next to a large white ornately carved swan, which was next to a large steering oar. He lay there thinking what he would discuss with Philo. What would Philo think of Yeshua and their missions to foreign lands? Suddenly, Yoseph heard splashing in the water. He jumped up and ran toward the port side of the ship. He observed V-shaped waves emanating from the splashing sound but couldn't recognize the shape as fish or human. A hand touched his shoulder and then Yoseph feared he was now the prey.

"*Shalom*, brother Yoseph," Hebron whispered. "I too heard the noise. Yet, I couldn't discern an image. Do you think it was our stalker?"

"I most certainly believe it was him. He's far stealthier and more dangerous than we give him credit. Evil can hide in any crevice or crack, or it can blend in with its surroundings. It is like a smokeless fire. You can see the flames but not the evil that burns from it."

Yoseph started shaking and now feared for his family even more. How could they fight something they couldn't see or recognize? He stood there and prayed for the morning sun to rise. Yoseph left Hebron and quietly stepped toward the large wooden carved swan. There he sat down and tried to calm himself. Hoping to distract himself, he tried to remember the last time he spoke to Philo the scholar. Yoseph had delivered a load of tin to the port of Alexandria several years before his Savior's crucifixion. They conversed long into the night about the prophets, especially Jeremiah. Philo spoke fluent Greek and his teachings reflected the Greek philosophers Plato, Aristotle, and Pythagoras. Some of what Philo said Yoseph had a hard time comprehending. He was always speaking about the truth and "the wise architect" *El Shaddai*.

"Yoseph," came a voice from the captain's quarter entrance. It was Captain Hiram.

"Rabbi Yoseph, are you ready to set sail? The morning tide is going out."

"Wait just a little longer. We expect Thomas and Philip to return. They should be here soon." Yoseph stared at the end of the quay and distinguished one person strolling toward their ship. It was Philip. What had happened to Thomas? Philip's face showed a downtrodden gaze the closer he came to the gangplank. "Where is Thomas?" Yoseph inquired.

"After we visited my daughters, he and I decided to preach in the synagogues and the streets. When we left the last synagogue, he seemed to go into a trance and said Yeshua told him to go east to the land of the elephants and tigers. Thomas said good-bye but didn't come back to wave or explain. I hollered several times for him to come back but he didn't. I think we will never see him again."

"Come, Philip, for we are about to depart." He slowly meandered up the gangplank, and then the sailors removed it. Yoseph felt the ship start to move with the tide just as one of the sailors removed the last rope to the harbor.

"Philip, please tell me more."

The stern oarsman pushed the ship from the harbor with large oars and then the wind caught the sail, and the ship jerked forward into the sea. "Did he give any further explanation?"

"No, but his body seemed to give off a radiant light as he walked into the dark streets. He appeared as Yeshua was guiding him. I hated to see him go, but you and I expected this to happen to any of us."

Yoseph rubbed his stubbled beard and thought what he would tell the remaining apostles. Thomas was an earlier follower of Yeshua and one of Yeshua's original twelve disciples. He thought it best to tell them now. Slowly, he gathered them around as their ship left all visible signs of land.

"My brothers and sisters of our *Maishiach*, hear well. What I am about to tell you is both disheartening and enlightening. Our fellow apostle, Thomas, won't be traveling with us to Alexandria. He has received a new calling from Yeshua. He has decided to preach the *Maishiach's* words in the east. Please pray for his protection and success."

Yoseph scrutinized all his fellow teachers for a reaction to what he had just said. There was the usual shaking of heads, open mouths of bewilderment, yet Miriam of Magdala's cheeks overflowed with tears. Yoseph went to see what troubled Miriam about Thomas leaving.

"Miriam, I see you are distressed about the news. What can I do to make you feel better?"

"Yoseph, two things occurred to me about his leaving. First, I am afraid it will happen to me, and second, he was such a promising young man. His mind thirsted for answers, and he wanted to know of the innermost wisdom of Yeshua."

"Miriam, don't worry, our *Maishiach* has a grand purpose for each one of us. Wisdom doesn't reside in one single place, and it isn't kept in a box. Yeshua wants you, me, and the rest of His apostles to experience and help the world. Besides, I will be there for you anytime you are troubled. Only you and your heart will know when that time comes."

Miriam seemed satisfied with Yoseph's answer and left to go speak with Lazarus and Martha.

Their ship was making excellent time. Its bow sliced the waves like a Roman *gladius* sword. Yoseph knew it would take 3,061 Roman *stadia* to reach Alexandria, which meant another two nights and two days travel time.

CHAPTER XXXIX

Alexandria, Egypt

Anno Domini 38

During dusk, the ship *King Solomon* approached the harbor guided by the gigantic Pharos lighthouse of Alexandria. Yoseph enjoyed seeing this spectacle, especially toward nightfall. The lighthouse's bronze mirror radiated an enormous beam of light that appeared to travel all the way to Anatolia. The structure seemed to touch the stars with a large statue of Jupiter garnishing the top. An immense cloud of white smoke spiraled upward into the dusky sky as they docked in the harbor. He noticed the colossal middle section of the tower displayed an octagonal shape. He remembered what Yeshua had whispered into his ear about *octa* at their last supper together. Was this a good sign for Yoseph's ministry? It appeared like a signpost.

The *King Solomon* ship was quickly secured to the dock and Captain Hiram approached Yoseph about his living accommodations. Some of Yoseph's fellow apostle had voiced their opinions about staying aboard their ship, while others wanted to explore the city. Miriam of Magdala wanted to go with Yoseph and speak with Philo. This intrigued Yoseph. What questions would she ask him?

"Yoseph, do you know where the stoic scholar lives?" she asked.

"Yes, but it is getting dark, and the city has grown since the last time I docked here. Hiram has told me that parts of the city are rioting. Some of the Jewish areas have been destroyed. Especially those with synagogues. He advises me to send one of his Greek Gentile crewmen to see if Philo is at home. I am sure this is the safest way. The captain said we would be here for less than a week or we might leave sooner. It depends if the riots spread farther. If they do, we will be taking on more Jewish people who want to escape."

Yoseph felt uneasy about this new threatening circumstance. He spoke to his fellow apostles about the current crisis. Philip shouted he wanted to go with Yoseph, Yohanan Marcus, and Miriam.

"Philip, why do you desire to risk your life?" Yoseph asked.

"Rabbi, it appears our band of followers want to learn from this venerable sage. I'll take the risk to further our ministry. Besides, I am sure he will also learn from us about our *Maishiach*."

Philip was right and he always had a thirst for knowledge. A short time later, the Greek sailor returned and spoke to his captain. Afterward, Hiram approached them looking concerned.

"Rabbi Yoseph, it is not good news. My sailor says the fire is approaching our direction, but he found a separate way to approach Philo's house unseen. It is still dangerous for you to travel."

"Did I hear the word travel?" Nicodemus said. "Yoseph, where are you going?"

"We are traveling to see my old friend Philo."

"I desire to go with you. I have heard much about this scholar of the Greek philosophers. Yoseph, maybe he can spread the word for us, and I know Yohanan Marcus would like to be our scribe. All he has communicated about is the great library here in Alexandria."

"Yoseph, you must leave now. The fires are getting closer," Captain Hiram announced.

Yoseph looked toward the city horizon and observed larger flames of fire racing toward the shore. His decision was instant.

"Let us leave immediately!" Yoseph shouted. He prayed he wouldn't regret his choice. They dashed down the gangplank, followed by Hebron shouting, "Yoseph, wait for me." They had now lost the advantage of stealth. Yoseph and his entourage rushed through the lesser-known narrow passageways of Alexandria, avoiding most of the fires and screaming rioters. The Greek sailor stopped at a sizable stone block house with a large, tiled roof. On the entrance door was a brass-shaped pentagram door knocker. Yoseph stood there, momentarily wondering if this risk was worth the reward in how to better teach the Gentiles. He knocked and then the door slowly opened revealing a young boy of about thirteen summers.

"My master has been expecting you, please hurry inside."

Yoseph thanked and dismissed the Greek sailor, and the rest of them quickly entered. A lone brass oil lamp lit the reception area and Yoseph heard footsteps. He squinted down a long hallway and noticed a dark moving figure. Then he heard a voice.

"Yoseph, it is an honor you have come to my house, but you could have picked a better time. I see you have brought your big brother-in-law, Hebron, with you. Who are the others with you? I don't recognize them. Pardon me for inquiring, for I know you traveled from afar and need rest and refreshment. Follow me to my study and we can sit down."

"Philo, thank you for your concern, but neither of us has much time," Yoseph said.

Quickly, they followed Philo, who was wearing an egg-shaped hat, to his well-lit study. It was quite enormous, and scrolls were neatly filed in wooden shelving that reached the ceiling. Yoseph noticed he had strange geometric drawings stacked on his desk. He pointed to each one to sit on amply supplied, intricately carved wooden chair.

"Yoseph, I will have my student Demetrius get us some wine that will help our conversation. Demetrius, hurry and obtain some good red wine for our guests." The young boy trotted out of the study and disappeared.

"Yoseph, introduce me to your friends, for I am anxious to meet them."

Yoseph introduced everyone except Hebron, but he noticed that Philo stared at Miriam a moment longer.

Philo then apologized to everyone sitting there about the tense situation in Alexandria. "The Jewish community was in uproar because the Roman emperor, Caligula, wanted his statue and their gods worshipped in Jewish synagogues. This gave the Greek ancestral Gentiles an excuse to confiscate Jewish property. The Jewish community wants me to negotiate a truce with the Romans and come up with a solution. I'd rather be Atlas in trying to hold up the world on my shoulders than solve this chaos." He shook his head sadly. "Enough of my problems, please tell me about your life, Yoseph. Is your tin and olive oil business still thriving?"

"No, I lost it, but I have gained much more. A new person has changed my *kavanah*. We now follow a true *Maishiach*. We have become teachers, apostles, and now I'm a rabbi. This *Maishiach* is called Yeshua ben Yoseph. He is or was my nephew."

Yoseph explained what had happened to him over the past four summers. He explained about his prison sentence, the secret numbers *octa* and *penta*, and the miraculous gifts he had been given. He thought Philo might think he was crazy and ask him and his followers to leave. Instead, he requested that Demetrius refill their cups with more wine.

"Yoseph, or should I say Rabbi Yoseph, I have studied the ancient Greek philosophers and mathematicians all my life. Especially Pythagoras, Plato, and Aristotle. Also the Torah and its mathematical gematria. There are deeper meanings with these men and the breath of *El Shaddai* written in the Torah. The Torah is not of men, but the logos of *El Shaddai*. The great Prophet Enoch received from *El Shaddai* and His angels writing and mathematics. *El Shaddai* was his Light and Grand Architect. So it was for *Melech* Solomon. He had a ring that displayed a pentagram resembling mine on my door. We have been influenced longer by the ancient Greek philosophers in seeking the truth than these heretical heathen upstart Romans. Yet, my Greek contemporary citizens have ignored their ancestral knowledge."

Demetrius returned and refilled their cups with the ease of a graceful swan. Yoseph could see his retinue of teachers were quite relaxed. They all seemed isolated from the city's tumult. Philo's great wisdom continued.

"Yoseph, my friend, all that man accomplishes, time destroys, just like the Pharos lighthouse will be someday. Yet, the Torah will go on through eternity. How ephemeral are our greatest monuments built by humans, but how permanent is the least spoken word of *El Shaddai*.

"The senses of man will never be satisfied; there is a loss of will and judgment. Sensual things are placed above spiritual things. However, humans are still striving for a higher purity, even if their body and soul are still tied to earthly things. There is a triad of methods whereby one can rise toward the divine: through teaching, through practicing, and natural goodness.

"Yoseph, tell me more about this *Maishiach* Yeshua."

"I am authoring a book about His life and our travels after His death and resurrection. He wants me and my fellow teachers to speak of His new logos to Gentiles and Jews alike. Yet He left me with the puzzling words *octa* and *penta*. It has to do with starting a new synagogue, but I know not where. Possibly on a faraway island I once obtained tin as a merchant."

"Yoseph, don't you see? He is telling you about starting a New Jerusalem, a new Temple for *El Shaddai*. The numbers five and eight are sacred numbers of the Old Tabernacle and the First Temple. Both housed the Ark of the Covenant. The Temple and the Tent of Meeting were both built on the multiple dimensions of five and eight, *penta* and *octa*. Did Yeshua divulge the names of the builders of the Ark of the Covenant and the Tabernacle?"

"Yes, he did. They were Bezalel and Oholiab."

"Yoseph, what do you get when you cube two items?"

"Philo, you get eight."

"What is the size of the *Kodesh Hakodashim*?

"The Holy of Holies is 8,000 square cubits."

"Yoseph, you will be building a new Holy of Holies to house your sacred cup! Also to build an additional room for your other sacred items. Plato spoke of his platonic solids composing all things and Enoch being shown all mathematic numbers by the Angel Uriel. Later Enoch was taken for eternity by *El Shaddai* and is now *El Shaddai's* personal scribe. He was renamed the Angel Metatron, and it is said his cube contained all things that *El Shaddai* had given him. Some say it is the symbol of all creation."

Yoseph thought Philo's exegesis was quite profound, but how did His Holy Lord's cup fit into Yoseph and his apostle's ministry?

"What number of people were on Noah's ark when they landed on dry land, and what did they start?"

"There were eight."

"Yes, and they started a new order or beginning. Yeshua is telling and showing you the way for His logos. Your holy cup will be a beacon just like the Pharos lighthouse and draw many people. From your Holy Book you will tell of the *Maishiach's* life and what He expects of humanity. His truth and wisdom will be a pillar that is never destroyed. Search for the acrostic meaning in His words. I believe He has hidden many things in what you have said so far.

"Yoseph, I am so glad you came to visit. I feel my spirit has entered a new age. I wish I could travel with you, but our Jewish people in Alexandria need me in Rome."

"Philosopher Philo," said Miriam as she reached into her purse. "Please accept this egg to give to the emperor. It represents our *Maishiach*. He will send a new governor to quiet things for the people of Alexandria. Tell him that you can turn this white egg into a red one if he agrees to a new procurator. This will show him the power of the Son of Man." Miriam got up and then placed the egg into his palm. "May our *Maishiach* bless your endeavor."

"Miriam, thank you very much, but I don't think new Emperor Caligula will agree."

"Philosopher Philo, remember my eyes when you speak to the emperor. What you will see is my *Maishiach*. The egg will change color and he will agree to your request."

Yoseph didn't expect this from Miriam, but he knew how much she loved Yeshua and knew little of the sacred knowledge Yeshua had quitted to her.

"Yoseph, are you able to show me this most precious cup you possess?" Philo asked. "It would be an honor for me to observe it. From what you have told me, you have sacrificed a great deal to be its custodian."

Yoseph hesitated before answering, fearing the chalice might hurt his good friend. However, Philo was quite wise on the advice he had given Yoseph and his apostles. He knew Philo was an *El Shaddai*-fearing Jew and Yeshua's cup would accept him.

"Yes," Yoseph replied. Slowly he withdrew the warm cup from his satchel and raised it above his head. A tremendous emanating light came forth from its rim and started spinning around Philo's study. The walls appeared to have thousands of tiny flaming lights issuing forth and they produced a dizzy swirling effect on the mind.

Philo fell on his knees and bowed his head.

"*Kodesh*, *kodesh*, it is truly *El Shaddai* and His Son's glory. *El Shaddai's* presence is in this room declaring his *kodesh* directives."

The light and flames changed to an orange color and then finally a deep purple. Afterward, the light diminished and retained a light golden orange color. Everybody in the room, including Demetrious, froze like a statue. Nobody moved until there came a thunderous pounding on the front door.

"Demetrious, hurry and answer the door!" exclaimed Philo.

The sudden knocking startled Yoseph and he feared it wasn't good news. Quickly, the young boy returned and approached Yoseph.

"Rabbi, there is a man at the door by the name of Captain Hiram and he wants to speak to you now."

Yoseph jumped up and then proceeded to the front door.

Standing in the entranceway was Hiram. His face spoke of danger and nothing else.

"Rabbi Yoseph, we must leave without hesitation. My sailors are fighting off a mob of rioters who are threatening to burn my ship. We must leave now. Soon, the ship may be burned to the water line."

Yoseph ran back to warn the rest of his fellow teachers.

"My friends, we must leave now. The dock and our ship are in peril of being burned."

Yoseph thanked Philo for his hospitality and the excellent revelations he had given him. He gave Philo a large embrace.

"Go, my friend, with the words of *El Shaddai*. Don't worry about Demetrius and me. We have a secret passageway that Demetrius and I can escape to if necessary."

Everybody had gathered at the entrance surrounding Captain Hiram, except Yohanan Marcus. He was still writing on his parchment. "Marcus, come we must leave right now!" Yoseph demanded.

"Rabbi Yoseph, I am not going. My ministry begins right here with Philo, for Yeshua has spoken to me. Good-bye, my friend, I will meet you in our next life."

Yoseph started to move toward him to convince him otherwise, but a strong arm of Hebron prevented him doing so. Out the front door they raced into the burning abyss of *sheol*. The heat was so intense, Yoseph felt the hair on his arms singe. Hiram led the way with the rest of them dashing behind him. They came to a dark alley and heard female screams of horror. Hebron hastened toward the dark images and the spine-tingling shrieks.

"Yoseph, bring Philip and Hiram, there appears to be trouble!" he shouted. The three of them sprinted toward Hebron. They approached two men raping two young women. The first man spotted Hebron, only to be met with Hebron's large fist then followed by a knee kick to the rapist's groin. The other man made a failed attempt to strike Yoseph's brother-in-law, but Hebron grabbed his arm and jerked it back behind him with a cracking sound. This man scurried off holding his arm.

"Yoseph, what will we do with these young women?" Miriam of Magdala asked.

"We'll need to leave with them before these men alert a large mob."

Yoseph didn't hesitate. "Hebron, you carry one and Philip the other. We'll take them with us on the ship. Now hurry. Pray that we will have a ship to leave on."

They rushed all the way to the dock, but rioters had surrounded the dock entrance. The gangplank was missing so the mob couldn't board the ship. Yoseph knew what to do, but he had to act quickly. He reached into his satchel and pulled out the cup of Christ. Instantly, the light blinded the mob, and many fell to the dock and grabbed their ears screaming. The rest started vomiting and bent over with pain. Quickly Hebron and Philip cleared the path to the ship. Immediately, Captain Hiram ordered his sailors to put the gangplank back and to prepare to set sail. Rapidly it was replaced with a thud, and Yoseph and his fellow teachers raced across, followed once again by its withdrawal. The unfurled sails caught the hot wind from the many fires and their ship surged toward the open bay where they set the ship's anchor for the night far from the dock.

Yoseph's mind was assailed with a myriad of emotions and his breath shortened. What was he to tell the others about Yohanan Marcus? Who were the young women they just rescued? How would he explain to his teacher what Philo revealed? What would Captain Hiram do now? He couldn't unload his cargo. Miriam quickly removed the young women below deck where her sister, Martha, was sleeping.

"Yoseph, tomorrow morning what are you going to tell the others about what happened tonight?" Hebron asked.

"I am going to tell them the truth. It is a long journey to the Glass Isle, and much can happen before we get there. I believe tonight has shown us thus. It appears our band of teachers will wax and wane according to Yeshua's destiny He has planned for us." Yoseph, so overcome with exhaustion, proceeded to lay down on the deck and fall fast asleep.

The next thing Yoseph heard was the *screeching* of the seagulls and then he opened his eyes to the morning rays of the sunshine. How was he going to explain the truth of last night in a coherent manner? This immensely distressed Yoseph. His hands started to shake.

"Rabbi Yoseph," came the voice of Captain Hiram. "It appears we won't be unloading my cargo. The dock went up in flames last night."

Yoseph gazed over his shoulder and spied a long dark smoldering dirt bank. "Where are you going to sell your cargo?"

"It won't be in Alexandria, besides the merchant quarters are in ashes too. It appears we are on our way to the ports of Massalia and Gaul. I know both Greek merchants and the People of the Book who would desire my payload."

Hiram just answered one of Yoseph's questions he could explain, but how would he properly explain to the others? He feared his nascent band of teachers would not go any farther and wanted to disband and return to Yehudah. This doubt scared Yoseph, and his tongue and throat drew up.

CHAPTER XL

Hebron gathered all the teachers and Hiram so Yoseph could tell them what happened last night. He explained who Philo was and what the philosopher and mathematician had revealed about the shape and dimension of their new temple. He noticed Miriam of Magdala embracing both women they had rescued last night.

"Rabbi," she said. "May I interrupt and explain where these two young women are from and their occupations?"

"Yes, please do. I think all of us would like to know."

"One is an Egyptian and the other is from the country of Abyssinia. Her land was once ruled by the queen of Sheba and her name is Sarah. The other young woman's name is Marcella, and she is from the old Ptolemy line of Cleopatra. Before the fires, they worked as servants for various Greek masters. They have no husbands, and both their parents are dead. They were trying to escape from the fires when they were attacked. We need to welcome them as sisters of our group."

Yoseph noticed his fellow teachers nod their heads in agreement and then rush forth and give hugs of acceptance. Yoseph didn't have any objections and hugged them both.

"My fellow teachers, I have some disquieting news about our fellow brother, Yohanan Marcus. He has a new calling from Yeshua and will stay in Alexandria and study with the philosopher,

Philo. The truth-seeker will protect and keep him safe from the fires, so please don't worry for his safety. Yeshua touched his soul and wants him to study at the ancient library in Alexandria and preach to the Gentiles and the Jews."

Yoseph prayed to himself with the hope that one day they would meet again in the physical world. His fellow teachers seemed some confused with the pronouncement and their voices buzzed with whispers.

"Note closely, my fellow friends and teachers. Our journey will be long and fraught with dangers, but we'll strengthen our way with faith and the truth. Come to me any time if you hear *El Shaddai's* call. I will not be disappointed in you if you decide to leave. As you can see, we now have two new members."

Yoseph introduced Sarah and Marcella to their teachers: Shimon the Zealot, Lazarus, Martha, Nathan, Philip, Shimon of Cyrene, Enygeus, Alein Yosephe, Yosa, Zechariah, Clotho, Georgeus, Miriam Salome, and Miriam Cleopas. Then all eyes focused on Yoseph.

"Philo has revealed to me what we must do when we reach our final destination. We'll build the First Temple to our *Maishiach,* and its dimensions will be a smaller version of Solomon's great temple. It is still a far distant to the Isle of the Apples or Glass Isle, but we are a determined band of teachers and have truth on our side."

By this time Captain Hiram's ship had distanced itself from the powerful white beam of the Pharos lighthouse. Their next port was Cyrene, Shimon's hometown. He knew Shimon, Yoseph's good friend who had helped carry Yeshua's cross, longed for his home after five years in *Yerushalayim.* They docked there about two days out from Alexandria. The port had a lighthouse, small and in a Grecian design. The shore was crowded with Greek and Roman temples, and the ancient name of the harbor and town was named Apollonia, named after the Greek god Apollo. To Yoseph's surprise, there were two harbors, which had made docking easy. It allowed merchant ships to quickly dock. They said their good-byes to Shimon while Captain Hiram loaded additional cargo that didn't take long as it was already at ship's capacity.

"Shimon, go with God and our *Maishiach*," Yoseph said. "Go to the Gentiles and Jews and preach our new way. We will always remember what you did for Yeshua. We will pray for you every day."

"I too will do the same. Travel in peace."

He hugged each one of the teachers and reluctantly ambled down the gangplank. Yoseph felt the gloom of his departure crawl up his spine and into his heart. Many tears were shed, especially among Yoseph's family, even Hebron.

The next morning, the ship headed due north into a cold northwesterly breeze. Whitecap waves increased in size as they continued in the ship's direction. The second day of travel, the waves grew larger and so did the dark clouds. Yoseph noted these weather signs indicated rough seas and lightning ahead of them. His many years of sea travel told him this was an omen of impending disaster. He must consult with Captain Hiram immediately. Yoseph proceeded to the tiller deck where Captain Hiram was struggling with the rudder.

"Captain Hiram, I am concerned about the sea ahead of us. The dark clouds are moving quite fast, and this doesn't bode well."

"Rabbi, it appears as a fast-moving squall, and we should pass through it quite soon. I have traveled this route during this time every year, and I haven't had any problems. Just relax; it will blow over soon."

Yoseph didn't want to doubt this experienced sea captain, but his intuition told him otherwise. He observed many large, whitecapped swells followed by deep dives of the ship's bow. This motion continued for more than half a day. Several of his fellow teachers were perilously close to the gunwales retching up their stomach contents. At any time, he feared that one of them would go overboard. Then to Yoseph's chagrin, he witnessed Yosa teetering close to the ship's railing, vomiting. He instantly shouted to Yosa and his cohorts.

"Everybody, below deck at once!" He rushed toward his

daughter and grabbed her waist just as she fell forward. "Yosa, you could have tumbled overboard and washed away. Please dear, we must go below." Just as Yoseph finished saying this a large wave washed on deck and swept away several large amphoras. Everybody rushed down the dark narrow steps as the timbers of the ship started to crack and groan. Toward the far corner of the stern, his teachers were squatting down in a huddle.

"Rabbi, what should we do?" several teachers asked. "We need to pray now for our survival and the completion of our holy mission. Philip, what would our Yeshua say to us in a time of trial?"

"Once, many years ago, we were in Shimon the Rock's boat on Lake Galilee when a storm like this one came upon us. Our *Maishiach* woke from His sleep after His fellow disciples feared they might sink. They asked Him to save them from drowning. To their amazement He admonished them. He told them, 'All of you have little faith and why do you fear this storm?' Then He rebuked the waves and wind, and then it was completely calm. The disciples were stupefied and asked, 'What kind of man is this? Even the wind and waves obey him!' In another storm on Lake Galilee, Shimon the Rock's faith was tested. During the tempest he perceived Yeshua coming to him on the surface of the lake. As He approached the boat, He told Shimon to stride toward Him. Shimon started out toddling on the water, but the wind and waves terrified him, and he began to sink. My brothers and sisters, both lessons reveal that just saying you have faith doesn't mean it is etched in your heart. Let us now etch this in our hearts and pray."

Yoseph and his fellow teachers bowed their heads and prayed for a continuous day, only stopping for food and to relieve themselves. At the beginning of the fourth day, the storm intensified in its fury. Water started coming in through the hull boards. Captain Hiram told the women to abandon the ship and launch his emergency boat. The last thing Yoseph remembered was Yosa's scream, a loud cracking sound, and the sinking into the sea. The taste of sea water and darkness covered Yoseph's eyes.

CHAPTER XLI

La Rochelle
Duchy of Aquitaine
Spring
Anno Domini 1191

Our ship's bow parted the constant waves with a *swishing* sound, which lulled me into thinking about my *épouse* and two *fils*, Brian and Henri. I missed Marie so much my heart ached every day wanting to hold her in my arms. Alongside my saddened heart, the thickness in my throat, from fear of their danger, reminded me how helpless I was. Shortly, we would dock at La Rochelle, and I would be in Gaul once again. My emotions told me I must protect them at any cost, yet an unseen force far stronger pulled me toward the British Isles.

"Lord Robert, what are you ruminating about?" asked Grand Master Gilbért. Right behind him was Muhammad gazing toward the landward horizon probably expecting that any moment one or more of the killer *Hashishiyya* might appear out of the water and come aboard our ship.

"I was thinking about home and my family. I still fear for their safety and wish I could hold them all."

"Observe!" Muhammad shouted. "I see the harbor. We will make port soon."

The sun above us held its highest point possible as all our eyes squinted toward the harbor entrance. Flocking white seagulls were squawking their usual high-pitched sounds, diving between the many masted ships maneuvering to dock into their slips. A smile came over Grand Master Gilbért as he stared into the distance. I knew he was improving each day, especially when he started explaining the history of the harbor and the Duchy of Aquitaine.

"Lord Robert, this port was constructed and improved by *Duc* Guillaume the Tenth many years ago. He was the *père* of the dowager Queen Eleanor, *mère* to *Roi* Richard and Prince John of England. Do you see behind the harbor bay there is a four-towered fortress? That is the *Château* Vauclair, which guards the port. It is our naval headquarters and Admiral Hidalgo de Fernando's headquarters too."

"Did I hear my name?" came the reply from admiral. "We will dock soon, and I can unload my horses. Muhammad has agreed to help me and my *frères*. This will shorten our time here. Afterward, I am loading numerous casks of Iberian *vin* to take to England. The *roi* and his *frère* pay handsomely for my cargo. The weather appears clear, so we'll leave tomorrow. I will add some barges so you and your compatriots can unload your horses before landing. Grand Master Gilbért, you said you and your men want to disembark off the English coast, *sí*?"

"*Sí*, and at night. We have some distance from there before we reach our destination. Muhammad will see to the arrangement with the horses. *Merci, mon frère*; you have been kind."

When the admiral mentioned loading the Iberian *vin*, my mind raced back to the departed *Marquésa* Helena chatting about her *vignoble* with smiles of delight. Forthwith, a sinking feeling formed in my stomach. Chaplain Jeremiah approached me.

"You seem troubled, *mon ami*. Why don't we sample some of this *vin*? They'll load it soon. I am sure there is a *vin* shop somewhere along the harbor. Besides, I suspect the loud neighing of the disembarking horses won't allow you to contemplate. You need some *vin* and company. Let's leave the boat and seek out a quiet shop to converse."

This sounded agreeable to me, and I had some questions I wanted to ask him. We traveled down the wooden wharf until we reached a wattle-and-daub building with a sign displaying a large *vin* jug above the entrance. We entered and found a quiet table at the back of the shop. Promptly, a dark-haired *mademoiselle* approached and procured our request. Before starting our conversation, she returned with our *vin*, along with some crusty bread and Camembert cheese.

"Chaplain Jeremiah, how is Grand Master Gilbért emotionally progressing?"

"I believe he is fine. The reunion with my aunt changed him immensely. That part of his life is now complete, and there are no more ghosts to haunt him. It helped me as well. Part of my past is no longer missing. However, you didn't come here to discuss my *père*."

"*Oui,* you are a wise observer. Guilt, shame, and a lustful longing have weighed on my soul for more than a month. I need you to hear my confession." I confessed my feelings for *Marquésa* Helena and even the truth of her being murdered in my bed. There was a long pause before he replied to my confession, which included another pouring of *vin*.

"Lord Robert, we are men, and most men are suspectable to loneliness, and this leads to desire. All of us have been under a great strain. Men of the holy orders are trained not to be tempted. You have not had this schooling. *Marquésa* Helena too had lonely desires, which weakened her. You didn't consummate this relationship and should not feel guilty for her murder and your lust. I will have you pray fifty *Pater Nosters* tonight and contemplate what Saint Joseph of Arimathea has so far revealed. We need your clear thoughts on the next stage of our quest."

He made the sign of the cross and then kissed the pattée cross around his neck. Afterward, we left the *vin* store and silently strolled back to the ship. I left feeling much relieved in him hearing my confession. The night came fast and by now most of the horses were unloaded except for our own horses. I said my fifty *Pater Nosters* and then reclined in one of the ship's hammocks. What would the English isles tell me about Saint Joseph of Arimathea? Did he successfully reach there? The Apostle Philip desired for him and Rabbi Joseph to preach there. Where did he live and to whom did he teach? How far did he travel there? What mode of transportation did he use?

All my questions were predicated on whether he survived his journey. Then I remembered about the location of the tin and lead mines that Joseph visited with his great nephew, our Lord and Savior, Jesus the Christ. This may be the exact spot where Saint Joseph of Arimathea constructed the first Christian church. Would I find it there at the *abbaye-cathédrale*? My quest had started out as a search of long hidden scrolls with new holy information. Then a mysterious *église* and finally the Last Supper cup with its ceremony. All that we had discovered was leading us to this town of Glastonbury. My mind now left me with great satisfaction that we were close to completing our months of searching.

Quickly, I fell asleep with my contentment. Sometime during the night my fitful dream started. It displayed Chaplain Jeremiah trying to kill me for the final tome of Saint Joseph of Arimathea's story. He told me he spied for Cardinal Folquet and had contempt for Grand Master Gilbért for abandoning him as a baby. The cardinal promised him great wealth and would appoint him as a bishop. After explaining his reasons, he lunged at me with a dagger while I was laying in the hammock. Immediately I woke up.

I couldn't sleep the rest of the night, so I proceeded above the ship's deck while it was still dark. I heard a slight murmur of voices and glanced to see who it might be. It was Admiral Hidalgo and Grand Master Gilbért speaking. I wanted no company but silence. This nightmare vision shook my bones, and I prayed it wasn't a portent. Chaplain Jeremiah gave me no provocation to think of him as a traitor. However, I had just confessed my innermost thoughts to him a brief time ago. I told myself not to let my many suspicions jar my judgment. Stay alert and maintain my objective manner. Our goal was now within our hands' reach.

"Lord Robert, I see you are awake," announced Admiral Hidalgo.

"*Si*, admiral, and I couldn't sleep. I was awakened by a nightmare. You must have launched your ship while I was sleeping."

"*Si*. Grand Master Gilbért and I were discussing the possibility of dangerous weather ahead. I hope your nightmare wasn't about stormy ocean waves?"

"*Non*, it is something I'd rather not discuss. Besides, where are we and why do you suspect severe weather?"

"Lord Robert, observe. See the many fleeing flocks of seagulls coming from the north and their loud squawking. A storm is heading in our direction. I have charted a course for a safe harbor at Saint-Nazaire. We should reach our destination late tonight."

I knew the area well, and he told me we'd be docking in the *Duché* de Bretagne. We were now entering the domain of *Roi* Richard and Prince John of England.

The rest of the day was uneventful, with me viewing the swiftly approaching dark odd-shaped clouds. To take my mind off the approaching squall, I counted the dolphins jumping in front of our bow. They seemed not as concerned as me about the forthwith storm. Their facial expressions were a permanent smile, which never left them. Toward late evening, the storm arrived, starting off with icy pebbles making a *clicking* sound as they bounced off the deck. This followed with bolts of lightning and thunder, then the ship started violently rocking back and forth. The sky got darker and then I heard a *buzzing* sound. The noise surrounded me from all directions.

"Observe, fellow *Frères* of Christ!" shouted both the admiral and Grand Master Gilbért. "It is Saint Elmo's Fire."

I followed their hands upward and observed an unbelievable sight. A luminous torch-like fire coming from all the masts and spars. Anything with a tipped point exuded fingers of bluish-violet lights. The *buzzing* sound intensified and so did the lights. Chaplain Jeremiah and *Abad* Miguel were both kneeling. The strange sound kept me from hearing their prayers and the entire sight made my body start shaking with fear. Was this event from heaven or hell? I prayed it was from heaven. Then I noticed both Admiral Hidalgo and Grand Master Gilbért smiling during the conflagration. I believed this was my demise and both men were mocking us. My fear now turned to anger. Yet, to my horror the sparks and fire surrounded my entire body. My ears couldn't hear anything but excessive *buzzing*. This continued to the next watch before it subsided.

"Lord Robert, this a good omen and nothing to fear. As sailors for many years, we are used to seeing this happen. This sign will mean the storm will rapidly pass. In a short time, we'll anchor in the bay of Saint-Nazaire and check our *vino* cargo. It won't take long to anchor and check it. We'll then continue to the English coast. It is a three-and-a-half day journey or 141 nautical leagues. But I don't know where to drop you off. What is the name of the English port you wish to disembark?"

I didn't know what to say, for Grand Master Gilbért had not told me or anyone else. He kept those thoughts to himself for good reasons. Our betrayals and loss of life had cost us dearly. I don't think he would even tell me until the last moment before we landed. I referred Admiral Hidalgo's questions to Grand Master Gilbért.

"Admiral, I think he would prefer to tell you that destination in private. It is quite a confidential matter why we are traveling to England." Just then Grand Master Gilbért came by as the storm was subsiding. I motioned for him to come closer and then repeated Admiral Hidalgo's question. Immediately, they traveled toward the admiral's headquarters.

Our ship steered into the bay and then placed her *clanking* anchor and chain down into the splashing sea. Shortly after anchoring, the storm passed and the firmaments sparkled with numerous diamond-shaped stars. After the last watch, Grand Master Gilbért and Admiral Hidalgo appeared back on deck.

Admiral Hidalgo spoke first.

"Lord Robert, I told you the storm would cease soon. Now you can discern a multitude of stars. Experience can stop fear no matter how great it is. Grand Master Gilbért and I have agreed on a charted course. If a steady wind holds for several days, we may reach your destination sooner. Now I must go check my cargo. *Buenas noches*, my *amigos*."

Grand Master Gilbért said nothing about our destination port and suggested I speak to our fellow compatriots about the storm, Saint Elmo's Fire, and how many days until we made land. After squeezing my arm, he left and went to his quarters. I did the same after speaking to my *amis*. Shortly after falling asleep, I was awakened by the noisy *clanking* of the anchor chain being withdrawn from the water and then the ship lurched forward. Quickly, I fell back to a quiet sleep.

The next morning the cloudless sky, the salty tantalizing sea air, and a good night's sleep had invigorated me. My ears heard the *flapping* sounds of our large white pattée red cross sails. I witnessed Admiral Hidalgo and Grand Master Gilbért pointing to a distance spot on the ocean horizon. Chaplain Jeremiah had joined me, and we strolled toward the stern of the ship.

"It appears a ship is following us," stated our admiral. Yet, Grand Master Gilbért stared at us knowing all too well who this might be.

"Can you make out the origin of the ship?" I asked the admiral.

"*Si*, and now I can see it. It's flying the cross of Toulouse."

"Will they overtake us soon?"

"Possibly but see how high it sails in the ocean. It is not carrying any cargo, which means it's faster. We both have excellent winds, and we both have the same number of sails. However, I know the currents off the coast of *Duché* de Bretagne. We should reach the tip of the peninsula by tomorrow and lose the Toulouse ship." Instantly, he signaled his rudder man to change directions. The ship sailed northeast and then picked up speed. We continued this way most of the day into the early morning of the next day and then headed due north. The sunrise revealed some islands to our port side, followed by a pointed tip of a large land mass. Once reaching here we increased our speed and the pointed land mass disappeared.

Muhammad came on deck and assured us that our horses were doing well. They had survived the storm and long voyage and were anxious to be ridden. He then approached Admiral Hidalgo and asked him when we would dock off the English coast.

"Emir Muhammad, it will be late tonight. I suggest you prepare your horses for debarkation. We'll be unloading at high tide. It is a dark moon tonight, which will make landfall further dangerous. I do not know what to expect. You and Grand Master Gilbért will make sure you are heavily armed in case of the *rey's* men. My sailors won't have much time to let you off before the tide goes out. I beg you to be prepared to leave."

The admiral's last couple of warnings caused my heart to race with anxiety. Why the urgency? Did he know something I wasn't aware of? He could have waited until morning before we left. This did not bode well. My mouth turned dry.

PART SEVEN

The Final Destination

CHAPTER XLII

Off the Coast of Weymouth, England
March
Anno Domini 1191

Late that night our ship sliced through the *swishing* water as we approached a dark isle land mass. The admiral murmured that we'd outwitted the other ship and to not speak a word. The small isle appeared as a large black leviathan ready to swallow our entire ship without warning. His sailors lowered several large anchors with thick ropes. He said to quiet the horses as we started hauling them into the barges. Muhammad's sweet whispers did their job and the sole noise I heard was the *thumping* of their hooves on the bottom of the barge. The ship's block and tackle made this a smooth task.

Muhammad slowly entered the barge and continued his soft words. The block and tackle lowered me and *Noir Ombre* along with Sergeant Jacque de Hoult in the next barge. The dog licked my face, as if giving his approval. Grand Master Gilbért, Chaplain Jeremiah, and *Abad* Miguel entered the second barge. Admiral Hidalgo slid into the second barge and gave us final instructions where to row, while several of his sailors followed.

We rowed until my arms started throbbing and that's when I heard a *grinding* thud followed by waves flooding into the bottom hull. The barges were beached, and we disembarked with Muhammad carefully leading the horses out of the shallow hull.

"I guess this is where we say good-bye," whispered Admiral Hidalgo. That's when Grand Master Gilbért gave the admiral a large embrace.

"*Mon ami*, there is not enough thanks my men and I can give you. *Vaya con Dios,* my *hermano*." Quietly the admiral stepped back into a barge with his fellow sailors and rowed back toward his firefly-like lit ship. We guided our horses down the beach with *crunching* footfalls until we reached a copse of trees, which then led into a pitch-black forest.

"Grand Master Gilbért, where are we going?" I asked after we traveled some distance heading north before lighting our torches.

His horse strode up next to me. "Lord Robert, ride up ahead with me." After separating from the rest of our compatriots, he said, "Our next destination will be the Templar training camp at Templecombe, England, with its small church of *Sainte* Mary. We will stop there in two days before we go on to Glastonbury *Abbaye*. You are the only person who knows of this destination. I don't want to make this easy for our enemies. We are so close to completing our quest, and I fear the woods have a thousand sets of ears listening. I know the preceptor from my fighting days in the Levant. He survived the Battle of Hattin and after transferred to the preceptory of Templecombe to train new *frère chevaliers* for combat. His name is *Chevalier* Roger de Shelborne, and I know I have said this before, he is a trusted Poor-Soldier of Christ. Sergeant Jacque de Hoult knew him also from our days of fighting in the Outremer. We must trust some people in order to complete our holy search."

He was right, but I had an uneasy feeling that I hadn't felt since we left Toledo, Iberia. I knew Prince John Lackland wasn't as sympathetic as his *frère Roi* Richard I *le Coeur de Lion* to the Knights of the Temple. Also, according to Sergeant de Hoult, the *abbaye* was one of the largest in England, and somewhat isolated in the countryside. This wouldn't make our search any easier and the closest Templar headquarters was in London, forty-six leagues due northeast away from the *abbaye*. Anybody and everybody could become our enemy between that distance. According to Grand Master Gilbért, the Templecombe Preceptory had a few good teachers from the Levant, but the rest were students.

We camped in a dense wood as the sun rose and then slept most of the day. That night we traveled once more, after feeding our horses and our war dog, *Noir Ombre*. We continued forward several leagues after midnight until we reached a high hill with the black silhouette of a Christian cross-topped dark building. I assumed this was the *église* of Sainte Mary. We camped in the church graveyard to obtain some rest until daylight.

I didn't get much rest because I kept hearing noises and *Noir Ombre* whined until daylight. He didn't leave my sight until after sunrise. We strolled the short distance to the preceptory and met Preceptor Roger de Shelborne. He was in a large, fenced area training his new recruits. The *chevaliers* were riding their horses while striking a stationary human-shaped target. Each young man held a spike-headed mace, which they were ordered to batter the head portion of the heavy wooden statue.

"Grand Master Gilbért de Érail, Your Excellency, it is good to see you once more!" Preceptor Roger shouted. "Your Saracen scout told us you were coming. Come and see the next new recruits to go to the Levant. *Roi* Richard will need them to fight against our old enemy, Saladin."

"*Oui*, but we have urgent business to discuss with you. May we speak in private?"

"*Oui*, Grand Master, please follow me to my headquarters."

We continued to saunter through the tall grass toward a small stone-built preceptory. I spied the Green Man's head carved above the entranceway. Once inside, we climbed a tight-fitting stairway toward the second floor. Once there, we had to stand in order for all of us to fit in the room.

"Grand Master Gilbért, what led you to my humble abode?" Commander Roger asked.

"It is a sensitive nature and concerns the Holy See. That is all that I can say. My men and I need to rest and would appreciate several days of your hospitality. You were an excellent fighter in the Levant, and I know I can trust you. We will be here just a couple of days."

"*Merci beaucoup, mon ami.* My men and preceptory at your disposal. Let us know if you need anything. We retire quite early so that my men will have a full day of combat training. Your men can sleep anywhere in the preceptory or in the *église*. Now I must go back to my *chevaliers* and finish their training."

We followed him back down the small spiral steps and went to our horses to unpack them and then we were ready to rest. Muhammad and *Noir Ombre* proceeded to search the surrounding area on foot. The sun was high above the trees, and I searched for a quiet place to write, contemplate, and just relax. I sat under a bare leaf oak tree with its buds just beginning to swell. I wondered what our destination *abbaye's* allure might be. According to Chaplain Jeremiah, many saints were buried there, including Saints Patrick and Dunstan. Most assuredly Saint Joseph de Arimathea was there. Yet, I sensed something else was pulling us there. It felt as if an unseen tide was drawing us to an isle that we couldn't escape from. Part of this tidal pull gave me a foreboding dread and the other portion a coming sense of euphoria. I never knew of such a sensation. I spotted Chaplain Jeremiah and motioned for him to join me. He sat down next to a scaly root and asked what I was contemplating.

"I see you are either in prayer or contemplation. Which is it?"

"It is contemplation. Why do you think this *abbaye* is pulling us toward it? We have visited numerous *abbayes* before and I didn't have such a keen sense of attraction. This pull is coming from my gut and heart. Do you feel this same sensation?"

"*Oui*, I do, and my senses are telling me it is God's *shekhinah* or the Holy Place of God, which like Moses and his tribes led them to the Promised Land. We are in its power, and we can't escape from it. Remember we are seeking a New Jerusalem and its tabernacle. The Old Testament has given us many clues to its dimensions and its great whirlpool is pulling us in to solve its hidden meanings. You must wrap yourself in its waves and seek its conclusion. This is how I explain my feelings. I think there are greater things, which to our astonishment will be revealed. Rest easy, *mon ami,* we are about to end our quest."

Chaplain Jeremiah always made my angst disappear and his *père's* past assuredness made me at ease. I stayed under the tree until the sun set. Suddenly, there was a *cracking* sound of broken branches. I got up to investigate and crept into the nearby dense woods. Darkness had covered the forest first, leaving nothing but dark tree trunks. I took one more step then felt a sharp pain in the back of my head and my mind was black. Later this was followed by a *buzzing* sound in my ears and the sensation of my body bouncing on a wooden platform. My eyes opened and still there was no light. My mouth was stuffed with rags and my head was covered with a black cloth and ropes tightly cut into my wrist. Also my ankles were the same. I heard wagon wheels turning and the *clopping* of several horses. Who had kidnapped me? Why had Grand Master Gilbért let this happen? How long had I been unconscious? Where was I and where was I going? Did Sergeant Jacque de Hoult tip off the cardinal to our location? How could he have done it while being onboard the ship?

After some distance, I heard whispers coming from two unknown drivers. Their whispers were a different language, which had the same dialect as Muhammad Nur Adin. I recognized just one word, "London."

Both men lifted me out of the wagon and then tied me to a roughed-barked tree. After a fleeting period, I heard the horses and wagon leave. The sole sound I heard was an owl hooting in the distance. My teeth started chattering from the cold and my body shook violently against the tight ropes. Had they abandoned me? My question was answered shortly after I heard riders approach.

"Here is a cloak," came a loud Norman-sounding voice. I felt the ropes around the tree loosening and the ones around my ankles, but not my hands. The mask stayed on my head as they put the heavy cloak around my shoulders.

"Get him on the horse, we must leave now!" ordered the same voice to his silent conspirator. This other man was quite strong as he quickly mounted me on the saddle. We left at a steady trot and must have traveled until morning. The sun's warmer rays let me know it was daylight and we continued for some time until I once again felt colder. That is when we stopped.

"Get him down and tie him to that tree. We need to feed the horses and cook our meal." Once again, the same man lifted me off my horse and proceeded to tie me to another tree.

"Acquire him some food and water, but don't let him see us. Prince John is paying a decent price for this Burgundian spy. We want him alive so the prince can question him. I hear tell an important cardinal wants to speak to him also. You must be most important to several people."

I felt part of my mask coming loose and then a piece of dried pork was shoved into my mouth along with a gulp of *vin*.

"Lord Robert de Borron, are you full?"

"*Oui*, but I demand to know who you are and where are you taking me?"

"That, I cannot say, but you will find out in two days. You are my prisoner and nobody else's. Keep your mouth shut and my compatriot won't have to test the sharpness of his knife on your fingers. Now go take a piss so we can leave. I know that Saracen scout and your dog will be on our trail soon."

They untied me and I was led behind a tree. After relieving myself, they tied my hands behind me. Once again, we rode all day and only stopped to feed our horses and feed me their tough-dried food. The steady *clopping* pace continued until I heard coursing water. I knew we were going in an easterly direction because each morning I could feel the warmth of the rising sun and later in the day the coldness on my back. The lapping water became louder and then we stopped.

"You take the horses overland, and I will load him in the boat," said the now familiar voice. "We will meet at our agreed location after I obtain our silver coin payment."

The other man must have given an agreeing nod, for there wasn't a verbal reply. I was once again unloaded from my horse, then I heard numerous horses galloping away. I felt a different grip pull my body toward what I thought was a steep riverbank. He guided my legs into a wooden boat and forced me to sit down on a wide seat. Quickly, he put a noose rope around my legs and tightened it until I felt a burning sensation. I could hear oars splashing in the water and afterward the *flapping* of a sail. There was nothing said, but long periods of silence. I prayed Muhammad Nur Adin and *Noir Ombre's* nose were on my trail, yet I realized it was harder to track me on a river. We would stop each night to eat, sleep, and warm ourselves near a *crackling* fire. This routine persisted for several more days and nights until we reached a section of the river where I heard other boats being paddled and faint voices. Where was I being taken? I prayed not to London as a spy. Wherever they took me it didn't bode well for me.

CHAPTER XLIII

The Tower, London, England

March

Anno Domini 1191

Suddenly, several wooden *clunking* sounds woke me from a dream about *mon épouse*, Marie, and my two *fils*, Brian and Henri. The noise was followed by voices.

"I see you trapped our spy, Lord Robert de Borron. Both Prince John and Cardinal Folquet will pay handsomely for this prisoner. Take him to the tower. I will follow right behind you."

Both men lifted me out of the boat and led me a short distance before I heard a large roar. "What is that roar?" I asked.

"That is our new interrogator. Several years ago, we received our new lion guard from the Outremer. Several *chevaliers* brought him back from their crusades. He is kept well fed with curious strangers and our torture team seeking answers. *Seigneur* Robert de Borron, you may get to meet him if you don't cooperate."

"What is your name?!" I demanded.

"My name is Guillaume de Longchamp. I am bishop of Ely, lord chancellor, chief justiciar of England, and the English legate authorized by Rome. Cardinal Folquet and Prince John have ordered me to hold you indefinitely. They didn't say why. If you comply with our demands, you will have a pleasurable time at our great keep, the Tower of London. Now follow our tower guard to your new accommodation."

"Have your knavish guard take this hood from my head!"

"As you wish, but not until you reach your living quarter. *Au revoir*, Lord Robert. You've made me quite wealthy. The business of ransom is growing by the day."

I strode toward my new prison, realizing that now I was a captive just like Saint Joseph of Arimathea once was. I prayed my Savior would give me sustenance and see after my release. My guard appeared to lead me down a long hallway, for our boots echoed off the walls. Then we proceeded down a set of steps and into a large chamber, which reeked of urine.

"Here's your new lodgings for now." I heard a squeaking gate open, and the guard pushed me into my cell. "Let me change your ropes for these nice fitting chains. This metal collar will enhance your neck."

He ripped the hood off my head with one hand and with his other locked the collar to the chain embedded into the tower's wall. His breath stunk of stale ale as he started to chain my feet.

"Lord Robert, enjoy your newfound friends. I hear tell one of the spiders in your cell is as big as your hand. I will be back tomorrow to obtain some answers why you are spying on us."

One thing I didn't want to hear about was the giant spider, yet the bishop didn't know why I was here in England. This gave me an advantage. Had the cardinal revealed any information to him? I hoped he assumed my stealthy presence came from *Roi* Philip II. The guard's ignorance might give me a few days of peace before being rescued.

I sat down against the cold dark wall with my chains *clanging* like noisy pellets of hail. Yet it wasn't the noise that distracted me but the feeling of hundreds of spiders scuttling across my arms. Quickly, I brushed them off with my hands, only to my horror they were replaced by hundreds more. How could I get them to stop? Their tingling sensations would quickly make me irrational. Slowly, I slid down the stone wall and sat and their legs stopped moving. This gave me some relief until I fell asleep.

I didn't wake up until the next morning, which might not have been the morning, when something smacked my boot. My eyes gazed upon my guard, who then unshackled my neck collar, but not my hand and leg chains.

"I've a special hot treat for you today. Just something to help warm you up from the cold." He unlocked my cell, and we proceeded down a dark dank corridor until we came to a brazier of red-hot burning coals.

"I want you to tell me who sent you, why you traveled to England, and what are you seeking? If you answer to my satisfaction, I will take you back to your cell. Lord Robert, do you understand?"

"*Oui,* I think, but I was just traveling with my fellow *frères* of the Temple."

"That is not the answer I want. Stalling will only give you pain."

Instantly the guard pulled out the glowing orange poker from the brazier and laid it on my left hand. Horrified, the smell of my burning flesh and excoriating pain shot up my arm and I passed out. I don't know how long I had lain unconscious, but I appeared back in my cell with a bowl of black creamy liquid in front of me. Once again, I was chained against the same stone wall with many spiders swimming in my bowl of liquid. The pain in my left hand hurt even more. One of my chain handcuffs was digging into my festering burned bleeding hand. I lay there feeling quite hopeless and thinking about when I might be rescued. Would *Noir Ombre* get my cold scent? Would he lead Grand Master Gilbért, Sergeant Jacque de Hoult, and Muhammad Nur Adin to the Tower of London before my demise or what I might confess? I didn't know, yet my dolorous thoughts were interrupted by a gigantic growl, which seemed just down the dark hallway from me.

My next visitor was Bishop Guillaume de Longchamp. I assumed another day had passed when he entered my cell, for the way he greeted me.

"*Bonjour, Seigneur* Robert de Borron. I hope you slept well?"

"*Non*, your *bâtard* burned my hand. What do you want from me?"

"My guard now knows what I want from you. You have some valuable information about a fifth gospel written by Saint Joseph of Arimathea, and I suspect it will reveal some never known before hidden information. Cardinal Folquet didn't specially say what its contents might divulge but said you would know. Also he promised a new archbishopric for me if we could convince your tongue to reveal such. Your new *ami*, my guard, will be rewarded handsomely. Let's not waste any more time or pain; tell me the secrets or write the content down for me. Right now, you still have the use of your writing hand. I hear from many authors and troubadours that you are quite talented. It would be a shame if you lost that ability. When tomorrow comes, I will return for an answer. In the meanwhile, my guard will get you something to write with. For now, *au revoir*."

The pock-faced bishop left with a sneer, leaving me with my burning pain. With care I slid back down knowing I had another day before he returned. I told myself that I would prefabricate something to stall for time. Obviously, it had to be believable, yet lead him astray. A brief time later the guard returned with a quill, ink, and several parchments.

"If you can convince the bishop of the truth with what you write, I'll let you go visit our cat friend. He gets lonely and enjoys people chatting with him. Now do what the damn bishop wants. Just rattle your chains when done."

I put all my writing skills to bear to come up with a believable lie. The bishop must think that the remaining Saint Joseph parchments were near an *iglesia* in *Scotia* and that was our destination before my capture. The parchments would be hidden in a stone beehive hut of the monastery *iglesia* of *Sainte* Mary near Saint Andrews. Chaplain Jeremiah Santiago de Compostela once mentioned to me a group of *moines* called the *Céli Dé.* He said they went by many names: the Vassals of God, Clients of God, and Culdees. He thought their founder was Saint Patrick. *Oui*, this would work quite well. Chaplain Jeremiah said later Saint Patrick would become the *abbé* or leader of Glastonbury *Abbaye.* This solved my dilemma. The bishop now faced a long believable trip that gave me some extra time from being tortured. Hurriedly, I wrote on the given parchments and even drew a map that gave the exact location. The details even convinced me there might be something there. A fleeting time later the guard returned with a grin on his face.

"Lord Robert, do you have something for the bishop? *Mon ami*, the lion would like to see you. He likes meeting strangers."

"You sadistic *bâtard*, here is the finished directions and information."

He glanced over the pages, folded them, and stuck them inside his surcoat. The grin on his face vanished and he turned to leave. "If this a trick, I'll be back and personally escort you to the lion's den."

As the iron gate slammed behind him, a sick feeling struck my stomach like a mace. I knew that if I had written the detailed truth, I was already a dead man. My only hope now was Grand Master Gilbért and Muhammad Nur Adin.

Several days passed with no further torture. In the meantime, I met the palm-sized spider and crushed him with my boot heel. Two more days went by without torture. On the fifth day, I heard loud shouting and several unfamiliar demanding voices. Was this my end, becoming a meal for a hungry beast?

CHAPTER XLIV

Southeast Coast of Gaul near Massalia

Anno Domini 37

Yoseph tasted gritty sand in his mouth and then saltwater brushed against his lips. Was he dead? No, another small wave splashed over his prone body and suddenly he reared up, coughing out sand and seawater. Where was he? The sun appeared rising from the east with red-streaked clouds over the sea. He gazed down at the snow-white beach and found wooden wreckage everywhere. What about his precious satchel? Did he still have it? Yoseph felt around his body and with a tingling sensation found it. He peeked inside and every *kodesh* item was accounted for.

"Glory be to *El Shaddai*!" He shouted and stood up, raising his arms to heaven. Yoseph was alive and still had his *kodesh* relics. What about his writings? Were they readable?

"Yes!" the goatskins had protected them. He could see the legible words. Yet his elation dropped like a shooting star when he thought about his family and fellow teachers. Were they all alive? What about Captain Hiram? Yoseph forthwith started searching for them. The sandy beach was low and swept inland some distance. After hiking a piece, he observed three women and a younger girl with dark skin. At this point, he started racing and shouting at the same time.

"It's Yoseph, it's Yoseph, it's Yoseph of Arimathea, and I am still alive!"

"Yoseph, is that you?!" shouted Miriam of Magdala. "I see you survived. Bless our *Maishiach*, Yeshua. He never fails my prayers."

Next, Yoseph saw Miriam Cleopas, Miriam Salome, and the young girl Sarah all running toward him. Yoseph viewed another female lying on the beach some distance from where they stood. He raced over to where she lay and quickly turned her over. It was Clotho holding baby Yoseph, his name's sake. She started coughing up water and raised from her waist. She was alive and so was little Yoseph. "Praise *El Shaddai*! Where is Georgeus?" she asked.

"Right here, my love."

Yoseph was startled to see that Georgeus had crept behind him before declaring his presence. He picked up his wife and son and squeezed both in his arms.

"Georgeus, are there any more survivors?" Yoseph reluctantly asked.

"Yes, I believe a woman by the name of Marcella, who is a servant now of the house of Bethany. Also two sailors named Maximus and Martial. Your family and I were discussing this earlier with Philip, Lazarus, Martha, Shimon the Zealot, and your good friend Nicodemus. Nathan was building a fire farther up the beach for our warmth."

Yoseph stood relieved beyond all understanding that his family, friends, and fellow teachers survived the storm and the ship's sinking. *El Shaddai* had truly blessed them and their cause. His small group of teachers started strolling inland toward the smoke rising from Nathan's fire. All were holding hands with smiles of joy on their faces, pleased to see one another alive. It seemed like both a nightmare and a pleasant dream that followed their ordeal. The waves were calm, the sky azure blue, and the beach's sand a white powder pulling them toward their additional reunion. The white sea gulls *screeched* and started following them to their destination. In the distance, from a roaring fire, came a dozen or more scampering people. Yoseph's adulation forced him to start racing toward the crowd. They all surrounded Yoseph and his group, paused, then started crying, and then crashed into one another's arms forcing Yoseph to his knees.

"Blessed be to *El Shaddai* and our Redeemer for letting us meet again. Let us pray for our current survival and continued preaching.

"*Our Maishiach, let us give thanks to You for our survival and bless us as strangers in a strange land. We are wayfarers from the land of Your birth and our old religion. Please endeavor to protect our band of teachers so we can teach Your logos to others who have not heard your words. Omein.*"

"Yoseph, are you hurt or sick?" Yoseph's sister asked.

"No, I am fine and quite giddy now. What about the rest of you?" Yoseph studied the many heads nodding their approval. "This is another blessing from our Redeemer, my teachers."

"Yoseph, Miriam Salome, Miriam of Magdala, Miriam Cleopas, and the rest of you, please join us near the fire," Nathan said as they trudged near the *crackling* flames.

"So, we are all accounted for and now we must figure where we have landed. Wait! Where's Captain Hiram?" Yoseph's eyes searched the sandy horizon, which was followed by a prolonged silence.

"Yoseph, he and several of his sailors went down with his ship. I saw a large spar fall on his head as the ship sank. Not all his men perished. Two survived the storm and are now with us," Hebron said. Straightaway we prayed for their eternal souls.

Yoseph's *kodesh* cup had saved Hiram's life once, yet his ending destiny gave life to Yeshua's logos. Yoseph was quite sad for his demise and the future bereavement of his *amma*, Tabitha. After their prayer, Hebron motioned for Yoseph and Alein Yosephe to follow him.

"I believe all our teachers have survived, but where are we?" Hebron asked.

"It appears we are close to the community of Massalia," Yoseph said. "I recognize the terrain from my past trips along the coastline. Let's plan how we will travel, search for a small village, and obtain food provisions."

Just then Zechariah appeared with a string of fish he had caught. "Note, Uncle Yoseph, we can smoke them and eat them during the day. Let me prepare them now. Food is quite plentiful here in this new country. See those horses on top of the beach? Maybe we can use them for transportation."

"Yes, Zechariah, we must do that, but first we must build some shelters. You go seek out some ground sheltered from the wind. Hurry back when you find something appropriate. Now go, but first give Hebron the fish." The young boy handed Hebron his fish and raced farther inland. Yoseph admired Zechariah's speed and enthusiasm. He knew the boy would find a great spot, setting an example for the rest of the adult teachers. Yoseph and most of the male teachers then combed the beach for any wreckage they could use. Farther on the upper part of the beach they found wineskins, amphoras of water, pieces of sails, broken wood, a few Roman coins, and strangely, part of the ship's wood timbers shaped like a Roman crucifixion cross. They gathered all items that had washed up on the shore and hauled them toward Nathan's fire.

"I see we will have some provisions the next several days!" Nathan hollered.

"Yes, you are right, my friend," acknowledged Philip. "But we must be frugal with our sorrowful bounty. By using it wisely we'll maintain our strength for our new ministry ahead."

"Uncle Yoseph, Uncle Yoseph," Zechariah called as he approached. "I have found an ideal spot for us to shelter ourselves for the next several days. Come, I will show you. Have Yosa and Miriam of Magdala come too."

Yoseph raced up the sand dune toward a thicket of bushes and his eyes noticed large, crude lean-tos of bush tents with Zechariah finishing a fifth tent bush enclosure. Yoseph was quite proud of the young man. His ancestry showed his leadership qualities.

"Let's notify the rest of our teachers and survivors. I am sure they will add some salvageable items for our comfort." Yoseph was starting to feel more comfortable in their survival. The surrounding food, shelter, and a possible mode of transportation would help strengthen their *kodesh* mission. He would have to seek out other members of his old faith to direct them to their final destinations. Yoseph knew this wouldn't be easy and the Roman army was always over the next hill.

"Yoseph, I see the baptizer's son has already set up our night's lodging," Hebron announced. "I brought along part of a sail and a keg of fresh water. Alein Yosephe has a catch of fish from the tidal pools. Also I have several lengths of rope, which we might use for the horses. I will go ask Philip to bring the fire and flint for tonight's supper. Later tonight we must tentatively plan and discuss what we might build for a religious sanctuary when we reach *Malach* Arvriragus's land. Gaul is an enormous land and I suspect inhabited by thousands of potential new believers. We will need some organized thoughts in how to section it off for maximum teaching."

Yoseph knew their planning might take one or two years for its realization, but this would give them hope for the fulfilment of Yeshua's teachings.

As Yoseph gazed toward the seashore embankment, he caught an odd but pleasant sight. In front of him strolled a group of women, their uncovered long hair blowing in the sea breeze. There was Miriam of Magdala, Miriam Cleopas, Martha, Enygeus carrying Enoch, Yosa, Miriam Salome, Clotho carrying little Yoseph, Marcella, and Sarah. All of them had smiles of confidence and determination. Oh! How Yoseph was thrilled. Such a beautiful vision. His heart pounded loudly, and his hope soared to the heavens.

"Rabbi Yoseph, what can we do to help set up our new temporary home?" Miriam of Magdala asked. Each woman had brought some salvage supplies and Yoseph told them how they could help. Before a small time had passed, the camp appeared to have a lived-in appearance and they rested after their diligent efforts. The men continued to feed the fire while the women prepared the grilling of many fish. Before eating the fish, Yoseph's original followers prepared for the *kodesh* cup procession and honor. He double-checked his cup and cruets, sword, paten, spear, oil lamp, and checked his *kodesh* written words. Here now would the *kodesh* ceremony be observed in a new land. Several of the surviving sailors wanted to attend the service, which Yoseph welcomed. The procession started with the lighted lamp and ended with the radiant cup before they kneeled for the *kodesh* elements. The two sailors, Maximus and Martial, didn't just kneel but prostrated themselves on the ground. It was always a wonder to Yoseph to see the incredulousness stare in these men's eyes, along with their expressions of awe.

After the ceremony they eagerly consumed their grilled fish.

"*Abba*, you wanted to discuss our land gifted to us from *Malach* Arviragus," Alein Yosephe said.

"He said we owned twelve hides of land near the Glass Isle. My understanding is each hide or plotted land section could support twelve members to live out an existence. Just like the twelve tribes of our fore-*abbas*. The isle is surrounded by an enormous lake with various plots of dry land suitable for building our shelter and a place to worship and honor Yeshua. As you know, the Celts use this ground for fishing, hunting deer, and taking of fowl. Tomorrow Hebron, Zechariah, Shimon the Zealot, and I will try to capture some horses for transportation. This is necessary if we are to get off this beach and travel to our destination. It may take a month to break the horses, for they appear quite wild. Also Shimon told me he knew how to handle horses after his days of being pursued by the Roman cavalry."

Yoseph knew his son was correct. Faith must push a God-given brain to accomplish such a *kodesh* task. He now knew how *Moshe* felt when he left Egypt. His people seized everything they had on their backs and then some. They made use of whatever they could find, just like they were doing now with the shipwreck. Yoseph now realized his tribe would spread out like the spokes of wheel planting new ones wherever they traveled. And these smaller wheels would continue their growth in Yeshua's logos. Each hub of the new wheel formed the center point of the new faith, ever-increasing. What might be the length and width of each center hub sanctuary? He must discuss this with Nicodemus. Where was Nicodemus? He wasn't at their recent ceremony.

Yoseph hurriedly searched for him, shouting his name. "Nicodemus, Nicodemus, where are you?" Yet no reply. He asked Yosa if she knew.

"*Abba*, I believe he is praying in the last brush lean-to.

"Bless you, daughter, for I am worried about him."

Yoseph entered the last lean-to see Nicodemus sitting with his pointed chin pressing on his chest.

"What is going on, my friend? You are not acting right." Ever so slowly he raised his head, and his dark hollow eyes met Yoseph's.

"I am so tired, Yoseph. I don't know if it is physically or my faith. Everything seems a struggle. Before we left Yoppa, I received news that my only surviving daughter died. I didn't want to mention it because of the fear of the daggerman. I guess the trauma caught up with me after the shipwreck. During the storm I thought I had lost you too, my friend."

"Well, I am here to comfort you about your loss. I'm so sorry." He embraced his old friend.

"Thank you, dear Yoseph. Now what have you sought me out for?"

"Let's confer about what is ahead of us. I have some exciting thoughts and need your religious scholastic knowledge."

Yoseph explained to him his epiphany about growing their tabernacles and how their new faith would spread. Nicodemus's face gave a small grin before replying.

"Yeshua was telling you this the night of His betrayal. Remember the names Bezalel and Oholiab. These two men constructed the first Tabernacle, *Mishkan*, or Tent of Meeting. It has been called several names over the millennia. These men designed *El Shaddai's kodesh* Ark of the Covenant and its many vessels and clothes when *El Shaddai* was in their presence. Bezalel's name means protection of *El Shaddai*. Bezalel possessed great wisdom that could combine letters with numbers sent from *El Shaddai*. Just like Bezalel and Oholiab, we will be building our sanctuary after the *Maishiach* has already given us our new ark, the cup. I am intrigued by the many measurements of five and eight. Yoseph, remember the Greek words *penta* and *octa* that Yeshua mentioned. In the Book of *Moshe*, Exodus 26:1–37, we have numerous measurement combinations mentioning the numbers five and eight."

Just then Miriam of Magdala entered the shelter and sat next to Nicodemus.

"Nicodemus, I just felt sadness concerning somebody in your family. Was there a recent death?"

"Yes, my daughter died. She was thirty years old and died having a son. Her name was Hannah. I didn't mention it sooner because of our sea catastrophe. Yoseph knew I had a daughter, yet I hadn't spoken to her recently because she went to live with my sister south of Bethany. It was an abusive marriage and her husband left her to go live in Damascus and sell carpets for rich clients. I understand I now have a grandson, named Ezekiel. He is healthy and well taken care of by my sister."

"Nicodemus, you have my upmost sympathy," Miriam said, a tear rolling down her cheeks. They both hugged him for a long time and then Yoseph said a prayer.

"Yeshua, the Maishiach and Ancient of Days, take the soul of Hannah and hold her in Your everlasting arms. Comfort her with the knowledge of her newborn son and protect him with Your grace. Let no evil harm him and may he meet her when he is born again. Omein."

The embrace and prayer seemed to lift Nicodemus's spirits for he smiled and hugged them once more. Yoseph still knew he was hurting, but Miriam's intuition along with their comfort helped clear his mind of his paralyzing grief. He entered back into the conversation about the tabernacle.

"Yoseph, several thoughts about the old Tabernacle. There were forty-eight acacia boards plated with gold that made up three sides of the Tabernacle and they were secured by fifteen bars total to hold the gold-plated wood together and mounted in five bars on the south side, five bars on the north side, and five bars on the west. This totals fifteen bars, which go through rings of gold on all sides. The east will have five golden columns, which will be hung curtains with blue, purple, and crimson yarn and fine twisted linen embroidered with cherubim on each of the four curtains between the five posts. All the framing boards were mortised to go into weighted wedges of silver."

"Don't forget the *kodesh* of *kodeshes,*" Miriam said. "It was shaped like a cube and had divine surface dimensions of 10 cubits externally. Also a cube has eight vertices. There is one of your eights or octaves. Nine cubits internally where the Ark of the Covenant was kept." She grinned. "My *abba* taught me this, for he was well tutored in numbers when I was a child. Yet, Yeshua told me this dimension was a sign of perfection that we must strive for our salvation."

Yoseph thought to himself that this woman never ceased to amaze him. Miriam could use her emotions to push her intellect and wisdom way beyond most mortal men. It was a great blessing to have her in their midst.

They stayed at this new seaside camp for two months. During this time, they roped and trained a dozen horses to be ridden and loaded with supplies. Zechariah, the baptizer's son, quickly became their horse expert. Miriam, Martha, Sarah, and Marcella grilled and dried many fish caught by Nathan and the surviving sailors. Hebron and Enygeus cut some of the sails to form tents to take with them. The other two Miriams dried berries and numerous hares for their meat. Travel provisions were increasing by the day and after two months, they decided to explore a large river that headed due north. The Gauls called it Rodonos or the Romans called it the Rhône. They met only one man curious enough to talk to them. He went by the name of Adair, who said he was once a Druid, but all his fellow teachers and bards were killed by the Romans. He was the last one to practice his faith.

Yoseph thought Adair might be his first convert in the land of Gaul. He told Yoseph he had a written map that might show the location of the Isle of the Apples and how to travel to the big Isle of Britannia, as the Romans called it. He knew there were fellow Druid priests there like himself, but he was too old to travel alone. Yoseph asked him to journey with them and his band of teachers would take care of him. Yoseph was glad he spoke some Greek, which helped convince him to come with them. To Yoseph's surprise, the priest could also speak Hebrew. He was nearly a hundred summers old and thought he wouldn't see any of his kind again. A large grin came over his long, white-bearded mouth. He told Yoseph about a range of mountains where fire erupted from the earth and steamy hot springs were often seen.

Yoseph didn't know whether to believe the old Druid or not, but it sounded like something to investigate. He would discuss this with Hebron and the others. Right now, it was important to gather as many supplies as possible and enough food to go anywhere. All their means of evangelizing were coming together and Yoseph's confidence soared.

That night he gathered Hebron, Alein Yosephe, and Philip to talk about traveling east into the mountains. Adair joined them in case anybody had questions.

"Yoseph, why are you asking us here tonight? Is it important news?" Hebron asked.

"I have asked all of you to come here to let you know about our new friend. Adair has a map to take us to the Glass Isle in Britannia. In exchange, he desires us to help him find more of his people. He thinks his son's family may be in the mountains to the west, which he calls the Great Pyrénées. He says there is a hidden cave where they might live. He also has a map for this location."

"Yoseph, won't this delay our arrival to the Glass Isle?" Philip asked.

"No, my friend. We are still gathering supplies for our trip. It is a long journey there, and we will need our strength to reach our ordained destination. The rest of our teachers can search here in the local countryside and preach. We will be back in a month, and I pray we ourselves will have gathered some new converts too."

"What does Nicodemus think of this, and by the way where is he?" asked Hebron.

"Right now, Miriam of Magdala is speaking with him. I will tell him if we decide to leave. Besides, Miriam is a great leader."

"Adair, I would desire to see these maps," Alein Yosephe demanded.

The old priest with shaking hands pulled them out of his leather satchel. He handed them to Alein Yoseph, while Hebron glanced over his shoulder.

"These are both excellent maps," Alein Yosephe commented. "The one to the Glass Isle will help our ministry in the most efficient way. I have seen a lot of maps during my travel days, and this is the best. The other appears to be of the same quality. I have no objections to helping Adair find his family. What say the rest of you?" Philip and Hebron nodded in agreement, and they all decided to leave in the morning. Adair, once again, smiled and embraced everybody there.

That night, Yoseph mentioned this expedition to Nicodemus, and he agreed to go with them. Yoseph thought this would help his state of mind. So many tragic things transpired in such a short length of time. Hebron convinced Enygeus he should go with Adair and the rest of them. Philip told Yoseph that his good friend Nathan wanted to go too.

The next day, all the volunteers left their new community. Some of them left with lined faces of reluctance and much sobbing from relatives. The first day they traveled four leagues on foot and alternated with two horses that Zechariah had tamed. They followed the coastline of the *Mare Magnum,* as the Romans called it. After fifteen days, they then turned due west, while gradually increasing their daily elevation. In those fifteen days, Yoseph and his compatriots viewed more strange appearing animals than any member could recognize. Numerous large, sharp-pointed beaked birds with gangly long legs. Packs of wolves, vultures, and enormous curved-pointed horned deer-like animals that appeared to be an ibex. Creatures Yoseph and his exploring party of teachers hadn't seen before. As the days increased, so did the elevation, and the air around them grew cooler. One day, they reached a large cirque covered with snow. They climbed to the top along a rocky path and came upon a cave entrance. After Adair checked his map, he told them at one time his relatives resided there. Hebron crept forward and then gazed into the cave. Afterward he threw a large rock in the direction of the dark interior. This was followed by silence. Adair slowly came forth and spoke in his native tongue. A short silent moment followed, then a moving dark phantom slunk forward. Was it a bear, monster, or wolf? Everyone braced for a fight.

Then came a voice associated with the shadow. Adair recognized the voice and replied to it in Greek.

"Is that you, my grandson?" Suddenly, a man with grayish-white hair and the same colored beard darted out of the dark opening. Pursuing the man was a dark-haired woman of about thirty-five summers. Right behind her were two children. They all surrounded Adair with hugs and eyes flowing tears. The man and woman were dressed in dull white ankle-length tunics and brown sandals.

"This is my grandson, and the woman is my great-granddaughter along with their children. My son left Gaul as a baby five years after the general and Gaius Julius Caesar conquered our home. I escaped to the *Mare Nostrum* chased by the Roman cavalry, or *equites* as they called themselves, into the wetlands where I found you two months ago. My son died some time ago fighting the Roman cavalry in Iberia. My grandson says he has a sister and an uncle who escaped by sea to Britannia, or as the native people call it Albion. I told him you and your teachers were traveling to Albion. He and his daughter want to go with us. He perused my map and told me the same map appeared in the stars a few nights ago."

Yoseph didn't know if he was excited about his new traveling friends or not. Roman outlaws didn't bode well for his new apostles. Yet, he laughed at himself, for all his present teachers and himself were outlaws to the authorities. That was one of the risks Yeshua spoke of before His resurrection. Once again, the teachers and Yoseph spoke in privacy about taking all of them back to the *Mare Nostrum* and then on to Britannia.

The next day, they left with their new friends. To Yoseph's surprise, they all spoke several languages, including Hebrew. Adair's grandson and great-granddaughter were trained as a Druid priest and priestess. This made for increasing conversation on their return to the sea. Yoseph thought of his earlier days with young Yeshua and both visiting the Isle of the Apples or Glass Isle. He wondered if the young Druid priest, Fin, and the priestess, Morrigan, were still alive.

During their remaining trip to the sea, Yoseph didn't know who was training whom in the ways of their *Maishiach*. Even one of their Celtic deities was called Hesus. They believed in an afterlife and each Celt had a soul. There was a concept of a trinity of gods. Yoseph noticed Adair's grandson had a golden circle cross embroidered on the back of his white-hooded cloak. Also two earrings shaped into triple spirals. On his neck and top chest were revealed numerous gold necklaces, which appeared as a shield. In his hair was a copper half-crown with three rays pointing upward from a single point. He said his name was Beli, which meant shining one. His daughter, Enid, said her name meant soul. They said they would have to change their clothes the closer they came to the *Mare Nostrum*. Both said the Roman army might capture and then kill them. This included Adair.

"My friends, did you bring other clothes with you?" Yoseph asked.

"Yes," answered Beli, "and we can hide the Druid clothes in our bags."

So, onward Yoseph and his new friends uneventfully traveled for many days until they spotted Yosa dashing toward their group.

"*Abba*, may *El Shaddai* and Yeshua be praised. Did you have any trouble?"

Before Yoseph could answer, she kissed him all over his face.

"No," replied her brother, Alein Yosephe.

"We have some new friends who are related to Adair. They are Druids and his relatives. He, Beli, knows the maps that Adair has brought quite well. His daughter's name is Enid, and, Yosa, she is about your age and a Druid priestess."

Yoseph witnessed the rest of his fellow teachers gather around asking questions from their fellow traveling teachers. He thought it best to announce to the entire group that the newcomers were leaving with them northwest into Gaul. He would later explain the second reason why they were accompanying them.

For another month they gathered supplies, more horses, and made portable tents from the remailing sails. Adair said he knew several places along the lower Rhône River where they could camp before heading into the interior of Gaul. He said the fishing there would provide them with plenty of food. Alein Yosephe found a new convert who wanted to travel with them before they left. His name was Azazel, which Yoseph didn't like. Alein Yosephe said the man was Hebrew and had lived among Greeks and Romans and had previously traveled to northern Gaul. Yoseph knew his name meant a desolate place where nothing holy came from, yet he remembered Yeshua's words, "Love thy neighbor as thy self and learn to turn the other cheek when displeased." So, he ignored his suspicions and found a suitable horse to use.

The first day Yoseph and his fellow teachers traveled about six leagues and camped along a large section of the Rhône. There, Nicodemus approached Yoseph in the privacy of his tent.

"Yoseph, my friend, we have an issue we should discuss."

Nicodemus's face seemed troubled but not as upset as before on the death of his daughter. His dark eyes didn't reflect as much pain, and a slight facial expression of confidence came over his demeanor.

"Yoseph, we have taken on several new students, but we know nothing of their characters or backgrounds. When we left Yoppa, our pursuer was a faceless killer and monster. I don't underestimate his evil intentions and tenacity. You need to discuss with our teachers and new followers what happens to evil in the presence of our *Maishiach*. Especially the new ones joining us. You will have to show them the past errors of their ways and how to obtain the *Maishiach's* grace. If our killer is among us, he will be revealed."

Nicodemus was right and that evening Yoseph gathered the new members together and started speaking of Yeshua's life and the *kodesh* deeds He accomplished. All the recent travelers nodded in agreement with what Yoseph said, and they asked many questions, especially the Druid members of their group. They wanted to know more about Yeshua and Yoseph's traveling days in Britannia.

After Yoseph finished, the *kodesh* grail procession began. Eight pitch tar torches were lit, then Miriam of Magdala led the way holding the blood-tipped spear of Longinus. Miriam was followed by Zechariah, who gyrated the executioner's sword of the baptizer. Next came Philip holding the empty silver paten. Yosa carried over her head the written scrolls that Yoseph so preciously had written of his life and Yeshua's. Alein Yosephe came next holding the glowing glass cruets. Yoseph came from behind a tree while holding over his head the brilliant glowing cup of salvation. Its blue, orange, yellow, and purple glow was a thousand times brighter than the eight torches. Every person bowed their head from fear of blindness and out of respect. Yoseph stopped and placed the cup on a large flat rock. Philip and Alein Yosephe placed the paten and cruets on each side of the cup.

"My friends and beloved teachers," said Yoseph, "come, see, taste, and feel the miraculous *kodesh* items our *Maishiach* has blessed. Each please come forward and accept His blood and body."

The last words Yoseph spoke caused whispering among the newest supporters. Some appeared to hesitate and held back from going forth.

"Fear not, my new students; we are not cannibals, but seekers of truth and love. Please come now and know your heart will have no ill feelings toward your fellow man or woman. Now come forward."

The recalcitrate people now moved forward and stood behind the first group of people. Each received the *kodesh* dinner and then returned to their former place around the ceremony. Their faces reflected smiles of happiness and wonder. Azazel was the last to come forward to partake of Yeshua's dinner. Yoseph held the precious cup steady as Azazel dipped his bread into the glowing cup. After he placed the bread in his mouth, Yoseph stared into his eyes and thought he perceived the evil flames of Baal's fire in the man's eyes. Azazel returned to his former place in the circle. Yoseph started to say a prayer, but suddenly a loud *rumbling* sound came from deep below them. The trees began to sway, and the roosted birds flew from their perches. Small ground animals raced around in circles as they approached them. The *kodesh* cup ceased glowing and the wine and bread disappeared. Blood stopped dripping from the spear of Longinus. A shivering fear rushed down Yoseph' s spine.

"Hebron, beware!" Yoseph shouted. "A tree is about to topple on you!"

Hebron dodged just in time as the large tree came crashing forward. The ground around them moved like the stormy waves in the sea. Was Yoseph having a fitful dream? The fear caused his hands to shake, and he quickly placed the cup on its side on the ground. Behind Azazel appeared streams of white light coming from the moving ground. Each appeared as five apparitions twisting and turning as if to break free from their earthly bounds. The ghastly lights began to emit screams, which was followed by a *ripping* noise coming from beneath Azazel's feet. By now, everyone was on the ground hugging each waving chunk of earth. Purple and orange-colored flames encircled the standing Azazel. He raised his arms to the heavens and then his mouth and lips contorted into the shape of a Roman crucifixion cross. He tried to scream, but no words came forth. A *hissing* sound, similar to boiling water, issued forth just as his body dropped into a large hole with red hot flames grabbing his legs and pulling him down from sight. The earth where he once stood closed with no visible signs of damage. The *rumbling* sounds, ground movements, and the white-colored light beams ceased. The birds returned to their roosts and the small animals returned to the dark forest.

"Yoseph, what happened here?" Enygeus asked. "Was this evil or good?"

Yoseph's suspicions told him to answer now, but he needed to compose himself. He knew the Druids comprehended what had just happened, but they would have a harder time convincing the others. He said a short prayer to himself before delivering the entire horrid explanation.

CHAPTER XLV

The Tower

London, England

I said a quick prayer, knowing this was my demise. My beloved *épouse*, *fils*, and Saint Joseph's quest were no more. I hoped my brother-in-law would raise Brian and Henri and give them a suitable education. I wanted them to cut my throat, so I prayed to make it a quick death, but I knew otherwise.

"Lord Robert, are you in there?" It was the voice of Grand Master Gilbért. My heart jumped into my throat. In front of my prison cell appeared four men. One was Gilbért, two others were Chaplain Jeremiah and a tall, gray-bearded *chevalier*. The stranger's surcoat bore a red rampant lion on a field of vert and yellow, and he held his arm around Bishop Guillaume de Longchamp's neck, causing the veins on the bishop's forehead to bulge. The *chevalier's* other hand grasped the hilt of a dagger, which penetrated the palm of the bishop. Blood streamed down his vestments creating a red streak that dripped onto the stone floor.

"Let me introduce you to this *chevalier* and *seigneur*," said the grand master. "This is to be the first earl of Pembroke, errant *chevalier*, and the only man to beat me with a lance and, I might add, *Roi* Richard. Here is Guillaume le Maréchal, the *roi's* maréchal, diplomat, and the *royaume's* fixer. He oversees *Roi* Richard's properties while the *roi* is in the Levant taking the cross. I am sure the bishop would disagree with me on this, but he is in no position to do anything concerning this matter." He glanced at the bishop. "Isn't this right, Your Excellency?"

A muffled *oui* came from his mouth.

"*Salut*, *Seigneur* Guillaume," I said. "An *ami* of Grand Master Gilbért's is an *ami* of mine."

"Oh, I forgot to mention," Grand Master Gilbért said. "He too fought in the Outremer and one day will join our order. That is where I noticed him, he was at our Temple Preceptory yesterday. He helped me track you to the Tower of London." He narrowed his eyes at the bishop. "*Seigneur* Robert, I am sure you are wondering why there is a dagger penetrating the bishop's palm. He refused to give the key to your cell and where you were located. The marshal decided he should make Guillaume de Longchamp concentrate on where you were imprisoned. We convinced him to show us. Isn't that correct, *Seigneur* Maréchal?"

"*Oui*, but he hasn't given us the key, yet I think I can persuade him to change his mind."

Slowly, he started turning the dagger in the bishop's palm. The bishop's eyes became bug-like with fear.

"Bishop Guillaume, you should thank me for only stabbing your left hand. This will still leave you to sign your damnable letters and arrest warrants for innocent souls. I think another turn will get our answer where he hid the key." Earl Guillaume le Maréchal's face seemed stone-frozen as he started to twist the sharp blade. The bishop pointed his head toward an iron torch holder and whispered a pained "There." Grand Master Gilbért reached into the empty rusted receptacle and pulled out a key. The earl didn't release his grip even after I was let out.

"Where is Cardinal Folquet?" Grand Master Gilbért insisted. He placed his nose right in front of the bishop's nose. "*Seigneur* Robert and I don't have much time. I am only asking you once, and you just heard it."

His feet started shuffling back and forth and once again a smothered sound of "I will tell" came from his mouth. The earl's forearm released its grip, but not his hand from the dagger.

"I have an answer to your question, Grand Master Gilbért," Robert said. "I told the guard a lie and gave him a fake map to deliver to the cardinal. The question now is when did the cardinal leave?"

All heads turned to the bishop. This time he didn't hesitate to answer, "Glastonbury *Abbaye* and then to the Augustinian priory at Lanercost near the ancient Roman Hadrian's Wall. He left yesterday with the cardinal's guard. All of them were on horseback."

"We must leave forthwith," Grand Master Gilbért said. "There are some fresh pack horses at the London Temple. Earl Guillaume, will you go with us?"

"I'm ready right now, and I know Glastonbury *Abbaye's* head *abbé* quite well. Before we leave for the Temple, I need to take care of the bishop. Bishop Guillaume, *Roi* Richard barely tolerates your bishopric see and performance. All I would have to do is send him a letter about your mistress and her babies. Keep your mouth shut and everything will be fine. Besides, you can go back to your dioceses and show them your holy stigmata. They will all think you pious and your bishopric will grow. Now let me bandage it."

Quickly the earl removed his dagger and then found a piece of clean cloth to cover the puncture hole. I wondered what Cardinal Folquet promised this greedy and power-seeking man.

I followed Earl Guillaume and Grand Master Gilbért as they ran through small villages and towns along the river, called the Thames. Before I could catch my breath, we approached a giant drum-shaped stone tower with various stone buildings butted up against it. I observed numerous Poor-Soldiers of Christ entering and exiting the squat-shaped cylinder building. The number of men and the size of the compound led me to believe this was their headquarters for all of England.

Grand Master Gilbért pointed at the structure. "This is an *église* and financial center for England and *Roi* Richard's rents and land holdings in Normandy, Gascony, Aquitaine, and of course, England. Let's go in and meet Sergeant de Hoult, Muhammad Nur Adin, and *Abad* Miguel. They are waiting for us, but we don't have time for a reunion."

I entered the stone-built west portico revealing a black-painted arch-shaped large and thick wooden door. Inside the circular nave stood a small stone altar with a gold-colored pattée cross. High up and all around the circle-shaped perimeter were stone-colored heads. Each head had a grotesque expression on its face. However, one head caught my attention. It was of a man whose ear was being bitten off by some wild beast. I wondered why the *chevaliers* of the Temple had such an obsession with heads.

We were then greeted by the grand master of England, Guillaume de Newham. He was a small man with marked numbers on a scroll, which he held under his arm.

"Grand Master Gilbért tells me you need fresh horses, new Templar clothes, victuals, and quarrels for your crossbows. Promptly, I will have my drapier and armorer furnish you with these items," he said. Right away, he called a black-robed fellow *moine*. "Follow this man and he will get you what you need. I'm quite busy right now for I have just received word from *Roi* Richard that he still needs more money after he conquered some island called Cyprus and the city of Acre in the Levant. It appears he is quite successful so far on his crusade. So sorry not to entertain you, but we both have urgent business elsewhere. *Merci beaucoup*, fellow *chevaliers*."

Quickly, the grand master of England scurried off and we continued to follow the drapier *moine*. We exited the *église* and entered a noisy counting house. I estimated at least fifty black-robed *moines* sitting at tables stacked with silver coins and various scrolled documents next to each man. White-robed *chevaliers* stood at each entrance and exit with swords drawn. Every strong box that left, the *chevaliers* would check against their parchment documents. Heaven forbid the man or men who might try to steal this money. Unexpectantly, I spied Sergeant Jacque de Hoult chatting with an unknown *moine*.

"*Seigneur* Robert, let me introduce you to *mon* blood *frère*."

While Grand Master Gilbért gathered the new clothes, quarrels, and food, I strode over where they were saying their good-byes.

"This is *Frère* Cedric; he oversees this counting house and the order's promissory notes. That is a great responsibility and an extremely trusted position. I am proud of him, which I know is a sin in our order." I shook his hand just as Grand Master Gilbért came back into the hall.

"We must leave now. Muhammad has already saddled our horses and packed our supplies." We exited, and then mounted our steeds. I spurred my horse and all seven of us raced toward Glastonbury. We stopped after four leagues and rested our horses and ourselves. It was a grueling pace we'd just finished. The horses were fagged, and lather dripped from their flanks. Grand Master Gilbért believed we needed to travel another thirty-three of thirty-four leagues before we reached Glastonbury. This left us with another two or three days of travel time. I knew Grand Master Gilbért wanted to capture the monster cardinal and bring him before the *Santo Père* and have him tried, disgraced, and put in prison. However, all of us had our endurance levels after numerous trying months being pursued by the cardinal and his demons. In addition, we had to catch him first. He was as slippery as a river eel and as cunning as a fox.

"Let's camp here tonight and get some rest. *Seigneur* Robert and *Abbé* Jeremiah, you take the first watch. Earl Guillaume and I will take the second watch. Then Sergeant Jacque de Hoult and *Abad* Miguel will take the last watch. Muhammad will report after the last watch." After Grand Master Gilbért assigned our watches, we had a hardy meal of dried venison and some dark red *vin*.

After our meal, I approached *Abbé* Jeremiah about our traitor matter. We walked into a grove of chestnut trees, and I brought up the subject of our unknown spy. I wanted his opinion on who he might be.

"You want to ask me about Sergeant Jacque de Hoult's blood *frère* at the Temple," he said to my surprise.

"*Oui*, how did you know? I hadn't mentioned it before."

"I know that you have been scrutinizing all of us. Besides, I overheard you conversing with him and Cedric. As far as the traitor is concerned, any one of us could be that person. I feel he won't divulge himself until the end of our quest. To ponder who it is, is a waste of time. Our energies and prayers should concentrate on obtaining the last of Saint Joseph of Arimathea's parchments. This is where you and Grand Master Gilbért's visions have led us. The last set I know will reveal things beyond our comprehension."

Abbé Jeremiah surprised me and made a valuable point at the same time. We needed to devote our time and strength to search for the final parchments. I too believed like him that we would read about never known before epiphanies that the Roman Church never knew about or wanted to know. This didn't mean careless protection on our part, but we should remain focused.

We finished our watch and returned to the campfire for some sleep. During the night, I had fitful dreams about the earth splitting apart and dark fiery holes appearing behind me. I woke up with a fuzzy black muzzle licking my face. *Noir Ombre* wanted to leave. Quickly, we doused our campfire and then covered it with dirt.

Another day's hard riding and we came upon a vast plain. There were a few rolling hills, but mostly plains with little wildlife. Our east-to-northeast direction didn't change much. We decided to camp in a large eerie-appearing stone circle. This gave us concealment for tonight, but the gigantic monoliths and capstones left me with a sense of dread. The winds during dusk blew out our campfire and it didn't help us keep warm from the unexpected sleet. Later, that night, after the wind and sleet ceased, Muhammad started a fire.

We traveled another two days, until the terrain changed to a copse of trees and hillocks. In between the hillocks were coombes, that *Abbé* Jeremiah called them. To me they were narrow valleys. The hillocks continued to increase as the sun sliced through the horizon. Ahead of us the coombes were filling up with fog and the moors appeared to be waves of water. A small hamlet struggled to maintain its rooftop view, but next to the fog-covered chimneys there revealed a long-jagged stone structure, and I wondered what it could possibly be. To my right, I observed a square-towered *église* steeple jutting from a gigantic hillock, which *Abbé* Jeremiah called a tor. We decided to camp for the night, and that is when Grand Master Gilbért said we had reached the Glastonbury *Abbaye* and village. Once the sunset completed itself, guard duty assignments were set. Gilbért thought it wise to not go to the *abbaye* until dawn. Cardinal Folquet and his men may be hiding, and the darkness and fog would conceal them enough for an ambush. Also he knew the Benedictine *moines* were finishing up their holy office of Vespers.

Once again, I drew guard duty with *Abbé* Jeremiah. We positioned ourselves to overlook an old Roman road that snaked itself into the hamlet. The half-moon gave some visibility to see the partial foggy road and hear anyone coming and going down the lane.

"*Seigneur* Robert," *Abbé* Jeremiah began. "There are several things I would prefer to discuss with you while we are alone. I want to do so now in case tomorrow we get separated or our traitor causes us to be captured. If one of us survives, he may be able to complete our quest."

I nodded for him to continue.

"I believe there's some information at Saint Dunston's *chapelle* on the *abbaye* grounds. When we stayed at the fortress at Ponferrada, I spoke about Saint Dunstan. He left a cryptic sentence which said, 'all will be revealed at Lanercost.' He foresaw a future vision about this yet-built priory. I mentioned some of this to you. It is a priory in northern England near the old Roman Hadrian's Wall. However, I didn't want to tell you this until now, fearing our traitor or capture."

Oh, how I wish he had told me this earlier. The evil cardinal was possibly on his way to this very spot that *Abbé* Jeremiah just spoke about. I sat there in silence, until *Abbé* Jeremiah asked me what was wrong.

"I have a confession to make, and you will not like what I am about to tell you. When my life was threatened back at the Tower of London, I wrote a description of where we were traveling. I thought my instructions would have the cardinal go on a fruitless journey to northern England and give us time to search for Saint Joseph of Arimathea's last parchments at Glastonbury *Abbaye.* Please forgive me, *Abbé* Jeremiah."

"*Seigneur* Robert, I am the one who should ask forgiveness. Neither of us can turn back time. Besides, let's discuss what tomorrow might bring and I will try to remember what else the old tome from Ponferrada told me.'"

"The giant hillock with the church on top was once a Druid college. Saint Michael's Church was built many years ago after the Druids abandoned the college. The Roman army persecuted the Celts and their Druid faith to oblivion. As you well know, the Celtic Silures tribe dominated this area at the time of Saint Joseph and had powerful rulers. I believe there are few places on earth that heaven dips down to share its holy secrets and Glastonbury *Abbaye* and its environs are one of them. Tomorrow we will see the *chapelle* of Saint Joseph of Arimathea. The *abbaye* was extensively remodeled and expanded by *Abbé* Henri de Blois. His *frère* was *Roi* Stephen of England and his *grand-père* was Guillaume the Conqueror, *Duc* de Normandy. Henri was appointed bishop and *abbé* to Glastonbury *Abbaye* in the year of our Lord 1126. He was truly Norman in his artistic abilities and architecture. At one time he was more powerful than the *roi.* Being a papal legate, he answered only to the Holy *Père* in Rome."

"What does all this have to do with Saint Joseph of Arimathea and the last scrolls?"

"Be patient, *mon ami.* I will explain. Bishop Henri was educated at Cluny. His foresighted intellectual acumen freely let other religious scholars visit the great library and scriptorium. The *moine*, Guillaume de Malmesbury, from the Malmesbury *Abbaye* spent several years here at Glastonbury writing the history of this *abbaye*. He called it *De Antiquitate Glastoniensis Ecclesiae*. I believe his history of the Glastonbury *Abbaye* may help us find the final scrolls of Saint Joseph or tell us more about the first Christian *église* and the end of the fifth gospel."

"I must apologize for my impatience, but I am anxious to complete our quest, and we have ridden quite hard this past week. Please continue with your information."

"*Seigneur* Guillaume le Maréchal knows the current *abbé*, *Abbé* Henri de Sully, quite well. Tomorrow, Grand Master Gilbért will send Sergeant Jacque to scout close to the *abbaye* for the cardinal's *chevaliers*. Muhammad would attract too much attention."

The fog continued to thicken until our shift was complete and we were relieved for some sleep. Yet, I couldn't sleep, for my mind filled with apprehension about what we might face tomorrow. My thoughts were pulling me to the *abbaye* this instant as if an invisible rope held my body. Was this my curiosity or a phantom that I couldn't see? Either way, this sensation was eerie. Sometime during the night, I fell asleep, but not for long. Once again, our trusty war dog *Noir Ombre* licked my face to the rising sun. Sergeant Jacque de Hoult was just starting his scouting mission and raced down the hillock on his horse. The fog hadn't dissipated, so he completely disappeared halfway down the hill.

"*Seigneur* Robert, are you ready to finish our holy quest?" Grand Master Gilbért asked.

"*Oui*, but I fear the unexpected from Cardinal Folquet. His evil is so mercurial and vicious."

"*Oui*, however, we have the saints and the Lord's angels on our side. Now hurry up and saddle your horse. Observe, *Noir Ombre* is wagging his tail to lead us. As soon as Sergeant Jacque returns, we'll leave whether the cardinal is there or not."

From my horse, as I gazed over the valley below, I heard *thumping* horse hooves coming from the fog. As a precautionary measure, we withdrew our swords from our scabbards.

CHAPTER XLVI

Quickly, Sergeant Jacque arrived, and he said the *abbaye* seemed clear of the cardinal or his men. He estimated there were about thirty *moines* doing their early morning chores and oblivious of our presence. We sheathed our swords as Grand Master Gilbért spoke to *Abad* Miguel.

"I want you and *Abbé* Jeremiah to initially do the speaking. These men may fear Templar *chevaliers*, especially with a Saracen scout. Also, *Abad* Miguel, don't they belong to the same order as you?"

"*Si,* or I mean *oui*. They belong to the Benedictine order. However, what am I to say why we are visiting their *abbaye*?"

"Tell them we come from the London Temple and the earl of Pembroke was left with instructions to inventory the *roi's monastère*. The earl knows *Abbé* Henri de Sully and he will ask for him. Isn't this right, *mon Seigneur* Guillaume?"

"*Oui,* that is right, but be careful what you say. *Abbé* Henri is a shrewd man."

After their conversation, I felt like I was riding into a trap, and I wasn't sure what to do about it. We continued down the hill toward the *monastère* with the fog starting to lift. Then to my shock I viewed the *abbaye*. As I was told, the once large structure was now in shambles. Numerous large *cathédrale* timbers were charred and stuck into the earth still emitting their acrid smell.

So too were many brown-scorched large stone blocks. Both broken and unbroken where they fell. It appeared something tragic befell this once proud *abbaye*. Yet, I observed in the still foggy grounds several building cranes, but no workmen scurrying back and forth. *How strange*. This thinking was replaced with a feeling of disappointment. In what way would a fire-ravaged *abbaye* help us find the last pages of Saint Joseph of Arimathea's gospel? But something caught my eye as the wind and sunlight chased the fog away. At the very end of the ruins was a newly built free-standing *chapelle*. At each corner was a slender pointed tower. All the building stones gave off an eerie flashing sheen of pale purple. Immediately, I was drawn to this *chapelle*. Once again, I felt my body pulled by an invisible rope wanting me to investigate.

We were greeted by two black-robed *moines*. One, who was quite older than the other, greeted us first. His almost bald-tonsured head said he was a senior member of their *abbaye*. His shepherd crook staff revealed he was in charge. *Abad* Miguel dismounted and gave his fellow *abbé* the kiss of peace. While they spoke, *Abbé* Henri kept glancing over the shoulder of Miguel and staring in our direction. Especially at the earl of Pembroke and Muhammad. Several more *moines* approached and glared at Muhammad and me. Why me? For my surcoat bore the same likeness of Grand Master Gilbért. A tall *moine* approached me and whispered.

"We must speak. My name is *Frère* Ambrosius, but some call me Padraic, for I am from Cymru or Wales. My fellow *frères* named me after Saint Ambrosius, an ancient doctor in our church and a reader like me. Meet me in the back of the Saint Joseph of Arimathea *chapelle*. You will be staying for some food and refreshing your horses."

Somehow this stranger *moine* knew we would take a short rest, for Grand Master Gilbért told us to dismount. We followed several of the *moines*, including Padraic, to a wooden makeshift barn. There, we turned the horses over to two black-robed *frères*, while I slipped away to the shiny *chapelle,* which drew me to its entrance. Shortly after reaching the archivolt, *Frère* Padraic suddenly appeared in front of me.

"*Seigneur* Robert de Borron, I know who you are and why you are here! My late armarius mentioned your name before he died in the fire." He stopped talking and crossed himself.

"How he knew your name, I don't know. He said only you could read the ancient documents."

"How can this be, for today is the first time I have seen your face and this *abbaye*? Where do you know me from?"

"I saw your face in a dream two days ago. You are here about Saint Joseph of Arimathea's fifth gospel and the Holy Grail objects. Am I right, *Frère* Templar?"

"Why should I answer your questions? I am here on private business, which doesn't concern you or this *abbaye*."

"Yet it does concern you and me. As you can see, this great *abbaye* was consumed by fire for the secrets and knowledge it once contained. In *Anno Domini* 1184, on Saint Urban's Day, May 25, the fires of hell consumed this *église* and *monastère*. I was a young novitiate, and this conflagration almost killed me. I worked in the scriptorium and aided the armarius in helping copy manuscripts and the cantor in filing scrolls and tomes in the library. *Sainte* Mary Magdaleine has visited you and is guiding you to your destination, *oui*?"

I hesitated in answering him even though he had a canny mind. I didn't need to add another spy to the cardinal's retinue. *Does this man want to help me or hurt me*?

"If you have had dreams about me; tell me where I am going."

"You are traveling to the Lanercost Priory in northern England. I was ordered to take a rescued tome from the great fire in *Anno Domini* 1184 and hide it there. I buried other papers from the great library before the fire consumed them and only I know their whereabouts. The cantor died in the fire and never told me specifically what they contained. I suspect they have something to do with the founder of this church. I know the pages were quite brittle and I didn't want to read them because of their fragile condition. Also this place then was as hot as brimstones, and I expected the Devil himself would appear at any moment. In my dream, I heard you chatting about Saint

Joseph of Arimathea. That saint has a long folklore association with this *abbaye*. What do you know about this saint, *Seigneur* Robert de Borron?"

"I know very little about him," I lied.

"It appears we have an impasse," the wary *moine* replied. "I know you are in a hurry and time is of the essence. We can solve this by trusting each other and satisfy both our curiosities."

"One last question before you can earn my trust. Was your family wealthy before you joined the Benedictine order?"

"*Oui*, they were, and I entered this *monastère* at the age of twelve summers. Before then, I was tutored by one of their scholars. I had three older blood *frères* and knew I wouldn't inherit anything. My family continued to donate to this *abbaye* until they died. By then I enjoyed being surrounded by ancient writings, scrolls, and tomes. I knew God ordained me to this career. Knowing knowledge and the wisdom it conveys separates us from the heathens and their dark abodes. Wouldn't you agree, *Seigneur* Robert?"

"*Oui*, I agree, but can you answer me how long ago Cardinal Folquet and his men visited here?"

"What cardinal? I just arrived before you reached here. Some of us are living and praying with the Carthusian *frères* at the Witham Priory. It's about five leagues from here. Some of us travel on foot, others by horseback. You can see we have no habitable refectory or dormitory. Many of the *moines* are skilled in masonry and we use them to help rebuild the Cathedral of Saints Peter and Paul. Hopefully soon, we will have living quarters. I am sure a cardinal would have spoken to *Abbé* Sully and not me."

I could see my conversation was futile for new information, so I tried another approach. "May I see inside this magnificent *chapelle* of Saint Joseph of Arimathea?"

"*Oui*, and afterward you will want to ask me some questions." The *moine* used a large, black-colored skeleton key attached to his robe and opened the Celtic designed iron braced wooden side door. We both entered, but to my astonishment this was like nothing I had seen before. The interior was painted with colors of ochre, red, blue, green, white, black, and gold. Many of the stained-glass windows were of rounded old-style arches. However, each window had scenes from the Old and New Testaments. In each stained-glass panel were inserted roundels of *Sainte* Mary with alternated roundels of Saint Joseph of Arimathea. Above the chancel and altar was a lancet-shaped vaulted ribbed arch. It was colored evening blue with a multitude of golden-painted stars. The altar area was laid out into a strange-shaped cube, with a large curtain rod traversing one side of the cube. On the rod hung a red velvet pulled-back curtain displaying the altar. Numerous gilded lead-shaped spinning stars were positioned just below the chevron intersecting blind arcades. A large, amber colored Eastern designed lantern hung down from an ornate gold chain, which emanated from the Green Man-faced boss in the ceiling arch junction.

"What do you think of this unusual *chapelle, Seigneur* Robert?"

"I am speechless in its appearance. The exterior and interior are of the old-style Romanesque from many years ago, yet I can see the building materials and paint are new. It reminds me of the small *églises* from home."

Suddenly, I felt faint, leaned over, and that is when I noticed the floor. Below my feet were large circles and geometric designs. A significant-sized heptagram emanated from a smaller center circle. The seven points of the heptagram either touched or their points touched the center of twelve other rotating circles. They were all backgrounded by a larger circle contained in a large square. Each of the twelve circles had some unrecognizable symbols on them. The colors of this enormous geometric form were gold, reds, and blues. Surrounding the outer perimeter of this large design were square-colored tiles of red and white. The next thing I knew, I was standing next to a snow white-haired hooded man. On the right side of the man were two women. One I recognized; it was Miriam of Magdala. The other I didn't know. I spoke to them, but they didn't answer. My hand reached to touch the old man, yet he didn't acknowledge it. All three spoke Aramaic, which I knew. The conversation discussed the coming frigid winter and how much wood they needed for their fires. I could see outside the hut, but it wasn't a Levant forest or grounds. A large lake backed up against other huts, maybe a dozen of them. Then a hand grabbed my wrist and said my name.

"*Seigneur* Robert, you didn't answer me. Are you sick? You almost fainted and then you succumbed to some kind of trance."

When I glanced up and focused on the face of *Frère* Ambrosius, the hut and the people disappeared.

"Your eyes and mind were captured by the floor's design. Others have experienced the same enchantment. I have been told the great writer and holy *Frère* Guillaume de Malmesbury had the same experience. However, he was in the ancient *chapelle* before the great fire. He spent numerous years as a guest *moine* here writing about the history of this *cathédrale* and *monastère*. He said there might be something hidden under this geometric design. Do you want to trust me now?"

"What do you think I glimpsed when I swooned?"

"I don't know, maybe a saint. There were many holy men and women buried under this *chapelle* during the last five hundred years or more. Tonight, I hope you can join me after Compline. I believe you are the new messenger to divulge what mysteries are hidden on these grounds. In my dream you and I discovered some wondrous clue near the Saint Dunston *Chapelle* burned ruins. As I told you I hid numerous scrolls, documents, and tomes during the fire. The Saint Dunston *Chapelle*'s stone floor remained intact. There I placed a large trunk under the flooring. In that trunk were precious, written words. A man died in that fire telling me where they should be buried. I think you can trust me now."

I knew then I had to trust this *moine*. "I must apologize, *Frère* Ambrosius. I lied to you about knowing Joseph of Arimathea. For six month or more fellow Templars and I have scoured three kingdoms chasing down two parts of the fifth gospel secretly written by Saint Joseph. His gospel revealed never known before information about our *Maishiach*, Jesus the Christ. I have his confirmation that he traveled here to this holy isle and built the first Christian church. Don't you see he was the first bishop, *abbé*, and the pastor of these entire island kingdoms? I must have Chaplain Jeremiah examine this floor design. He is an educated scholar of these things. Is it all right if he meets with us tonight?"

"*Oui*, and I know the three of us will learn new revelations. After Compline, in the *chapelle*, we will meet at Saint Dunston's ruins, but now let us leave the *chapelle* and go our separate ways. I will take an unlit lantern and then light it to signal I am there."

Frère Ambrosius's plan sounded simple, yet nothing was simple anymore. We commenced to leave and to my uneasy surprise it was almost sundown. *How could this happen*?

We entered the *chapelle* just this morning and now the sun was setting. Time had literally disappeared with no explanation. I stared at *Frère* Ambrosius, and his expression displayed his own confusion and disbelief.

"You caused this to happen," he told me. "Truly, you have gifts from our Savior." He crossed himself and bowed.

"Please stand; I am mortal just like you. Other different holy events have happened to me before, and I get quite embarrassed."

"Time doesn't exist with our God. It has no meaning for Him. He is the One who created time for us mortals. His kingdom is timeless, and you just entered His kingdom, *Frère* Robert."

Just as he locked the entrance door, Muhammad walked toward us. He, his horse, and *Noir Ombre* were partially obscured by a large bush. Our war dog's tail started wagging when he heard me call his name. *Frère* Ambrosius jumped against the side of the *chapelle* and he started praying.

"Fear not, *mon ami*," I reassured him. "The man is a Saracen prince from the Levant and both the dog and he are traveling with us." They walked away as we traveled down a different path.

We met Chaplain Jeremiah in the burned-out cloister as he observed some broken columns that once held the cloister roof. I introduced him to *Frère* Ambrosius, and they shook hands.

"*Frère* Ambrosius, how many carrels did you have before the fire?" Chaplain Jeremiah asked.

"We had twelve before the fire and two more in the library preparing the parchment hides. Two armarius and the cantor died in the flames. How do you know I worked the carrels and library?"

"Observe, all six of our hands with ink-stained fingertips. We are all writers and men of letters," Chaplain Jeremiah replied with a knowing grin.

I told the chaplain about our most recent time slip and the *chapelle's* geometric-designed floor. His arched eyebrows indicated his curiosity and he wanted to know more. Chaplain Jeremiah agreed to meet us after Compline and investigate the trunk's contents.

"*Frère* Ambrosius," the chaplain said. "I am sure you know the names of the saints who were claimed by this ground. One you already mention, Saint Dunston, who gave us the horseshoe for our good blessings. The others are Saints Patrick; possibly Brigid; Indract; Gildas the Wise; Aidan; Paulinus; *Roi* Coel, *grand-père* of Constantine the Great; and Saint Joseph of Arimathea."

"*Oui*, but the fire destroyed many of their relics. However, if we can find written proof, our claim and their resurrection will help rebuild our *abbaye*.

"I would like to measure the *Sainte* Mary floor plan as well as study the floor's unusual geometric patten," Chaplain Jeremiah told us. "There are two Old Testament biblical passages, which will confirm what exists here. One is from the Book of Zechariah where he says, 'I lifted my eyes again and beheld a man with a measuring line in his hand. Then said I, whither goest thou? And he said unto me, to measure Jerusalem, to see what the breath is thereof, and what is the length there of.' Also a passage from the Book of Revelation written by Saint John. 'And the one who spoke with me had a measuring rod of gold to measure the city and its gates and walls. The city lies foursquare, its length the same as its width. And he measured the city with his rod, 12,000 *stadia*. Its length and width and height are equal. He also measured its walls, 144 cubits by human measurements, which are also an angel's measurement.' I suspect Glastonbury was a New Jerusalem for Saint Joseph of Arimathea and his followers." He turned to me. "*Seigneur* Robert, didn't you tell me that our beloved Joseph was a *bon ami* of Saint John the Writer?"

"*Oui,* and I feel at some time in their relationship, Saint John revealed to Saint Joseph his innermost dreams and thoughts."

By now, the few surrounding *moines* started converging on the *chapelle* for Compline. Less than a dozen plus *Abbé* Henri Sully were leading the black-hooded *moines* to their destination. We joined in the procession with *Abad* Miguel leading our way. Chaplain Jeremiah followed, with Grand Master Gilbért, the earl of Pembroke next, and then Sergeant de Hoult and me. I waited for Chaplain Jeremiah's reaction upon entering, but there was none. The *chapelle's* darkened floor prevented him from seeing it until all the candles were lit and the curtain pulled back from the altar. Then he frowned and quickly crossed himself. He and Grand Master Gilbért sat next to the altar table and *Abbé* Henri de Sully and *Abad* Miguel sat to the left. Our chaplain stayed focused on the seven-pointed geometric design in front of his feet. He mumbled his psalms from rote, yet his body leaned forward pulled by some invisible force. I too sensed the same sensation. Toward the end of Compline, Chaplain Jeremiah didn't even chant the *Ave Regina caelorum*. His body appeared as if it was made of stone, like the victim of one of the Greek mythological Medusa's gazes. The office shortly ended, and we proceeded to leave. The rest of the *moines* went to their tents along with the *abbé*. Then I told Grand Master Gilbért what we planned to do while waiting for our signal.

"See. there is his signal," Chaplain Jeremiah whispered. Out of the blackness appeared a flickering spark of light. We crept toward the diminutive flame while *Noir Ombre* trotted ahead.

"I didn't think you would arrive. Especially after I observed you and your chaplain at Compline," *Frère* Ambrosius whispered.

"*Oui*, the floor design held me in its grip," Chaplain Jeremiah announced. "I have not seen a geometric design similar to this before. There are new numbers embedded in that design. I believe it wants us to investigate further."

"I told *Frère* Robert that several years ago the great historian, *Frère* Guillaume de Malmesbury, called it a sacred enigma to be contained."

"*Oui*, it is an enigma that projects many things; especially the number seven and any multiple thereof and the twelve circles or moons," Chaplain Jeremiah surprisingly revealed. "Now let's see what this chest might tell us."

I pulled away several scorched tiles that bore no recognizable designs. *Frère* Ambrosius lifted several pieces of charred wood, which gave off a burned oaky smell. We dug an arm's length of dirt that exposed the top of a large trunk with a huge rusty padlock. Each of us gathered at the ends of the chest and used its handles and lifted it straight up. Whatever it contained; there was no weight to its contents. It was decided to break the padlock later at our camp because of the noise.

"*Frère* Ambrosius, we need to take this chest back to our hilltop campsite for further scrutiny," Grand Master Gilbért insisted. "We are exposed here, and I know *Seigneur* Robert and Chaplain Jeremiah could read its contents better by our campfire light. I recommend you come with us and further aid us."

"*Oui*, but I don't know what's in it. My superior ordered me to bury it and not read it until a new library was completed."

"That's not important to us; we must leave now. You can ride with Chaplain Jeremiah. Now let's hurry." Grand Master Gilbért rushed toward the makeshift stable and to my surprise Muhammad had readied our horses. We strapped the chest to one of the pack steeds, then mounted, and I noticed *Noir Ombre* race toward the top of the hillock and our camp.

We reached the summit in just a brief time, dismounted, then unloaded the chest in front of the embers of our fire. Muhammad quickly gathered some dry twigs and got the fire roaring in an instant. That is when the anticipation struck me. It just seemed we were back in Toledo digging up the second set of Saint Joseph of Arimathea's parchments in the old *Iglesia* de Santiago del Arrabal. Grand Master Gilbért gave the honor of opening the chest to *Frère* Ambrosius, but a large padlock prevented him from opening it. Quickly, Muhammad retrieved a large iron hammer from his saddlebag and then smashed the lock with a loud *clang*. Slowly *Frère* Ambrosius lifted the squeaky lid and reached for the dark contents.

CHAPTER XLVII

Frère Ambrosius's trembling hands pulled out numerous sealed scrolls. In the flame light it appeared as if the scrolls were contained in a waterproof covering. Carefully he tore it apart to reveal several illuminated manuscripts.

"Aha, they are written in my native language of Cymru. Note, there is an angel on the first page. What does it mean?"

Chaplain Jeremiah and I tilted our heads for a closer look. The angel wings were red and gold colored. He wore a crimson red shawl and a buff-colored tunic. His head bore a sun-shaped crimson nimbus with long gold-colored, dagger-shaped rays coming from it. Most unusual yet were his hands. One palm had flames coming from it; the other hand grasped a rolled-up scroll.

"That is the Archangel Uriel," declared Chaplain Jeremiah. "Sometimes Uriel carries a flaming sword that guards Eden and signifies repentance. Other times the flames in his palm light our way for the books and scrolls he carries. When I attended Oxford, they had a motto based on this angel. It said *Dominus illuminatio mea*, which means the Lord is my light. I have observed other pictures in which one hand carries a chalice similar to Archangel Gabriel's. *Seigneur* Robert, you encountered him on your Kabbalah journey in Toledo. This is a good sign for us, *mes amis*."

"What does it say, Chaplain Jeremiah?" I asked.

"Let *Frère* Ambrosius tell you. I believe it is written in his language, which I don't know."

Ambrosius perused the document then looked up at us. "My fellow *frères* this is the long-lost Prophecy of Melkin. He was a Druid bard before Merlin and knew where Saint Joseph of Arimathea was buried. Right here, he tells the exact location of Saint Joseph, which is near the old *chapelle*. He says another holy of holies is buried here but doesn't mention who it is or where."

"Is there any mention of Saint Joseph's final parchments?" Grand Master Gilbért asked.

"Tomorrow, while Chaplain Jeremiah is measuring the *chapelle* inside and out, *Frère* Ambrosius and I will examine these papers more in the daylight. It is getting late, and we need our rest."

I can't say the day was long for me, but my strange short day left me emotionally exhausted. I settled into a deep sleep but was awakened by a female voice coming from a fog bank.

"Robert, you are so close to the completion of your quest. However, the closer you are, the greater the dangers you and your brethren will face. Beware of a traitor, the men of the shadows, and the women of the dark mist. Especially the women of the dark mist. Stay close to the words of Saint Joseph of Arimathea."

Then there was silence. *Sainte* Mary Magdalene had given me a warning. What did she mean by the women of the dark mist? This warning I feared above the others. The tone in her voice spoke of great danger.

The sunrise over the tor *église* appeared as a lit torch. It was a site to behold. Quickly, we broke fast and then Grand Master Gilbért, along with Chaplain Jeremiah, Guillaume le Maréchal, and Sergeant de Hoult saddled themselves.

"What are you going to tell the *Abbé* Henri de Sully about why you are measuring his *chapelle*?" I asked Grand Master Gilbért.

"The earl de Pembroke and I will tell him we are here to survey the damage of the *abbaye* and its grounds. *Roi* Richard wants him to obtain periodic appraisals while he is on crusade. Also the grand master of England has authorized me to record the dimensions of the *abbaye* and environs for our order's recordkeeping. *Frère* Ambrosius told me we'll meet some *frère* architects and masons when we arrive. They will have the proper measuring rods and lines. This is something I have knowledge of from measuring *châteaus* in the Levant."

Quickly they raced down the hill while *Frère* Ambrosius and I investigated the remaining contents of the chest. To my surprise, Bard Melkin predicted the burial location of *Roi* Arthur and *Reine* Guinevere. Melkin said that his spheres were revelations of future events. He said the first two were about the burial place of Saint Joseph of Arimathea and *Roi* Arthur and his *épouse*. Both places were in the burial grounds of the *chapelle* graveyard. His measurements were quite detailed.

"I can't believe this information about *Roi* Arthur. Most of my life he and his *chevaliers* of the roundtable have been my life's written work!" I exclaimed. *Frère* Ambrosius and I both stood up and hugged each other. Not only had the specific location of Joseph of Arimathea's burial place been divulged, but also the bear *roi*. That name bear, most people knew as his cognomen. Arthur in the Celtic language was Artorius or bear. *Frère* Ambrosius and I continued to read the old scroll until we came across a heptagram design surrounded by twelve spheres and a large sphere in the center of the seven-pointed heptagram. The geometric design almost matched the one on the *chapelle* floor.

This floor had a little more detail, as if further information was later discovered. Once again, we shouted our amazement. I couldn't wait for Chaplain Jeremiah and Grand Master Gilbért to return. We decided we must ride down and tell them our *bon* news. However, there were two remaining parchments for us to investigate. One page started to reveal the prophecy of the remaining spheres, but moisture had erased the ink. The other spoke of the numbers seven and twelve, which would solve an even greater mystery that would shock the world.

My hands started to shake, making it difficult to place the scrolls back into the chest. *Frère* Ambrosius assisted me and afterward we raced to our horses. We quickly mounted and then galloped down the hill to the precinct of the *chapelle*. We met Chaplain Jeremiah working with an unfamiliar *moine* holding a measuring line. Grand Master Gilbért had started down the steps of the well.

"*Seigneur* Robert, this is Radulphus. He helped build the second Arimathean Mary *Chapelle*." Radulphus moved away to continue his measurements.

"He knows the measurements of the original *chapelle* and the new. He says they slightly expanded the second *chapelle* but with the same floor plan. The measurements are 64 feet by 37 feet. Radulphus says the exterior width and length mimic the ancient Jewish Tabernacle, sometimes called the Hebrew *Mishkan* or Tent of Meeting. *Seigneur* Robert, as you well know God, Moses, Bezalel, and Oholiab were the original designers to house the Ark of the Covenant. They came from Egypt, and Moses grew up in the pharaoh's court. They knew to use the Egyptian royal cubit for a measuring rod. The royal cubit is 20.6 inches. In the Book of Exodus, chapters 25 and 26 give us some of the measures of the Ark of the Covenant and the Tabernacle. If we divide 37 feet into 64 feet, we obtain 1.7, which is the square root of three. The square of three is the sign of the fish or *vesica piscis*. This tells us that Joseph's Tabernacle kept some of the old traditions and he wanted to show the new teachings of Jesus the Christ. These numbers are telling us many things."

This new information was quite illuminating, which further increased my trembling hands. Yet, I still blurted out our new disclosure.

"We discovered some new information about Melkin's prophecies! One of his documents had a similar heptagram design as the one on the floor in this *chapelle*. He said his spheres were prophecy spheres, which he explained several. The burial place of Saint Joseph of Arimathea, next to the *chapelle*, and the exact burial place of *Roi* Arthur and Reine Guinevere."

All eyes turned in my direction and all faces froze in disbelief. Grand Master Gilbért did the same as he came up the well steps.

"More important, Melkin said there was somebody buried in the *chapelle* whose importance would shock the world. Who might that be?"

Nobody responded to my question, but all the Glastonbury *moines* inquired about *Roi* Arthur's specific whereabouts. To my surprise nothing more was said regarding the unknown person. Chaplain Jeremiah, *Frère* Ambrosius, and Grand Master Gilbért wanted to know, but I didn't have any more information. We decided to continue our *chapelle* investigation and seek out more about the heptagram design and the *chapelle's* length and width, both externally and internally.

"*Seigneur* Robert, it appears we have a new set of numbers in solving our quest. The numbers seven and twelve are leading us further into this biblical mathematical mystery. The numbers five and eight still have meaning, and I am sure we may need them again. Many of our past prophets, saints, and elders were privy to God's holy numbers and shapes. For example, how many hides did *Roi* Arviragus give him?"

"Twelve," I replied.

"How many acres in a hide?" Our chaplain asked me again.

"I estimate 120 acres, why do you ask?"

"What does twelve times 120 acres equal?"

"It's 1,440 acres."

"*Oui*, which can be verified in the *Domesday Book* by the Norman conquerors. Yet, more important, Saint John's Book of Revelation says the New Jerusalem was a cube, 12,000 *stadia* in height and 12,000 *stadia* in length and width, and the walls were 144 cubits thick. It resembled a colossal cube coming out of the clouds. Also the number twelve is used many times in both the Old and New Testaments. The Tree of Life bears twelve different fruits in the New Jerusalem, the gates are twelve with pearls, twelve towers on the gates, twelve jewels on the high priest's breastplate, twelve tribes of Israel, twelve pieces of show bread in the Tabernacle and the Temple, and twelve disciples of Jesus the Christ. Also how many elect were from the tribes of Israel? They were 144,000 total sealed with the name of God and the Lamb written on their foreheads. These numbers get stranger. If you divide the internal volume of the Ark of the Covenant, which is 5.625 cubic cubits, into the internal volume of the Holy of Holies, which is 810 cubic cubits, you obtain the number 144, which is twelve times twelve. You have told me about Saint Joseph of Arimathea using gematria. How many letters in the Greek alphabet?"

"There are twenty-four, which is two times twelve. Also don't forget the twelve *chevaliers* of *Roi* Arthur's roundtable," I added.

"What do all these numbers have to do with finding the last section of Joseph's fifth gospel? It seems like we are wasting time," Grand Master Gilbért said as he paced back and forth in front of the entrance door.

"Your Excellency, be patient and I will finish my hypothesis," Chaplain Jeremiah said quietly. "I am presenting mathematical and geometric evidence that will verify that Saint Joseph of Arimathea and his small band of teachers did arrive here on this small isle."

Grand Master Gilbért mumbled some unrecognizable words and then strolled back down the well steps. Chaplain Jeremiah's face remained passive, which I couldn't tell if he too felt the same frustration as his *père*.

"*Seigneur* Robert, please stroll with me in private, and I will explain the rest of my theory."

We ambled toward the burned-out cloister, continuing our conversation, as a cold breeze buffeted my face.

"My theorem about the *Sainte* Mary *chapelle* has many facets," Chaplain Jeremiah said. "Let me explain some more strange marvels about sacred numbers. If you measure the square area of *Sainte* Mary's *chapelle*, which is 37 feet by 67 feet, you obtain 2,368 square feet. The Greek letter gematria equivalent spells Jesus Christ. Saint Joseph and his teachers were replicating the old Jewish Tabernacle for their new Savior. A section of this *chapelle* formed the altar where they conducted their eucharist. The cubic-shaped area of the *chapelle* became their Holy of Holies. If you unfold a cube, you will see a cross. Saint Joseph's *chapelle* held a circular design with a square within this circle, thus the cube. This is called *ad quadratum* in shape. From there, we add hexagon triangles, which are called *ad triangulum*. This helps us create our fish design and another symbol for Jesus the Christ.

"The heptagram design is in this area. I haven't figured out what this design means, but similar to *Frère* Guillaume de Malmesbury's conjecture, it is enormously important. Maybe the next set of Saint Joseph's parchments will tell us more. However, the number seven enters into my theorem and so does the number five, but we know that already. There were seven candlestick holders in the menorah. Seven sacraments in the Roman church. Our God resides in the seventh heaven. He is surrounded on His *merkavah* or throne by seven archangels. Jesus told Peter to forgive not seven times, but seventy times seven. Saint Joseph of Arimathea was one of Christ's original seventy. The high priest entering the Holy of Holies of the Tabernacle sprinkled blood seven times on the mercy throne of the Ark of the Covenant. There are seven colors in the rainbow, seven stars in the great bear constellation, and seven notes of music plus five sharps and flats. From the Book of Revelation and the New Jerusalem, there were seven seals that secure the Holy Scroll, seven eyes of the Lamb of God, and fifty times the number seven appears in the Book of Revelation. Enoch was the seventh person from Adam and Moses, who were seventh from Abraham. The feast of the Tabernacle is seven days. The flower of life has seven circles in it. The year of the jubilee is recognized as forty-nine years, which is seven times seven. Between Passover and Pentecost is seven weeks or forty-nine days. And finally, Joshua had the Tabernacle priests march around Jericho once a day for seven days. On the seventh day they were to march around Jericho seven times. Then seven priests were to blow their seven trumpets and the Israelites shouted a war cry."

"All these numbers—five, seven, eight, and twelve—are God speaking to us mortals," I commented. "He is truly the Grand Architect of the universe. Didn't Saint Thomas say, 'We will behold wonders and numbers that *rois*, princes, and men of God will be puzzled and then astonished, after which they will comprehend what God is telling them.'"

"*Oui*, that is true, and the Book of Exodus tells us the number five was used extensively in the construction of the Tabernacle of old. However, these digits only disclose what Saint Joseph of Arimathea and his followers planned to do using the nascent teachings of Jesus the Christ. It doesn't tell us what he experienced, pictured, or who his new followers of the way were and their reactions to his final parchment of his gospel."

I knew I must now convince *Frère* Ambrosius to accompany our band of *chevaliers* and lone sergeant to go on this dangerous trip to Lanercost Priory. We headed back to the holy *chapelle* where we met Grand Master Gilbért, the earl of Pembroke, *Frère* Ambrosius, and several other *moines* helping with the measurements. Privately, I drew *Frère* Ambrosius aside to note my proposal.

"How would you like to know the contents of the book you hid in northern England, and would you be willing to leave now? We can depart right after you finish your final measurements."

There was a silent pause before a large smile appeared on his face. "*Oui*, but what will I tell the other *frères*?"

"Tell them that *Seigneur* de Pembroke requests your presence back in London to help him with his survey for *Roi* Richard's report. Now, let's tell Grand Master Gilbért and *Seigneur* Guillaume." I discreetly pulled both men away from the *chapelle* and gave them all the information Chaplain Jeremiah and I had discussed at the cloister. Both men agreed with my plan to leave, but Grand Master Gilbért wanted me to hear him on something he had just found out.

"Earlier, one of the *frères* told me several interesting pieces of information. He said the steps to the holy well have a hidden stone partition on one side of it. He believed the partition moved, which led to a tunnel that ended some distance at the tor mound. He assumed this was a secret meeting place. This doesn't bode well for us. It sounds like a hiding place for an ambush. Both Muhammad Nur Adin and Sergeant Jacque de Hoult agreed with me."

"Even a better reason for us to leave sooner, but what will you tell *Abad* Miguel?"

"He told me he can't travel today because of his back pains. He'll stay in *Abbé* Sully's house until we return. Let's leave immediately, for it is time to end this holy quest."

Grand Master Gilbért signaled Sergeant Jacque to bring the horses. *Frère* Ambrosius told the rest of the *moines* his destination and why he was leaving. Grand Master Gilbért had Chaplain Jeremiah swear *Seigneur* Guillaume to secrecy about Saint Joseph's fifth gospel before we left, to which he agreed. We hopped on our horses and then raced back to our old camp. *Frère* Ambrosius stored his parchments in his saddlebag and afterward we headed north.

"How many miles or leagues to the Lanercost Priory?" I asked Grand Master Gilbért.

"It is 107 leagues or 320 miles, but most of it is on well-traveled Roman roads. It will require a fortnight or better to reach the priory."

After just one league, the earl of Pembroke, Guillaume le Maréchal was startled by the sudden appearance of Muhammad Nur Adin by a side copse of dense trees. "*Salam, Seigneur* Pembroke. It is I, Emir Muhammad, fear not."

Right behind him, wagging his tail, stood *Noir Ombre*. Muhammad's swarthy face betrayed him with a wrinkled brow of concern.

"I fear we are being followed, Your Excellencies, but I have yet to determine who it might be. Even *Noir Ombre* seems calm and happy. I will continue to scout our rear, Grand Master Gilbért." Muhammad galloped off with our war dog from hence we came.

I felt some apprehension, but this feeling had occurred many times before. However, we were now close to our final objective of obtaining Saint Joseph's manuscripts and me returning home to my loved ones. A giddy feeling came over me as we galloped down the old Roman road.

CHAPTER XLVIII

Southern Gaul

Anno Domini 38

"My fellow teachers," Yoseph declared. "What you just observed shows the power of this holy chalice. It will not tolerate killers, liars, and people who wish to harm us. It can't be in the presence of such evil humans. It will remove them instantly. I say this not to scare you but to guide you on the proper way to conduct your good behavior. Some of you who were of the Jewish faith know the power of the Ark of the Covenant. The *Maishiach's* chalice has that same *El Shaddai*-given power to destroy. Yet, it has a saving grace of restoring life. Some of you can testify to this power. We now have a symbol, which will give us peace."

This seemed to calm the group of teachers after their fiery earthquake experience. Yoseph put the holy cup back into his satchel and moved on to speak to Alein Yosephe. He wanted to know more about their new follower. As he walked back toward Alein, he noticed a twisted look of surprise, disappointment, and bewilderment on his son's face.

"*Abba*, I had no idea about this evil man. He spoke of being a simple Gentile farmer. He said he had traveled from Greece to grow his produce for the local markets. The only thing unusual I noticed about him was a quite small spread-eagle tattoo on his wrist. I am sorry I asked him to join us."

"My son, you wouldn't know his evil intent. I suspect the eagle designated him as a Roman spy. The cup of our *Maishiach* will always know their motives and thoughts."

"*Abba*, I failed to mention, because of the horrible earthquake, that your early disciples want to speak to you tonight. They must speak to you before we go any farther."

Yoseph was afraid what this meeting might be about. He hoped their recent staggering experiences hadn't slackened their faith. He spoke to each one of them and told them to meet him a short distance from the camp. Yoseph knew the meeting was serious for they hadn't had one since the shipwreck.

Yoseph's family of Zechariah, Hebron, Enygeus, little Enoch, and Yosa stood next to him. Miriam of Magdala spoke first.

"Rabbi Yoseph, was he the man stalking us from Palestine?"

"No, he may have been a Roman spy. The holy cup knows those who are evil and will sort out all our enemies. Alein said he was Greek and pretended to be a farmer. Pray Barabbas hasn't followed us here."

"Rabbi Yoseph," said Philip. "Alein and I want to convey to you the wishes of some of our teachers, including Miriam of Magdala, Lazarus, Philip, Martha, Marcella, Sarah, Maximus, Miriam Cleopas, Miriam Salome, Nicodemus, Nathan, Trophimus, Sidonius, Martial, Saturninus, Clotho, Georgeus, little Yoseph, and Cleon.

"Rabbi, we decided as a group that some of us will stay here in southern Gaul. I know you and your family want to travel to the Isle of the Apples and King Arviragus's gifted land. The rest of us think it is best for spreading the logos of our *Maishiach* if we separate. Besides, you have the Druid's map, and they want to return to their family in Albion. Some of us do want to go with your group of teachers, comprising Nathan, Clotho, Georgeus, Nicodemus, Shimon the Zealot, and two of the sailors called Martial and Maximus, both friends of Lazarus."

"Miriam of Magdala, do you agree with this idea?" Yoseph asked.

"Yes, Rabbi Yoseph, and our decision didn't have anything to do with the dreadful earthquake. Yoseph, I am not abandoning you. I promise to come to visit at the appropriate time. Our *Maishiach* wants us to travel another path. You have comforted me in times of great turmoil and sadness. We have made our decisions by *El Shaddai* and our *Maishiach's* will for us. Please don't hold this decision against us. I beg you not to think ill of us."

"Daughter and teachers of Zion. I wish you the joy, happiness, blessings, and future accomplishments given to you by the Holy Spirit. I will miss all of you."

A tear rolled down Yoseph's cheek, which prompted him to stroll over and hug each one of them. Especially Miriam of Magdala. He thought of her as another daughter and didn't want to leave her embrace.

The next day they all hugged one another once more. There were promises to visit Yoseph and his band at some future time. Yoseph then watched his friends, who helped him start his ministry, disappear down the trail from whence they came a day earlier. Once again, tears rolled down his cheeks.

"Yoseph, how long do you estimate it will take us to reach the Isle of the Apples?" Hebron asked.

"Hebron, according to Adair it is about 7,829 *stadia* or forty-five days of travel time. That calculation is based on no delays, which I know we'll have."

"Yoseph, are you sure you are emotionally fit for this arduous trip?" Hebron asked.

"Hebron, I have you and the rest of my family to help me teach the *Maishiach's* wisdom. Also I must keep Nicodemus's happiness intact. The loss of his daughter is not an easy situation to contend with."

Yoseph gathered the rest of his teachers, postulants, and his new Druid friends and headed north along the Rhône River until they came to a Roman port town called Arelate in the Roman tongue. The noisy arena and forum, they were told by Beli to avoid. He was afraid the Roman authorities would spot them. Also he said it was originally a Celtic town. From his map, they headed northwest for a full day. They reached the outskirts of a large Roman town, which the Romans called Nemausus, and camped in a cave near a small brook. As they sat around a small campfire, Beli explained the town was named after a Celtic god who protected rivers and streams.

Hebron rushed over and sat next to Yoseph. "Yoseph, did you see the large Roman aqueduct coming out of the hills into the walled city?"

"Yes, why do you ask?"

"According to Adair, this town is built similar to Rome and settled by retired legionnaires after the Egyptian campaign by Gaius Julius Caesar. He gave this land to them for their service. We should leave tonight. There are spies everywhere."

"Yet, my friends, let me warn you about the Massif Central," Adair said. "That's a rugged range of mountains, which travels perpendicular to the sea. They get higher and higher the farther northwest we go. See here on the map, it shows them." His bony finger stopped on a long band of sharp-peaked mountains.

"From what both you and Beli have told me," Yoseph said, "we are in the proverbial Roman hornet's nest. We can't waste any more time and need to move on to remoter areas. What do you say, Hebron and Nicodemus?"

Both nodded agreement and then rose to leave.

"Adair, I appreciate your caution, however, the risk is worth saving the time and I don't want to be in prison again," Yoseph stated.

Their band of teachers left and headed northwest that night. They made numerous torches to light the way and continued until dawn. As the sun rose over the mountaintops, Yoseph realized how high they were. Snow lay in the shadows and the air was quite cold. They entered a secluded snow-covered valley.

"Yoseph," Alein Yosephe said. "We need to stop . . . here . . . and rest. Adair stumbled several times coming down this side of the mountain. The paths around these peaks are quite narrow and any of us could fall."

Yoseph agreed, so they stopped near a gurgling brook and pitched their camp and started a fire. There they broke their fast just as the moon disappeared over the mountaintops and the sun pushed its way above the sky horizon. That is when they heard a bloodcurdling howl from a close peak near them. Then the horses started neighing and stamping in fear.

"*Abba*," Alein Yosephe observed. "It sounds like we have company for breaking our fast. A pack of wolves is quite close. What shall we do to protect ourselves?"

"My son, go tell the others we have nothing to fear. If we should fear anything, tell them it strides on two legs."

They rested two full days and gained their strength to sojourn over the rest of the massif. During this time, they replenished their water supply and caught some fish in the icy stream. After two days they left, and the land started to flatten out. They hoped to come across some isolated villages, but not until the third day did they spy five round straw-thatched mud huts. The villagers were hesitant at first to come out of their huts, but Beli spoke to them in their Celtic tongue. Most of them warmed to the presence of strangers after Adair and Beli spoke to them about where they came from and that most were Culdees, which meant strangers from afar. Yoseph and his teachers spent an entire day with them showing the various symbols of their nascent faith. They were most intrigued about the story behind the symbol of the cross and their fish symbol. The next day they left on amical terms and said others like them would come to visit. As a departing gift, they gave Yoseph's band one of their horses.

They continued until reaching a windy hillock and camped there for the night. The additional horse helped gain them some time.

Nicodemus approached Yoseph and spoke. "Yoseph, have you thought anymore about our new synagogue to honor the *Maishiach*?"

"Yes, my friend. Just like you and Miriam suggested. It should be on the dimensions of the ancient Tabernacle. We will have limited materials, but we'll start with a round hut like the ones in the village we just left, except bigger. As our new group of teachers grows, so will the sacred hut. Also there will be twelve huts for the teachers who knew Yeshua. Similar to Moses's twelve tribes."

Yoseph realized their dream of Yeshua's wishes neared reality. Yet, they had only reached half their journey's destination. After another two days, they reached a sizable hamlet with approximately a hundred people. They repeated the same teachings as the previous smaller village, but this time they held the wondrous supper of their *Maishiach*. Afterward, three people decided to join them. Yoseph and their band were quite happy. The new postulants said there was an even bigger city farther north.

Two days later they reached a high gorge that overlooked a river below. To Yoseph's amazement, there were numerous homes and buildings hanging on the gorge's cliffs.

"Rabbi Yoseph," said Shimon the Zealot. "I had a dream last night about this place. Numerous years ago, Yeshua and our band of disciples visited Jericho and observed a man sitting in a sycamore tree. Yeshua knew his name, but he didn't know Yeshua's. In my dream his name was Zacchaeus and he collected taxes in Jericho. My dream told me this man would later become a powerful leader here in this town several years after we left. It appears our words will leave an impression on these people. I thought this dream would reassure our band of teachers."

"Thank you, Rabbi Shimon, for this information. We must relay your good presentiment to the townspeople when we teach."

Yoseph and his teachers spent three days there and made new friends. Once again, they taught about Yeshua's holy philosophy, signs, and their symbolism. Before leaving, Rabbi Shimon the Zealot spoke about his dream and the future coming of Zacchaeus. This left the townspeople excited for the future. With *El Shaddai's* blessing, three new postulants joined their band.

Yoseph's band of teachers and new postulants then headed in a more northernly direction. After a month of traveling they reached the old Celtic capitol of the Limovices tribe or as the Romans called it Augustoritum. Beli and Adair said we should avoid this city too. The Roman army used this town as a major staging area. We rested some distance from the city in a dense grove of trees. We didn't light any campfires.

That evening, Yoseph approached Adair and Beli with some questions in his mind. They were surrounded by their family, speaking in their Celtic tongue. Yoseph wanted to learn more about the Isle of the Apples and its environs.

"Venerable Adair," Yoseph asked in the Greek language. "Can you and Beli tell me more about the Glass Isle, or as you call it the Isle of the Apples, and why your people venerate it so much?"

"Rabbi Yoseph, it is a holy place for our ancient Celt ancestors, the Silures tribe, and there are twelve colleges of learning centered around the great tor. It is a place of good and evil. Underneath the tor is another world called Annwn, where *Roi Gwyn ap Nudd* reigns in darkness. Some call him *Seigneur Arawn*. If you aren't careful, once you enter this world, time there stands still. In this dark realm is the domain of the fair folk, the black hounds with orange-red eyes, and wild white stallions. At night they search for lost souls to capture and take back to their chthonic lair."

"Why is this wonderful place also evil like a spiderweb?" Yoseph asked.

"For you to have good," Beli replied, "you must have evil. It is left to man to see to it there's more good than evil. Faith and good conscience are the tools that drive evil away. Men and women must be diligent in using these instruments. Don't you agree, Rabbi Yoseph?"

"Yes, I agree and that is why my devotion is so important to my nascent faith. I hope we can discuss my religion further, but I have another question, elder Adair. Where did your people come from before settling on the Glass Isle?"

"We came from the east, close to where you once lived. We were once called the shining ones and traveled to a great river called the Danube. I am curious about your powerful chalice and the sacred items you carry in your satchel. We need to discuss more about your *Maishiach Hesus,* or Yeshua as you call Him."

The next day, they left Augustoritum and then Yoseph's back started hurting. He obtained his walking staff from the back of one of the horses. After leaving prison, he had found the straight wooden rod. The staff helped his limp after he tread numerous *stadia*. It seemed like a lifetime ago he had found this sturdy thorn branch.

After several more days, they headed in a more westerly direction, but still headed north. They had traveled five weeks when Yoseph noticed two seagulls flying in the cerulean blue sky.

"Hebron, observe in the sky!" Yoseph shouted. They were now close to the ocean and another week of hard traveling. Yoseph felt giddy with anticipation, but fears of another disastrous sea voyage tempered his enthusiasm. They continued until nightfall and then camped near a cave. The clear night sky projected a gorgeous slanting firmament, which Beli said was an auspicious sign. Before they sat down to have their holy supper, Adair pointed on his map to a piece of thumb-sized shape land, which jutted out from the coast of Gaul near the coast of Albion, or Britannia as the Romans called it. He said this thumb of land was called Armorica, which means land in front of the sea, and a Celtic tribe called the Veneti once lived there. Adair said most were captured and pressed into Roman slavery in the time of Gaius Julius Caesar. Some whose ancestors escaped still spoke their language and traded with their tribe at Ynys Wydryn or the Glass Isle in Albion. A boat would be available there for them to travel in.

"I am sure it will cost us some money, which we have little of," Yoseph stated.

Without warning a dirt-covered man appeared from the cave opening. He stumbled toward their campfire to further reveal his face. His dark hair was matted like moss and his eyes were large like the size of black walnuts. They could see his bony cheekbones and spindle-shaped arms reach for the warm fire.

"Who are you, stranger?" asked Hebron.

He didn't say his name until he reached the *crackling* flame of the fire.

"My name is Ammon, and I am hiding from debt collectors. They seized my house, sold my wife and children to the Romans, and for many *stadia,* I rushed from a pack of wolves. Please, let me stay for the night and feed me. Six days ago, I had my last meal, and it was thirteen berries. I see you are from the people of Abraham and so am I. Last summer, I worked for the Roman army and sold them spices. The army paid me well, but I lost all my profits in a fake land deal. Please accept me as a son of Abraham."

Yoseph didn't know what to think about this man. Yet, he seemed in need of help and Yeshua's teachings said to help the needy, the downtrodden, and the poor. This man met all those categories. Yet, he felt uneasy.

"Ammon, let me confer with our council of elders and see what they say."

The man seemed satisfied with Yoseph's reply and sat down near the fire. Yoseph gathered Nicodemus, Shimon the Zealot, Hebron, Alein Yosephe, Enygeus, Nathan, Georgeus, Clotho, Yosa, and even Adair.

"Rabbi Yoseph, you know what that man's name means in Greek. It means hidden one," Adair stated.

Yoseph nodded. "Well, the man's name surely fits him. If it's true, he definitely has hidden himself well."

"Brother Yoseph, I don't trust this man," Enygeus warned. "His mannerisms seem familiar to me."

"Rabbi Yoseph, don't forget what Yeshua once said," Nicodemus reminded Yoseph. "'I am the *Melech,* and I tell you the truth, whatever you did or didn't do for one of the least of these brothers of mine, you did to Me.'"

Yoseph knew he should always help the unfortunate, but he also had faith in his sacred chalice.

"I think we should accept this poor downtrodden soul and have him became one of our postulants," Yoseph decided, his palm tightening around his thorn tree staff.

"*Abba*, this man could do us harm!" Yosa pleaded.

"Daughter, you have little faith in Yeshua's logos. He is more farsighted than we could ever imagine. Our faith is being tested, but Yeshua also said, 'Behold, I send you forth as sheep in the midst of wolves. Be therefore wise as serpents and harmless as doves.'"

"Yes, *abba*, you are right. I'll go help and prepare the holy supper."

Yosa left to go join the other apostles to start the procession. Those who weren't participating obtained their places around the fire. Yoseph stood some distance to observe the new postulants' reactions. Yosa carried the broken spear shank, Enygeus carried the paten, Zechariah held the sword, Clotho presented the red and white cruets containing blood and sweat of their Savior, and Hebron clasped the holy cup above his head. Yoseph then followed with his holy written parchments. After a couple of steps by Yoseph, the chalice appeared to be struck by lightning. A large bluish white bolt bounced off the chalice and cracked the ground. The cup glowed a fiery orange color, but Hebron seemed not affected by the lightning. Once again, there was a collective "aha" followed by bowed heads from the light. He continued and then placed the cup on a large rock next to the paten.

Yoseph carefully placed his parchments on the ground and moved to his place as officiant. Strangely the chalice wasn't hot to his touch but kept its fiery orange iridescent color. Each person came forward to partake in their holy supper. Ammon was the last to reach for the sacred supper of bread and wine. As he bent forward, he pulled out a large dagger from his cloak,

"Yoseph!" Hebron shouted. "Beware, he has a large blade!" Suddenly, the earth started to shake. Ammon stumbled backward and Hebron tried to grab the knife. However, Ammon wobbled to one side.

"Now I will get my brother Judas's revenge. I will kill everyone here including the children."

Once again, he lunged at Yoseph with his knife. "I, Barabbas, will destroy every one of you and torture the last person in the end."

Another bolt of bluish white lightning struck at the feet of Barabbas. His face gave off a *sizzling* sound and his mouth gaped open with his tongue emitting sparks. The ground under him split with zigzag lines and the earth shook. This time, nobody else experienced any movement under their feet. An additional bolt struck once again, and his entire body started melting. Quickly, the holy cup changed to a lava red color and emitted a *screeching* sound. Barabbas's body dissolved further, then, to everyone's horror, the zigzag line opened, and a green scaly arm grabbed his murky image and pulled it into the ground.

Yoseph and his band of teachers were speechless with stunned silence. Rapid breathing became the only sound heard. The smell of sweaty fear permeated the entire campsite.

"Fellow teachers and postulants, this event just now revealed the supremacy of our *Maishiach* and His holy cup's power. It is like the old Ark of the Covenant. It won't allow deceit, murder, lies, imposters, or anything that goes against *El Shaddai's* ways. Evil can't find a home in the chalice's presence."

"Rabbi Yoseph, indeed, your power of faith is stronger than anything I've seen in many summers," Adair said. "My people will be amazed and those throughout Albion will be astonished in what you say."

"My friends, this evil man has stalked us for almost a year. He was responsible for the murder of many innocent men. My family lived in fear under his terrible knife and now we are set free from harm. All should sleep well tonight and pray to *El Shaddai* and His Son for our deliverance from hatred. Tomorrow, we embark on our last road to the coast and on to Albion."

Yoseph fell fast asleep with relief but was awoken near dawn by a golden shimmering light. The shining light began to speak. "Yoseph, you have done well. The King of Gloria is pleased and has sent me."

"Who are you?"

"I am the messenger for *El Shaddai* and some call me Gabriel. You will prosper in the land of the shining ones and will be remembered as a holy man and Yeshua's cupbearer. Many will call you the fisher king."

The light and voice vanished and Yoseph fell back to sleep with a feeling of contentment.

The next day, Yoseph left with his band of teachers and his Druid friends. They traveled another two days until they finally reached a cliff that overlooked an ocean bay. Below them stretched a wide river that flowed into a vast sea. A small village rested on one side of the river. As they traveled down a well-worn traveled path to the village, Yoseph observed numerous fishing boats with nets hung over their sides. There appeared more boats docked than the number of mud huts. Nobody greeted them as they entered the village. Yoseph sensed the villagers were cautious of strangers and didn't want to greet them. Three men and two women darted toward their boats to escape. That's when Adair shouted out in his Celtic language. "Peace, my brothers and sisters, I am an old priest from the Glass Isle." Beli, the priest said the same and then slowly they crept out of their smoky-filled huts.

Yoseph thought it best that Adair and Beli did all the discussion. After a short conversation, smiles appeared on the villagers' faces, yet some of the children hid behind their mother's skirts until they noticed the babies and children traveling with us.

Adair said that they agreed to let the band stay the night and feed them fish, which they had caught earlier in morning. Now all that was left to do was arrange passage to Albion.

The next day, Adair and Beli arranged for passage to the Isle of the Apples or Glass Isle, which were both thrilling and apprehensive. So many of them had faced near drowning and loved the ones who did drown that Yoseph, Nicodemus, Alein Yosephe, and Hebron faced an insurmountable job convincing many of their teachers to sail. Especially the ones with children, who included Yoseph's sister. Yoseph asked them to pray to Yeshua and trust in His will. Just as they finished their prayer, a white dove flew down and perched on Yoseph's shoulder. The dove rested there for a while, cooed, then flew away. That holy sign convinced the recalcitrant teachers to agree. The boatmen said they would sail the group to Albion if they gave them their horses. The council of elders agreed but Hebron added a caveat.

"Yoseph, since we have Adair with us and he knows the land but can't travel far without a horse, they should sail us directly to the Glass Isle."

Yoseph agreed and so did Adair. Everyone decided to leave immediately because the tide was going out. The sailors accepted the horses and agreed to take Yoseph's band to their destination. They embarked in two boats and left the bay. Adair said there were 3,000 stadia by land or ten to fifteen days of travel on the sea.

With joyous smiles Yoseph and his teachers headed west. What would the strangers from afar find on this new holy isle?

CHAPTER XLIX

Middle Britain

April

Anno Domini 1191

"We stopped for the night at Temple Balsall and the Earl de Pembroke Guillaume le Maréchal, who once knew the preceptor and the temple's late benefactor, *Seigneur* Roger de Mowbray, told us about him. The earl said his *bon ami*, Roger, died shortly after the Battle of Hattin in the Levant. I crossed myself and thought about the thousands of *chevaliers* who wouldn't see their families and homelands again.

We stayed there just one night and continued on the next day. Muhammad joined us about midday and gave his report to Grand Master Gilbért.

"Your Excellency, we are still being followed. I don't know by whom. My suspicions tell me they're the dark *seigneurs* of the night."

Grand Master Gilbért nodded his head in agreement, which left me puzzled.

"Grand Master Gilbért," I asked, "who are the dark *seigneurs* of the night?"

"*Seigneur* Robert, let us whisper when we converse about them. Right now, their presence may be among us. It is a secret group within the *Hashishiyya*. They are called the *Fida'is*. They have a *fatwa* on Muhammad, Sergeant de Hoult, you, and me. They're not like the *Hashishiyya*, but worse. They strike only at night like a poisonous snake in the darkness.

"They're older experienced killers who have survived many battles. They train rigorously at night, and some say they can see like a black leopard in the dark. Muhammad, Sergeant Jacque, and I fear them the most. *Seigneur* Robert, don't fear, it is still daylight, and the earl of Pembroke has fought them. He has unhorsed five hundred *chevaliers* in combat in his lifetime."

This made me feel some better, but these noted fighters, their fighting prowess increased each time they told of their exploits. I didn't want to doubt their abilities, for I had seen their tenacity, apart from the earl of Pembroke and he didn't fear a bishop of the church. His face had two deep scars across his forehead, a bent nose, and one hand with a crooked finger. He and Grand Master Gilbért were the same size and both as agile as a powerful stag. The earl handled a horse as well as Muhammad and his mount's size dwarfed ours.

That night nobody slept, including *Noir Ombre*, who paced back and forth in front of our fire. To my relief, the sun popped up above some distance hillocks and we proceeded toward the Templar Penhill Preceptory. According to the earl, another preceptory was funded by the late *Seigneur* Roger de Mowbray. The preceptory would require two days of riding time before we reached its location. That was another two nights of silent threats. Muhammad continued to scout ahead and behind each day. That evening we camped near a large copse of trees and made our fire. *Noir Ombre* stayed close to me, which was unusual. His shiny, black walnut-colored eyes kept staring into the high tree limbs above.

Suddenly, Muhammad shouted, "*Allahu Akbar, Allahu Akbar, Allahu Akbar*!" He drew both of his scimitars from his back and rushed into the woods, with *Noir Ombre* snapping his teeth as he raced into the dark forest. This is it, I told myself, but I didn't see anything or hear anything. Sergeant Jacque and the earl of Pembroke drew close to me as I too raised my sword. We stood there against the flame of our fire and perceived nothing. *Frère* Ambrosius's face was as white as snow and his body frozen like a chuck of ice.

"*Seigneur* Robert, they are coming for us," Grand Master Gilbért whispered.

"I don't see or hear anything," I replied. Just as I said that a dark-dressed man fell from the stygian night sky and drew two swords from behind his back. He crouched like a predator ready to kill his prey. I reached for my long dagger, only to drop it into the fire. All around me these men were dropping from the trees surrounding us. Each one was followed by a quiet *thump*. Not a word or scream emanated from their black-covered mouths. The man in front of me swung his narrow scimitar that ripped through my chain mail as I jumped back. The earl's large sword swung one time and his evil opponent's head flew off into the fire. My man fought like Muhammad with his scythe like rotating swords. The earl of Pembroke threw me a single mace and a chain mace weapon.

"*Seigneur* Robert, use these weapons."

I used the chain mace to wrap around one sword and pull him forward, the other I struck his head, which made a *cracking* sound like an egg. Just as I finished him off, another appeared behind me. They were dropping as fast as if I was shaking an apple tree. Sergeant Jacque de Hoult retrieved two crossbows and shot the man behind me and shot another leaping from a tree limb. This is when I heard a loud bloodcurdling howl coming from *Noir Ombre*. It wasn't a howl of pain, but as if our war hound was signaling something or somebody. The earl used his large horse to trample two of the *Fida'is*, using its steel-covered hooves as maces. Grand Master Gilbért used his misericord Damascus dagger and sword to eviscerate one man.

"Where is Muhammad?" I shouted to Grand Master Gilbért.

"I don't know," came back his reply.

"How many are they?"

Once again, he replied the same.

To my chagrin, two more appeared in front of me. I threw a stick of fire at one of them and he started to burn. He kept coming at me with flames burning from his front. Then I remembered what Muhammad once said. He told me these *Hashishiyya* swallow something called opiated hashish, which makes them impervious to pain. I used my chain mace and swung it around his neck and pulled his head into the campfire. He didn't scream but was blinded. I finished him off with a sword blow to his head. This left the other man, who hesitated to come forward and meet me. Sergeant Jacque threw me a loaded crossbow, quickly I aimed it, and shot a quarrel between his eyes.

There was a pause in the fighting, and it became deathly still. Then a shiver raced down my spine when an eruption of howls came from all directions. In the distant dark woods, I glimpsed movement. I prayed it wasn't a second wave of these dark demons. Yet, what I observed were moving glowing eyes and snapping of teeth, and I heard the throaty guttural noise of wolves. I distinctly remembered those sounds from the cold Pyrénées *Montagnes*. The howls continued as more wolves penetrated the darkness. Out of the darkness came *Noir Ombre* with several wolves at his side. He seemed to know them. Behind them were sixty sets of glowing, orange-colored eyes. The attacks had ceased, and Muhammad parted the large pack as he came forward. None of the wolves growled at his presence or ours.

"Muhammad, *mon ami,* where did you get reinforcements?" I asked.

"It wasn't me, *Seigneur* Robert. My specialty is horses. You can thank *Noir Ombre* for the help. His *jinn* must be part wolf. That first howl summoned his *bon amis*."

It never ceased to amaze me about God's creatures.

Strangely, Muhammad's face was bleeding with a large gash across his cheek. Of the many battles we had fought, this was the first time I noticed an injury.

"Robert, Grand Master Gilbért, and Earl Guillaume, I retrieved some documents from their deceased leader. It lists how many were sent to capture you and kill us, which tallies with the number of dead. Also it mentions us killing their brethren in Toledo, the killing of my entire family, and taking my land. Tonight, I revenged the disgrace on my family and regained my honor. However, another revealing line says the cardinal hired them and this document bears his religious seal. It discloses they were sent by an unnamed person from Glastonbury."

All heads turned toward *Frère* Ambrosius who looked surprised.

"I didn't tell this cardinal or anybody else where we were traveling. I still don't know this evil man. Grand Master Gilbért and Earl Guillaume, I did as you instructed me. I am not responsible for these godless men. Please believe me."

"We'll discuss this further when we reach the Penhill Preceptory," Grand Master Gilbért said. "Let's ride now. I want to reach there by noon tomorrow!" We jumped on our horses and then spurred them hard. Muhammad made some quick torches and caught up with us in no time. He handed several out as we raced along in the still dark night. Nobody spoke a word until we reached a large escarpment overlooking the preceptory in the morning sun.

However, the earl of Pembroke broke the silence as we stopped to rest our horses. "Grand Master Gilbért, answer for me a question. Why are every damn Moor and Saracen from Iberia and the Levant chasing you? When I traveled on crusade to Levant, I never noticed this many Arabic-speaking people. You left there, traveled the entire Mediterranean Sea, Gaul, Iberia, and now England, and they all followed you. You didn't leave anybody in the Levant for *Roi* Richard to fight. All you left him was a caravan of camels."

I noticed Grand Master Gilbért smiling for the first time in months and he replied with a slight laugh.

"*Mon ami*, I left him the great army of Saladin and their camels, which are faster than our horses."

We reached Penhill just as the sun beamed overhead. Once again, the earl of Pembroke knew the preceptor. He accommodated us quite well with food, *vin*, water, and horses. This preceptory trained *chevaliers* to fight on horseback. All of us spoke to *Frère* Ambrosius, but he still said he didn't know the cardinal. We left that evening fully supplied with new quarrels for our crossbows. The daylight increased because of the change of seasons, but the weather turned colder because we were heading further north.

"*Seigneur* Robert," Grand Master Gilbért whispered as he trotted up next to me. "I spoke to *Frère* Ambrosius while loading our supplies at Penhill. I don't think he is our traitor."

"Who is it then, Grand Master Gilbért? We keep playing this guessing game, but there is no definitive evidence. How many hundreds of leagues have we discussed this? I still think it is a useless waste of time. The Roman language once had a saying, *id est quod id est,* it is what it is. I want to stay focused on the final road to our sacred quest. However, give me your evidence." I felt my mind couldn't assimilate any more conjecture, especially after our horrific attack.

"Unbeknownst to you, *Seigneur* Robert, I spoke to one of the Carthusian *moines* who accompanied *Frère* Ambrosius from the Witham Priory. He wasn't out of sight of *Frère* Ambrosius, except when you two were together in the *chapelle.* Like he said, he arrived after the cardinal and his men left."

We rode another two days until it started snowing. That evening we camped a short distance from Lanercost Priory. Muhammad had scouted the area but did tell us he believed the cardinal's men were here earlier and left. The tracks headed further north toward the old Roman Hadrian's Wall. Why this direction, he didn't know. Yet, he said they weren't anywhere close to the priory. This *monastère* gave me a tight feeling in my stomach. Besides being isolated in a large copse of woods, the buildings seemed to blend in with the dark evergreen trees. The canopy of trees covered the night sky.

"Well, *Frère* Ambrosius, it is time for you to lead us to our final quest." Grand Master Gilbért whispered. He then tramped the small campfire with his boot. "Tell us where you hid your secret tome."

"It is in the alcove tomb of the late *Seigneur* Hubert de Vaux. He was instrumental in seeing to an order of Augustinian canons to start a priory here. He donated the land on the condition that he and his family were to be buried in the *église* here and prayers be said for him forever. At the time I hid them, the priory wasn't entirely finished. The alcove is on the north transept side. His effigy is visible on top of the stone sarcophagus."

"Why did you come all this way with the tome?" I asked. "You could have hidden it anywhere in England."

"That is true, *Seigneur* Robert, but I did as I was told by my armarius and my cantor before they died in the flames. They knew this priory was quite unknown, and like today, still quite hidden. There aren't many canons living here, which should make it easy to go in unseen. Also we must fetch a pry bar so we can lift the tomb lid."

"*Frère* Ambrosius, very few things have been easy on this holy quest. You'll do your job so we can get the hell out of here!" Grand Master Gilbért demanded.

Grand Master Gilbért, Sergeant de Hoult, Chaplain Jeremiah, *Frère* Ambrosius, and I crept through the empty priory gatehouse with relief that the snow had ceased. Muhammad stayed in front to guard the entrance. We reached the archivolt steps, paused, and peeked around before pushing open the door. Once inside the narthex, everything was pitch black, except a small beam of light coming from the north transept, which reflected on the crossing floor. Slowly we tread down the central aisle before reaching the crossing. As we turned north at the crossing, we spied *Seigneur* Hubert de Vaux's effigy tomb. Rows of lit candles had burned a whiteish mass of wax, which covered the floor next to his final resting place. We immediately approached the sarcophagus, stared at the human stone image, and then put our pry bars that Muhammad had given us under the lid. Forthwith the *grinding* sound echoed throughout the *église,* and we paused before continuing further.

"*Seigneur* . . . Robert, can you get both your hands inside and grab the book?" Grand Master Gilbért whispered. "Help him,

Frère Ambrosius," once again Grand Master Gilbért whispered.

"*Oui*, but since his face is peering east, you must tip the lid toward you."

Without another word they used their pry bars to tilt the lid. A terrible moldy smell issued forth, which burned my eyes and caught my breath. I had to use my touch to find the tome. Rotten clothes and cold bone encompassed my hand. Then I touched cold leather, grabbed it with both my hands, and lifted it straight up with an elated sense of accomplishment. The written part of our quest was finally over after many months of danger. I hugged it to body. Carefully the others placed the lid back and made sure the lid matched with the tomb opening.

Just as I slid down from the elevated alcove, one of our pry bars slid off the top and *clattered* across the stone tile floor. I grabbed the pry bar in my free hand, and then we raced for the door. In the distance we heard scurrying footsteps and shouting voices. We opened the door and there mounted was Muhammad who held the reins of our horses. I slipped our precious cargo into my saddlebag and then leaped on my horse to leave. Quickly, I spurred her flanks, and we galloped off into darkness. I glanced back and viewed five swinging lanterns in the distance, and they too disappeared into the ink-black night. My excitement moved faster than the horse under me. An elated feeling of anticipation surged through my entire being. What new revelations would Saint Joseph of Arimathea disclose? Yet, many more leagues lay from here to Glastonbury *Abbaye*.

CHAPTER L

Off the Coast of Britannia in the Severn Sea

Early Winter

Anno Domini 38

Sailing from the coast of Armorica around the land's end of Albion to the Severn Sea and the cliffs of Britannia left all the teachers relaxed. The captain of the ship said he would be sailing up an estuary river called the Brue where the Glass Isle stood. The ship would reach it in a day's time. Yoseph noticed his fellow teachers had smiles on their faces and were constantly chatting about their new destination. Yoseph felt exhilarated knowing his final destination was within one day's sailing time.

Toward sunset, Beli and Adair pointed in a northeasterly direction toward a hovering sun above a large hill. "Rabbi Yoseph, there is the tor." Yoseph followed their pointed fingers and observed a large peak of land jutting straight up out a glassy sea or huge lake. However, from this distance he didn't see anything else. Adair said they would dock soon and must trek the rest of the way to the Glass Isle.

After a short distance, they came upon a long narrow dock extending out from the shore. Quickly, everybody collected their sparse belongings and disembarked to dry land. Yoseph thanked the captain of the ship for a safe delivery. Quickly, they left the salient dock before the tide turned, waved farewell to the sailors, and then turned to follow a narrow well-trod path to the top of a hillock. Halfway up the hill, Yoseph scanned back, and all his postulants, teachers, and apostles seemed like ants following their leader with anticipation. What they foresaw, he knew not, which he felt the same.

He reached the summit first, stopped, then gazed across a large valley covered with water. The tor island or Glass Isle appeared as a gigantic ship sailing across a piece of large precious glass. A cold wind blew into his face causing him to shiver. Adair said it was close to the winter solstice and the snows would come soon. To Yoseph's right, in the distance, were forty round yellow-thatched huts. The village lay on a smaller island in the glassy sea. It appeared this gave the occupants some protection from attack. Yoseph and his band were now ready to take possession of the land that King Arviragus had given him.

"Yoseph, what will we do next?" Hebron asked. Yoseph didn't reply but trudged to a muddy spot and formed two fish shapes in the mud.

"I declare this new land for Yeshua, our *Maishiach.* May He reign over it for all eternity." Then Yoseph seized his staff from his homeland and shoved it into the soft sod. Immediately, white flower blossoms appeared on the staff. By now, everyone had surrounded Yoseph and bowed in amazement at the miracle that Yoseph had performed. Even the Druid priests and priestess exhibited openmouthed wonder.

"Hebron, I want you and Alein Yosephe to go with Beli, Adair, and Enid down to that village and tell them we are coming. Tell them we are strangers from afar and we used to mine tin in these hills. I hope Adair and Beli still have relatives alive in this village. Now go, for the weather is changing and nightfall will come soon."

They left, racing toward the small island in the bigger lake. The rest of them trudged carefully down the other side.

"*Abba*, are you going to retrieve your miraculous staff?" Yosa asked.

"No, my daughter, it will remain there for all new and old followers of the *Maishiach*."

At the edge of large lake, they were met by what appeared to be the local chieftain. He wore long checkered pants, a golden torc around his neck, a cloak fastened with a large snake-designed silver broach embedded with an amethyst stone. At his belt, Yoseph spied a silver and ivory hilted sword. In one hand he held a brass embossed wooden shield with a red dragon painted on it. He said he was Beli's cousin named Bedwyr. He welcomed the group to his island village and asked them to join him on the island. Yoseph noticed he had a strange tattoo on his wrist. A blue-colored eagle with a spear thrust through its chest.

Yoseph and his teachers piled into several dugout wooden boats and crossed to the small island. They were hungry and cold. A large fire in the center of the village greeted them. Men, women, and children had come out of their mud-built homes to surround Beli. Yoseph found out it was a happy reunion with his brother. They didn't stare at the strange dress but invited the group to come and celebrate Beli's return. Quickly the group sat around the large fire and then a large plate of cooked meat became their first meal in their new home. Large horns of golden liquid accompanied the food.

Chief Bedwyr raised his horn for a toast and shouted, "*Slàinte mhòr*, my new friends, and to Adair, Beli, and Enid. We are happy on your return to your homeland."

They feasted the rest of the night as the village women sang a high-pitched rueful sound, which Beli called keening: mourning the long absence of their kinfolk, Beli.

The first couple of nights they stayed in the huts of the villagers. This gave Yoseph time to do several things. He observed the men and women's daily routine. There were distinct levels of labor. Some men worked with metals, both precious and ordinary. Even then some of these men were jewelers and others made swords, spears, helmets, and shields. Farming had ceased for the season, but others were still fishing with their nets. Fish was a big part of their food supply.

During those winter days, Yoseph continued to write about his past travels and how many they had converted to their *Maishiach's* logos. This fascinated the villagers observing Yoseph scratch on his parchment paper. According to Beli they had no written language, but every bit of their knowledge came from oral history passed down millennia or longer. Yet, he divulged that the Druid priest and priestess used a secret written language called *ogham*. Only the priests and priestesses understood the alphabet.

One warm winter day Hebron and Alein Yosephe approached Yoseph as he finished a page of his gospel of Yeshua.

Hebron spoke, "Rabbi Yoseph, we need to build our own huts. Our women teachers want some privacy and have come to us to ask you. Their men have several wives, and they aren't embarrassed of their nudity in front of other men. They don't want to criticize the Celts, because of their great hospitality. Beli said their men and women would help us build our own village as the weather warmed."

Yoseph agreed and wanted to discuss with Nicodemus the layout of their new village. After sunset he and Nicodemus met with Beli and Adair. Yoseph thought it best that they didn't build on an island in the lake.

"I believe we should build as our forefathers did a thousand summers ago. We array our huts as the twelve tribes of Israel did. We'll have our *Maishiach's* new tabernacle face east, then twelve disciple huts surround the tabernacle where we'll build an altar and enclose it in a cube-shaped sanctuary. There we can keep the holy items in this cube space and the holy cup of Christ in a small wooden cube until the holy supper is needed. The altar won't be separated by preventative curtains, but open to all who believe in our *Maishiach*. Later we'll expand and add a rectangular shape to it when more space is needed. Nicodemus suggested this idea when we first washed ashore in southern Gaul."

Nobody disagreed with Yoseph's suggestions.

"We'll start tomorrow with this construction," Beli stated. "I have a twelve-knotted measuring cord we Druids use for measuring. This will help keep the measurement precise."

"I too have a stake and some measuring line to make perfect circles," Adair added. "The villagers can make a wattle-and-mud hut in a day; possibly two huts. Also they store spare dry thatch in one of their barns. This just leaves a holy location for your village. I have some special metal rods of gold we can use to map out the location. Mother Earth has special power centers only we Druid priests and priestesses can locate. From what I have seen from the power of your holy cup, it needs an extraordinary place to rest." Beli and Enid nodded their agreement.

Yoseph's skepticism at first invaded his mind, for he feared the holy cup might be stolen, but only for a fleeting moment. It wouldn't have entered if Yoseph and the teachers hadn't faced murder or harm to protect this cup. Demons appeared in many disguises and spoke lies.

All of them retired early for the long day ahead. Yet, Yoseph's happy anticipation prevented him from sleeping. At dawn, Yoseph arose to face a crowd of villagers ready to work. Beli held in his fists two gleaming golden rods. The rods were held horizontally with the bent portions buried in both fists. Quicky, everybody piled into all the dugout boats and paddled to shore. Beli was the first to disembark and then slowly shuffled forward to hunt for the appropriate spot. Not until the sun rose overhead did the thin rods started moving. At one level location, the rods seemed to move so fast they were a blur.

"Rabbi Yoseph, Mother Earth says to build your tabernacle here. I will put a stake in this spot, yet I must seek the boundaries of your village. The force of this place will see many revelations." Slowly, Beli moved around the outer limits of this power and placed stakes in a circular fashion. When he finished, the outer circle was huge. At the very center was the first stake. From there he used his Druid cord to create a straight line that ran horizontal through the altar stake north and south, then from there he used his Druid cord to form a right angle east and west, which aligned with the stakes' sun shadow. He then created a large circle, which the altar would encompass. From there, he squared that circle, which would be the altar area for Yoseph or any of the disciples to perform the supper ceremony.

Yoseph glimpsed with fascination as Beli expanded that circle to be the diameter and circumference of the holy hut's boundaries. He created some other fish-shaped edges and then he ceased measuring.

"Now you have the layout for your tabernacle. Are you pleased, my friend?" Beli asked.

"Yes, I am elated with joy!" Yoseph said, noticing the broad smile on Beli's face.

"What are the fish-shaped designs, and where did you learn do this measuring?"

"Rabbi Yoseph, the fish-shaped design came to me in a trance, but the rim of your holy cup has this design. As far as knowing how to measure things, this verbally came to some of us Druid priests and priestesses. The old ones said the ancient Greek philosophers gave them this secret knowledge."

The building continued for three or four new moons, which Yoseph used the time to preach to travelers and the surrounding villages. The rest of his teachers did the same.

After four new moons they were ready to occupy their village. Yoseph said a blessing for their well-being. Part of the village workers were there to witness what Yoseph was to say. In Greek, he blessed the crowd and their fine work, asked for *El Shaddai's* blessing, and spoke their *Maishiach's* words to the Gentiles. Beli translated the Greek words into the native Celtic language, then arose a loud shout of approval.

Suddenly, a bright light streamed down through the clouds and the beam stopped in front of Yoseph's face. A white dove appeared, fluttering its wing and cooing its approval. The crowd fell to their knees and bowed in Yoseph's direction. The air got deathly quiet except for the dove's *flapping* wings. Then the dove disappeared. Shortly thereafter, Beli explained to the crowd that Yoseph and his followers were priests and priestesses just like his Druid family. Henceforth from that day, Yoseph and his teachers were honored with respect similar to their Druid friends.

Chief Bedwyr suggested they build a wooden stockade around their village. He said there were warring tribes and wild animals that would enter without the stockade. Hebron and Yoseph agreed and shortly thereafter, it was built. Yet, Yoseph let the chief know that anybody who was hungry, thirsty, or wanted to hear the words of their *Maishiach* was welcome.

That late spring, Beli, Adair, and Enid came to Yoseph and asked if he and Nicodemus would celebrate the longest daylight of the year. He called it *Alban Hefin,* which means the sun sits still.

"It is not one of our official fire festivals," Beli explained, "but we celebrate it with fires anyway. Having you both there would honor our college of Druids. It commences in seven sunsets. The event starts on summer's eve. All our religious celebrations start when the stars are first visible."

Was it a coincidence that Yoseph's old faith and Druid celebrations both started in the evening? In Yoseph's heart he knew more similarities were to come.

"Rabbi Yoseph, please come to my hut this evening, just as the sun is starting to set," Beli asked. "Also bring Nicodemus with you. It's quite important for both of you to be there."

"Yes, we'll be there before sunset, and I will let Nicodemus know of your request." The three Druids left and didn't say anything more. Yoseph wondered why they wanted him there. Shortly thereafter, he met Nicodemus near the new tabernacle.

"Nicodemus, may I speak with you?"

"Yes, Yoseph, what do you want to speak about?"

"Beli asked us to meet him this evening in his hut. Also he invited us in seven sunsets to meet with him in celebration of *Alban Hefin*, which means the sun sits still. What do say, my friend?"

"The celebration sounds fine, but why does he want to speak to us in private?"

"I don't know, but I guess we'll find out!"

That evening came and the sun hung low on the horizon. They both entered a partially dark interior with Beli, Adair, and Enid standing around a large clay bowl of still water. The smell of burned sage permeated the small residence.

"Adair told me when he first met both of you; he knew you were both holy men," Beli said. "Now I will tell you of your future." He pointed to the still water in the clay bowl. "In our Celtic faith we can see into the future by staring into this water that creatures must have. We Druids call this scrying. Please do not say anything until I am finished."

"Why do we need to see the future?" Nicodemus asked.

"Both your futures are entwined with the three of us," Beli answered with a stoic expression. Forthwith, Enid started a high-pitched chant followed by Adair's deep hum as he beat on a deerskin drum. Beli gazed just above the water. Then he began to speak with his head twisting back and forth and his arms shaking at Yoseph and Nicodemus.

"I discern an old man holding a fish-edged chalice and giving it to a young man who is a bard. They are in a tunnel fraught with evil men. Some of the men are purported to be holy men, but I see them as servants of darkness. There are other men there who are the servants of light. I also see you, Yoseph of Arimathea, but there is a blinding light that won't let me see any farther."

Suddenly, Beli's arm movement ceased. What remained was excruciating silence. His head rose straight up with beads of sweat trinkling down his nose.

"Do you have any questions, Rabbi Yoseph?"

"Yes, I do. Why is our future entwined with yours?"

"We three are the channel that your new faith expands. There may be more revealed in the future, but this all I understand for now."

Yoseph and Nicodemus ambled away from Beli's hut in silence and then paddled across the lake. Not until they reached their stockaded village did Yoseph speak.

"My friend, what do you make of these prophecies?"

"I don't know, Yoseph. Yet, I do believe it has something to do with our *Maishiach's* future tabernacles. We are the first of many who will follow in the path of Yeshua. Britannia and the Isle of Albion, as the Celts call it, will be the first organized tabernacle of Yeshua. It will be the first New *Yerushalayim*. Yet, there will be newer *Yerushalayims* to come. These *Yerushalayims* will exist long after we are no more of this earth."

"My good friend, you're right, but I sense the *Maishiach* and *El Shaddai* will have a final New *Yerushalayim* for the chosen ones." Yoseph felt his prophecy came from his heart.

On the seventh day, Beli, Adair, and Enid came to Yoseph's hut. All three had looks of anticipation as they stood inside his hut.

"Rabbi Yoseph, we desire you and Rabbi Nicodemus be present at our Nemeton or longest day ceremony. There will be numerous Druid priests and priestesses from other *touta* or tribes and the Cymru region. The word of your holy accomplishments has preceded you and your followers. My colleagues want to hear your holy words and see your miraculous cup. We always have this gathering before any festival. Our deities are mostly from the earth, and we want to hear about your three sky deities. I believe you call them your Father, the Son, and the Holy Spirit. Could you and Rabbi Nicodemus follow us to our sacred grove?"

Yoseph thought this was an excellent opportunity to discuss each other's faith. Nicodemus nodded his approval and off they departed to this unknown grove. They traveled to a nearby hillock covered with oak, beech, and hazelnut trees. They came to an open clearing with a gurgling spring passing close by. At the corners of a large rectangle mat were ditches with poles on each corner with mounted skulls. On the mat were three different fires in three different directions, an axe, a wooden cut trunk with a carved man's face, stacked firewood, a small black cauldron, a homemade well with water, a clay bowl filled with water perched on a small mound of earth, and a separate drinking horn. At the far end was a small rectangular-shaped stone. High above the mat was a brush arbor attached to the four skulls.

Suddenly, Yoseph and Nicodemus jumped when twenty-one additional white-hooded robes appeared from behind the many different trees. Each of their hands held a golden-colored hand sickle and the other hand held a small, strange ear-shaped leaf on a branch with white-covered pearl-like berries. Beli explained this ceremony was to bless the strength of the sun king and its fertility put forth for its Celtic people. Yoseph relaxed after Beli's explanation for the gathering.

At the completion of the event, Yoseph heard Yeshua's voice prompt him to place the holy chalice on the Druid mat. Slowly, he eased the cup out of his bag and bent over to place it on a level space. Without warning, a great burst of bluish rays shot straight up and then changed to rotating beams of orange, red, yellow, and blue rays. A collective gasp emanated from all the white-hooded Druids. Then the chalice levitated to Yoseph's height and stopped. Once again, there came an even louder gasp that approached a shout.

"Rabbi Yoseph, indeed, you are a holy man and have the power to move things," Beli stated.

"My God works through me and my heart opens to let Him enter," Yoseph replied.

"After the festival my fellow priests and priestesses would be honored to have you speak more about your God man and nephew, Yeshua. It's almost time for the *Alban Hefin* festival to start."

They walked toward the base of the tor, and that is when Yoseph glanced up and spied a large pile of wood stacked at the very top.

"Rabbi Yoseph, my fellow colleagues have requested you and Rabbi Nicodemus to lead the way."

As he and Nicodemus started, there appeared a grooved earthen pathway, which ever-so-slightly elevated itself, circling the entire tor. As they approached the top, Yoseph peered back, and observed hundreds of people holding torches. Their presence appeared as a gigantic fiery dragon. As he and Nicodemus stood in front of the woodpile, suddenly a bolt of lightning struck the wood. Immediately, large roaring flames issued forth and then a collective shout of "*Taranis*" roared across the valley floor. Yoseph and Nicodemus stepped aside and let the brightly lit torchbearers come forth and throw their torches into the flames. Several individuals lit straw-shaped wheels and rolled them down the tor. Other villagers twirled their torches before placing them into the bonfire. Young men and women jumped through big hoops of fire. Finally, a white stallion horse and a white mare raced up opposite sides of the tor. Once meeting, the stallion started copulating with the mare. Beli said this was a good sign of fertility and the land would provide a great harvest. Yoseph had never seen such a sight as this. Then he heard a long-forgotten voice call his name in the Greek tongue. The white-hooded robe concealed the voice's face as he walked toward Yoseph.

"Yoseph of Arimathea, it is I, Arch Druid Finn! We met many years ago with your young nephew. Do you have time to speak?"

"Yes, but first follow Beli. He has your colleagues waiting to hear about Yeshua, whom we call *Christo* in the Greek tongue."

Nicodemus, the Arch Druid Finn, and Yoseph traveled back down the tor into a torch-lit grove of oaks. There waiting were the priests and priestesses holding hands. A larger circle of priests and priestesses surrounded that circle. They parted both circles for Yoseph and Nicodemus to stand in the center. Yoseph spoke of their long journey, Yeshua's death and resurrection, His teachings, their fellow disciples, and the dangers they faced along the way. Nicodemus spoke about Yeshua's resurrection and the act of being born again. This subject acquired the most questions and lengthy discussions. Several Druids wanted to know more about the holy cup. Yoseph invited them to his services at their newly built tabernacle. It became quite late before the crowd adjourned. Finn was the last to leave.

"Rabbi Yoseph, I am sorry to hear how your nephew died and the earth's sorrows He shouldered. Yet, he or she who believes in Him will never die and will be reborn for an eternity. Yoseph, good-bye, my friend, and I hope to see you again. When you least expect me, I will return."

Finn melted into the woods just as his colleagues had once appeared. Yoseph felt sadness thinking about long ago and young Yeshua.

CHAPTER LI

The Glass Isle

Anno Domini 43

Six summers had passed since Yoseph and his teachers survived the treacherous waves of southern Gaul's beaches. Yoseph sat in his wooden dugout boat fishing. He now had several cognomens. Some called him the fisher king, because of his holy chalice rim, others for drawing his secret sigil of a fish, and some called him rabbi. Beli and Enid called him the prophet from a far land.

Yoseph's tabernacle had grown. The eastern side extended outward into a rectangular-shaped mud-and-wattle roofed structure. Yoseph and his teachers and apostles had baptized many new acolytes. Even King Arviragus was personally baptized by Yoseph. Some of the tribal chiefs came to join his holy cup services. His logos of Yeshua had quickly spread like a windy fire. Shimon the Zealot went northeast to the tribe of the Iceni to speak of his time with Yeshua and the miracles their *Maishiach* had performed. Hebron and Enygeus had another child and called her Deborah. Alein Yosephe married a local village woman, and they had their handfasting or marriage on the fifth *Alban*

Hefin and now she was with child. Zechariah, the baptizer's son held office in the local tribal council. Yosa had a male companion, the son of the tribal chief Bedwyr.

"Yoseph," shouted Nicodemus from the shore. "I have a message from Philip. Please come and read it."

Yoseph withdrew his line, and then paddled to their earthen slip. He got out of the boat with his fish and greeted Nicodemus, whose trembling hands handed his missive to Yoseph.

Fearing unwelcome news, he read the note.

> *Dear Yoseph and Bishop of Britannia,*
>
> *I have some good news to relay. Miriam of Magdala, Martha, and Lazarus are coming to visit you. I suspect they will arrive there soon. They are also bringing a surprise visitor who will make you quite happy. Give my regards to Nicodemus, Hebron, Alein Yosephe, and the rest of your family.*
>
> *Your servant in Christo,*
> *Philip of Gaul*

Yoseph's heart pounded like a drum as he and Nicodemus's upbeat footsteps turned into a sprint. He met his sister, Hebron, Yosa, and Alein Yosephe standing in front of his hut.

"Great news!" Yoseph yelled. "Miriam, Lazarus, and Martha are arriving soon. Philip just sent us a note. We must get everything ready for their arrival."

Over the next two days they hunted deer, caught fish, and obtained some more of the Celtic liquid called mead. He and Nicodemus prepared the tabernacle area for worship and made it as presentable as possible. On the third day, Yoseph was in his boat fishing when he glanced up to see three robed women and three men coming down from the top of the hillock near Yoseph's now bushy thorn staff. Quickly Yoseph paddled his boat to shore, and then raced to tell the others.

"They're here, they're here, they're here!" hollered Yoseph. All the teachers emerged from their huts and congregated near the holy tabernacle. Yoseph, Hebron, Alein, Yosa, Enygeus, and Nicodemus traveled outside of the stockade to greet them. Shimon the Zealot was not far behind along with Zechariah. Yoseph rushed the rest of the way until he reached them.

"Miriam, Lazarus, Philip, and I can't believe it, my niece . . . *Amma* Miriam. My heart is *thumping* so fast it feels like it will come out of my chest."

They all hugged, cried, and kissed one another until *Amma* Miriam just laid her head on Yoseph's shoulder and whispered into Yoseph's ear.

"My Uncle Yoseph, I am so tired."

Yoseph immediately pointed in the direction of their stockade village, and they slowly followed Yoseph's lead. After they entered the stockade, an uproar of cheers went forth, which continued each time they found out *Amma* Miriam appeared in their midst. All of Philip's party shuffled toward their new *Yerushalayim*. Yoseph noticed nodding eyes from each one of his visitors and suggested they rest in his hut for now.

The rest of the day, Yoseph's fellow teachers quietly brought portions of their meals for the newcomers.

That night, first out of Yoseph's hut appeared the Magdalener. Her hair seemed grayer and many wrinkled lines of worry on her face reflected deeply from the village fire.

"Yoseph, I returned as promised. My heart is filled with happiness in seeing your face once more. How often I missed your comfort in times of trial." She then kissed him on his forehead. "However, I have mixed feelings right now. *Amma* Miriam is sick. This trip didn't help her health and the situation in *Yudah* is dire for our *Maishiach's* followers. Yohanan the Writer is hiding from both Roman and Temple priest authorities. Philip returned there upon hearing Yohanan was pursued by the new procurator. He brought *Amma* Miriam to Gaul, where she lived with us for several summers. She requested to come here to be with you."

Yoseph didn't know what to think about this latest information. He assumed she lived with Yohanan as Yeshua had asked.

Then a sinking sensation of sorrow grabbed hold of Yoseph. He was her last living relative from the old days.

"Yoseph, Philip will discuss several important things tomorrow morning. Most of it is good news. Now I want you to show me around your village. You and your teachers have helped spiritually change the entire land of Gaul."

Yoseph grabbed a staked torch from the ground and proceeded to show her the stockade, the teachers' twelve huts, and the tabernacle. In the dark center of the altar stood the golden glowing chalice. As both approached the wooden table, the cup's rays grew higher and brighter.

"Philip has approached several Celt artisans who have made duplicates of our *Maishiach's* Seder cup," Miriam informed him. "We now use them in our services like the last supper conducted by Yeshua. We say its same ceremony and have duplicated and blessed the holy items."

After the tour, Yoseph felt proud of his accomplishment, but pride only led to sin, so he asked for forgiveness. Then he excused himself and told the Magdalener he must rest. That night he slept next to the holy cup, so others could sleep in his hut until dawn came through the east doorway.

"Yoseph," came Philip's voice outside the tabernacle door. "May I come in?"

"Please do, my good friend and fellow teacher. Come and see our new *Yerushalayim*."

The early morning rays of sunlight streamed in and reflected off the chalice, sword, spear, paten, and glass cruets.

"Yoseph, we need to speak. I have ordained and documented you as bishop and apostle of Britain and northern Gaul. Your tabernacle is only the first of our *El Shaddai* and *Maishiach's* houses of worship. Lazarus is the bishop of Massalia, the Magdalener is the bishop of central and part of southern Gaul, and Martha just started building her tabernacle in Gaul. Your magnificent work and teachings are now reaping their rewards. Yoseph, please accept my humble gratitude. I see you have blessed this holy land, and your name won't be forgotten through the ages."

"Thank you, my friend, and I am so glad you have received your chance to come to the land of the Druids and Celts. I remember many springs ago, on the Mount of Olives, you asked about this land when we entertained Yeshua and some of His disciples."

"Yes, I do remember and now I have disturbing news. Roman Emperor Claudius has massed the second, ninth, fourteenth, and twentieth legions and two thousand cavalrymen plus four auxiliary legions totaling 60,000 men on the northern seacoast of Gaul. Beware, Yoseph, the Roman army is planning an invasion of Britannia. I don't know their military planned target. They want to wipe out all followers of our *Maishiach*, Jews, Druids, and anybody else who gets in their way."

Yoseph started pondering this unsettling news, but he didn't want to contemplate this now. "Philip, I won't tell the others about your disquieting news until after you leave. Please join us this evening for our holy supper meal."

"Yes, Yoseph, I'll be there. Once again, I can't wait to see the cup of our *Maishiach*."

Yoseph decided that morning to paddle over and ask their water tribe friends to attend the holy evening supper. After docking, he went to speak to Chief Bedwyr. He enthusiastically agreed to tell the others and said he would be there himself. Yoseph decided to ask Philip to go fishing with him that afternoon. They paddled out into the estuary.

"Philip, I believe you will like these Celts. Spiritually we have many things in common."

"Yes, you are right, Yoseph. My numerous years teaching in Gaul has revealed their religion. They trust me now and share their beliefs. Theirs is an *Amma* Earth faith in nature. They see things on a different plain than some of us do. They know things we do not know, and we know and see things they do not know. It is tantamount that we and their Druid priests coexist together. I believe the survival of the Celts, their priests, and our neophyte followers of Yeshua will necessitate syncretism or the combining of our faiths. Let's show them what is in the heavens."

Philip and Yoseph discussed a path for the future of Albion, or as the Romans called it Britannia. They caught numerous fish that afternoon, but not the one hundred and fifty-three that Yeshua helped the disciples to catch many years earlier in Galilee.

That evening, Yoseph witnessed an enormous number of burning torches snaking their way toward the stockade. The clan chief, Bedwyr, led the way. Yoseph's heart *thumped* as fast as one of the Celt's beating drums. Hebron and Alein Yosephe already had placed a long table from the tabernacle.

After everyone had assembled, Yosa asked Yoseph to carry the holy cup over his head while the rest of the teachers proceeded behind him. It was a wondrous sight to behold as they marched and gathered around the supper table. As he lowered the holy cup, rays of blue and yellow lights penetrated the heavens. A collective shout came from the crowd. Those whom Yoseph had baptized came forward to partake in the sacred supper. Afterward, Philip spoke to the crowd in Greek and several Druid priests translated into the Celtic tongue. Philip then kissed Yoseph on the cheek and spoke of Yoseph's authority to the crowd. This followed the tremendous sounds of "huzzah."

The next morning, a messenger from the tribe of the Atrebates spoke to Bedwyr and told him the Roman legions had landed and they were on the march to the Roman city of Londinium. Yoseph notified Philip immediately. Philip, Miriam of Magdala, and Lazarus decided to leave and travel back to southern Gaul by boat and then overland. Both Miriams were crying and Yoseph felt a large lump in his throat. They all hugged and prayed to see one another again. *Amma* Miriam grabbed Yoseph's arm and squeezed. They both knew she wouldn't see Philip, Lazarus, Miriam of Magdala again, or the land of *Judah*.

Everyone kissed one another and then waved good-bye. Yoseph viewed them for some time trudging up the tall hillock where he'd once planted his staff, which was now a small tree. Slowly, he ambled back to his hut and sat on his mat and tasted salty tears rolling over his lips. A brief time later, Nicodemus and *Amma* Miriam joined him in his sadness.

The next day, Nicodemus suggested Yoseph update his writing about his new teaching to the Celts to distract his mind from his sorrow. Yoseph thought this would be an excellent idea and commenced to update his writings.

This became daily therapy for Yoseph, which turned into weeks, months, and years. The Roman legions never penetrated the Glass Isle and Yoseph knew the holy cup had kept them away. He saw his grandchildren grow into adults. Clotho's son replaced Zechariah's place on the tribal council and then Zechariah became clan chief. It seemed to Yoseph each sunset and sunrise seemed to pass like the seasons.

Then one day Nicodemus limped into Yoseph's hut and told him he was leaving for Palestine. He had gotten word that his sister had died, and he wanted to see his daughter before he no longer could travel. Yoseph was heartbroken once more, and tears streamed down his cheeks. Another good friend from the old days was leaving his presence. He promised Nicodemus a departing banquet and invited everybody in both villages, which had grown considerably. Numerous Druid priests and many newly baptized Celts came from far and wide. Martial, one of the original people who came with them to this holy isle and a good friend of Lazarus, helped him arrange the going-away festivities. Martial did most of the work. Sadly, Shimon the Zealot couldn't attend, because the Roman authorities had executed him on one of his teaching trips to the east coast of Albion.

As the date drew closer, Yoseph approached Martial. "Martial, how are you coming with our forthcoming celebration?"

"Most things are falling into place, even *Amma* Miriam has strength to help me. Also I found this triad that Bishop Lazarus left for you sometime back. I suspect he forgot to give you this since he left in such a hurry." Martial handed him the missive, and then Yoseph read it. The perfect triad to read tonight, he thought.

Their tabernacle had increased in size and now the interior cubic space, their Holy of Holies, and the round hut was covered with a long rectangular basilica space. Tonight, would be an excellent night to have a holy service. The afternoon sky radiated a cerulean blue and there was no wind.

Once again, the night sky illuminated with hundreds of burning torches. This time, white-haired Hebron and Alein Yosephe set up three tables for Yoseph to officiate. Hundreds of teachers baptized the Celts, as their youthful children waited to receive the holy blood and body of their *Mashiach*. Martial stood at Yoseph's far left and *Amma* Miriam to his far right with Hebron and Alein Yosephe in between. However, Nicodemus was shoulder to shoulder with Yoseph as co-officiants. Oh, how they had depended on each other through their many summers of life. As the *crackling* bonfire grew larger with the discarded torches, each member at the table held sacred objects. Zechariah held his *abba's* sword, Hebron the holy lance, Nicodemus holding high Yoseph's gospel, Alein Yosephe one of the cruets, *Amma* Miriam held the cruet of blood, and Martial held the holy paten. There was no need for a lighted lamp, for the light of the world had settled on their Glass Isle.

"Behold the vessel of truth who seizes the sins of *Amma* Earth. It is this truth in our *Maishiach* that we bring against the world of sin and its demons. In your mercy, *El Shaddai*, forgive our sins and cleanse us with Your holy chalice. Lead us once again to Your humble table and unite us with the *Mashiach*, who is the bread of existence and the vine from which we grow in mercifulness."

After Yoseph said his opening words, he raised the chalice higher, and the entire isle turned into a brilliant glow of daylight. When he lowered it, nightfall returned. This sign prompted the masses to come forward and accept the holy blood and body of *Christo*. The cup never failed in its drafts of ruby-colored liquid or the bread in its shape. Most of the night, they spent officiating. Just before dawn, the last person partook of the holy elements. Yoseph ended the service with the Triad of Lazarus.

"My friends, believe in *El Shaddai* who made thee, love *El Shaddai* who saved thee, and fear *El Shaddai* who will judge thee."

After he finished, the entire crowd shouted good-bye to Nicodemus in their Celtic language and wished him *sláinte* or good health.

The next day after many hugs and kisses, Nicodemus departed the same route as Philip did, the fifth disciple called by Yeshua. He climbed the same hillock as did the Magdalener when she left with Philip. Yoseph observed him disappear over the hill with his two guides. For some odd reason, he didn't feel as melancholy this time when his good friend left. Events were happening so fast. His family, whom he loved most, suddenly had gotten older. Then one night, he heard a whispering voice. It sounded like Yeshua's.

"Yoseph, you will not die but live in another world until the next grail writer comes. The grail will make you one of the holy sleepers. Fear not, my uncle, a thousand or more summers will pass before this predestined man comes." That night, after his encounter with Yeshua, he couldn't sleep. The moon was full, and then he started walking toward the forest. Suddenly, he heard the rustle of leaves in the trees. Then came the hooting sound of a large owl that flew past Yoseph with its enormous round yellow eyes gazing at him. It was the exact same portent as the owl that night before Yeshua's crucifixion.

The next day, he spoke to *Amma* Miriam about his foreknowledge, experience, or dream. She didn't know what to make of it, yet said her son always did the most unexpected things. Yoseph noticed she was bedridden. He tried to help her up, yet she stumbled and fell back onto her bed. Her eyes were cloudy and her arms the size of small tree limbs.

"Uncle Yoseph, please come closer," her raspy voice asked. "Please bury me under the cup in your tabernacle. I want to be with my son once more." Her head reached up, and she kissed him on his cheek.

Yoseph answered, "Yes."

She fell back against her pillow and was no more of this earthly plain. Joseph's tears dripped down his face and the Glass Isle became deathly silent. He and Martial carried her frail body to the tabernacle floor next to the high altar. Hebron and his son, Alein Yosephe, Yosa, and Enygeus helped prepare her body for burial. Zechariah had brought the council elders. That night a tall column of white light ascended toward the heavens from her body through the roof and into the starry night sky. Everyone gasped and then bowed their heads. During the vigil, Yoseph heard a commotion at the entrance of the tabernacle. The crowd quickly parted, and a dark silhouette appeared against the outside vigil fire.

"It is I, Arch Druid Finn. I come to pay my respects to the mother of your God and mine. If you let me, my retinue of acolytes and I would like to say a prayer."

"Yes, yes indeed. Please come forward," Yoseph answered. Arch Druid Finn and twelve white-dressed pupils strolled forward. Inside, the entire crowd bowed in respect.

"Most honorable Yoseph, I observed the shaft of burning light and came just as I did when the King of Glory saved that young woman from death's grip."

Finn's gold breastplate, golden belt sickle, white robes, his hand holding a carved wooden staff of office, a tiara on his head, and a long white beard made him appear as *Moshe*. Without warning, they chanted the word "*Modron*," which meant *amma*, repeatedly until dawn came. Yoseph and his family then commenced to dig *Amma* Miriam's grave. To his surprise, Yoseph's shovel broke a wooden log. Hebron and Alein dug around the log and discovered a tunnel. Martial thought the tunnel went to the tor. Arch Druid Finn confirmed this. It led to the Celts' underworld, he said.

"Most revered Yoseph, this is a natural hiding place for us if the Roman soldiers come," Martial stated. Yoseph agreed with him for future needs.

With ropes and a wide flat board, they lowered the holy body into the tunnel. Hebron, Alein, and Zechariah scrambled down the ropes into the tunnel with heavy bags of rocks to cover the body. Then began the final good-byes. A long procession of people dropped flowers into the tunnel hole. After the last person expressed their grief, heavy pieces of flat slate were shoved over the opening. It was now over. Yoseph had buried his niece fifteen summers after his great nephew. Yoseph knew his life span would be extended for a greater purpose, yet whatever that purpose, it didn't matter, for wisdom would come from it.

The next day, Martial, Hebron, Alein, and Zechariah started

digging a hidden entrance down to the tunnel and tor. The tor beckoned him to ascend to its top. As he trudged up its labyrinth, a large gust of wind struck him as he reached its peak. He sat down on the soft cool grass and let his eyes survey the stunning countryside. Yoseph thought he viewed the Severn Sea as he stared west. Once again, he knew what *Moshe* felt like on Mount Sinai. Then came a slight *buzzing* sound, which he thought might be the wind or a bee. The noise grew louder, so he decided to leave the tor. Once on level ground the noise sounded like someone humming. He didn't recognize any distinct words. None of the sounds made sense. Yoseph decided to lay down for a while in his hut, thinking this might clear his head.

He awoke late in the afternoon and noticed the leaves on the trees had changed. How odd he thought. The noises were still there, which now sounded like music. He realized it originated from the sky and surrounded the whole isle. Yoseph gazed in the distance and spotted what he thought was his daughter, Yosa. Yet, her hair was snow white and she limped while holding a small staff. *How could this happen*? Then he observed a white-robed man going down some steps next to Yoseph's tabernacle. Hurriedly, Yoseph followed him into the dark cavernous tunnel that held a sole melting candle visible on the tunnel floor. The stones on *Amma* Miriam's grave were gone and there were no bones. *Where did they go*? Then Yoseph heard a familiar voice, turned, and observed Yeshua standing with two angelic glowing beings, one on each side of Him.

"Uncle Yoseph, I have planned a place for you in My kingdom." His arm pointed to a glowing mat next to the dripping candle. "Uncle Yoseph, you will be given what few mortals have received."

With Yeshua's last word, Yoseph felt the mat pulling him toward it. The *buzzing* and whispering grew louder. He started to recognize some words, but the mat pulled him down. As Yoseph lay there, he started having visions of wooden and stone tabernacles, caves, and then an auburn-haired man appeared, reaching out with an open hand and in the other hand grasping a book. On his body he wore a white tunic with an equal-armed splayed red cross. Then Yoseph spoke.

"Pilgrim, you finally found what you seek."

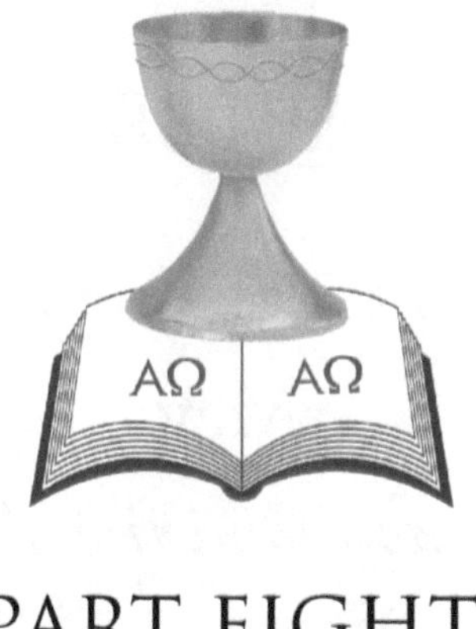

PART EIGHT

The Beginning of The End

CHAPTER LII

Center of England
May
Anno Domini 1191

We rode for two days nonstop from Lanercost Priory, only stopping for water for us and our horses. Muhammad said we must let our lathered steeds rest for the night. We made camp at sundown, next to a gurgling stream. I unsaddled my horse and joined the others around a *crackling* campfire. *Noir Ombre* snuggled up next to me while I now had a chance to read the last segment of Saint Joseph of Arimathea's gospel. My hands trembled with anticipation as each chapter came to light.

Without warning, a white stag appeared out of nowhere. It startled everyone as it trotted up to the fire. Its glistening black eyes reflected the flames, and suddenly the animal's antlers beckoned me to follow. The rest of my companions and *Noir Ombre* remained as if they were paralyzed. Slowly, I rose and quietly followed the white animal into the dark woods. *Frère* Ambrosius had mentioned to me about a white stag on our way to Lanercost Priory. If we witnessed one, it indicated we were on the right spiritual quest. The stag led me farther into the woods and away from the light of our campfire. Then I heard a loud *yipping* sound and the scampering of a small animal's feet. I stared down and glimpsed a red fox curling its white-tipped tail around my ankle. After a moment, both the fox and the stag vanished.

Then I heard the snapping of sticks behind me, drew my sword, and turned around. To my utmost horror a demon-like monster stared me in the face. The abominable creature wore the horns of the stag, bearing an open muzzle of a deer, a golden torc around its neck, dressed in deer skins, standing as a human with buckskinned boots. In one hand it held another golden torc, but in the other hand it grasped a black and white *hissing* serpent. Its antlers displayed both boughs of holly and mistletoe. I moved to slay the hideous creature, but he spoke.

"Peace, *frère*, I do not mean to harm you."

"Why should I trust you? For almost nine months my life and family have been threatened. What are you and who are you?"

"Don't you recognize me? I have had many names over the centuries and some you know. Hern the Hunter, Cernunnos, Green Man, Ambrosius, Myrddin Wyllt, and Merlin. Your *mère* knew me many seasons ago when she lived. I am here as a messenger and seer for your welfare. So, Robert, listen closely. The old ways are quickly disappearing and there is much you should know. First, beware of an old broken-down *chapelle* and the ghostly *succubi* that inhabit it. Their evil will not let you finish your quest. You and your companions will be trapped there for all eternity. Second, don't trust any Roman clerical authorities at the Glastonbury *Abbaye* that you now seek. Stay close to the men of the blood-red cross."

With his last words of blood-red cross, he turned, took one step, and then vanished into the ink-black night. Once again, I felt the rustle of the red fox's tail. He too took one step and disappeared. I crept back to the fire expecting any moment, another apparition or shapeshifter. Upon my arrival, my companions were smiling and joking with one another. They acted as if nothing strange had happened.

Before going to bed, I confided in *Frère* Ambrosius about my recent encounter and thought it was from lack of sleep. Nobody else in the camp commented about the white deer.

"I don't doubt your happenchance and what Merlin said. The Cymru people have spoken of this mystic for hundreds of years. We must show our vigilance this coming fortnight."

Another two days we rode in the saddle, only stopping for water and *vin* and on the third day we rested. We followed this procedure for a week until we reached the Preceptory de Sanford. The earl of Pembroke decided we should approach Glastonbury *Abbaye* from a different direction for safety reasons. The entire area lay on swampy land, and it didn't bode well for me. The air smelled like human waste. The horses gave out low *whinny* sounds of fear. Their nervousness heightened my nervousness too, causing my palms to sweat. The stench didn't dissipate until we reached the Templar preceptory. However, nobody came out to greet us. The stone-and-wattle buildings had an eerie silence. A few horses were *nickering* and the sounds of sheep *baying*, but no *moines*. Last night's cooking fire felt warm in the small refectory chimney. This didn't bode well for us. I asked Grand Master Gilbért what he thought.

"*Seigneur* Robert, two things happened here. One, the *moines* hurried away from something or they were lured away. I see numerous shoe impressions heading toward those dense woods growing on the hillock. I don't detect hurrying strides of fright, but curiosity. Muhammad and Earl de Pembroke Guillaume, what do you say?"

They both nodded their head and said, "*Oui*." Muhammad studied the track some more and then told *Noir Ombre* to follow the tracks. Off he galloped toward the hillock. The sun had started setting behind the hills by the time our war dog returned. At first, I didn't see him because of his black coat against the dark trees, yet I heard him. He gave out a high-pitched *whimper*. Then I met him racing with his tail between his legs in fear. His entire body trembled, and he lay down next to my feet still *whimpering*. Our dog had faced all kinds of fear in the past and never *whimpered* like this.

"What scared *Noir Ombre*?" I asked my companions. All I received in return were stone-like faces.

"I guess the only way to find out is to follow the tracks before nightfall," replied the earl of Pembroke.

Muhammad stayed with our war dog as the rest of my cohorts and I followed the trail. Along the way we made some torches to light the tracks. After darkness descended, we stopped at a clearing and investigated some cracked stones that were an old foundation. All of us entered the broken-down structure and searched for any sign of human activity. A numb, tired sensation came over me and my legs and feet seemed to be heavier. The ground pulled me toward it, and I teetered forward on one knee. My *amis* did the same. Then I fell forward, striking the cold ground. I touched something hard with my hands and to my horror I grasped a broken stone cross. One of Merlin's prophecies had come true. We had stumbled into the cursed *chapelle* he had warned me about. I tried to get up, but my body hardly moved. My companions were in the same physical state. Only our hands and voices functioned.

"*Seigneur* Robert, what is happening to us?!" cried out Grand Master Gilbért.

"I don't know," I replied. Then my eyelids became heavy and edged down across my eyeballs. I fought to stay awake. In the distance, past the *chapelle* foundation came a foggy swirling mist. At first, I thought it a fog and nothing more. Yet, the swirls started forming human shapes. I tried to edge my fingertips toward my writing satchel, but they were frozen with fear. Then my ears heard a slight shrill noise and the whirling shapes then formed naked female bodies.

"We are surrounded by *succubi*!" hollered *Frère* Ambrosius. "They will seduce us, and we will be trapped here through all eternity."

The shrill sound grew more intense and hypnotic, and each naked female hovered right above each of us. My eyes remained slightly open, and I still couldn't raise up. My memory harkened back to Homer and *The Odyssey*. I now realized how Odysseus felt when confronted with the Sirens. The shapes then drew closer with both hands extended. They were starting to undress us. My fingertips had reached the lip of my satchel. With what little strength I had, my hand finally reached in and grasped Saint Joseph of Arimathea's holy words. Slowly, I pulled out the book and it slid to my side. Immediately, the melodious shrills stopped and the naked flesh-like apparitions paused, and their beautiful faces turned pus-pocked. The rest of their bodies started shriveling inward like a demonic hag. Then as suddenly as they first appeared, they at once disappeared. I raised my back and proceeded to stand. Each of my fellow *frères* did likewise.

"*Seigneur* Robert, what did you do to vanish those enchant-resses?" the earl of Pembroke asked.

"I displayed Saint Yoseph of Arimathea's holy words of God."

"*Seigneur* Robert, God has truly blessed you. Now let's get the hell out of this evil place!" retorted the earl.

We raced back to our horses, mounted, then spurred them to hurry. We rode the rest of the night with newly lit torches. We rested all the next day, which let me read the remaining content of our holy tome.

My fingertips rubbed the outside carved leather cover. The front cover's tooled image was that of an angel; which angel I didn't know. In one hand, the angel held a bowl of fire and the other hand held a book. Carefully, I turned the pages and commenced to read its content. Earlier, I had read about Yoseph's ministry after leaving the port of Yoffa, his meeting with Philo, the fire, and the disastrous sea voyage. Now I read about God's retribution on the assassin Barabbas and other enemies of Saint Yoseph. Then I came upon his Celtic Druid companions. Near the end, I nearly dropped the book and then I had to pinch myself to make sure I wasn't dreaming. Yoseph had buried the *Mère* of God at Glastonbury. *How could this be*? Other legends and Holy *Pères* said otherwise. At first, it shocked me on an emotional level, yet now all the clues, symbols, cryptic words, arcane religions, and the cup of truth put together made this irrefutable. Some of what I had seen, heard, and felt over the past seasons, I couldn't explain.

Quickly, I called Grand Master Gilbért to come forth. I motioned for him to follow me into the woods so we could speak in private. Once I stopped, I told him what I had found. After my explanation, I noted his face for a reaction. His eyes stared down as if lost in thought. His pursed lips held tight, and his forehead squished with lines. He then raised his head and stared into my eyes.

"We must tell only *Frère* Chaplain Jeremiah and no one else. Is that clear, *Seigneur* Robert?" Grand Master Gilbért demanded. "This goes against twelve hundred years of church orthodoxy, and we will be hunted down until we are all dead."

"*Oui*, I understand, but what will we tell the others?"

"Nothing, just leave her out of Saint Yoseph's narrative about the *Mère* of our Lord. Tear the page out and dispose of it as you wish."

He said no more but turned to go back to our camp. Nothing was said the rest of the evening. I slept with the holy book next to me the following two nights.

CHAPTER LIII

Glastonbury *Abbaye*
May 1191

We reached the *abbaye* about midday, and to our surprise there were numerous *moines* from several different orders participating in a mass on one side of the Saints Mary and Joseph *chapelle*. Their habits were numerous blacks, some whites, and a few brown scapulars. To my shock, I observed a large rectangular-shaped hole they had dug. Off to the side of the hole was an enormous pile of dirt. After *Frère* Ambrosius dismounted, he raced toward the crowd.

"What are you doing to our sacred grounds?!" he yelled. All heads then turned in his direction. From my mount, I noticed *Abbé* Henri de Sully come forward and speak to him. Afterward, they hugged and their leader patted *Frère* Ambrosius on his back. He trod toward me and the rest of us. His frown didn't bode well for what he was about to tell us.

"*Abbé* Henri said they found the grave of *Roi* Arthur and *Reine* Guinevere and a lead cross with *Roi* Arthur's name. Both were buried together. When he observed the Poor-Soldiers of

Christ here along with the earl of Pembroke measuring outside the *chapelle*, he knew something important might be buried there. They didn't trust our explanation about surveying *Roi* Richard's precincts. I pray he doesn't know about the inside of the *chapelle*. Does the ancient tome tell us anymore about who may be buried inside?"

I didn't want to lie to the *moine* Ambrosius, but what could I say?

"All I can tell you," I replied, "is you'll be astonished. Someday, I will write and reveal the name, however, now is too dangerous. I owe that to you for helping us. I suspect this dig is a hoax to draw more money to the *abbaye*. Yet, you never know. The *abbaye* has surprised us with its revelations, *oui*. We know Saint Joseph of Arimathea is buried here along with more saints than anywhere on earth."

"*Oui*, *Seigneur* Robert."

Frère Ambrosius rejoined his fellow *moines* to make sure they didn't disturb anything else. The dug-up area seemed odd. Here lay a large mound of earth between two unknown written stelas or obelisks. The Greeks had written a description about these kinds of stone columns in a faraway land call Egypt.

My body ached from the many leagues we had traveled. Slowly, I dismounted and observed a lone oak tree some distance from the *chapelle* of Saints Mary and Joseph. The trunk measured the diameter of five standing men, and I mentally visualized it as a sapling when *Amma* Mary and Joseph of Arimathea were here. Each of my feet felt like the weight of boulders as I trudged in its direction. Upon reaching its gnarly roots, I slumped between the two of them, almost hiding me. My frayed mind told me our quest wasn't completed, but why?

I decided to write to my *épouse* and tell her I would arrive in a fortnight. I reached into my satchel, touched the tooled leather of the holy tome, and then found paper, ink, and quill pen. Just as I started to pen my missive, a black and white-striped badger ambled toward me. He kept digging holes as he approached. My eyes became fixated on his activities. He would dig down and disappear, then after a brief period reappear and repeat the same process. The badger made twelve holes and on the twelfth, he reappeared and then stared at me. It was if he wanted me to come forward and admire his work.

That is when I heard faint voices coming from the ground. I traipsed over to each hole, and heard sounds, human voices, coming from the earth. The words were muffled from the depth of the ground. Then I remembered what Grand Master Gilbért mentioned when we first arrived, about a possible secret underground passageway to the tor. Silently, I backed away from the holes until I reached the *chapelle*. There I motioned for the grand master, Sergeant Jacque, *Abbé* Jeremiah, and the earl of Pembroke to follow me toward the oak tree. I put my index finger up to my lips to signal them to be quiet. All of us slinked toward the holes with the badger making a hasty retreat into the woods. We stood between the holes waiting for more conversation. When voices started once more, Grand Master Gilbért pointed for us to follow him into the woods.

"I think we know who is down there hiding. It is a trap to steal the *Santo* tome. Those *bâtards* are too cowardly to confront us here in daylight. Let's wait until all the workmen and digging are done, then we give them what they want, but it won't be the tome!" Grand Master Gilbért exclaimed. "We'll meet back at close to sunset."

I left to ponder our up-and-coming final battle. There in the distance, where the cloister once stood, I spied a broken column and its ornate stone top, which once was part of many that held up the cloister enclosure. After sitting back down between the oak trees, my mind could visualize many black-robed *moine* scribes working tirelessly each day. Their ghosts or bodies started to appear until *Noir Ombre* scampered up and licked my face. After he settled down, I finished my letter to my *épouse*, and then folded it and put my wax seal on the edges. Afterward, I walked toward my horse's saddlebags. There, I placed my missive in one of the bags, while obtaining *vin* and cheese from the other. *Noir Ombre* followed, hugging me next to my legs until we headed toward the ivy-infested woods. His ears told me that he too heard the belowground voices. Immediately, he started *whimpering*, which forced me to start feeding him my cheese, so he'd stay quiet. I drew him into the woods when suddenly Muhammad leaped out of some holly bushes.

"Damn it, Muhammad, I thought you were one of the cardinal's men."

"*Seigneur* Robert, are you ready to end this holy quest?"

"*Oui*!"

"I made some torches and brought two crossbows. I believe the passageway is narrow, dark, and could cave in on us. Yet, all of this could be in our favor. The ancient peoples always constructed large chambers in their tunnels for their food, water, weapons, and shelter from raiders."

With the stealth of a large cat, Muhammad moved from the woods into the green pasture of the *abbaye* grounds. I glanced westward and viewed the sinking sun. In the distance came my companions. After nine long months we were ready to end this horrid odyssey. I crossed myself and said a prayer to Saint Joseph of Arimathea for his blessing. Once again, we met in the woods to have me tell *Frère* Ambrosius to distract any remaining *moines* so we would be out of their line of sight. That would let us enter the *chapelle's* well house and its secret stone door, which Grand Master Gilbért had mentioned a fortnight ago. To my surprise, Muhammad told us he had already been in a small length of the tunnel. Quickly, I told *Moine* Ambrosius what I wanted him to do. He, with no questions asked, started surveying the grounds for any late departing *moines*.

We hurried toward the well house, then entered the entrance facing a small spiraling staircase. Muhammad lit our torches, and we crept down the steps.

"*Seigneur* Robert, please help me push this small stone wall," said Grand Master Gilbért. I squeezed past Sergeant de Hoult, and then placed my hands on the cool stone. Slowly and quietly, the stone moved backward, giving us enough room to enter bent over. The dank musty smell reminded me of when we were in *Roi* Alfonso de Chaste's secret *château* tunnel, but safer then. As I shined my torch, numerous spiderwebs appeared on the ceiling with spiders as large as the ones in the Tower of London. *Noir Ombre* brushed up against my leg, staying close, and Chaplain Jeremiah held out his pewter cross. Muhammad carried his crossbows and Sergeant Jacque de Hoult rested his hand on his dagger. Our swords were useless in the tunnel's narrow confines. We crept some distance before hearing faint voices. *Noir Ombre* started to growl, but Muhammad and I grabbed his muzzle several times. Grand Master Gilbért whispered into my ear.

"I believe we are getting close. I estimate there are five voices. One of them I recognize." He didn't say anymore, but he clenched his jaw hard.

In my mind there was no doubt about this ancient tunnel to the tor. Both Joseph and the Druids were right in Saint Joseph's writings. It led to another world. After another twenty paces Grand Master Gilbért once again whispered into my ear.

"They don't know we are here. Let's rush them now and not give them a chance to fight. It is now the moment of truth!" Then he yelled, "*Non nobis Domine, non nobis, sed nomini tuo da gloriam.*"

I watched two of the cardinal's *chevaliers* jump up from their wooden benches just as two of Muhammad's crossbow quarrels struck them in the chest with a thud. Sergeant Jacque killed the third while he rose from his bed. To my horror and surprise, sitting against the wall, appeared *Abad* Miguel speaking to, I presumed, Cardinal Folquet. Finally, there was our traitor, but why? The cardinal lunged at Grand Master Gilbért with a hidden dagger, only to have it twisted from his hand by Gilbért's larger, powerful hand. The prince of the church then shouted at him.

"I'll have you executed if you touch me again. Besides I have the *Santo Père's* backing!"

"I don't think so," Grand Master Gilbért retorted. "There is enough testimony and written evidence to disgrace you for all eternity." He then glared at the *abad.* "Yet, Miguel, why did you betray all of us? I have known you since childhood. Also the evil shame of having your blood *frère* murdered. Why did you have him murdered?"

"He didn't want me to work with the cardinal's men and tried to expose my actions. I didn't give a damn about that nowhere place of an *abadia*. Cardinal Folquet promised me a bishopric in Toledo and later an archbishop position. For forty years I was penniless. I couldn't say no. Besides, the cardinal wouldn't reward me until Lord Robert translated the final book. I had to keep all of you alive and keep me from being the obvious traitor."

Grand Master Gilbért raced over and *slapped* Miguel along the side of his head with his gauntlet. "You *bâtard*! You are no longer an *abad* or anything else of holy nature. I want you out of my sight."

Just as Grand Master Gilbért said his last word, a bright light cast its shadow of an image accompanied by the sound of *shuffling* feet. Could there be more of the cardinal's men hidden? We braced ourselves for an attack. The footfall seemed forever before a hooded *moine*-like figure appeared holding a lantern in an outstretched arm. To my incredulity, this was the *moine* whom I had observed in several past places.

"Don't harm this man, I know of him. He is a prophet and holy man. Yet, I don't know your name." I smiled at him.

"Pilgrim, you have done well. The Holy Spirit has protected you and your companions to complete your holy quest. I have come for several reasons. First, my name is Joseph of Arimathea. Second, I am the final judge of your tormentors. Third, I'll reveal my secrets to you and your fellow *frères*. And finally, the fourth secret only you'll know until the next grail bearer comes, and you will tell him or her your secret."

"Saint Joseph de Arimathea, how could you live so long?"

"My son, there is more than one kind of flesh and the cup giveth immortality and also taketh away life."

His bony arm reached into his robe and pulled out the same type of cup as he did in the Cathar cave and the one in Iberia. A sudden burst of bluish light filled the tunnel, and we bowed our heads from the intense orange and blue rays. Cardinal Folquet and

Abad Miguel lunged for the cup while holding their arms close to their eyes, but a violent rumble from the tunnel floor caused them to stop. A vaporous outline appeared of two images standing behind Joseph de Arimathea. Both materialized into human forms, yet they glowed the same colors as the cup.

"Behold, the messengers of God," bellowed Saint Joseph. "To my right is Uriel, the flame of God, and to my left is Gabriel, the cupbearer of God." He stared at the cardinal and *abbé*. "You two evil men will now see the retribution of God!" Suddenly, two large holes opened under the feet of Cardinal Folquet and *Abad* Miguel. For a moment they were suspended above the holes only to view in horror as long arms of fire grabbed their shoulders and sucked them downward into the depths of the chthonic earth. The air became as cold as a grave digger's pit. We glanced at one another with astonishment, but also with relief. After a silent moment, my curiosity overcame my fear.

"Holy one, who sent you?

"You did," replied the spindly limbed Joseph. "From the moment of your birth, you were predestined to come here. Jesus the Christ marked you at your beginning. Now that you have uncovered my final writings, I ask you do one thing in secret for me." The cup's eye-aching light ceased, and he strolled toward me and whispered his request. He wanted me to hide the two cruets of blood and water, which came from our Lord and Savior's crucifixion. Also not to reveal what was inside the Holy Grail cup. Carefully, he put the glass cruets into my palms and then raised the chalice rim to my eyes. At first, all that I perceived was a dark *vin*-colored liquid. Suddenly, it transformed to golden fluid and started to glow. My entire body shook with euphoria and a sense of calm came over my entire being. Inside the golden liquid were the moving faces of Jesus and his *mère*, Mary. Afterward there was darkness, followed by a point of light growing larger until I was once more conscious. I found myself prone on the tunnel floor clutching the two cruets. The holy saint and the angels had vanished.

"*Seigneur* Robert, what happened here?" asked Grand Master Gilbért.

"I don't know, yet I have been sworn to secrecy by Saint Joseph of Arimathea. After I gazed into the cup, I must have fainted. What you witnessed, *mes amis,* must be sworn to secrecy." Everyone there crossed themselves twice and said, "*Oui.*"

I put the cruets into my sword belt as we left, not wanting to explore the tunnel any farther. Nothing was said as we reached the secret door entrance and daylight. We exited it unnoticed and congregated to the rear of *chapelle.*

"What are you going to do next?" asked Chaplain Jeremiah.

"Mail my letter to *mon épouse* and tell her I am coming home and then grant Saint Joseph his secret request. I haven't had time to mentally assimilate my nine months of experiences so I must do that and just rest. What about yourself, *mon ami*?"

"Grand Master Gilbért wants me to join him in returning to the Levant. If *Roi* Richard doesn't win back Jerusalem, he could possibly broker a peaceful settlement with Saladin. I am sure Sergeant Jacque de Hoult will return with him. Pray for us, *mon ami.*"

I approached both the earl of Pembroke and Grand Master Gilbért and hugged each.

"Both of you have saved my life on numerous occasions and I will miss you."

"What are you going to do with the Holy Grail book of Saint Joseph's writings?" asked Guillaume le Maréchal, the earl de Pembroke.

"I will hide them so when the next Holy Grail servant comes, I will reveal everything I have read, seen, and heard. I was just part of the servants before me and in the future I will pass off my holy wisdom to another."

The next day, we prepared to leave. Just as the sun rose from the pink-colored horizon, I ambled around the tor and adjacent woods to spy for some hiding places. Near the tor, I heard a babbling stream originating from an opening. The stream flowed into a large hole in the ground that appeared bottomless. There, I dropped one cruet, said a prayer, and then crossed myself twice. Slowly, it sank into the watery abyss and disappeared. I searched for another hole, and not far came upon a different stream and a smaller hole.

Both streams were just far enough away to not be obvious. Once more, I repeated the same prayer and crossed myself twice. I had completed my work in England, and now it just left me to hide the Holy Grail book. Or should I now call it the fifth gospel? As I turned around, I jumped back to see Muhammad facing me. His cat-like stealth hadn't weakened but seemed quieter.

"*Wali Taqi* Robert, are you ready to leave? The horses are saddled."

"*Oui, mon ami*, but first let me tell *Frère* Ambrosius farewell." I strolled back to the *chapelle* and met *Frère* Ambrosius supervising the *Roi* Arthur dig. He stood there shouting orders not to dig too close to the *chapelle* walls.

"I am leaving right now and want to say *mon au revoirs*. You have no idea how you helped us. *Au revoir* and *merci beaucoup*, *mon ami*. Someday soon, I'll write and tell you what happened. For now, I must leave. I know in the future this *abbaye-cathédrale* will contain more books than it did before the disastrous fire."

I put my foot in the horse's stirrup, mounted, and then spurred her as we raced away. Once I stared back and viewed the dark foreboding tor and Saint Joseph's remaining thorn tree, yet there are a few places on earth that heaven dips down to share its holy secrets and Glastonbury *Abbaye* is one of them. My fellow companions and I traveled for four days before parting to catch our separate sailing ships. At that juncture we dismounted, shook hands, hugged, and got misty-eyed together. I knew I wouldn't see them again, or would I?

"Just as I now live a hidden life, and always shall, from those to whom I do not wish to reveal myself, so too the holy book will remain obscure and only rarely will anyone reap all its benefits."

—*Seigneur* Robert de Borron
Anno Domini 1192

GLOSSARY

Latin Terms

Ad quadratum—architectural term for designing medieval buildings using the geometry of a square

Ad triangulum—architectural term for designing medieval buildings using the geometry of a square in a circle using the triangle lines in the square

Anno Domini—in the year of our Lord

Ave Regina caelorum—hail O' Queen of Heaven

Britannia—Britain

Cognomens—nicknames used by ancient Greeks and Romans

Dominus firmamentum meum—the Lord is my strength

Dominus illuminatio mea—the Lord is my light

Dominus vobiscum—the Lord be with you

Equites—Roman calvary

Gladius—Roman sword used by a legionnaire

In nomine Patris et Filii et Spiritus Sancti—in the name of the Father and the Son and the Holy Spirit

Id est quod id est—it is what it is

Laus perennis—perpetual prayer

League—unit of measure equaling three miles

Logos—divine reason implicit in the cosmos (holy words)

Mare Nostrum or Mare Magnum—Roman for our sea and aka the Mediterranean

Non nobis Domine, non nobis, sed nomini tuo da gloriam—Not unto us, O Lord not unto us, but to your name we give glory

Octa—the number eight

Opus Dei—work of God

Paravi lucernam Christo meo—I have prepared a lamp for my Christ

Pater Noster—Lord's Prayer

Pax vobiscum—peace be with you

Penta—the number five

Vesica piscis—bladder of fish which is a geometric shape

Vetusta ecclesia—the name the original ancient church at Glastonbury, England

Satanas—adversary (the devil)

Stadia—Roman measurement of 606.9 feet or 185 meters

Iberian (Spanish) Terms

Abad—abbot

Abadia—abbey

Abuelo—grandfather

Adios—good-bye

Almendro tree—almond tree

Altesse—noble woman (highness)

Alteza—high king

Buenas noches—good night

Buenas Tardes—good afternoon

Buenos dias—good morning

Caballero—gentleman or knight

Castillo—castle

Conde—count

Condesa—countess

Cortez amores—chivalrous love

Detener—arrest

Diable—characteristics of the Devil

Don—gentleman

El Camino—the way to St. James Cathedral

El Diablo—the Devil

Esposa—wife

Excelencia—excellency

Hermana—sister

Hermano—brother

Hijo—son

Hogueras—bonfires

Hola—hello

Iglesia—church

Judios—Jewish people

Madre—mother

Marquésa—marquess, female royal title

Marqués—marquis, royal title

Mezquita—mosque

Momento—be there shortly

Monasterio—monastery

Muchacho—young boy

Muchas gracias—thank you so much

Mudéjar—Iberian Muslims

Mujer—woman

Nieto—grandchild

Ninguno—none

Niños—children

Nochebuena—Christmas Eve

Palacio—palace

Parada—stop

Perdón—I'm sorry

Princesa—princess

Queso Manchego—Manchego cheese

Santo Padre—Holy Father (pope)

Salud—to your health

Señor—mister

Su Excelencia—Your Excellency

Tio—uncle

Torre—tower

Ulamas—scholars

Vaya con Dios—go with God

Zuda Tower—former Mudéjar fortress in Aragón

Medieval Terms

Aketon—long quilt-padded shirt covered with chain mail

Apse—rounded alcove behind a church altar

Arbalest—large and stronger crossbow

Archivolt—a religious ornamental molding on an arched entrance to a Christian church

Armarius—monk librarian at a monastery scriptorium

Bailey—castle courtyard

Barbican—gateway or outer works defending a drawbridge

Beauséant—Knights Templar battle flag

Cantor—monk in charge of music and religious writings

Carrell—monk's copying cell

Center of the earth—another name of Jerusalem

Coif—hood of chain mail

Culdees—Celtic word for *stranger from afar*

Dame—a lady, wife of a knight, or a female knight

Fitchée cross—pattée cross with a pointed end

Gematria—an alphanumeric code of assigning numerical values to names, words, or phrases according to its letters

Keep—heavily fortified tower in the interior of a castle

Merlon—a solid stone or brick toothlike section of a castle battlement

Nave—central part of a church

Portcullis—heavy wooden-grilled gate that can be raised and lowered

Quarrel—thick metal tip of a crossbow arrow

Refectory—common hall where monks eat

Romany—Gypsies

Sacristy—room in a church where sacred vestments and vessels are kept

Sain—make the sign of the cross or bless

Scriptorium—room where monks prepare manuscripts

Seneschal—top administrator or steward in a noble or religious household

Succubi—mythological demon-like women with wings and claws for feet who seduce mortal men

Transept—either one of two parts of a church forming the design of arms of a cross

Tarida—medieval ship which could transport horses to the shore

Tympanum—area of a church between the lintel of a doorway and the arch above it. May have biblical scenes carved in this area

Visigoths—ruled Iberia (Spain) from 418 through 711 A.D.

Jewish and Aramaic Terms

Abba—father

Achoti—sister

Adonai—our Lord

Almanah—widow

Amma—mother

Ashrei—praying a psalm

Ben or *bar*—son of

Brit chadashah—new covenant

Chayot ha kodesh—highest ranking angels in Heaven who hold up God's throne

Chokmah—meaning wisdom or one of the *sefirot* for wisdom in the mystical Jewish Kabbalah

Doh-dah—aunt

El Shaddai—The Almighty

Eloheinu—meaning our God, which is used in the Jewish Shema

Elohim—the almighty

Etz Chaim—Tree of Life

Judah—tribe or province in Palestine

Kabbalah—to receive

Kabod—halo or bright light

Kavanah—direction, intention, or purpose

Kodesh Hakodashim—Holy of Holies in the ancient Tabernacle, the cube-shaped area the Ark of the Covenant stayed

Kodesh—holy

Kohen—an ancestor of Moses's brother Aaron

Maishiach—anointed one (the Messiah)

Malach—angel

Melech—king

Merkavah—throne of God surrounded by seven angels

Metatron—the name of the Prophet Enoch after his transformation to the highest angel

Mishkan—ancient Jewish tabernacle

Moshe—Moses

Navi—prophet

Omein—amen or so be it

Pesach—Jewish Passover

Ruach ha-kodesh—holy wind or spirit

Seder—order for Passover service

Shabbat—Jewish Sabbath

Shalom—peace

Sefirah or Sefirot—orbs or gates guarded by an angel in the Kabbalah

Shekhinah—the presence of God in the world or the dwelling place of God

Shema—"Hear, O Israel, the Lord is our God, the Lord is One! Blessed is the name of His glorious kingdom for ever and ever," prayer recited twice a day by Jews

Sheol—hell or burning pit

Shiva—the seven-day period of formalized mourning by the immediate family of a deceased Jew

Tefillin—worn leather prayer boxes attached to the forehead and arms

Tikkun—fixing the world

Ya'akov—name for James

Yudah or Yehudah—Judea

Yerushalayim—Jerusalem

Frankish Gaul Terms

Abbaye—abbey

Abbé—priest (father)

Adieu—good-bye

Amande—almond

Amis—friends

Amant—lover

Ami—friend or amis (friends)

Amour—love affair

Au revoir—good-bye

Baron—another nobility title for lord

Bâtard—bastard

Beau-frère—brother-in-law

Bien sûr affectueux—of course my affectionate

Bienvenu—welcome

Bon ami—good friend

Bon—good

Bonjour—hello

Bonne nuit—good night

Bonsoir—good evening

Cathédrale—cathedral

Chapeau—hat

Capellán—chaplain

Château—castle

Chevalier—knight

Coeur—heart

Comte—count (title)

Contraire—disagree

Duc—duke

Duché—duchy or dukedom

Église—church

Épouse—wife
Fils—son or sons (des *fils*)
Fin amor—courtly love
Frère—brother
Fromage—cheese
Garçon—young boy
Halte—stop
Juive—Jewish woman
Le Coeur de Lion—war name of King Richard the First of England
Lé Sangraal—the cup of Christ (the Holy Grail)
Les Maries de le mare—Maries of the sea
Majesté—majesty
Mari—husband
Marquise—lord of the border
Merci beaucoup—thanks a lot
Mère—mother
Mère de Dieu—mother of God
Mère supérieure—mother superior, head of a nunnery
Mon chéri—my darling
Moine—monk
Montagne(s)—mountain or mountains
Monastère—monastery
Neveux—nephews
Nom de guerre—battle name
Non—no
Oubliette—dirty basement prison
Père supérieure—superior father (pope)
Père—father
Petit-fils—grandson
Prêtre—priest
Princesse—princess

Provence—geographical region in southwestern Gaul (France) facing the Mediterranean

Reine—queen

Roi—king

Royaume—kingdom

Santo Père—holy father

Seigneur—lord (title)

Soeur—sister

Tante—aunt

Très bien—very good

Trouvère—poet/singer

Vin/vino—wine

Vignoble—vineyard

Muslim Terms

Ahl al-bayt—People of the House aka followers of Muhmmad

Alhamdulillah—praise be to Allah

Allah—God

Allahu Akbar—God is Great or Greatest

Asr—afternoon prayer

Basmala—in the name of God, the Merciful, the most Compassion

Bāṭin—hidden meaning as in the Koran

Dajjal—evil force or deceiver

Dawah—issuing call or summon

Fatwa—death decree—on an individual or individuals

Fida'is—special forces of the Brethren of Purity

Grand Mufti—great judge of wisdom

Hamsa—amulet to ward off the evil eye

Hashishiyya—assassins (Brethren of Purity)—

Ikhwān as-Safā—another name for the Brethren of Purity

Issa—the Prophet Jesus the Christ

Jambiya—large, curved dagger

Jinn—evil spirit

Khalifa—king overlord

Lataif—spiritual journey

Madrasa—school or college

Mahdi—a spiritual leader who is hidden and will reveal himself before the end times

Madrasa—school or college

Malahidas—infidels

Maymum—blessed by Allah

Mujahidin—a Muslim who fights for his faith

Musa—prophet Moses

Nass—secret knowledge passed on to Mohammad's successor

Qadar—destiny

Qahwa—coffee

Qiblah—fixed design in a mosque pointing toward Mecca

Qur'an—Koran

Rasā'il Ikhwān as-Safā'—esoteric faction and philosophy of Nazari Isma'ili or branch of the Shia Muslims (Brethren of Purity)

Rasul—spiritually gifted

Sa'ada—a good or charitable person

Salam—peace

Salaam alaikum—peace be upon you

Salat—a ritual prayer by a Muslim

Sassanian—early kings who ruled Persia after the fall of the Roman empire

Shaytan—the devil

Shaheed—martyr

Surah—chapters in the Koran

Taqiyya—appear and disappear at will

Tasbih—either 33 prayer beads or 99 with the different names of *Allah*

Tolati-tola—city of Toledo in Iberia

Wali taqi—holy man

Yusuf—Joseph

Celtic Terms

Alban Hefin—summer solstice (the sun sits still)

Albion—Britannia (England)

Annwn—Celtic underworld

Avalon—Isle of the Apples, aka Glastonbury, Ynys Wydryn (Glass Isle), and Isle of the Dead

Céli Dé—strangers from afar

Cymru—Wales

Drunemetons—groups of druid priest meet in oak forests

Keltoi—Greek name for Celts

Modron—Celtic goddess of fertility and maternity

Ogham—Druid secret alphabet

Scrying—the art of seeing into the future or past

Slàinte mhòr—to your health

Taranis—Celtic god of thunder and lightning

Touta—Celtic word for tribe

WRITER'S NOTES

All three books of the Cup of Christ Mystery/Thriller series reflect the ancient author Homer's *The Odyssey,* except centuries later. Lord Robert de Borron and Saint Joseph of Arimathea are on a spiritual journey with trials and tribulations similar to Ulysses. All three men want to go *home* or find a new *home*. You will see several references and vignettes to Homer's ageless journey. I believe most quests in the past and present are self-induced for fame, power, or money and maybe all three. Yet, Saint Joseph of Arimathea, Lord Robert de Borron, and I are pulled by something more spiritual in nature. It is a longing you have to help others and experience something far greater than yourself. Some psychologists say it's something deep in our ancestry DNA prompting us to express or complete our destiny.

However, this book has more citations from the Old Testament, and numerous notes from the New Testament and the Book of Revelation. Once again, the reader experiences Spanish, Muslim, and Jewish cultures, and scholars in the late twelfth-century Iberia. From there Lord Robert and Saint Joseph make their final journey (different time periods) to the magical Celtic land of Britannia, or is it magic? Once again, the reader will be exposed to hidden numeral truths of the Old and New Testaments, and the *bāṭin* (hidden) meanings of the Koran. The reader should contemplate on geometry and mathematics as the "universal language," which most ancient and current cultures understood and understand. This is God's language throughout the universe and why many earthly cultures incorporated it into their religious text and traditions.

My third book emphasizes numbers more than the other two books for climactic purposes. Previously, the reader was told about the power of the numbers five and eight (*penta* and *octa*), the gematria number code of Greek and Hebrew letters, but this book reveals the power of the numbers seven (heptagon) and twelve (dodecagon). The Hebrews used the royal cubit (20.64 inches or 525 millimeters) in constructing the ancient Egyptian's monuments. This was to my surprise, since there were various lengths for the cubit. Moses knew this and used the royal cubit to construct the Tabernacle to house the Ark of the Covenant. His Holy of Holies was in the shape of a cube where the Ark of the Covenant was stored with one side of the cube covered with curtains. If you unfold a geometric cube, you will get a cross. If you divide the Ark of the Covenant's cubic cubits (5.625) into the internal volume of the Holy of Holies of the Tabernacle (810 cubic cubits), you'll get the number 144. Yoseph was given twelve hides, which is 1,440 acres by Celtic King Arviragus (this number is a multiple of twelve). This was later recorded in the *Domesday Book* of William the Conqueror. There are many examples of seven and twelve in Part Seven of this book. They are so much mathematical evidence that it's overwhelming. There is a word called *euhemerism,* which means legendary events are presumed to have originated from historical evidence. Especially after many retellings.

Later, Saint Joseph of Arimathea uses these measurements and geometric polygons to build his Christian chapel in Britannia. Much of the math and geometric calculations has been done by the geometer Dr. John Michell and his groundbreaking books: *City of Revelation* by John Michell, *The Dimensions of Paradise* by John Michell, *The Temple at Jerusalem: A Revelation* by John Michell, and *How the World Is Made* by John Michell and Allan Brown. His seven-pointed star and twelve spheres is a sacred enigma, and its design was used as a tile floor in the Lady Chapel at Glastonbury. At one time, there was something mysterious buried under this geometric design, which is the sacred enigma. This was recorded by William of Malmesbury in the early to mid-eleven hundreds.

Today, the secretive abbey ruins of Glastonbury exude clues and irrefutable numerical values to lay claim to the oldest aboveground Christian church. Also the once possible burial places of Mary the mother of Jesus, Saint Joseph of Arimathea, and the Holy Grail. The ancient Jewish Tabernacle design and Saint Joseph (as the high priest) and Mary the mother of Christ along with the Holy Grail have similarities that are not coincidences.

I have listed some amazing books that have helped me in my research. The lengthy, but germane, list helped my trilogy and its plot lines.

Rose Guide to the Tabernacle by Rose Publishing
Glastonbury Abbey by Glastonbury Abbey
Glastonbury by Philip Rahtz
The Isle of Avalon by Nicholas R. Mann
The Gate of Remembrance by Frederick Bligh Bond
Servants of the Grail by Philip Coppens
Merlin and the Grail by Robert de Boron and translated by Nigel Bryant
Discovering William of Malmesbury by Rodney M. Thomson, Emily Dolmans, and Emily A. Winkler
Sacred Geometry by Iva Kenaz
Signs, Symbols, and Sacred Geometry by Mari Silva
Sacred Geometry (An A-Z Reference Guide) by Marilyn Walker
The Book of Celtic Symbols by Joules Taylor
Secrets of the Druids by Teresa Cross
Celt, Druid and Culdee by Isabel Hill Elder, Merch O Lundam Derri
Atlas of the Celtic World by John Haywood
The Celtic Book of Living and Dying by Juliette Wood
Druids: Preachers of Immortality by Anne Ross

"The knowledge at which geometry aims is knowledge of the eternal . . . Then, my noble friend, geometry will draw the soul towards the truth, and create the spirit of philosophy, and raise up that which is now unhappily allowed to fall down."

The Republic, VII
Plato
375 BCE

COMING SOON

The Other Side of Nowhere

What shameful malevolent secrets does a rural Kentucky county have during the 1920s? There is a revengeful evil spirit stalking families who wanted to forget about a hanging that took place numerous years earlier. How does a suicide enter into all this? Was the protagonist responsible for his wife's death or did she murder their children then kill herself? Come and discovery if there is a supernatural connection in another Jack Holt mystery/thriller.

Thank you for reading the third book in my trilogy series and please sign up for my newsletter at my web page for book discounts.

jackmholt.com

www.ingramcontent.com/pod-product-compliance
Lightning Source LLC
Chambersburg PA
CBHW020616310726
48979CB00008B/1517/J